INDIAN GIVER

19 Nov '86

For Marsha,
a student of human
behavior — may you find
some behaving humans
herein —

Love,
Gerald

INDIAN GIVER

GERALD DUFF

INDIANA UNIVERSITY PRESS

Bloomington

Library of Congress Cataloging in Publication Data

Duff, Gerald.
  Indian giver.

    1. Alibamu Indians—Fiction.   2. Koasati Indians—
Fiction.   I. Title:
PS3554.U317715   1983   813'.54   83-47829
ISBN 0-253-13999-6
1 2 3 4 5 87 86 85 84 83

And who would eat a cleaner meat
Must grabble in the hollows of underwater stumps and roots,

Must cram his arm and hand beneath the scum
And go by touch where eye cannot reach. . .

from "Grabbling in Yokna Bottom"
by James Seay

"Don't look behind," he said to his brothers. But, as
they went along, one of them looked back, turned into
a wildcat, and ran away growling. Another looked
back, turned into a panther, and went off howling. The
third looked back and turned into an alligator. In the
same manner the fourth changed into an owl. Likewise,
the fifth became a chicken-hawk and flew away. The
sixth brother returned home alone.

from the Alabama-Coushatta tale
"Outwitting the Cannibals" collected
by Howard N. Martin

For Vereen Bell, Roy Blount, and Jim Seay
and for Judson Battise
who rode the bus with me

CONTENTS

INDIAN
GIVER

1

How Fire Came

"This time," Coach Dodge said out loud as he drove the purple and white station wagon into Cooper Leaping Deer's yard, "this time, by doggies, that ornery flathead'll play." He pulled the wagon around the body of a '50 Ford pickup and stopped, listening to hear if anyone was home. The sound of a basketball bouncing against hard-packed earth came from around the side of the house, letting Dodge know that Sam was there, shooting at the goal put up on a pole near the house. Like every other male child in the Alabama-Coushatta Nation, Sam had been shooting at an outdoor basket ever since he could get a ball or a pine cone or a discarded shoe up to it. Dodge got out of the car and walked to the side of the house to say howdy to him.

As Dodge rounded the corner of the house, Sam was just finishing a drive into the right corner of the court he had laid out with staked-down rope around the backboard. He stopped short, jumped off his left foot and as he turned, drifting out of bounds, let loose with a right-handed jump shot. The net hardly moved as the ball fell through it. Retrieving the ball, Sam looked at Dodge and this time drove to the left corner and made the same shot left-handed.

"How many in a row, Sam?" Dodge asked. Sam held up his left hand and closed it twice.

"Nice, mighty nice, Sam, but don't you see, when you shoot that shot as you go out of bounds there ain't no way for you to get a chance at a follow-up."

Sam picked up the ball and didn't answer, except to drive the left corner again, this time landing even further out of bounds after the shot. "Where's Cooper?" Coach Dodge asked and picked up a stick of stove wood to ward off a skinny long-haired dog that was crawling from underneath the house toward him, what teeth it had, bared. Sam jerked his head toward the house and walked out twenty-five feet from the backboard to work on his set shot. Coach Dodge heard the whisper of the first one through the net as he knocked on Cooper's door. The dog kept about a six-foot distance behind him, its eyes set on the back of Coach Dodge's neck.

"Cooper, Cooper Leaping Deer, L. A. Dodge here to see you," the coach hollered through the frame that had once held screen wire in the door. Cooper had removed the wire several years before in hopes of fashioning a dip net for fish like the ones he had seen the white fishermen using on Lake Franklin. Coushatta County was dry, and the nearest liquor store was on the county line on the banks of the huge government lake about thirty miles south. About twice a year Cooper was able to join a group of other elders in the Nation and make the trip over there. Many factors influenced the chance and success of these excursions, the chief one being the simultaneous coincidence of transportation and the monthly fifty-dollar government check. The screen wire dip net hadn't worked out, and Cooper hadn't got around to replacing it.

"See 'em," Cooper called from inside the house in his Coushatta talking-to-white-man voice. Coach Dodge pulled open the door and walked in, blinking to get his eyes used to the wood smoke drifting into the front room from the kitchen. Cooper's wife was cooking something in a pot on a stove which Dodge could see through the door into the next room. The flue pipe had broken loose from the stove some time back, and about as much smoke stayed in the house as got out the hole in the roof where the pipe had been. Cooper was sitting cross-legged on the floor, dressed only in a white undershirt turned inside out and backward with the Fruit of the Loom label in the middle of his chest like a medal. As Dodge walked in, Cooper stood up with dignity and stepped into a pair of blue overalls.

"Hot, Cooper?" Coach Dodge asked, but Cooper didn't bother to explain. Instead he pointed at Dodge with his left hand turned palm down and asked, "Extract?"

"Beaucoup extract, Cooper, after a while. Talk first." Coach Dodge wasn't exactly nervous, but he was keyed up a little. What he had to say to Cooper he had to put in such a way as to enlist his aid in getting Sam to win that state championship while at the same time not causing Cooper to think that the bait he was using would lead to Sam's leaving the Alabama-Coushatta's land for good. Coach Dodge had had this problem before when he had tried to use basketball scholarships to various colleges as incentives and reward. It was never a problem with white players, of course, but the Alabama-Coushattas just didn't seem to be able to appreciate the value of a college education. Hell, he thought, they'd rather see a boy of theirs get married to some little squaw and set right here on this reservation the rest of his life, drawing his government allotment and dancing in them damn corn festivals ever' spring and fall, instead of waiting around for that degree in Phys Ed and coaching basketball at Kountze or Goodrich or maybe even Lufkin. The college scholarship was the only thing that Coach Dodge had ever seen work at all in dealing with an Indian player's family, though, and this one was a good deal different from most of them. Maybe it had a chance.

"Cooper," he began, "Sam Houston Leaping Deer chicamau basketball player."

"Beaucoup chicamau," Cooper agreed.

Coach Dodge heard Cooper's wife back in the kitchen move closer to the door. Outside the sound of the basketball splatting on the red clay continued:

"I'm gonna tell you straight, Cooper. I want to win state. Sam can do it for me. He could have last year, but he pulled that stunt. Sitting there in that bedsheet. I know it was corn planting time, but. . . ." Looking closely at Cooper's eyes, Dodge suddenly stopped his talk of last year, and shifted his weight back and forth from heel to toe.

"Here it is then, Mister and Miz Leaping Deer. You make Sam play now, and I'll get him a free education at a special college." Cooper bowed his head and looked at his Fruit of the Loom label. In the kitchen Mrs. Leaping Deer stirred whatever it was she was cooking in the blackened pot, and threw another stick of wood into the stove, causing a puff of smoke to roll through the door. Dodge hurried on, "Now, it ain't no Texas college. It ain't Huntsville, and it ain't Nacogdoches, and it sure ain't Rice University."

Several years before, one of the Coushatta players, Elton Redd, had left the Nation on a basketball scholarship to Rice, and everything had gone completely wrong with his life. After playing out his four years he had refused to come back to get his plot of land and his allotment, and when he did return on a visit, he was enrolled at some California college, writing what he called "a dissertation on tribal variations in corn dance ritual" and doing "basic research." Afterward his family was treated fairly kindly by most of the Nation, but his father no longer took part in the corn dances and left his shotgun house only at night. Elton's sisters went unmarried, and his mother chanted the death song almost every night. Scholarship deals could go bad, and Coach Dodge knew it. Elton Redd was still hurting the basketball program at Big Muddy, and Dodge knew he had to convince Cooper the same kind of catastrophe wouldn't strike his lodge.

"No sir, not Rice, no sir," Dodge repeated in a strong voice, hoping to drive the idea home to Cooper. Cooper was sitting on the floor again, picking at the undershirt label. He slowly lifted his eyes to Dodge's face and looked at him for half a minute. "No base search," Cooper said finally.

"No, no, no chance of that kind of foolishness a-tall, Cooper. Not a-tall. Let me tell you some more about this deal. I got to go out to the car to get some stuff about it." Coach Dodge pushed out through the screen door frame and as he stepped off the porch he almost tripped over one of the younger children of the Leaping Deer family. The child held a knife with a six-inch blade in one hand and a shoe upper in the other. "Play 'em ball?" Dodge asked loud enough for Cooper to hear in the house. The child, boy or girl Dodge couldn't tell, looked up with Cooper's eyes, and stabbed the point of the blade through the leather in his hand. "Chicamau," Dodge said, exhausting half of his knowledge of the vocabulary of the Coushatta language. He hurried on to the car to get the brochures, catalog, and photographs the basketball scout had given him. Along with the printed material, Coach Dodge also brought back a pint of vanilla extract when he returned to the house. He had meant to get a fifth of some kind of cheap brand of whiskey for this job, but he had been unable to get to the lake before the liquor store closed. "Extract'll have to do," he said under his breath as he pulled the door open. Cooper waited in the same spot, acknowledging the coach's return with a nod. Dodge handed him the extract bottle and went into his pitch.

"Now, you remember Mr. Barlow? Works for the sawmill? Well, his girl got married to a fellow in the Army, and this fellow is a basketball scout now. He was in Franklin at Christmas visiting his wife's folks and saw Sam play in that tournament. He wants Sam to go there where he works at."

Coach Dodge began fumbling through the material he had brought in, and stopped at an 8 by 10 color photograph of an Indian chief in full headdress. He wore buckskin clothing trimmed with long fringes, each of which was closely sewn with colored beads. The feathers of his bonnet were twice as long as the ones Coach Dodge had seen the Alabama-Coushattas wear at their corn dances, and no Alabama-Coushatta had ever worn moccasins decorated in the rich fashion of those on the man in the picture. In fact Converse All-Star tennis shoes swiped from the Big Muddy athletic department were traditional at these functions. The chief in the picture was standing in the middle of a basketball court with his arms extended in front of him at about a 45 degree angle. Each foot was balanced on a brand-new basketball colored with orange and blue stripes. This picture was only one of many of the chief in his costume. Others showed him waving a tomahawk around his head and dancing with his feet pushed so high off the floor his knees were almost touching his chin. One photograph showed the chief about to bury his axe in the head of a papier-mâché animal that looked something like a large rat with an M on its chest. Another pictured the chief standing triumphant over a large bean-shaped object that had obviously just felt the wrath of the chief's weapon.

Cooper studied each picture carefully as Coach Dodge handed them to him one by one. When he had seen the last one, he pointed to the words which were printed at the bottom of each and looked at the coach. "It says Chief Illy . . . Eye-lee . . . or something like that, Cooper," Dodge said.

"What he is, see, is he is the head man there of all the school. He's a real Indian, and he's the one that runs the whole show up there in Illinois." Coach Dodge sounded the s as he pronounced the word. "That's what that scout told me. The whole school is Indian-oriented, he says. What he means is that the Indians there are the main ones. Not like at these Texas schools." Dodge stopped to judge the effect of his words on Cooper and tried to think of something to add. "Look at them decorations," he offered. "Now, that ain't all," he hurried on. Cooper broke the seal on the bottle of extract.

"Let me show these pictures of a different thing." Coach Dodge pushed several more photos toward Cooper. After taking a swig from the extract bottle, Cooper began to look through them. "Sha towea," he said.

"That's right," Dodge said, offering up the rest of his proficiency in Coushatta. "Corn. It's corn. That field you see there with that fence around it is right there on the schoolyard. It's the only experimental cornfield right slap on the schoolyard in the whole country. That scout says it's been there a long time, ever since they made that university in the first place. What they do, see, is they think it's the most important thing there on the grounds, and they take care of it just like your people do."

"Have dance?"

"Yes, they do," Dodge said, not knowing if they did or not. "Ever' spring and fall, same time as y'all do. Have their dance, yessir."

"Chief Ill-ee dance then?"

"He leads it, just like Miller Sylestine does here. Only he's got better clothes and all, like you see." Dodge pointed to the pile of photographs on the floor beside Cooper. "Cooper, if Sam goes there it'll be just like being here at home on the reservation. Got the dances, got the corn growing right there. And I flat guarantee you, he ain't the only one to get something out of this neither." Cooper looked up again. "I mean you, Cooper. Get Sam to play that game in the state tournament like he can if he will, and plenty of extract."

Cooper looked at the photograph of the cornfield, tapped it with a fingernail and said, "He play."

"Best thing you ever said, for you *and* Sam, Cooper. I mean it. Come out to the car and get the rest of that extract. You can keep them pictures if you want to and show them to Sam."

After unloading the rest of the bottles, Coach Dodge guided the station wagon around the dead cars in the front yard back toward the state highway. He could hear Sam and the basketball as he started up the hill to get to the dirt road leading out. Through his rearview mirror he caught a glimpse of the skinny dog and the child with the knife stalking each other. He picked up a photograph of Chief Illini that had fallen to the car floor when he had taken the others inside. He took his eyes off the road to look at it. Chief Illini seemed to be dancing and cavorting especially for the Big Muddy Bobcats and for him. Reaching up, Coach Dodge stuck the edge of the picture under the sunvisor, making it easy for him to look up at as he started back to Big Muddy.

Sam watched the brake lights of the station wagon come on as Coach Dodge slowed to maneuver around a chuckhole, and then turned to speak to the younger Leaping Deer child.

"You see that man, little brother?"

"You mean the White Eyes?" asked the boy, reaching out to the skinny dog with his left hand while he tried to balance his knife on the back of the other. "Yes, I see him. And I see him talk to our father. Why?"

"Just this thing, little brother," said Sam. "Never show him your best move."

Sam half turned toward the basketball goal and tossed up a fifteen footer left-handed. It hit the edge of the hoop with a flat metallic sound and bounced away toward the side of the house.

"You do and that man will try to buy it," Sam said to his brother and moved off to retrieve the rolling ball from underneath the edge of Cooper Leaping Deer's house.

The big gymnasium on the University of Texas campus was only about half-filled with rooters on the afternoon of the Class C championship game. The large crowds showed up only for the higher divisions of the play-offs, which were scheduled at night in order to allow local television and radio coverage. Big Muddy belonged to the lowest division, which was made up of schools with enrollments of less than two hundred. The largest division, the AAAA, always received the most attention in the state play-offs because it included the big city schools, such as Houston and Dallas. The founding fathers of the classification system had thought it only fair to allow the small schools to play each other for one of the six state crowns because of the disparity in the number of students from which each school had to select its play-ers. The whole classification system had been a sore point to Big Muddy partisans for a long time. This year, for example, the two schools scheduled to play for the AAAA championship had each lost only one game during the regular season, and in both cases, to the Big Muddy Bobcats. Coach Dodge didn't bother himself with this irony, however, for all he wanted was the Class C champion-ship, and he believed this year he would get it. That is, if Sam Leaping Deer did what Cooper had promised he would.

Last year when Coach Dodge had gone to the motel room at noon to get Sam and his roommate Homer Cloud, he found Sam sitting in the middle of the floor wrapped in a bed sheet singing some sort of song over and over in the Coushatta tongue. Dodge had finally got him to the gymnasium, but Sam wouldn't play a lick, and the Bobcats lost by six points. Not again this year, please Lord.

Sam sat in the dressing room listening to Coach Dodge's in-structions a few minutes before the game with David Crockett High. At least Coach Dodge thought Sam was listening as much as he ever did. He was sitting on a bench with the other players from the Alabama-Coushatta Nation, the four token whites from the sawmill camp, and the twin sons of the Big Muddy school superin-tendent. The look on Sam's face reminded Coach Dodge uncom-fortably of the look on the face of the child with the six-inch blade. But Sam was looking up as Dodge talked, and that was a lot better than what he had done last year at this time.

Once Coach Dodge had attended what they called a "coach-ing clinic" over at Huntsville because the Big Muddy School had paid him to go, and there he had learned in one session entitled "The Psychology of Winning Basketball" a model speech winning coaches were supposed to make before big games. Dodge had never really bothered with speeches before, but this time he thought he would try to remember what he had heard then. A reporter from one of the Austin newspapers sat in the dressing room with a notepad on his knee. "Men," Coach Dodge began, remembering that the coach of the clinic had said always to call your players that, "men, we have come a long way to this moment of deciding." He looked over at the reporter who held his ballpoint poised over the paper. "It's a long road from here in Austin back to Big Muddy. And I don't mean just miles." The reporter scribbled on his pad. "You have all took up the slack when the going was rough." One of the white substitutes yelled "Yea, Bobcats!" Coach Dodge looked over at him and frowned, trying to remember what came next. "Pulled in the slack. Yes sir. This here is the big one. Make your school proud of this bunch of bo . . . *men* this afternoon in this beautiful gymnasium on the campus of the University of Texas in Austin." He looked over at the reporter and added, "Home of the Longhorns." The sons of the sawmill hands and foremen and strawbosses and the superintendent's twins jumped up and yelled various things. The four Coushattas and the two Alabamas stared at their new white basketball shoes, which had been donated by the lumber company commissary right before they left Big Muddy.

"O.K., men. That's all. Let's go out there now," Coach Dodge said in a loud voice, catapulting the white players toward the tunnel leading to the basketball court.

"You sure got them fired up, Coach," the reporter said. "They sound like they came to play." Coach Dodge nodded sagely as he listened to the war whoops of the white players fading down the tunnel and the squeak of the new shoes on the Coushattas trailing behind.

As Sam walked out on the court for warmup, he could hear the Big Muddy cheerleaders across the floor starting up their yells. The cheerleading squad was composed of four white girls dressed in purple and white costumes and one boy, H. W. Dillard, whose teeth protruded so much he was known at the school among the whites as Picket Fence. The Indians didn't have a name for him at all. H. W. dropped to one knee and began to lead the crowd of about two hundred fans who had followed the team to Austin:

> Crockett will die tonight.
> Crockett will die.
> When the sun goes down
> And the moon comes up
> Crockett will die.

H. W. then tried a back flip, inspired as he was, and almost made it over, but one of the girls got a pompom in the way and instead he banged into the first row of seats with his left shoulder.

Sam Leaping Deer thought about the corn dance, which had begun the day before right at the time the team was playing Uvalde, and then he thought about his father's command. He took a jump shot, retrieved the ball, and with it in his left hand he walked over to the Big Muddy bench and said a phrase in the common language of the Alabama and Coushatta tribes to the team manager, President Polk, an Alabama too fat and slow to play but not too proud to fetch and carry in order to get to ride on the yellow school bus on which the team made its trips. President Polk reached into the front of his shirt and drew out a small leather bag hanging from a drawstring around his neck. He loosened the mouth of the bag and pulled out what looked like a piece of blackened tree root. Sam broke off a piece about the size of a dime and put it under his tongue, as President Polk replaced the substance in the bag. "Chicamau," Sam said.

And then he played basketball for thirty-two minutes.

The Class C Texas State Champions left Austin almost immediately after the game with Crockett ended. The Alabama-Coushatta players wanted to get back to the reservation to take part in as much of the corn dance as remained, and the white players and Coach Dodge were looking forward to the homecoming they would get in Big Muddy. The play-by-play account of the game had been broadcast by the radio station in Franklin, and already passenger cars and pickups were crawling up the red clay roads of the school district toward the gymnasium where the team was expected to arrive before midnight. The school superintendent had even allowed the fleet of buses which most of the students rode to and from school to be pressed into service to bring in fans who couldn't make it any other way.

The school bus carrying the Bobcats, the cheerleaders, and various other Big Muddy people had reached as far as Navasota by about nightfall. Sam sat near the rear by a window looking out at the rolling country covered with small scrubby oaks. The tall pines and the thickets would begin to appear abruptly a few miles west of Huntsville. The land here looked to Sam too open, too light. He could see for hundreds of feet into the small clumps of trees that flashed past the school bus. It seemed to him that a person would not be able to hide from sight if he wanted to, here. The pastures on each side of the highway were not friendly like the deep gullies and the interwoven grapevines, saw grass, and youpon bushes covering the reservation. Here was no protection, no cover.

Sam drew his eyes away from the window to try to stop thinking about open spaces, and as he did, he saw that across the aisle Mary Ethel Matlock was leaning so far in his direction that she was almost sitting in the seat beside him. In fact, she sat turned sideways in the seat, her knees pushed up against Sam's seat across the narrow aisle. Just above the red pressure marks on her knees caused by the edge of the seat cutting into them were grainy white splotches. Sam looked at Mary Ethel's face and then quickly fixed his eyes on the back of the seat in front of him. Mary Ethel said, "Hi, Sam."

She was the daughter of Mr. Tibb Matlock, one of the wealthy of the Big Muddy community, so wealthy in fact, that Mary Ethel drove her own car to school every day instead of riding a school bus. Despite Mary Ethel's wealth, however, she was not a pleasing girl to look at. She weighed close to two hundred pounds, it was rumored, and the dresses she habitually wore with broad vertical stripes did little to conceal the fact. Her hair was always nicely done up each week at a beauty shop in Franklin, but the extra layers of fatty tissue in her face made her mouth look even smaller than it really was. It was pulled down at the corners by the load of blubber her chin and throat muscles were forced to support, so that she always looked as though she was about to burst into tears. She did often do just that, particularly in class when an academic or social failure took place. She would lay her head on her desk and cry until suddenly with a great lurch she would flounder up and run out into the hall, snickers of her classmates sounding behind her.

Mary Ethel had enjoyed a sort of renaissance of attention and sympathy recently, however, because her mother had died within the last month of cancer of the brain. Mary Ethel had bravely insisted on following the Bobcats to Austin for the state tournament in spite of her grief, and several of the white girls in the school had felt it their duty to cheer her up even if she did weigh so much and have so much money. Her greeting to Sam was partly a result of the haze of well-being in which Mary Ethel had recently found herself wandering.

She never went out with boys, except twice as blind dates in Houston when she had visited her cousin, but it was universally acknowledged among the white girls at Big Muddy that Mary Ethel had a real good personality. Now, riding on the darkened school bus back toward home with the State Champion Bobcats, Mary Ethel had gathered the courage to speak to Sam Leaping Deer, a flathead Indian. The other girls on the bus were all sitting near the front, some singing and some half-reclining by their boyfriends. Mary Ethel had earlier worked her way to the back of the bus seat by seat as the sky outside grew dimmer, and by the time the bus had left the lighted streets of Navasota, she had positioned herself right across the aisle from Sam. She had been watching the back of his head for several minutes before he had turned and seen her. When he looked away from her again, Mary Ethel shot a quick glance toward the front of the bus. No one was looking back. Coach Dodge was driving, so happy that every few hundred feet he gave the horn a little tap. When he did, several of the students in front would laugh and yell. Everyone seemed occupied. Mary Ethel could see the back of Nelda Bailey's head four seats up, but Nelda was busy holding off Ray Adcock's right arm with one hand and rubbing the back of his neck with the other. The darkness in the back of the bus was intensified by the light in front from the driver's instrument panel. Mary Ethel sucked in a deep breath and heaved herself into a crouching position between the two seats. Then adroitly and silently she swung herself into the seat by Sam.

"Do you mind, Sam? I just wanted to talk to you about the game." Sam had felt the seat cushion sink and tilt beneath him as Mary Ethel sat down, but he hadn't turned toward her. He said nothing and sat very still.

"You sure did play a good game, Sam. When you made that last jump shot, I just like to died." Mary Ethel spoke in a hoarse whisper, her tight little mouth dry. As her right arm jiggled to the swaying and bouncing of the bus, it touched Sam at intervals of a few seconds. Each time it did, Mary Ethel felt it burn all the way up her arm, through her armpit into her chest, and then up into her throat.

"I really admire your ball playing, Sam. My daddy says you're the best Indian—, best ballplayer Big Muddy ever had. The way you can dribble and shoot is real cool. I just love to see you do it." Sam seemed to be hugging his arms tighter against his side. Mary Ethel relaxed her shoulder muscles so that the motion of the bus had a better chance to push her arm against Sam's. "Wasn't you real scared when we got behind in the last quarter, Sam?" Sam spoke to her for the first time.

"When?" Actually Sam seldom kept up with the score of any game he played, and in this one, he could not have unscrambled the colored lights of the scoreboard if he had looked at it.

"You know. When that old referee called a technical on Coach Dodge and gave them two free throws and the ball." Mary Ethel tentatively shifted her weight to her left buttock, hoping to let gravity aid her right leg in its career toward Sam's left. The movement was a success. She now had maneuvered herself so that alternately her right arm and right leg were touching Sam. Her throat burned so much that she found it hard to talk at all. She swallowed twice, then again before she offered anything further.

"We're all just so proud of the boys for winning the state. Specially you. I mean if it wasn't for you old Crockett would be number one now 'stead of us." Sam still hadn't looked in her direction. She peered again toward the couple closest to the seat where she and Sam were and saw that Nelda Bailey now had both arms up around Ray's neck, rubbing the back of his head. Nelda had slumped lower in the seat so that by this time Mary Ethel could see only the very top of Nelda's head outlined against the bus window by the headlights of an oncoming car. The car passed, and Nelda's head disappeared completely from view. Mary Ethel allowed herself to sag further over toward Sam, who sat stiffly upright on his third of the seat, his face hidden in the shadows.

The shape his head made against the dim light coming through the window reminded Mary Ethel of the last blind date she had had in Houston. The first one had turned out to be not much fun because the boy had refused to talk or sit close to Mary Ethel at the drive-in movie her cousin's boyfriend had taken them to. On her next trip to Houston, though, Mary Ethel went to another drive-in with a different boy, Lupé Lopez, a Mexican boy in her cousin's class, who looked to Mary Ethel not too different from one of the reservation Indians back home. "Lupé has a real cute personality," Mary Ethel had told her cousin after this date, thinking of how he had grabbed her and wrestled her back and forth in the back seat of the car, all the while chewing on her lips and tongue.

"Oh, Sam," Mary Ethel forced words past the hot drought in her throat and mouth, "I'm just so grateful to you for winning the state for us. I just wish there was something I could do to show what it means to me. I mean, after my mother dying of brain cancer on the 27th of February and all. I just feel so cheered up."

Just at that point Coach Dodge began steering the bus into a steep left curve, tipping Mary Ethel even more to the right. Sam shifted his pinned shoulders, trying to find some extra space between the girl on his left and the steel wall on his right. As he brought his right shoulder forward, Mary Ethel's head collapsed against his left bicep and she voiced a low bubbly sigh. "Sam, I feel like you're a racing driver just won a race, and I ought to give you a kiss for it." She closed her eyes and pushed her chin up at Sam's face, the effort forcing her mouth open. The wetness of it glistened in the light coming over Sam's shoulder from the window, and he gazed at the dark line Mary Ethel's lower teeth made against the moon's reflection. The mouth made a swallowing sound, setting off a series of small clicks. "Oh," Mary Ethel's voice said damply, "Stick in your tongue if you want to." Instead Sam loudly broke into a chant used by the Coushattas to frighten off the big-bellied ghost men who prowled the winter nights in search of male children because they had lost their own.

"God damn," Coach Dodge said, jerking the steering wheel to the left to get back on the road from the shoulder where he had veered when the yelling began in the back of the bus. Gravel from the road-bed chattered against the underside of the chassis, and everyone sitting toward the front of the bus jerked around to stare into the darkness at the rear. Switching on the dome lights and peering into the rearview mirror, Coach Dodge saw Nelda Bailey patting her hair with one hand and making smoothing motions below his line of vision with the other. Several seats further back on the left side of the bus, Mary Ethel Matlock sat leaning over the back of the seat in front of her with both hands jammed into her eye sockets. Across the aisle Sam Houston Leaping Deer continued the racket he had started a few seconds earlier just before Mary Ethel called him a stinking flathead and lurched away to the opposite seat to collapse like a gut-shot doe.

"Wait for the corn dance, Sam," Coach Dodge said kindly, not being up on tonal variations in Alabama-Coushatta ritual chants. "We'll be back in Big Muddy pretty quick now, everybody. So just wait a spell." He increased the speed of the bus to what it had been before and turned off the interior lights. The white students aboard went back to their business. The girls in the front started up a new song, and Nelda Bailey again grabbed Ray Adcock's right hand with her left and settled back in the seat. Ray began to grumble about having to go back to first base again but soon got quiet.

Mary Ethel Matlock dug the heels of her hands into her eyes and thought about the big glob of red jello eating her mother's brain and about Lupé Lopez's quick tongue working its way to the back of her throat. Little quakes of emotion sent tremors hiccupping through her breathing apparatus as the bus pulled through Huntsville and on toward home. Sam continued to chant in a low monotone, and the other Alabama-Coushattas looked out the windows at the dark silent pine thickets, wondering if the makhantas Sam had seen were following them all the way back to the reservation.

By the time Coach Dodge pulled the yellow bus carrying the official Big Muddy party into the parking lot beside the school gymnasium, the passenger cars carrying the fans back from Austin had already arrived and met the folks gathered there. Some leader in the group had directed everyone to draw his vehicle into a huge U shape with the others facing the road, and at sight of the team bus all those waiting in the cars turned on their headlights. "Make sure you get them on high beam," the man who had thought of the maneuver directed. As the team bus slowed to a stop in the parking lot no one aboard could see anything but the blinding car lights and the dark bulk of the gymnasium at the edge of the bright half circle. The other school buildings were completely blotted out by the display. All the girls and some of the boys on Coach Dodge's bus began to laugh and squeal in high voices at the magnificence of the greeting.

"Would you look at that! Ain't it something?" Even Coach Dodge himself felt a tickle in the back of his throat, as he heard the crowd of people outside break into the Big Muddy school song. He pulled the door release and stood up in the aisle, fighting to keep the swarm of cheerleaders from pushing him back into the driver's seat. "Now, wait just a minute," he bellowed past a purple and white pompom which someone had jammed into his face. "Let the boys off first now, y'all. Let these folks get a look at them." By the time the white players and the cheerleaders and the other riders had ejected themselves from the bus into the knots of people out-side, several of the drivers of the cars in the U formation had switched their headlights off to save their batteries, so that as Coach Dodge followed President Polk down the steps, it was considerably darker outside than when the bus had first pulled up. Just before the yell went up from the crowd at the sight of the winning coach walking down the steps to the soil of Big Muddy, Dodge heard the bang of the emergency door at the rear of the bus as someone slammed it shut. This ain't no time to worry about them fool Indians, now, he thought, raising his hands above his head the way he had seen boxers do on the sports pages of the *Houston Chronicle.*

Sam and the other two Coushattas who had left through the emergency exit headed across the parking lot toward the farm-to-market road leading back to the state highway. Trotting a little ahead of the other two, Sam put his hand to his chest to touch the leather pouch he had retrieved from President Polk in the dressing room after the game. Behind the three Indians a string of firecrackers went off at the celebration and someone in the crowd let out a whoop. It must have been H. W. Dillard, because in a few seconds the sound of the cheerleaders starting up a yell began. Sam fumbled with the pouch as he moved in a trot down the gravel shoulders of the road, thinking ahead to the reservation and what remained of the last night of the corn dance. As he neared a fence line angling off the highway to the right, he veered off the shoulder and jumped a small dry ditch, his companions right behind him. A rabbit made a quick leap into the path ahead of Sam, zigzagging from side to side until it disappeared suddenly into a youpon thicket. Sam Leaping Deer looked up at the three-quarter moon and slightly quickened his pace. Behind him the Big Muddy Independent School Marching Band faintly hammered its way into "The Eyes of Texas." Slipping the leather pouch over his head, Sam handed it behind him like a relay runner making a pass in reverse. Frank Shoes took it perfectly, not breaking his stride, and a little later passed it back to Sam. The moon shone brighter.

In less than two hours Sam and the two other Coushattas reached Long King Creek, the stream which ran partway along one edge of the reservation and then cut across it toward the river to the east. Sam's ancestor, the mythical Leaping Deer who regularly cleared the thirty-foot creek on hunting trips, had made his leaps a few miles north of the trail Sam and the other two followed to the water's edge. Splashing through the knee-deep stream, Sam remembered Old Man Sylestine pointing out the patch of earth from which the original Leaping Deer had launched himself forever into the heavens, a pig from the white man's settlement under each arm. Sam looked up for the constellation the old man claimed as memorial to the leap, but the moon had hidden the stars with its light. Behind him, Frank Shoes said something to the other Coushatta and they both snorted, holding back their laughs. Their voices sounded slurred and slow to Sam, as if they came from under water. He looked down at the ground in front of him, watching first one foot, then the other poke itself into view and then vanish. Up ahead several yards, an armadillo heard the approach of the boys and ran grunting through the underbrush. The three heard it bounce off something with a metallic sound and continue off through the pines. "Fence," Sam said in English, not having the word in the language of the Nation.

The hurricane fence just ahead had been built by the government a few years before to replace the three strands of barbed wire which had encircled the reservation up until then. Hogs, of course, found barbed wire no hindrance, and over the years the half-wild hogs belonging in name to the white men who had cut notches of various design in the animals' ears roamed at will back and forth between the reservation and the country surrounding it. The hogs' favorite target was sha towea, the corn ground and the center of the Nation. Because of the rails the men of the tribe had piled around the plot, the hogs were generally unsuccessful, and the Indians had worried little about the random damage the corn suffered. At critical times in the yearly planting, cultivating, and harvest, the subchiefs assigned each family the task of providing someone to stand guard at night, and Sam had put in his time between the ages of six and fourteen along with the rest of the youths of the Alabamas and Coushattas at his station. There was seldom any trouble from the hogs owned by the Indian families. Very few of these animals lived long enough to be able to break out of the pens scattered near the houses of those who kept them. The hogs belonging to the Alabama-Coushattas generally perished one by one off and on during the winters as the corn ran out and the white man's pulpwood crews stopped operating in the muddy woods. During these months of the year, the white man's piney-woods rooters wisely stayed on the other side of the three strands of barbed wire, harking back to some sort of racial memory of red men with long knives and smoking fires.

The understanding between the white man's hogs and the Alabama-Coushattas endured with the exception of small incidents of corn theft and pig murder for years, until the event one summer which led to the government hurricane fence. McKinley Short Eyes, an old bachelor of the Nation to whom the sick went for herb remedies and faith healings, had himself died after his own medicine and prayers to the Old Ones had not worked. Before his death Short Eyes had instructed the people gathered in the sleeping room of his shotgun house about the kind of burial he wanted. He told them not to inform the agent who lived on the reservation in a brick house near the headquarters and post office that he had died until several days after the fact. In the meantime he wanted to be wrapped in a leather covering and raised up to lie upon a wooden platform near Long King Creek in the old way, long outlawed by the white man's health department. "After three days," he had told the men squatting near the quilt on the floor where he rested, "tell Hickson to give burying money to Chief Sylestine." Then Short Eyes had pointed out which personal effects he wanted placed on the grave mound when his body was put into the white man's box and buried in the government-approved cemetery near the agency headquarters.

After the old man died, some women had sewn him into the two cowhides he had been saving for the event. Sam, along with two other boys, had stood on a pine stump outside the unscreened window of McKinley Short Eyes' house and watched the process. That night several men of the Nation, Sam's father among them, had carried the cowhide bag, with the hair side turned inward as Short Eyes had directed, through the thickets toward the creek. Sam followed at a distance and watched them lift the old man's body up to shoulder level and place it on the platform made of pine saplings tied together with strips of rawhide and pieces of wire the white crew had left when they put up a telephone booth beside the post office. Sam had hidden behind a rotting sweetgum trunk as the four men walked back toward the village after they had finished their job. He waited until the moon rose just above the top of the tallest pine and then turned back toward home. He had seen no movement in the leather bag and heard no sounds from the Old Ones in the earth, the water, and the sky.

When he returned the next night to watch, he again could see no difference in the appearance of the bag and no sign of the Old Ones. They remained hidden. The next night, the last before the men would tell Mr. Hickson about Short Eyes' death and bury him where the white man said they must, Sam could tell there was a change near the creek long before he saw the platform. The water in Long King seemed full of splashing sounds, and the underbrush was moving in short jerks. He had stopped to listen, afraid to approach the Old Ones at their work. Stepping around the fallen log he had hidden behind two nights before, Sam moved so that he could see the platform more clearly. At first he thought the Old Ones had taken the old man and his platform completely, but then moving nearer he saw that one end had fallen and was resting on the ground. The telephone wire that had held the top of the platform to the supporting sapling was moving in a series of jerks, making a thrumming cracking sound as if a child were using a bowstring to pull something through the brush. A yellowish hog, long bristles standing in a ridge on its back, had caught one of its hind legs in the wire as it tore at the leather bag holding McKinley Short Eyes. Two other hogs, darker ones, were reared up with their front feet to the slanting platform, feeding with quick short jerks of their heads, their tusks yellow in the moonlight. Short Eyes' left arm, the one away from the hogs, had fallen out of the bag and moved rhythmically up and down as the snouts shook and worried the body. The beads the old man had fastened to the front of the shirt made a dry clicking as the hogs rooted at the flesh.

Sam had used a pine knot to club the hogs away and had sat guard all night until the men came next morning to take the body up to the village cemetery. All through the night the three hogs had stayed just outside the range of the club, snuffling in the dead sycamore leaves and drinking from Long King Creek. The Old Ones did not come to wait with Sam. The only sounds he had heard were those that hungry animals make in the dark.

The burying party had arrived just after sunup, and after putting what was left of McKinley Short Eyes back into the torn cowhide bag, two of them carried the load back through the woods to the village cemetery. At sight and smell of the four new men, the hogs had retreated across the creek to feed on beech shoots, occasionally lifting their long snouts to sniff the breeze coming across the water at them from the burial site. Cooper Leaping Deer and the other Indian, a fat young Alabama who worked off and on at the sawmill in Camp Mineola, had left Sam to watch the hogs and had gone back to their houses for weapons. For the rest of that day and most of the next there took place what Agent Hickson always referred to later as the Big Hog Massacre. "What I don't understand," he had written in the report to the Department of the Interior, "is not the fact that certain Alabama-Coushattas hunted down and killed every piney-wood rooter they could find on the reservation, but that they didn't butcher out a single one to eat. As best as I can determine from my investigation of the incident, what hogs they didn't mutilate and leave for the buzzards, they poured kerosene on and set fire to."

Agent Hickson had suffered a great deal of embarrassment and chastisement as a result of the brief war against hogs—and *marked* hogs, at that—so he pushed hard in the report to the government for a hog-proof fence. A few of the slain hogs had even belonged to the United States congressman from that district, who maintained a farm near Franklin, his childhood home. The congressman prided himself on his knowledge of the character and ways of the Alabama-Coushattas, but their actions in this case, he announced, gave him cause for great surprise and alarm. "I can accept the extermination of the hogs that ate up the old man," he had told Agent Hickson when he had come to the reservation to discuss the rush order for fencing, "but I am appalled at the senseless slaughter of innocent hogs. I had some high-bred boars killed in that action, and I want to see to it that no more of them perish." Agent Hickson had increased the frequency of the head-nodding he had begun as soon as the congressman had arrived at village headquarters.

"That nine-foot hurricane fence will do her," he swore to the congressman as he sat in his car ready to leave. "Sunk a foot in the ground too, so they can't root under it. You see, sir, the reason these hogs around here have formed the habit of coming into the reservation is mainly that big patch of corn the Indians grow every year. Not even good corn, neither. They won't use hybrid strains or even fertilizer."

"Well, no matter about that, Mr. Hickson. I'll make sure you get that fence put up. We can't have these citizens around here getting their stock killed." With that, the congressman had rolled up the window of the Lincoln and the driver had smoothly pulled away, leaving Hickson, a smallish man with oversized ears, standing in the gravel roadway with the smell of gasoline fumes in his nostrils.

The fencing crew had arrived soon after the congressman got back to Washington, and within a few weeks the Alabama-Coushatta reservation was encircled by a nine-foot steel hurricane fence, sunk one foot into the ground, anchored in concrete, and coated with an aluminum alloy to prevent rust. The white men had also built cattle guards of steel rails where the state highway cut across a corner of the reservation. Only one mistake had occurred in construction, and it was a small one. The angle irons at the top of the linked fence which supported three strands of barbed wire had in some unknown fashion been turned the wrong way. As a result, the barbed wire was no real hindrance to anything or anyone scaling the fence into the reservation, but it made a difficult job of climbing the fence to get out. Most of the young men of the Nation had, in fact, learned to avoid attempting to climb out of the reservation by means of the fence. The ones who did try it did so only under great duress, and in these moments usually suffered being snagged or torn by the white man's steel on the way over. The direction of the barbed wire had taught most of them to take the long way around, down the various unpaved roads of the section to the center of the village, up the blacktop road to the state highway, and then across the rail cattle guards, where it was necessary to look closely and step cautiously to avoid breaking an ankle or leg.

On the other hand, the direction of the barbed wire made it quite simple to scale the fence from outside the reservation on the way back in. It was so encouraging to the young Alabamas and Coushattas, in fact, that several one-way trails led from the various places the youths visited outside the reservation up to the steel fence. The trail that Sam and the other two Coushattas were following back to the reservation from the Big Muddy Independent School was one of the most traveled of these.

Sam fastened the top button of his shirt so that the pouch on the leather string would not catch on the barbed wire on his way over. He scrambled quickly up the chain link fence and paused at the top, standing almost straight up, one foot on a barbed wire support and the other on a strand of wire between two barbs. Frank Shoes shook the steel mesh behind him as he climbed. Sam launched himself into a pool of darkness at the base of a sycamore near the fence and landed in a half-crouch, his left foot tingling from the impact. As he rose and began to trot toward the village, looking up between the new leaves at the sky, he heard Frank hit behind him and a squeal from the barbed wire as Haskell balanced on it. In a few minutes they would be in the village at the corn dance, at the center of the Alabama-Coushatta Nation.

The light from the four fires built at each point of the compass was barely visible to the three members of the Class C Texas State Championship basketball team as they neared the big clearing. Sam raised his right hand, and they slowed to a walk in order not to disturb the major ceremony of the last night of the spring corn dance. They stopped short of the outer edge of the circle of people who squatted ahead, facing the center of the clearing like a crowd of spectators at a sporting event. A few of the younger children in the gathering slept on blankets scattered around the perimeter of the circle, and every few minutes one or the other of the young men would walk off into the darkness followed a few steps behind by a young woman of the Nation. The departures were all quiet. The young men never looked back to see if they were being followed, and the young girls always looked at the ground directly in their path as they walked from the open space into the dark thickets. For the most part, the crowd was quiet, its attention centered on the figures in the middle of the hard-packed dance ground. Sam could tell by the positions assumed by the two men wrapped in bearskins near one of the low fires that the story of why Fire came to the Alabama-Coushattas had just begun.

The two Bear Clan members were bent over from the waist, making deep snuffling noises in their throats. One of them held a stick of wood in each hand as though about to replenish the dying fire near them. Suddenly the other Bear actor moved away and began swinging his head from side to side. The Bear carrying the wood followed the other figure, and both disappeared into a small knot of people seated on the side of the clearing opposite to where Sam squatted. Fire called in a faint voice for help, but the Bears did not hear. He fluttered and grew dimmer as the minutes passed. A small boy near the inner edge of the circle of watchers shouted for the Bears to return, bringing low laughs from those near him. Sam pulled his chin with his right hand to stifle his smile. He sneaked a look at Haskell and Frank Shoes, but they were both avoiding looking at anyone. In the clearing Fire called again in a weaker voice. One year Sam had been Fire in the performance. No child was allowed the privilege more than once. This year's child made his voice quaver as the fire sank lower into itself. This time a voice answered from the darkness, and in a few seconds an Indian trotted into view with several sticks of wood in his arms. Sam recognized Austin Black Fox behind the carved wooden rack covering the top part of his face. Looking back toward the dying fire, Sam's eyes caught a glimpse of his father's face turned toward him from a part of the crowd several feet to his left. Cooper raised his head and made a circle with the first finger and thumb, his sign for Sam's basketball playing. Sam nodded once toward his father, and both looked back at the Indian now asking Fire where his custodians, the Bears, had gone. Fire was too weak to answer, so Indian fed him two sticks and left to bring more sticks from the other points of direction. After all of the four directions away from the heart had yielded their fuel, Fire grew into a large blaze, strong and warm again. Suddenly the two Bear figures reappeared, full from their feast of acorns and ready to reclaim Fire. Fire spoke in the language of the Nation, "I know the Bears no longer. I will stay with Man." Thus had Fire come again this year to live with the Alabama-Coushattas.

After Fire was safe, a few of the younger people gathered for the ritual applauded like white men, as they had learned to do at the basketball games in the Big Muddy gymnasium.

"Hey, Chief," someone called in a white man's voice. Sam turned in the direction of the sound and received the full benefit of a flash bulb at close range. It came from the strobe unit of a stubby white man wearing blue jeans, cowboy boots, three cameras, and a large leather carrying case.

"Hey, yeah, you," the man said and broke into a little trot as Sam retreated. "I mean you, old buddy. You're the basketball guy, right?" He fumbled with the flap to his case and began making adjustments to one of his cameras, different from the first one he had used.

"Can I get a couple of shots of you with one of these dancers? Maybe a couple of them in the costumes, you know? It'd be gangbusters." He swung his head back and forth as though it was on a swivel and asked the crowd of Alabamas and Coushattas at large if anyone could find him a basketball for a prop.

"How much you pay me?" someone called out in English. "A dollar is what it takes."

"Sure," the photographer said, "I'll give anybody a dollar for a basketball and a good pose."

A group of the younger people, President Polk at the center of the throng, moved toward the white man, waving their hands in the air as though they were in a Big Muddy classroom in home economics. "Come on, Sam," one of them called. "It'll be a dollar."

Sam took advantage of the response to the photographer to move out of the firelight and follow quickly behind a cluster of families walking away toward their homes. He fell in behind one in particular, a clump of people headed up a red clay road pointed north. It was the family of Thomas Two Tongues, led by the evangelist himself. Two Tongues had a vague sense that the corn dance rituals were not really in keeping with his position as a preacher of the Gospel of Christ. He also felt that if he didn't continue making an appearance at these gatherings of the Nation, attendance and collections might fall off at the Holiness Church. The result of his divided thinking was a compromise he had arrived at over the past few years. He and his family attended all ceremonies of the Nation as spectators, but Brother Two Tongues allowed none of them to take active part in the festivities. In particular, his daughter La Wanda never joined the couples who slipped away from the clearing into the nearby thickets during the spring and fall rites. La Wanda now walked at a slow pace at the rear of her family group, so slowly in fact that her smallest brother had already passed her. The moon was near setting, and away from the central fire in the clearing the light was almost gone. Sam had to look at a point a little above the figures in front of him to see them at all. As he came to within a few feet of La Wanda he spoke her name. She looked back quickly at him, then again toward her father a short distance ahead.

"I see you, Sam Leaping Deer."

"I see you," Sam answered formally.

Tom had heard the exchange, but he had not yet turned

around to see who was speaking to his daughter. The entire group walked several yards in silence.

"I see you, Thomas Two Tongues," Sam said.

"Who sees me? What voice is that?" Brother Two Tongues halted, as did the whole group except for one of La Wanda's half-asleep brothers. His mother jerked his arm to keep him from walking into the pine sapling.

"Sam Leaping Deer. He sees you."

"La Wanda," Thomas said, "walk ahead with your mother." He looked toward Sam.

"You are basketball boy. You play games with a piece of wire nailed to a tree. You are not a Christian. You don't have Jesus in your heart."

He paused to think of more flaws in Sam's character, and in a few seconds added, "You have many cars in your yard. Yet none goes on the highway. My daughter does not know you." He turned to follow his family, already past a bend in the road.

"Thomas Two Tongues," Sam called after him. "You pray to the white man's god each week in your church. Yet you eat Abba Mikko's corn."

"I got Jesus in my heart, basketball boy," Two Tongues said.

"But what is in your belly, white man's preacher? Answer that question," said Sam and left the road to plunge into the thickets between himself and his father's home. He was already asleep on the front porch by the time his family returned from the corn dance, his left hand resting on the leather pouch attached to the thong around his neck.

11

A Trip to the Bead-Spitter

The last two months of Sam's career at Big Muddy High School rolled by quickly, and one afternoon late in May he found himself sitting on the stage of the auditorium with the other scholarship winners, listening to Marsue Campbell deliver the valedictory address. The superintendent of the school had found reprinted in an American Legion magazine a prize-winning speech first spoken by a teenage leader somewhere in Pennsylvania. Marsue now stood before the assembly of parents, cousins, friends, and Alabama-Coushattas with her eyes half-closed in concentration, saying very rapidly the sentences which she had got by heart during the last six weeks. She ended with the last few words, "Remember, Foe, we are Americans," quickly said "Thank you" without pausing for the dramatic effect as she had been coached by Mrs. Richardson, and retreated to her chair.

Sam sat with his eyes fixed on a shaft of sunlight that entered high in a back window of the auditorium and illuminated the large painting of the Defense of the Alamo hanging on the back wall. Sam stared at the light, but the picture of the Alamo registered only on his retina and not in his mind. Superintendent Purkey was now introducing the scholarship winners, and as he announced each name and described each award, the student in question rose and faced the audience, walking at the end of the description of his triumph up to the speaker for a handshake and a blank sheet of paper. The real documents were in his office for safe keeping, Superintendent Purkey had explained earlier. "But act like you really *are* holding that scholarship in your hand, now," he had added. Sam heard the superintendent speak his name and begin the description of his scholarship. He shifted his gaze from the shaft of sunlight to the left edge of the lectern behind which Purkey was standing.

"... all-state guard for two years and most valuable player in the State Tournament at Austin his senior year, Samuel Houston Leaping Deer—." A spate of clapping broke into Purkey's speech at his mention of the state tournament, but died immediately as the applauders remembered the august nature of the occasion. Purkey continued, "Samuel Leaping Deer has been awarded a Big Ten grant-in-aid (the superintendent stumbled a bit at the strange phrase) to the University of Illinois. Sam is not only the first of his race, but also the first Big Muddy player to achieve this award. And may I be permitted to be the first to say to Sam—Claw 'em, Bobcats!" The audience broke into hoots and applause, with a few foot stompings and a loud whistle or two thrown in. Superintendent Purkey smiled benignly out at the crowd, and turned toward the seat where Sam was sitting. Sam rose suddenly, nearly upsetting his folding chair, and began to walk toward the lectern as he and the other winners had practiced during the previous week. He placed a limp right hand into that of Superintendent Purkey, who gave it a vigorous squeeze and shake and handed Sam the piece of blank paper with his left. The exchange was a bad one. The paper slipped from Sam's grip and fluttered off the platform to the floor. A twelve- or thirteen-year-old boy jumped from his seat, retrieved the paper and handed it back to Superintendent Purkey after giving both sides a good look. "It ain't got nothing on it," he announced to the front row of spectators in a stage whisper. "Neither side."

Superintendent Purkey quickly began to describe Billie Lou Hightower's achievement, the winning of the Shepherd's Landing Tuition Award for a course at Drew's Business College in Beaumont. Back in his chair Sam looked again at the ray of sunlight, and this time began to count the Texas defenders, but only those who were already dead or dying. By the time he had reached the last one, a soldier in the bottom left corner of the painting with his right hand staunching the flow of blood from a bayonet wound in the throat, the Big Muddy Independent School Band had launched into "Texas, Our Texas." The audience struggled to its feet, and in a few seconds Sam did the same.

Sam spent the summer after his graduation from Big Muddy High School doing little other than practicing various shots at the basketball goal beside his house. About once a week he would journey to the school gymnasium with a few other young men of the Nation and there play three- and four-hour games, mostly full-court. Not much happened to break this routine. Cooper Leaping Deer asked little of Sam during these months, his main concern being to finish off the case of extract Coach Dodge had left him and to tinker off and on with the various cars and parts of cars in the front yard. One Sunday afternoon after the morning services at Thomas Two Tongues' Holiness Church, Sam caught a glimpse of La Wanda from a distance as he waited in the grove of pines near the church building. She didn't see him as she walked out with her mother and sisters and brothers on the way to the Ford pickup which Brother Two Tongues had recently bought. Sam watched the group load into the truck and pull away with La Wanda and several of the children riding in the bed, and in a few minutes he started back toward the basketball court.

The most important event in connection with his collegiate future came one morning with the arrival of Coach Dodge at the Leaping Deer home. "I was heading this direction this morning, Sam," Dodge said, "and Mr. Purkey asked me to bring you over to the school with me when I come back." Dodge paused and waited for Sam to ask the reason for the trip. When Sam did nothing but stand there looking at him, a basketball in his left hand, Dodge was forced to speak again. "Don't you want to know why you still got to go over there? Ain't you scared they called your diploma back or something?" He offered a laugh, but Sam's face remained the same. Coach Dodge looked around the yard for the long-haired dog he suddenly remembered from his last official visit to Sam's home. It was nowhere in sight.

"Well, then, I'll tell you. That university you going to in September, they sent a letter and some other stuff to the school for you to take some kind of a test. Mr. Purkey said to tell you they said not to worry, because it ain't a test you can fail or nothing like that. It's got some kind of letters. C. B. or A. T. or something like that. But you got to take it before they'll pay you your laundry money up there." Sam continued to look at Coach Dodge for a few more seconds, and then turned to roll the basketball under the front porch of the shotgun house behind him. As Coach Dodge opened the door of the station wagon, he looked back at the porch and asked Sam whether or not that was a school basketball. Sam didn't answer, and Dodge headed the car toward Big Muddy.

When they arrived at the campus, Dodge let Sam out in front of the school and asked him if he needed a ride back home later on. "Walk," Sam said and went into the building to take whatever test it was that the white man in Illinois had devised.

Superintendent Purkey led Sam to a classroom full of broken desks waiting to be fixed and left him sitting at one with a sheaf of papers and a special pencil sent all the way from Urbana. "Use only the pencil furnished," Mr. Purkey read aloud from an instruction sheet and fixed Sam with a hard stare before he left to discourage any sneaking in of forbidden writing devices. Sam looked at the first page, saw that he was to color in one out of five little boxes printed after each question, and turned to the first page of test questions. The people in Illinois, he quickly learned, had a deep interest in various strange shapes and designs. After reading carefully through a question which asked him to color a box which would show what would happen if shape A were changed in the same way as shape B, Sam quickly colored the first box a solid gray. He studied the work he had just done and then carefully erased it. He reversed his pencil in his hand and poised it over the second small box, running his eyes back over the question. Somewhere outside the window of the classroom of broken desks, a mockingbird did an imitation of a jay. A drop of sweat gathered itself on Sam's forehead, hesitated, and then plopped onto the paper in front of him. He brushed at it with his left hand, releasing his grip on the desk top as he did so. It slid to the floor with a smack like an oak limb falling on the tin roof of a reservation house. Sam rebalanced the desk top on his knees, gave a part of his mind to Abba Mikko, chief among the Old Ones, and began to move his special pencil down the page. He filled one blank box for each question, the decision as to which one no longer in his hands. Superintendent Purkey gave Sam an approving smile a little later as he glanced over the exam, pleased to see the unmistakable metallic sheen of the special pencil. And they say these Alabama-Coushattas can't learn, he thought to himself. Out loud to Sam, he said, "I'll mail this back, and it will be there before you are." He then stuffed the papers into a heavy envelope especially provided by the taxpayers of Illinois for the occasion.

    The morning of Sam's departure for the land of the Illini came only a couple of weeks after his afternoon among the crippled desks. The day he was to leave according to the schedule he had received in an envelope marked "Athletic Department," Sam found another letter in the Leaping Deer mailbox. This one contained a one-way Trailways bus ticket from Franklin, Texas, to Urbana, Illinois, and a note stating that all inbound athletes were expected to furnish their own meal money for the trip. There was also a color photograph of what Sam took to be a large flying saucer sitting in a cornfield. Several white men were standing before it, dwarfed by its size and smiling happily at the camera. One of the men held a large coil of copper wire in front of his chest, obviously for display, and another offered a chunk of some white substance in his extended hands. The caption at the bottom said "Assembly Hall: Over four thousand miles of copper alloy wire and 40,000 tons of polyethylene." Sam studied the picture carefully for almost a minute, turning it over in his hand and holding it at different angles in order to highlight various features of it. After a minute or two of thought, he decided to give it to Miller Sylestine, for whatever use he might find for it in the ritual life of the Nation.

    Sam took the bus ticket inside his house and opened a greenish tin footlocker which had belonged to Homer Shoes until a few days before. Homer had bought it drunk one night several years before when he and a group of Coushattas had made it as far as Beaumont in and on a borrowed pulpwood truck. Sometime during the tour Homer had stumbled into a pawnshop and spent all the money he had remaining from his payday at the sawmill plus a beaded necklace from which he had earlier removed the Made in Japan label. Along with a large typewriter for seven dollars and a half, and a size six pair of hip boots for fifty cents, Homer had brought home the footlocker. When he had heard of Sam's great fortune in being able to travel northward to the college run by and for Indians, he had brought the box over to the Leaping Deer residence. Sam's father had forced a pint of lemon extract on him in appreciation, and the two had crawled into a '53 Chevrolet two-door sedan in the front yard to drink it.

On one side of the locker Sam had stacked the clothes he was to carry north. He was wearing his shoes, the same pair he had worn for the first time during the state tournament in March. He had put them on that morning for the first time since he had worn them in the Big Muddy school building during the examination. He kicked the top of his right foot against the tin box, and the rubber rebounded pleasantly. Sam turned his attention to the other end of the box, slipping his hand under the pile of pants and shirts and groping until he found what he wanted. He nodded and withdrew a large cigar box that one of his brothers had found in the dump near the village headquarters. Untying a leather thong fastened around it, Sam flipped back the lid and sniffed at the contents. The box held approximately twenty times as much of the rootlike substance as did the small leather pouch resting on his breastbone. Sam hoped it was enough to last until Christmas, the time he had been promised by the white man's letter from Illinois that he would be sent back to the reservation for his first visit. He retied the leather string and replaced the cigar box, careful to make certain that plenty of cloth padded it on all sides.

The other articles in the box—the three dried ears of corn, the handful of feathers bound by a rubber band, the Bull Durham sack filled with pebbles of three different colors, the special examination pencil—Sam checked only briefly. He gave the tin lid a push, and it fell shut with a heavy dull sound. Hoisted to his shoulder the casket filled with his possessions was not really heavy but was still hard to manage. He had trouble adjusting its bulk, and before he got it outside the house and into the front yard, he had to shift it from one shoulder to the other. His family stood outside in a group as though waiting for a picture to be snapped, watching Sam's struggle with the green trunk. The gray long-haired dog sat to one side of the group near Cooper, a hind leg thumping away as it scratched at a tick seized up at the base of an ear. Sam's father had the carburetor from one of his lame engines in one hand. With a screwdriver he held in the other, he made scraping motions on the top side of the mechanism. Sam lowered the tin box to the ground and stood beside it, letting his gaze fix on a wood chip lying about halfway between himself and his family. They all stood there for a full minute, the only sound that of the youngest Leaping Deer child mumbling over something he had crammed into his mouth and the dog which continued its scratching.

Cooper lowered himself into a squat and put aside the carburetor so that he could reach the dog. He grabbed it by one ear and pulled it toward him. The animal rolled over on its back, feet lolling in the air, and groaned comfortably as Cooper began to part the hair on its belly as he looked for the fat gray ticks. He pulled one loose with a jerk and spoke to Sam, whose attention had moved from the wood chip to the tick hunt. "The blank eyes' letter has money inside?"

"Ticket."

"You carry food in a paper sack?" Sam made a small gesture with his left hand toward his mother.

"I have food. Meat. Biscuit," Sam said to Cooper.

Cooper finished with the dog and stood up. It whined at his feet for more attention, and he pushed it away with the big toe of his right foot. The noisy child had stopped his teething and lay collapsed across his mother's shoulder. Across the reservation from the state highway came the sound of a diesel semi on its way to Houston changing into a lower gear as it started the run up the hill the Indians called Slow Man. Cooper took two steps toward Sam and stopped in front of him. He touched the boy on the left shoulder and then turned toward the greenish trunk. He picked up one end, Sam the other, and they walked toward the dirt road leading in the direction from which the sound of the truck had come and gone. Before they reached the turn in the road which put the Leaping Deer house out of view behind a grove of pines, one of Sam's brothers came running after them with the paper sack of pork and cold biscuits he had forgotten. Cooper allowed the younger Leaping Deer to follow all the way to the state blacktop, carrying Sam's provisions for the trip clutched to his chest.

When the three arrived at the point where the road from the center of the village intersected the highway, both Sam and his father had sweated through their shirts. They crossed the road and put down the footlocker in the shade of a sweetgum tree and sat down to cool off. The younger boy picked up a handful of gravel and began to throw at the stop sign, Cooper and Sam watching intently for a few mintues.

"Milton," Cooper finally called to the younger boy, "come sit with us."

Milton threw one last handful of gravel against the metal sign and then flopped down beside his father and Sam.

"Up there," Cooper said after a minute or so, "there will be much talk. In Illinois at the basketball."

"Yes," said Sam.

"It is their way," said Milton.

"But it means nothing," said Cooper. "It is the sound they want. The air is empty for them without words to fill it."

They all fell silent and watched two trucks running nose to tail thunder by on the highway sending a wash of hot air over them as they squatted on the gravel shoulder.

"I will talk to them," Sam finally said, "when I have to."

"I am interested in this corn they grow on the schoolyard," said Cooper. "You must see what it is like."

"I will do that, father," said Sam.

"Come," Cooper said to Milton, though he was looking at Sam. "We go home."

He and the younger boy rose and recrossed the highway, stepping carefully on the hot tacky asphalt. They walked a hundred yards down the village road and then turned off into the woods to go the short way home out of the sun. As they stepped into the shade of the thicket, Sam's brother looked back and waved. Cooper had already vanished. Sam lifted his right hand and then hunkered down beside the green trunk to wait for a ride to Franklin.

His stay in the shade of the sweetgum tree didn't last long, because after two or three cars and one truck had gone by, a large maroon station wagon slowed down as it passed him. It stopped a few hundred feet up the highway and waited. Sam stood up beside the trunk and looked at the rear window of the vehicle, making no move to hoist the box to his shoulder. In a few seconds the car began to back slowly toward him, the rear windows filled with faces of white children. After the driver had backed until the rear was parallel to where Sam stood, the right front window began to disappear with a slight hum, as though it were immersed in oil. A woman wearing a pair of sunglasses with lenses which covered the top half of her face and earrings shaped like medium-sized bananas poked her head out at Sam. Her earrings clashed in a way that reminded him of the spurs the riders wore at the county rodeo. The woman looked at Sam's face, down at his basketball shoes, and then at his green locker. "Are you," she said, "one of them?" When Sam did nothing except to bounce the left side of his shoe against the trunk, she continued. "I mean what the sign back there said. One of the whatever-you-call-them Indians?" One of the children whose faces Sam had watched growing larger as the sta-

tion wagon backed toward him yelled out, "He is! He is! I know
he is! Look at how he looks!"

"Hush," the woman said. Sam could hear the driver, the man
belonging to the woman, he supposed, say something to her in a
low voice. "All right, all right," she answered, "I'm getting hot
too!" She turned away from the back seat, into which she had been
leaning to swat at the children, and looked at Sam.

"You want a ride to town, Chief?" He opened his mouth to
decline, but catching a glimpse of the shadow cast by the sweetgum, instead asked, "What time is it?"

"I don't know. Ten ten." The sunglasses looked back from
the watch on the freckled arm.

"Yes," Sam said and lifted his footlocker to load it onto the
roof luggage carrier. The driver's door opened, and a short man in
a blue stretch shirt with a tiny red alligator on the left breast
crawled out. He helped Sam rearrange the trunk and suitcase already tied there, and tied the green locker into the new space they
had made. During the process of untying, unloading, rearranging,
and retying that went on, the short man kept repeating "Parn me"
every few seconds. Sam supposed that was either the short man's
name or a way he had of cursing when something got in his way.

While Sam and the driver were working outside the station
wagon, the children inside were screaming, crying, and fighting
over the problem of who got to sit by the Indian. As the driver was
tying down the last rope end, Sam reached up and inserted his left
hand in the leather loop at the end of the footlocker. He paused,
looked back at the sweetgum shadow, withdrew his hand and then
squeezed past the short man as he held open the door to the back
seat. "They're gonna take turns. You don't mind, do you?" The
woman spoke, leaning over the back of the front seat to hold one
of the children who was not sobbing on her shoulder.

"You're their first Indian. I mean, we're from Philly on our
way to L. A. You know? When they saw you, you really blew
their minds. Do you smoke? I mean cigarettes. No peace pipes in
this wagon." Her bananas jiggled as she laughed, swinging back
and forth from the little gold rings which Sam noticed were run
through holes in her earlobes. The short man joined her, "Yeah,
hey. Ho ho ho. Lou, you *are* quick." A sudden sharp pain in his
right side caused Sam to look from the woman's earlobes down at
the boy beside him. The child again dug the muzzle of the silver

cap pistol into his ribs. Looking up, he withdrew the weapon and spoke. "How," he said.

"Gareth," the woman snapped, "give him some peace. He's our guest." Her son drew back the hammer of the six-gun and clicked it in Sam's face. He flinched, but there was no report. "We don't allow them to put in the caps inside the car," the woman said, noting Sam's reaction. "That's only for roadside parks." Sam nodded at the sunglasses facing him across the three feet of space between the back and front seats. He had learned that if he nodded frequently when in close quarters with the white man, he never had to speak much. In most of Sam's encounters he had found it impossible to know how to respond to the questions the whites put to him, so through a long process of trial and error he had settled on nodding his head frequently as the best procedure. The mouth beneath the sunglasses seemed to be preparing to speak again.

"How far are you going, Mister . . . er?" She stopped to hear Sam's name. He nodded twice, then caught himself, realizing more was required.

"Town. Franklin."

"With that huge green tin thing? Are you leaving the reservation with that just to go to town?" With her right forefinger she pushed her sunglasses back up the bridge of her nose. The man with the red alligator shifted his weight and placed his arm up on the back of the seat. He had a deep dimple in his elbow.

"Yeah," he said. "That trunk doesn't weigh as much as it looks like it does, but it's more than I'd want to carry." He laughed loudly for several seconds, looking at his wife as he did.

"Don't run off the highway, Marv." She looked back at Sam.

"Well, is it personal or something? I ask only because I wondered if you're traveling further west. To the coast maybe. You know. Hollywood. Marv's brother-in-law has done some work in the motion-picture industry, and he tells us that young people still come there in droves. Of all types." The child at the other end of Sam's seat began to claim in a high whine that it was his turn to sit by the Indian. Several minutes of arguing between the parents and the children followed with the final result being that the original sitter was allowed to remain where he was for four more minutes. During the discussion both parents had occasion to slap at the two boys across the back of the front seat, but none of the father's blows landed because he had to keep some attention on the road. Sam noticed that both children defended themselves well, landing more telling blows than the woman did.

"You're not trying to break into the movies, then," the woman put to Sam after things had settled down.

"No," Sam said and thought of the movie career that Gemar Red Cloud had enjoyed a few years back. Gemar had come to the attention of a talent agent when he had appeared on a float in the parade at the Forestville Dogwood Festival. Gemar had ridden on the back of a large flatbed truck down the main street of Forestville, dressed in cutoff khaki pants and painted with lipstick and water-base latex, as representative of Texas' only Indian reservation. After his ride ended, a man who had come from Houston to judge the beauty contest for Dogwood Queen offered Gemar a chance to go to Hollywood and be in a picture. He had gone, and returned in a period of about three weeks, fetching with him the hundred dollars left from his pay, an autographed 8 by 10 still shot of him being hit with the butt of a rifle swung by John Wayne, and a letter of appreciation from the Governor of Texas for his services on behalf of the Alabama-Coushatta Nation.

"Lots of good parts in westerns. Some real juicy," the woman was saying. "Aren't I right, Marv?"

"You bet, Lou Lou. Ernest tells many stories of success." He laughed too loud and too long again. Sam looked out the window, away from the glint of the sunglasses. The station wagon was passing a large field surrounded by geometric rows of pine saplings on three sides. The sun flashed off a television tower which rose several hundred feet into the air, trailing silvery guy wires anchored to large blocks of cement sunk into the corners of the clearing in the tree farm. Sam strained to look up out of the window, trying to get a glimpse of the red light at the top. He couldn't see it, but the light didn't blink on and off in the daytime anyway. He leaned back in the seat and crossed his right arm over his left. The boy on the end of the seat leaned across his brother and pulled at Sam's shirt. "Hey," he asked, "do you live in a wigwam?"

"Come on, fellows," Marv said. "Give him a chance to talk. Maybe he can give you some pointers on what to do when you're lost."

"Right," Lou joined in. "You know, woodlore. Like in that

movie with Robert Redford. The one where he's a sheriff, chasing that Indian named Willie Boy." She turned her glasses toward Sam. "Do you know some woodlore to tell the boys? Like what to do when you're all by yourself in the wilderness?"

Sam looked at the dimple in Marv's right elbow and paused. The two boys stared up at him intently, and from the rearview mirror came the reflection of Marv's eyes looking into the back seat. They were pale blue and trusting, staring out of the deep pockets made by Marv's bushy blond eyebrows and the puffy freckles beneath. "Go to sleep," Sam carefully answered Lou, "and then go home." He watched the rearview mirror and saw Marv's hairline rise into view.

"What?" Lou said. She pushed her glasses back up on the bridge of her nose and gave her head a shake, which set the bananas to bobbing again. "You guys can change seats now," she told the children and turned her back to the passengers in the rear. She pulled a Pure Oil map from the sun visor on her side of the car and began unfolding it in quick jerks. Neither she nor Marv said anything else to Sam for the remaining five miles into Franklin.

Sam watched the fenced pastures and dirt farms roll by the window, waiting for the courthouse square in the middle of Franklin to appear. When in a few minutes of gas stations and Seven-Eleven stores it did, he asked Marv to let him out. Marv pulled the maroon wagon to a stop in front of the Sunset Cafe across from the courthouse and got out to help untie the trunk. The mother made the boys stay in the car until the operation was completed. "Leave the engine running, Marv," she said. "I want that air conditioner on in this heat." After they had unloaded the box of Sam's belongings, the short man turned to watch Sam lift it to his shoulder.

"Thank you," Sam remembered to say.

"Not at all. No problem. But I'll tell you what, Chief. I sure hope for your sake you don't get lost in the wilderness. You'll have to call for a forest ranger if you do." Sam heard Marv's long laugh for the last time as he got back in the station wagon and resumed the westward movement. The faces of the two children appeared again in the rear window and remained as the car turned left around the square. One of them stuck his tongue out.

The tin trunk on his shoulder, Sam walked up the street toward the bus station. The heat the trunk had picked up on the roof of the station wagon popped sweat out on Sam's cheek and neck. Up ahead a metal sign on the front of a white building announced that Trailways buses stopped there.

After pushing through the screen door, which swung both in and out, Sam set his trunk near a machine which told your weight and fortune for a penny. He retrieved the ticket from where it was stuck inside the lining of the trunk lid and rechecked it. Nothing seemed to have been jostled during the trip from the reservation, except that some of the clothing had been pushed closer to one end. Sam wedged the green box between the scale and a pinball machine and walked over to the counter near the cash register. A skinny girl wearing a Franklin High School football sweater over her waitress uniform was swabbing the top of the counter with a yellowish sponge. Her dishwater blonde hair was put up in a black hairnet which had come loose on one side from its bobby pins. Since Sam had come through the door with his trunk, she had been watching him with great interest, particularly when she had seen him remove something from the lid. "You want something to eat?" she said as Sam stopped and began looking at the bus schedule written on a piece of cardboard on the wall behind her. There were three entries under "Arrive" and four under "Depart." One of the departure times seemed to have been crossed out with a green crayon some time back. Someone had killed a fly on the second number of the time announced, making it difficult to tell whether it was a 3 or an 8 under the green wax.

Sam poked the ticket toward the dishwater blonde as she stood waiting for him to order. She looked down at it and then made a gesture of refusal with her upraised hands. "I don't do no tickets," she said. "He handles all that stuff." She looked in the direction of the green trunk. "Checking suitcases too. He does that too." Sam looked from the name stamped on the ticket to the cardboard square and then back again. Down the counter a woman in a flowered feedsack dress watched with interest, a doughnut with one bite out in her left hand. She lowered the doughnut to a saucer in front of her and leaned a few degrees more from the vertical toward the scene of the ticket negotiations.

"Urbana," Sam said. "What time?"

"There ain't no bus directly to Urbana. Just the morning one to Houston goes through there. But there ain't no bus station in Urbana. Don't even stop."

"No. Not Urbana. In Illinois," Sam said, pointing to the word on the ticket.

"That ain't the same one over by Shepherd?" The woman in the flowered dress looked at her doughnut, but spoke to Sam and the waitress.

"In Illinois," Sam repeated, again poking the ticket toward the girl behind the counter as though she had been the one speaking.

"Uh uh. I done learned not to mess with them Continental Trailways tickets." She backed away until a shelf behind her intersected the small of her back and tipped slightly, enough to rattle the row of thick-bottomed glasses sitting on it.

"Bus he wants," the customer in the flowered dress announced to no one in particular, "is that one goes through Lufkin, I reckon. My sister's youngest boy rode that same one once when he was stationed in the army in Fort Leonard Wood, Missouri. Illinois and Missouri's somewhere together up there, ain't they?" She finished the last bite of her doughnut and dabbed at her mouth with a paper napkin. Sam looked back at the cardboard and saw that the afternoon bus to Lufkin was scheduled for 12:30. He walked back to the trunk and leaned against the pinball machine beside it. The biscuits packed in the brown paper sack were still soft. He ate two of them, but left the meat for later.

As he was rerolling the brown paper around the remaining food, the woman who had given him the advice about the Lufkin bus left the Bus Station Cafe. She stopped in the door with the screen half-open before her and turned toward Sam. "Is they any army camps in Illinois? That why you going up yonder? To be a soldier boy?"

"No, not a soldier." The woman continued to stand where she was, feet planted as if she would wait for an answer until the bus came. Behind the counter, the waitress stopped rattling dishes and turned to hear what was said.

"Not a soldier," Sam repeated. "Just to play."

The woman gave the bottom of the screen door a kick with her right foot and sent it flying against the wall on the outside. "You might know," she said. "I didn't figure they'd draft Indians."

For the next hour and a half, Sam waited near his green footlocker, squatting with his back against one of the legs of the pinball machine. He left his position only once, just after two farmers had come in for coffee and pie. After they left, the waitress began clearing off the table where they had sat and watched Sam as she worked. He glanced up, saw her eyes on him, and quickly looked back at the tips of his fingers. She carried the cups and spoons back behind the counter and went into the kitchen to talk to the cook, standing so she could see out the opening cut in the wall behind the counter. After a few minutes Sam stood up, placed his sack of meat and biscuits on top of the trunk, and walked toward the rear of the dining room. The door had the word "Gents" lettered across it.

As he stood pissing on a cigarette butt lying in the urinal, Sam read the penciled and carved statements on the wall before him. One written in red crayon caught his eye. He learned from it that on some unspecified occasion Hilda Faye Gaston had taken eleven inches and declared it good. After he had finished pissing, Sam stood a minute and pondered. He had never heard of any girl of the Alabama-Coushatta Nation doing such a thing. He looked again at the number and lifted his shoulders.

Back in the large room, two other girls of high school age had entered the cafe and were leaning across the counter talking to the waitress. Their voices were pitched low, but frequently loud giggles erupted from the group. Sam heard one of the new ones say "O.K. I will," and then discovered that all three were turned in his direction. "Hi," the one who had just spoken said. Sam shifted his weight so that his left shoulder blade rested against the pinball machine.

"Hey," the girl spoke again, and all three collapsed into a spasm of giggling. "Oh, you crazy thing," one of them said high in her throat.

"Hey, ain't you from Big Muddy?" Sam nodded. "Didn't you make all-state in basketball this time?"

"He did, he did," the other interrupted. "I just know it was him."

"What's your name?" the waitress asked.

"I know," one of her friends said in Sam's direction. "It's Sam Houston Deer."

"Leaping Deer?"

"Yeah, right. Sam Houston Leaping Deer." All three squealled in unison and moved their feet up and down as if preparing to bolt and run. They remained in the same place, though, whispering into the spit curls dangling over each other's ears and twisting their bodies from side to side. The screen swung into the building and another customer for coffee came in. While the girl in the Franklin High School sweater waited on him, a man dressed in a dark green shirt and pants covered with large felt representations of bottle caps, the other two girls huddled together at their end of the counter, occasionally sneaking glances at Sam. One of them finally turned all the way around and faced him. She wore a light blue sweater which had lost most of its bulk and now showed clearly the outline detail of the underwear beneath it. Her bra was too big, Sam noted. On each side, the areas above the nipple point were dented. It looked as if the girl had been struck a severe blow in the chest with a baseball bat. Between the two damaged mounds rested a large man's ring supported by a green ribbon strung through it.

"We know who you are, now," she addressed Sam in a voice lowered because of the Seven-Up man. "Don't you want to know what my name is?"

"Hilda Faye Gaston?" Sam asked, his eyes fastened on the signet ring.

"It ain't neither!" She grabbed the ring in her right hand and swung back toward her friend at the counter. The waitress was looking back and forth between Sam and the blue sweater girl, puzzled as she stood out of hearing range.

"Did you hear what that Indian called me? That nasty old thing! Oh, I wish Opal Gene was home from the army to hear his steady girl friend called that!" The other girl who had heard Sam's reply was attempting to comfort her insulted friend, while directing a look of horror in Sam's direction. Her eyes were small and close together, but she was doing her best to open them as wide as possible.

"Let's get out of here," she said. "I never in all my life!" After the screen door slammed behind them, the Seven-Up man swivelled around on his stool and waved his right hand at Sam, who had remained just as he was except to lean far enough to the right to see the Coca-Cola clock near the cash register. Sam nodded at the Seven-Up man.

"Hilda Faye Gaston, huh? Boy, you sure put a bee in her bonnet. I deliver at the reservation. I sure wouldn't a guessed that Gaston girl was putting out to you all, though. She let everybody in Franklin have a crack at it already, so I expect why not." He stood up to leave and counted out some change on the counter. He walked to the door and stopped to light a cigarette. "Tell you one thing, though," he said, "if I's you, I wouldn't brag on it too much. Especially not to these little high school girls." The Seven-Up man took a long drag on his cigarette and waited to see if Sam would answer. Outside a honk sounded, the bus for Lufkin blocked by the Seven-Up truck. The driver of the truck stepped outside, and Sam lifted the greenish trunk to his back, delivered from his den between the machines by the bus for Lufkin and points north.

The bus driver, who examined Sam's ticket before he allowed him aboard, was certain that the ticket in its present condition would not get Sam to Urbana, Illinois. "Why, you got all kinds of layovers and transfers between here and way up yonder, I imagine," he said as he eyed Sam's trunk. He assured Sam that in Texarkana, which was as far as he ever drove the bus, there would be both a layover, a transfer, and the need to get his ticket reissued. "I only just drive from Cleveland to Texarkana and back, but I have carried plenty of folks who was going on through. New York, Chicago, Findlay, Ohio, everywhere. They all got separate tickets to get them from each transfer place to the other." When Sam looked back at him, unspeaking and uncomprehending in the midday heat, the driver tried to explain further.

"What it is, see, is there ain't one man owns all these buses. They got to divide the money up between each other. See what I mean?" Finally he had punched a single hole with the tool which hung from his belt in the edge of Sam's ticket and waved him aboard. "Let them worry about it," he said to the other passenger boarding in Franklin, a black woman who lived seven miles up the road and commuted by bus every day to keep house for an old blind judge in town. She pursed her lips and shook her head, her eyes on Sam's back as he walked up the steps in front of her. "He don't know *nothing*," she assured the driver and stepped up behind the Indian.

Once aboard the bus, Sam walked slowly toward the rear, blinking his eyes to adjust them to the sudden darkness of the shaded windows. Most of the seats were empty, so he sat in one about halfway back on the left. He moved near the window to look out and make certain the driver did not leave the green trunk he wouldn't allow Sam to carry aboard the bus. By the time Sam spotted the driver, he had already shoved the trunk into the carrying space in the side of the vehicle and was shaking his left hand rapidly back and forth because of the severe pinch his left thumb had received when he let down the compartment door. His mouth was open, but Sam wasn't able to make out what he was saying. In a few seconds he stuck the tip of his thumb to his mouth and walked toward the door of the bus. Sam settled back in his seat and looked through the blue tinted glass at the barber shop next to the Bus Station Cafe. The barber nearest the window was lathering the face of an elderly man with long strands of white hair combed up from one side and laid across the top of his head. As Sam watched the two, the barber leaned across the top of the chair and said something. Both of the men laughed, their chins moving up and down in silent cackles. By the time Sam felt the driver beginning to ease the bus away from the side of the station, the barber had finished stropping his razor and had raised it for the first stroke. A ray of sunlight made a blue flash off the blade as the barber shop slowly drew away from the window of the bus. In the front of the bus the driver was explaining to a passenger sitting just behind him how he had injured his thumb. Sam could see a sign above and to the right of the driver's brown cap identifying its wearer. "Safe, Reliable, Courteous," the sign read. "J. T. Owens, Do Not Talk to Driver While Vehicle is in Motion."

For most of the first forty miles of his journey, Sam looked out the window at the piney woods and the tin-roofed shacks with wringer washing machines on their front porches. Occasionally a black child or two standing in the yard of one of the houses would turn away from playing with a tin can or a piece of rope and watch the Continental Trailways bus pass by. At one house one of them waved as the bus came into sight, and J. T. Owens answered with a blast on his air horn. The man across the aisle from Sam jerked awake at the sound, rolled his eyes to one side and reclosed them. His eyelids quivered as his head lolled back, and he returned to sleep as quickly as he had left it. Sam opened the brown paper sack and took out a piece of the blackened pork. After he had eaten it he felt thirsty. The tips of his fingers were sticky from the grease. He wiped them on the edge of the seat, then his pants, but in a few minutes when he put a finger to the window glass to scratch at a flyspeck, he noticed that he left a greasy mark.

Every few miles, the reliable, safe, and courteous J. T. Owens would respond to the sound of a buzzer by his left ear by slowing and pulling the bus off on the shoulder of the road. One of the group of black women riding behind Sam would lurch down the aisle as the bus slowed, catching the backs of the seats for support as she made her way. When the one who had boarded the bus in Franklin came by, she looked down at Sam where he sat next to the window and chuckled. "Heh, heh," she said, "Lawd, Lawd." She walked on up the aisle and down the steps of the bus into the heat and dust outside, still shaking her head even after the driver sealed the door-closing mechanism behind her.

After the bus reached Lufkin, picked up a few more passengers downtown, and moved back onto 59 North, Sam got tired of looking out the window. He settled back into a rubber foam corner and closed his eyes. The regular bump of the asphalt expanders between the slabs of the highway soothed him in the shaded seat. He sank lower and fell asleep. The brown bag of food slipped unnoticed from his lap to the floor. He dreamed.

He was at the fall corn dance in the clearing at the center of the Nation. He felt cold, though all those around him seemed not to notice the north wind cutting through the dead leaves of the sycamores. For some reason he knew that it was the first night of the festival, but as he looked at the figures in the center of the clearing, he realized that they were dressed in the wrong costumes for the ceremonies of the first night, and there were also several more figures swaying and bobbing in the light from the four fires than were needed for the Crayfish and Buzzard play.

Sam drew the cloak he was wearing closer about him against the cold. The material of which it was made was slick and metallic. It held no warmth, but he bundled it around himself and walked nearer to the fire burning at the southern point of the clearing. A large crowd of people that he hadn't noticed before were suddenly between him and the fire. No matter how loudly he begged them to allow him nearer the fire, none heard. They talked quietly among themselves, just as the people of the Alabama-Coushatta Nation always did at the ceremonies. Occasionally one of the older men would put a piece of the root Sam had learned of from McKinley Short Eyes under his tongue. As one of them did so, Sam reached out to touch the old man on the shoulder so that he might share. The old man seemed not to feel the touch, and as Sam braced himself to give a strong tug to the old bones beneath the dry skin the old man was suddenly across the fire from where Sam stood.

Sam tried to get near the fire burning in the east, and then the one in the west, but at both spots large crowds of people suddenly appeared to shut him away from the warmth. The wind blew more fiercely and entered the cloak as though it were made of spider web. Shaking from cold, Sam turned toward the last fire and saw it roaring with heat and light. One person, wrapped in a long robe, stood facing it, his back to Sam as he approached. When he reached to within a few feet, Sam recognized the figure to be La Wanda Two Tongues, alone and waiting for him in the warmth. He called her name, but she continued to stare into the red flames licking up from a huge pile of hickory and oak logs. Sam stretched out his left hand and spoke her name again in a louder voice. When he touched the material of the robe on her shoulder, it seemed to twist beneath his fingers. La Wanda's head slowly turned to face Sam, and he smiled as he waited for her to see and recognize him. Her face was hidden in shadows as she began to turn, but as she turned halfway around, the fire flared higher and cast a bright light on what lay beneath the dark black hairline. The teeth were long and yellow, and a tatter of cloth hung from a lower tusk. The small eyes on each side of the snout darted rapidly from side to side just as they had the night Sam had first seen them above the teeth tearing at the leather covering over McKinley Short Eyes' body.

Someone beside him was talking, making the same sounds over and over. Sam sat up straight in the bus seat and felt in his lap and on the seat beside him for something that was lost. He remembered the bag of food and stopped looking. The man seated next to him in the aisle seat spoke again. "You all right, boy? You all right?" Sam nodded and bent forward to pick up the sack he had felt with his shoe.

"Well, I didn't know. Way you was groaning and sweating, I thought maybe you was having a heart seizure. But you O.K. now." The man must have gotten on somewhere after Lufkin, because Sam didn't remember seeing him on the bus before. Most of the seats that he could see from where he sat were now filled. The man in the next seat nodded at him again. "Yes sir, I didn't know but what you was having a fit or something." From the corner of his eye Sam could see that the man was wearing a tan straw dress hat shoved to the back of his head. The coat of his shiny blue suit was open enough to show the wrinkled white shirt beneath it and the maroon tie which hung halfway down his chest. He had unbuttoned his collar, and a tuft of gray hair poked through the top of his shirt. The man crossed one leg over the other and turned in Sam's direction. The two were sitting so close together that when the man opened his mouth to speak, Sam could see yellow ovals in the tops of one side of his lower teeth. The teeth in the other side of his mouth looked to be made of bathtub porcelain.

"Hidy," the man said. "Name's Newt Hampshire. Out of Tyler. Main office, I mean. The Universal Life Insurance Company of Tyler, Texas, with branch offices in Marshall and Liberty. That's me." He stuck out his right hand, and when Sam gave his in return, Mr. Hampshire turned further in the seat in order to get a better grip for the handshake. He had learned long ago that a firm handshake was always important.

"Ordinarily, I never ride the bus. They can't move just when you got to, and they's times I got to leave for somewhere without five minutes' notice. What it is, see, is my car, the company car I drive, is in the shop broke. I got to go all the way to Texarkana to see a fellow, and no car to drive up there in. Ain't that a kick in the old sitting-down place?" He waited for Sam's agreement with his mouth half-open. The back of the seat immediately in front of the insurance man suddenly slipped back several degrees, as its occupant pushed the recline button. Both Sam and Hampshire turned to watch the woman sitting there settle herself, and then Hampshire spoke again.

"You must be of Mexican-American extraction. Lots of my business is with your people. San Antone, Houston, any place where you fine folks get together to live. I purely love Mexican food."

"No," Sam answered.

"Well, I mean it *is* good. Kind of hard on the belly sometimes, all right, but you can't beat it for taste. Not in my opinion, no sir." He reached into his coat and withdrew a Lucky Strike and a kitchen match. "Don't smoke?" he asked, and when Sam shook his head, the agent lit up and inhaled sparingly. "Got to be careful about them tars," he explained a few minutes later as he stubbed out the half-smoked butt. "Insurance studies show that the real danger is in that last inch and a half." Newt Hampshire talked comfortably off and on for the next hundred miles, seldom asking a question he expected an answer to. Sam listened for the first few minutes to all he said, but after a while he found his attention centering on things about the man next to him rather than on what he was saying.

Sam's mind would wander from detail to detail of Hampshire's clothing, the objects he brought out of his various pockets to hold in his gesturing hands, various features of his face. Mainly, though, Sam's gaze kept returning to Newt's lower teeth and the way the artificial ones split the man's whole face into two parts—one made up of sweat and spit and skin pores and the other of manufactured plastic and porcelain hardware. The words which Sam no longer heard became sounds of a large animal being slowly eaten by a machine. The thought was so strangely powerful that Sam forced himself to open the bag of food and begin eating another biscuit. He listened to the sound of his own chewing and swallowing as he ate the last two remaining in the bag. They were harder than they had been a few hours earlier.

Sam turned his back to the insurance man and concentrated on the music which came with a thin metallic sound from a transistor radio somewhere in the rear of the bus. Whoever owned it kept changing the dial every few seconds to another frequency in search of something better. After a few minutes of alternating static, news reports, and bits of songs, the operator settled on a country music station. A deep voice sang about green grass and city lights. Various other kinds of voices and subjects and beats entertained the passengers the rest of the way into Marshall, the last rest stop before Texarkana and its transfers.

Sam stayed on the bus in the Marshall station, which was much more than just a cafe like the one in Franklin. Parked beside the bus were several others, and there were two arrivals and one departure during the fifteen-minute rest stop. The Universal Life man was one of the last passengers to reboard. He carried a Dr. Pepper bottle and a bag of peanuts in one hand and a *Time* magazine in the other. He offered Sam some peanuts, and Sam took two. Until it became too dark to see, the agent read *Time*, moving his lips over the series of facts he found there and occasionally wetting his finger to turn the pages.

When J. T. Owens reached downtown Texarkana and pulled the bus into the loading dock in the station, he rose from his seat and announced the destination in a solemn voice. "Texarkana, Texas," he said. "All passengers transfer for points north." The twenty or so people aboard crowded into the aisles quickly, as if afraid they would be hauled back south by J. T. Owens unless they moved fast. As he stepped off the bus in front of Sam, the insurance agent turned to say goodbye.

"Don't forget now, son," he urged, "Universal Life is just the ticket for people of your extraction. Satisfied customers all over Texas." He hitched up his belt, front and back, and was gone. Sam walked to the side of the bus where he had seen the driver store his trunk, his rubber soled shoes slipping on the dark grease on the terminal parking area. As he leaned against the side of the bus and waited for J. T. Owens, he looked one last time into the paper bag, now greasy enough to see through. He took out the last piece of pork and held it in his right hand for a few seconds. No one was watching him, so with a look around, he threw the greasy black chunk into a cluster of Nehi orange drink cases stacked by the building. A minute or so later, as the driver was pulling the tin trunk from the storage compartment, Sam could hear scuffling noises in the dark as something dragged the chunk of meat away from the cases. He shouldered the trunk and hurried into the station to get his ticket reissued, looking toward the place from where the sounds had come as he stepped through the door in the brightly lighted building.

After two hours of waiting inside, his reissued tickets in his shirt pocket, Sam boarded a bus on its way from Dallas to St. Louis. It was a new one with a row of seats jutting high up into the roof behind the driver. Most of the passengers were asleep, propped up against flat hard pillows. Sam found one of these in an empty seat, and after examining it closely, stuck it behind his head and leaned back. He pushed the recline button as he had seen the woman in front of him and the agent do earlier and stretched out as much as he could. He tapped the front of his shirt with one hand and relaxed as he felt the leather pouch. By the time the bus full of transients reached Hope, Arkansas, Sam was sound asleep, high above the roadway with the green trunk secure somewhere below.

He awoke just at daylight, the tail end of a dream tantalizing him as it faded. It seemed to have had something to do with a berdache, a half-man such as the Alabamas and Coushattas had fought on their way west to Texas. He put the thought out of his mind and looked out of the window at the flat scrubby country which unrolled alongside the divided highway. As the bus started into a curve Sam saw the rising sun flash against something silvery up ahead in the distance. There were no sounds from the other passengers except for someone whimpering in his sleep. Everyone on the bus but Sam and the driver was asleep. Sam straightened up in the seat, and a joint in his neck popped like a wet stick stepped on. Rubbing his eyes and stretching his shoulder muscles, Sam leaned forward to get a better look at whatever it was that had reflected the sunbeam. The traffic outside the bus began to thicken, and as he looked from one flash of light to another, a roadside sign flashed by. "Memphis" was the word written on it, and the next one had "Mississippi River" in block letters painted across it. As the bus rolled over the bridge, which was what Sam had seen earlier, he looked down at the brown water and realized that the Trinity River and Long King Creek together were nothing to this. In the middle of the bridge, his stomach began to rise as though it intended to crawl out of his mouth, and he was forced to tighten all his muscles and clench his teeth to hold things steady until the water crossing was complete. As soon as the bus rolled past the last section of bridge railing, he suddenly felt things resettle. He opened his tightly clenched eyes and saw a large plastic hamburger turning slowly on top of a steel pole as the bus swept by. Sam thought of the empty brown bag and reached into the front of his shirt. Later there would be food, later in Illinois, at the college the Indians ran.

Sam took no real interest in the scenery outside the window for several more hours. When he finally did read another road sign, the bus was somewhere in southern Illinois with St. Louis behind. For several miles the country outside looked much as it had all the way from East Texas. The only real difference Sam noticed was that there were now no pines and only occasional tin crosses with "Prepare to Meet Thy God" painted on the intersected arms. When a change came, it was sudden. Sam had turned his eyes away from the window to watch a lady soldier and her seatmate struggle against each other a few rows ahead, and when their heads slipped out of sight, he looked again at the scene framed by his window. What he saw was so foreign to his experience that he bumped his head against the window glass in surprise. He had seen flat land before on the yearly trips between Big Muddy and Austin for the state basketball tournaments, and he had also seen scattered stands of scrubby oaks. The view of central Illinois he had out the bus window, though, was as unlike what he had seen before as the ocean.

There was corn. There was corn planted as far as he could see, standing seven feet high, its leaves green and yellow in the sunlight. It grew on both sides of the highway, from the horizon in the distance to the gravel shoulder of the highway six feet from the bus. As he watched, an occasional puff of wind would move across the fields and the stalks would bow and sweep in unison like the ocean waves he had seen in movies in the Roundup Theater in Franklin. The farmhouses, built a mile or two apart, looked from the window like ships floating in green water. When the bus passed by them, Sam could see two, three, but never more than four trees clustered near the buildings, their branches cut and lopped into the shape of ice cream cones. The small towns that appeared were islands, sharply defined by the edges of the cornfields with definite beginnings and ends. You were either in town or out, never in between in central Illinois.

After several minutes of feeling himself moving deeper into the sea of corn, Sam leaned across his seat toward a soldier sitting across the aisle with his shirt unbuttoned and his shoes off. "Sha towea," Sam said, and then catching himself said the word in the language of the white man. "Corn."

"Huh?" the soldier sat up in his seat. He had a grayish thin face like a fox squirrel. "Wha'd you say?" He looked at Sam intently, scratching his long front teeth with his thumbnail and scraping off what he had garnered on the front of his shirt.

"Corn. Outside." Sam waved his hand slowly, palm down, at the window as though he were playing the part of Abba Mikko in the creation dance.

"Yeah, I see it all right," the squirrel-faced soldier said. "And that's all I want to do with that stuff. I've been seeing it all my life." Sam looked at him across the aisle with respect.

"Yeah, see, I was brought up in Homer. That's why I joined up as soon as I could get the old lady to sign the papers. I spent half my life handling corn. A-2 Hybrid. Nu-Grow 8. You name it. My old man tried all of them." The soldier shifted his scraping to his lower teeth, stopping every few seconds to inspect the signs of progress deposited on his thumbnail. He finished the job and brushed the fingertips of both hands on the knees of his summer issue khakis. He looked back at Sam with yellow eyes.

"Why? Do you like cornfields that much?" Sam shrugged and continued gazing out the window.

"Who eats it? All of it out there," he said, left hand again palm downward toward the window.

"Eats it? Nobody. That's just stock corn. Hogs eat it. I wouldn't set my teeth into a single ear of the damn stuff if I was starving to death."

"People don't eat the corn?" Sam asked in an amazed voice, his mind filled with pictures of piney-woods rooters tearing down stalk after stalk to rip at the fat ears.

"Hell, no," the squirrel-faced soldier answered. "Who wants to eat corn? That stuff breaks me out anyway. I get red dots all over my chest and everywhere else too, you know." He looked down at his crotch and made his eyes goggle. A woman riding in the seat ahead flounced noisily. "All over it, I mean, all over it," the soldier said in a louder voice, winking a yellow eye at Sam across the aisle.

The only large break in the sea of corn before the bus reached Champaign was the island made by Decatur. They made a fifteen-minute stop there, but Sam hurried inside to the men's room and back to the bus in less than a third of the time. The soldier had stood beside him in front of the urinals, telling him about his adventures with women of the Far East, but Sam had hardly listened. The sight of so much of what he had known always to be so scarce and powerful as to be sacred had unnerved him. He didn't remember whether he had rezipped his fly, so as he reboarded the bus he had an impulse to reach down and touch the reassuring row of metal teeth. As he did, he saw a middle-aged man in a light-colored suit lean forward in his seat behind the driver and grin broadly. "Gobble, gobble," the man said. But by the time Sam had walked up the aisle past him, he had forgotten the incident already. Corn. Corn and no trees. Corn and no thickets. An ocean of corn to be fed to hogs.

During the last fifty miles of his journey to Champaign, Illinois, Sam sat in an aisle seat, staring for the most part at the back of the seat immediately in front of him and only occasionally turning his head to look at the continuing sea rising and falling softly in the breezes of late August. The city limits of Champaign, marked with a large blue and orange sign, came as abruptly as had any of the previous small towns. One moment the corn stretched everywhere to each side of the highway, and the next, the bus was bumping down a short stretch of brick street between rows of two-story houses. In a few blocks the bus turned left, stopped by a low building, and began discharging its passengers. The squirrel-faced soldier, remaining where he was as Sam rose to leave, waited until Sam was halfway down the aisle before he spoke. "Hey, I hope you get all the corn you can stand," he said, his head tilted back so that his mouth was forced open to reveal his long yellow teeth, already in need of another scraping job. Sam nodded and walked to the front of the bus.

"Here you are," said the driver as Sam stepped down to the sidewalk. "Champaign-Urbana, home of the Fighting Illini. Claim your bags inside."

The Snake with Horns

After he retrieved the green trunk from inside the station, Sam asked the man who had shoved it at him through a gap in the counter the way to the university. The reply he received he didn't understand, but the man had pointed vaguely to his left, so when Sam left the building, the trunk heavy on his shoulder, he began walking in the direction he guessed to be the right one. Somewhere between Franklin and Champaign-Urbana, the leather strap handle at the end of the trunk had been pulled loose, making the handling of it even more troublesome. Sam walked less than a block before he had to lower the trunk to the sidewalk to attempt a better grip. As he did he could hear rustling and thumping sounds as the contents shifted inside. He began turning the tin box to a different position to get it out of the way of other people on the sidewalk. Looking up at the window in front of which he had stopped, he saw something which caused him to forget the trunk.

The window was filled with numerous small objects—guitars, ashtrays made of halved steer horns, small boxes of strange coins, satin pillows with various inscriptions embroidered on them, necklaces, bracelets, Bowie knives. What caught his eye was located far back in the display, almost hidden by a fringed plastic vest which lay partly across it. It was a small yellowed skull with most of the upper teeth intact, and with a lower jaw fastened to it by rusty wire. The sight of the skull itself was not unusual for Sam. Mr. Vilka, the biology teacher at Big Muddy High School, kept a complete skeleton in a storage room off the science lab along with cans of paint and nails and other building supplies.

The skull in the window was unlike others he had seen in various establishments of the white man in that the eye sockets were not empty. A white chalky material had been molded into the blank spaces, and a pattern in green and yellow had been painted on where the eyeballs were when the skull had been a living part of a man. The pattern was the exact one that the Coushatta tribe drew on the dried clay they stuck into the skulls of their enemies killed in battle in the days before they had come to live on the reservation. McKinley Short Eyes had several of these skulls, which he would show to the young men of the tribe in the last few years of his life. When Short Eyes had died and his home was given to a newly married couple, Agent Hickson had taken the collection away and given it to some professor in Houston. "It's kind of a bad influence on the children, anyways," he had told the elders who had objected.

Sam walked to the door of the shop and found it fastened with a large padlock. A painted sign taped to the inside of the glass said, "Closed until further notice." Sam stepped back and read that the name of the shop was Marty's Treasure and Junque. He repeated it to himself several times under his breath, and with a last look at the skull, wrestled the trunk up from the sidewalk and began walking.

After a few blocks he saw a sign on a corner with an arrow and the letters UI in blue and orange. He turned left as the arrow directed, the trunk cutting into his shoulder and sweat dripping from his eyebrows into the corners of his eyes. He stopped to rest and wiped his face on his shirt sleeve, pushing the trunk off the sidewalk onto the edge of a small lawn covered with bluish green grass. He hadn't been sitting on the trunk more than half a minute, watching the cars and people, when he heard a door slam behind him. A woman's voice began filling the air with indignant noises. "Hey, you, boy! I will not have you students ruining my grass. Where are you from anyway? This is the United States of America. My yard belongs to me." Sam scrambled up from his seat and picked up the trunk, looking at the short gray-haired woman who strained toward him as though she were on a tight leash. "Move on," she said, "keep moving." She waved a rolled-up newspaper in one hand with which she gestured threateningly. After he had gotten a block down the street, Sam looked back at her. She still leaned forward, as though supported by an invisible wire which kept her from falling on her face. As Sam walked on, she leaned further over and brushed at the grass where the trunk had been, making a smoothing motion with her newspaper.

At the end of the block Sam paused to let a car turn in front of him. Instead of turning it stopped, and the driver leaned across the seat to speak out the window. "Do you wish a ride?" he said very rapidly in a heavy accent. He had to ask the question twice more before Sam understood the words, but the meaning of his stopping was clear enough. The driver of the '57 Chevrolet was small, dark, and heavily bearded. After Sam and the trunk were inside, the driver turned before putting the engine into gear and looked closely into Sam's face. His black eyes were like polished chinquapins. One looked bigger and less alert than the other.

"Third Worlder, hey brother," he said.

"What?"

"I said, Third Worlder. You are Third Worlder, no? A man of color. You have definition in a sea of paleness." He paused for an answer, but Sam sat silently picking at a rip in the seat cover to give himself a chance to double-translate what he had just heard. He formed the words into the language of the Alabama-Coushatta Nation, but nothing clicked in his mind. He surrendered and nodded at the driver in agreement.

"I am called Fawzi Kahwli," the bearded man said and extended his right hand toward Sam, his eyes on the Buick in front of them. "How are you called?"

"Sam Deer," Sam answered, offering the form of his name which usually seemed to cause the least surprise to strangers.

"Zam Dehah," Fawzi Kahwli repeated in his strange accent. "Do not tell me where is your home. I will tell it to you." He stopped for a few seconds and bounced his small fist on and off the horn ring, causing no sound at all to come from beneath the hood. "Jordan," he said finally in a voice rich with triumph. "Jordan the Brave." He continued to speak without waiting for a confirmation from Sam.

"Why do you come to U of I? To free your people, I know. But in what way? Through which means of science will your cause be furthered? Will you study engineering? Pre-med? What?"

"No," Sam said, "not that."

"Then what? Animal husbandry? Hardware? Computer programming? What brings you from your nation to this place of snow and machines?"

"To play basketball," Sam answered carefully, pronouncing his words as distinctly as possible. "To play basketball on the Indian team." The driver said something in a foreign language and suddenly eased off the clutch to the sound of much backfiring.

"I don't understand what you say. How does this playing with balls help your people in the Third World struggle? Is this utilitarian?" Sam shrugged his shoulders and shot a quick glance at Fawzi Kahwli's face. It seemed darker and more bearded than ever as Kahwli scowled through a lacework pattern of cracks in the windshield in front of him. Suddenly he began pounding the horn ring again and grinning broadly, showing blindingly white teeth interspersed with iron fillings.

"I get it, as the Americans say. The Olympics. Of course. A shrewd plan. Most effective propaganda for Third World people. Why should the United States with its oppressed black athletes be allowed these victories? Of course, of course. Use their facilities and instruction to beat them before the whole Third World and all the non-aligned nations." He looked at Sam with great affection and nodded vigorously. For the last several blocks the Chevrolet had been passing a series of large boxlike buildings made of red and yellow bricks. Kahwli pulled the car to a stop in front of one of them near a telephone booth and opened the door. "I must make call here," he said. "Please wait. I drive you where you wish to go." He hurried to the booth, searching throuh a handful of change he pulled out of one of his pockets. While he talked on the telephone Sam managed to open the green trunk and find the letter he had received with the Trailways ticket for Champaign-Urbana. In it was a sheet of paper with instructions for what Sam and all the other "grant-in-aid recipients" were to do on arrival at the university. He reclosed and retied the trunk and read the sheet. "Huff Gym," he told Kahwli when he returned to the car.

In a few minutes Kahwli let him out in front of another large, boxlike building made of bricks of the same color as the others they had passed. Several trees of not more than ten feet in height were geometrically spaced near the structure. "Here," Kahwli said as Sam picked up the trunk. "Take this paper with two addresses, please. One is the rooming house where I and some other Third Worlders stay. The other is a special place for strategy and solidarity meeting. Make use, please." Sam nodded and stuck the sheet of paper in his shirt pocket. Kahwli drove off, the '57 Chevrolet backfiring sharply as he shifted gears.

A large crowd of young men filled the hallway of the building, making it hard for Sam to maneuver his trunk through the heavy door. Once inside he let the trunk slide to the floor and stood beside it, his back against a dark blue wall with an orange stripe painted along it. Only the people nearest the door seemed to notice him. The rest continued talking in loud voices as they pushed each other back and forth, occasionally punching each others' shoulders in a playful fashion. Sam had seen white students at Big Muddy High act the same way in the cafeteria line at lunch, so he began to feel more comfortable. He noticed immediately that almost all of the sixty or seventy men there had necks much too large for the heads they supported. One in particular, wearing an orange T-shirt with the word Tanya written across the back, seemed to have nothing at all between his shoulders and his shaven head. Looking randomly around the crowd by moving only his eyes and keeping his face pointed straight ahead, Sam discovered that almost all the rest of the young men also had shaven heads. After a minute or so, immediately in front of Sam one of the herd put his shoulder into the chest of another and pushed him backwards into the green trunk. The edge of the tin box caught him just behind the knees, and he half-fell against the wall, catching himself with a hand on the way down. Everyone who had seen him tripped brayed with laughter, heads back and mouths open. Everyone else joined in, asking people near what happened. The man closest to Sam had no front teeth at all, Sam noted. The one who had fallen cursed happily and laughed with the rest, most of whom turned away when they saw he wasn't going to attack the one who had pushed him. He banged on the trunk lid with his right hand and looked at Sam.

"Hey, man," he said, empty-eyed and friendly, "you track, huh? You not football with that build, huh?" He smiled by drawing the corners of his mouth down and tapped Sam on the left shoulder lightly.

"No," Sam agreed, "basketball. The Indian team."

"Huh? Indian team?"

"Illi-," Sam attempted the strange name he'd been seeing, "Illiniee."

"Huh? Oh yeah. Right. Fighting Illini. Hang tough, baby. Gotcha." He jutted his chin out and took a deep breath, holding it for several seconds and then expelling it with a deep whoosh, watching Sam's face during the whole operation. "Can't get too much. Doctor told me that. Trainer on our squad. Greg Township. State runners-up last year in hitting and shitting." Sam nodded politely, offering his talking-to-white-peers face, and moved back a step as another body crashed into the group standing near him. "Oxygen. Oh two," the deep breather said. "Where you from?"

Just then from somewhere down the hall on the other side of the mass of grant-in-aids came two shrill blasts on a referee's whistle. Instantly about a third of the waiting group launched into imitations of the sound, some better than others, the deep breather's among the loudest. The real whistle kept on blowing until the imitations quieted down and everyone stopped talking. Sam could see some sort of bright silver object above the heads of the crowd, slowly making its way to the center of the lobby area in jerks and starts. When the person carrying it stopped walking, Sam realized that the object was a stepladder, soon mounted by a man just a few inches over five feet tall. Like most of the others there, he too wore a T-shirt, but it looked to be almost twice as wide as it was long as it strained over his torso. The man turned and faced the area where Sam was standing for a minute or so, making no attempt to speak. Tufts of black hair stood up from all around the neck of the shirt, shading to gray toward the man's back. The face of the man looked profoundly sad from its left profile, but when he craned his head around to survey the crowd, his face from the right side was vengeful and angry, like the Abraham Lincoln portrait which Mrs. Hubbard always enjoyed covering first one side of, then the other with a piece of cardboard for the benefit of the American history class at Big Muddy High School. "The warrior," she'd say, "and the freer of the slaves. Enemy and friend. Light and darkness." Mrs. Hubbard greatly relished dichotomy. Glancing around at the crowd which had been so rowdy a minute before, Sam was surprised to see that most of them were now looking down at the floor in front of them, as though they had been scolded. The man on the stepladder began to speak, his sad profile toward Sam.

"Gentlemen," he said, "I am Coach Underwood. I am not the head football coach, nor basketball, nor any of the minor sports. But let me assure you now. I am the man you've got to deal with." The other profile swivelled into view. "You get your checks through me. And your meal ticket. You get your extra football and basketball tickets. And you get a friendly little counseling service with me when you get in trouble. See me after your meetings this afternoon with the staff for your first issue. Any questions?" Everyone studied the floor. "One other thing. I played right guard in the Rose Bowl in '52 and covered two fumbles. Which I caused." He looked around for challengers, first warrior-face, then slave-freer. None came. "All right. Get into your groups." The assembly broke into shuffling and murmuring sounds as Coach Underwood dragged his ladder back down the hall. The deep-breather tapped Sam on the shoulder again and hurried off with the largest bunch of the group, drawing a double lungful of air as he left.

Sam fell into step behind the group with the skinniest necks, figuring that to be a likely sign. He had not seen an Indian, except for the skull in Marty's Treasure and Junque, since he had arrived in town, but maybe they would all be wherever the basketball beginners were going. The brochures Coach Dodge had given him had not actually pictured Indian players, but at the time Sam had thought little about it. Now he looked closely at the people he was following down the long blue and orange hall. All but one were taller than he was, most by several inches. They wore differently colored jackets and sweaters which generally did not reach all the way down their arms to the wrists. Most of the hands dangling at the ends of the long arms were large, and, Sam thought, awkward, almost deformed. They reminded him of the way the ends of crane wings looked when the birds were beginning to flap their way out of the mud flats of Long King Creek. The people ahead neared the intersection of another hall and turned off to the right. As they did, suddenly a person shorter even than the player walking directly in front of Sam appeared. Sam had only time to notice that he was black, his skin several shades darker than Sam's, before the advance group turned into the door of a room. The black man's hair was long and bushy, unlike the hair of any black Sam had ever seen in Franklin or even in Austin on basketball trips. Sam set his green trunk down just outside the door and went into the room, looking only at the chairs lined across the room facing a small platform. He chose one in a back row and sat down. He looked back at the door and saw a corner of the trunk outside.

The whispering and chairs scraping died down suddenly when a man sitting behind a desk at the front of the room slowly rose to his feet and walked over to a portable blackboard covered with writing and figures. He picked up a piece of chalk and stood juggling it up and down in his hand as he looked out over his audience. Again, Sam noticed, the young men began looking down at the floor or at the tips of their shoes as the man gazed at them. Only one, the black with the bushy hair, sat looking upward, and he seemed to be counting the orange and blue tiles in the ceiling. He sat two seats to the right of Sam on the same row. As Sam watched him, he slowly turned his head in Sam's direction and looked at him for several seconds, no expression on his face. He had a small patch of hair growing beneath his lower lip. Sam held his gaze, and the black man turned back to his tile counting. The man at the blackboard cleared his throat loudly, as if he were trying to dislodge something bad-tasting.

"Gentlemen," he said, "welcome to the U of I. You are among the finest freshmen basketball players in the country. Potential-wise." He looked out at the group, letting his eyes sweep over each of them, a kind smile beneath his nose. "You are here to learn and grow, to develop," he paused and juggled the chalk in his left hand, "on the court," he shifted the chalk to his right hand, "and in the classroom. You come from Illinois. You come from Indiana. From Ohio. New Jersey. From families in all walks of life and in all conditions. You are fine young Americans." He stopped again and allowed his smile to blossom. Sam thought about the look on the face of a sulled possum he had once seen being worried by two black-and-tan coon dogs.

With a long pointer which he had picked up from the top of the desk, the man gestured toward the blackboard. "These are the facts and figures of you as individuals and as members of your group." He began reading numbers and percentages from the board in a lingering voice, savoring each syllable. From the back of the room Sam watched closely and attempted to listen carefully to what the smiling man was explaining. After the first couple of minutes of explanations of what the man called "vital stats," Sam found it hard to keep his attention on the front of the room. For one thing, he suddenly discovered that he was ragingly hungry. The effects of the root he had chewed had worn off several hours earlier, and by the time he sat down with the group of freshmen in the gym, the pork he had eaten in Texarkana was a dim event in the past. He fingered the pouch beneath his shirt for a few seconds, but his belly told him that now only food would do. An image of the corn he had ridden through for hours suddenly flashed into his mind, and a hollow pain gripped him just under his belt buckle. The man at the front of the room, whoever he was, had finished pointing to the blackboard and was now handing out sheets of paper to the people in the front row. Sam again tried to listen to what the man was saying.

"Here are your room assignments. See Coach Underwood for your first checks and meal tickets. We'll meet tomorrow for our first offensive talk, and then suit up for some shooting. Any questions?" He stood, the smile again beneath his nose, one foot resting on a vacant chair. A hand went up slowly from someone on the far side of the room. It belonged to a sandy-haired boy with a long nose and a high voice. "When do we register for classes?" For the first time the smile vanished.

"You'll get taken care of. We have some volunteers from the fraternities to take each of you around and get you signed up. That's a different subject altogether. I don't worry about that end of it at all." He glared at the sandy-haired boy, whose head sank lower and lower until it was almost hidden behind his jutting knees. "Anything else?" the man asked, and when no other hands went up, he put the smile back beneath his nose. "Dismissed," he said.

After receiving a check made out to S. H. L. Deer for sixty dollars with the word "Laundry" stamped in the space after "For" and an orange ticket book, Sam stood in the hall near the pay window studying a sheet of instructions. He found his name typed next to another one, F. D. Jones, under the designation MRH PA 415 SA. He remained there, staring at the sheet of paper and thinking of food, until almost all the shaven-headed men had picked up their checks and left. One of the last two still there, the lanky sandy-haired one who had asked about classes, walked past Sam slowly and then stopped.

"Say," he said, "do you know where the Pennsylvania Avenue Residence Hall is? I believe that's what these letters here mean." He pointed at the sheet in his left hand.

"I don't know," Sam answered, hoping to indicate that he had known the meaning of the letters already.

"I sort of know where it is. She told me the direction in there," the sandy-haired one said, gesturing toward the middle-aged woman who had issued the tickets through the window slot. "But I don't know exactly. You want to walk on down the street and look for it? We find it before six, we can still eat this afternoon." Sam stuffed the paper into his shirt pocket next to the one with Fawzi Kahwli's addresses and hoisted the green trunk. Sandy Hair held the door open for him as they left the building. Outside, the white man turned to the right and Sam followed, listening to the stream of words that came from him as they walked. Sandy Hair said his name, Martin Kroeber, that he was from Pekin, Illinois, played center, and that his main interest in basketball was getting a chance to study engineering. "That's where the real money is, see," he explained. "What I want to do is go into civil engineering and get married to my girl in Pekin and settle down right there. Where my contacts are. What about you?" Sam nodded and Martin seemed satisfied.

After a couple of blocks the large boxlike brick buildings gave way to smaller areas which looked a good deal like oversized houses. They were not at all like the shotgun houses on the reservation but like a few of the ones in Franklin, set far back from the sidewalk with large lawns in front. They reminded Sam of the mansions he had seen in movies about white men in uniforms and white women in long dresses. At the same time Mrs. Hubbard would show the Big Muddy history classes how Lincoln's face divided, she also would talk about the people who used to live in the sort of houses Sam thought of now as he looked around him. "Gone," she would say, "gone with the wind." Some of the white girls in the class would heave sighs and a few of the boys would look grim. "Ess Ay E," Martin said, pointing to one of the largest on the block, red brick with white columns across the front and lawn chairs scattered around the lawn between it and the sidewalk.

"Say?" Sam asked, putting the letters together.

"Ess Ay E. Sigma Alpha Epsilon. It's boss, man. My older brother was one at Iowa. Wasn't no good there, though. Dekes big there." Sam looked at the large house. Two young men dressed alike were tossing a football back and forth in the side yard.

"You going to pledge?" Martin asked in the midst of something he was saying about the iron fence surrounding the house.

"Uh," Sam said, and thought of the word. The only thing that came to his mind were the times in the lower grades when the teacher had led the children in placing their hands on their chests while repeating a series of words in the direction of the flag in the corner of the room. He could make no connection between those events and the way Martin seemed to be using the word now. "Pledge," Sam said, "I don't know."

"I'm pretty much with you on that. Wait awhile until you see what the rush has to offer. Of course, the athlete's frat is the BOM's. Not everybody gets a chance to pledge that one, though. Only the guys they think are really going to make it in the major sports. Not too many swimmers in the BOM's." Martin laughed at what he had just said, flapping his hands up and down. Up ahead a few yards several white girls turned onto the sidewalk in front of Sam and Martin, a couple of them glancing back over their shoulders. The large brick house out of which they had come had been painted white, Sam noticed. Except for color, their skirts and blouses looked the same. Sam stopped and set the trunk down. He began rubbing his right shoulder and looking down at a crack in the sidewalk. The sound of girls' talk and laughter moved further up the sidewalk.

"Hey, man. Don't stop now. Didn't you see that bunch of Tri Delts? They were looking back at us, man." Martin's voice was higher than before. He walked a few feet up the sidewalk and looked back at Sam, gesturing for him to come on. "They going to get away."

"You go," Sam said and propped his right foot up on the tin box. A streetlight on the corner of the block suddenly flashed on. Martin looked back and forth from the light to the girls disappearing around a corner up ahead.

"Shit," he said, "I'm hungry. I guess I'll go on with you right now." He helped Sam place the trunk back on his shoulder, and for the rest of the way to their destination he discussed various fine points of the girls he had spotted. "Did you see the calves on that short black-haired one with the lavender jumper?" he asked as they turned into the entrance of another flat box, this one with the right letters on the door. "I mean the way they flexed every time she took a step?"

In a few minutes, Sam found himself alone in a room on the third floor and freed at last from the green trunk. After checking the contents for damage and finding none to worry about, he shoved the box against one of the walls and felt relieved. The only thing really disturbed was the sheaf of feathers, and they were only battered about the edges, none broken. He sat on the edge of one of the beds and looked about at the place they had put him in. The room was smaller than the motel rooms the Big Muddy team occupied in Austin each year during the state tournament, but it seemed to have more in it. Besides the two single beds, there were two desks, bookshelves, and two chests of drawers, all built into the walls. The reigning color was green, the particular shade of which immediately reminded Sam of the film that came over the surface of the water which collected in gullies on the reservation during the winter rains. He bounced a little on the bed, and it gave mushily beneath him. He stood up, walked over to the light switch and snapped it on and off a few times. With the light on, the outside looked completely dark, the window pane as black as if it had been painted over. He left the light off and stepped out into the hall on the way to a larger room he had seen filled with people eating when he had come upstairs from the office.

Most of the eaters had finished and left by the time Sam arrived at the end of the cafeteria line. He went through it quickly, pointing at random containers of food without knowing what they held, and at the end of the line, handed the cashier the book of tickets he had been given. She told him that he was allowed only three vegetables and would therefore receive only two the next night. He carried his tray to an empty table and ate quickly, hardly tasting the food as he stared at his plate and chewed. One of the dishes he had chosen was corn, he discovered, but it had been treated in such a way as to make it unlike any he had had before. Chewing his last bite, Sam carried his tray across the room to a conveyor belt as he had seen others doing and deposited it there. It moved out of sight quickly toward a large dark hole in one wall. Sam stopped to watch, but by the time his tray had reached the

hole, he was unable to pick it out from the others which surrounded it. For some reason he felt as though he had lost something.

He turned away from the belt, almost bumping into a fat
short man behind him and headed back to the room. "Parn me,"
the fat man called after him in a sad voice. Sam looked back and
saw that he was scrubbing at a spot on the front of his shirt with a
paper napkin.

When he neared the door to his room Sam could tell that
something was different. A streak of light came from a crack between the door and the jamb and lay across the hall like a bar. Sam
looked from the key in his hand to the number on the door and
back, and then moved forward slowly until he stood a little to one
side of the streak of light. He could see nothing through the crack
but part of one of the desks and the edge of a table lamp. He placed
the tips of his fingers on the door and gave a small push. The sound
of springs creaking in one of the beds came from the room. The
door swung open slowly about halfway and stopped. "What's
happening," someone in the room said. Sam stepped in front of the
door so he could see inside and stopped, looking quickly from the
person lying across one of the beds to the green trunk against the
wall. It looked the same. The person in the bed was the black man
with the strange hair who had sat in the back of the room near Sam
a few hours before.

"Oh," the man said, "you, huh? It figures." He looked at Sam
with his head turned to one side and a look on his face as if he had
known everything worth knowing for so long that it had lost all
interest for him. Sam walked in and leaned against one of the
desks, his gaze still on the black face. A thought hit him, and he
pulled the sheet of instructions out of his shirt pocket. The Kahwli
addresses and the book of meal tickets fell out, but he caught them
at waist level. Sam searched the list of names until he found his
own, and then read the one next to it aloud. "F. D. Jones."

"You got it. The name. The slave name. My real name, the
one I picked for myself, I mean my rightful name is Akbar Ameer.
You know what the F. D. stand for?" Sam shook his head like a
white man. "Franklin Delano. That's right. Franklin Delano." He
stopped, seemed to wait for a reaction. Sam shrugged his shoulders
and shifted his eyes to a point on the wall a little above and to the
right of Akbar Ameer–Franklin Delano Jones's head. "Yeah, man.

I hand you no shit. My old grandfather was so fooled by these white so-called liberals he name me that. What you called? What you call yourself?"

"Sam Deer."

"Yeah? What them other letters mean? On the sheet there." Akbar pointed toward the paper in Sam's hand.

"Houston Leaping. Sam Houston Leaping Deer."

"Hey, man. Ain't he president too? You just like me. Both us name for presidents of this slave nation." Akbar sat up in the bed and leaned against the wall. He laughed with pleasure and bounced his head back and forth off the plaster behind him. "Your old man a liberal too?"

"No," Sam said, "a Coushatta."

"Huh?" Akbar sat up further in the bed and looked hard into Sam's face. He smiled again. "I dig, man. Right on." Sam moved over to the other bed and sat down on the edge of it. The bed gave and seemed to reach up and pull at him. He leaned forward and put his elbows on his knees.

"What that mean? What you just called your old man?"

"The tribe. Part of the Nation."

"Yeah?" Akbar scratched at the hair rising up into a ball around his head. "Rap," he said, "lay it on me. Who you be, man?"

"Sam Deer."

"Yeah, but I mean something else, you dig? Where your turf, man?" Sam pondered the question. The black man seemed to be talking a language he didn't follow, although the words were ones he had learned before from the white men in Big Muddy and Franklin and wherever else he had seen them. The way Akbar spoke, the sounds of his speech, the way he said his words and parts of words added up to something different. It reminded Sam of some of the music the white students at Big Muddy played on their car radios in the parking lot and at the school dances held during the year. Once Cooper had brought in a television set from some trade he had made, and the Leaping Deer family had listened to it off and on for three or four weeks despite the fact that no picture came on its mud-green face, until the sound had finally stopped. Some of the words Akbar used Sam had heard on the television set, but he had never worried about what they meant at all. The sounds and rhythms had been the only real interest during that month, not what they added up to. Now, as he sat listening to the black man, he found himself responding in the same way to the words he was hearing. The sounds were so entertaining in themselves that it was hard to keep attention on unraveling what the speaker meant by them. It was like listening to the music from the white dances held in the gym at Big Muddy as it filtered through the windows to the edge of the road where he had sometimes stood for a while to hear.

"Where you live, man?" Akbar asked.

"The reservation. Alabama-Coushatta reservation," Sam answered, and then remembering the phrase he always heard white men use when identifying the Nation, added, "Texas Only Indian Reservation."

"Too much. Uh Indian." Akbar shook his hands above his head. "You see what Charley done, don't you?" Sam rubbed his hands back and forth on his thighs and said nothing. No use. It was like the dying TV set.

"What?"

"I say, you dig what Charley is up to, putting us here in the same room?" The word *room* took Akbar fully two seconds to get out. He let his head bounce off the wall again as he laughed. "Shit, man. You figure it. We the only two dudes on the freshman roster who ain't ofay, right?"

"Ofay?"

"White, baby, white. Pig Latin, you dig? Comes out of jazz. Lots of our old stuff does. I learned all about origins in the Southside Liberation School. Look. These cats figuring a way to put everybody in rooms. Two to a room, you dig. You and me together solves all the problems, man."

Sam nodded, responding in the way he thought the general drift of the black man's words led. He shifted his weight on the bed, easing the pressure of the belt buckle cutting into his belly. The food he had eaten lay heavy inside. He was thirsty. Akbar was talking again.

"Like the man say, use the pigs. Use what weapons you got. Myself, I play basketball. It's a commodity. They got a demand for it, dig, so sell it for the most profit. Make them capitalist mothers play your game."

"Yes," Sam said, quickly picking up a series of words he recognized. Coach Dodge had often said much the same sort of thing to the team before games and at half-time, especially when Big Muddy was even or behind.

"Yeah, man," Akbar said, "we groove to the same beat. That where Charley always make his mistake. He think he put all us in one place he can keep a watch on us. Shit, man, he's a fool. What the brothers forced to do in the ghetto situation is organize. Charley make it possible, man."

"Charley," Sam repeated, trying to make his tone knowledgeable. Charley must be a coach of some sort, he decided, that he hadn't met yet.

"What we can be," Akbar broke into his thought, "in this room is a wedge." He reached down and scratched at his crotch. "Fighting Illini, shit. We'll see, baby, we see what's going to come down."

Sam leaned back and let the bed take him, surrendering to the heavy pull of the food in his stomach. The last thing he remembered before he fell asleep was Akbar's chuckling about the foolishness of Charley as illustrated in an anecdote that Sam made no effort to follow.

Sam spent most of the next day tagging after a guide provided by the Athletic Department to help get the grants-in-aid registered in classes. The guide was named M. M. Myers, and he was proud of his job. Between the sessions with clerks at different tables set up in a large building with a cinder floor, M. M. described his responsibilities, the origin of the program he was in, and his ambition to sell paper products in Chicago. "Something basic, something basic," he kept saying, looking into Sam's eyes earnestly and long. After telling Sam to call him at his number with any problems with classes or "orientating yourself" he left him at the door of Huff Gym at two o'clock.

Sam put on the practice uniform he was issued by the equipment clerk and walked toward the sound of bouncing basketballs and splatting shoes. He looked down at the orange letters on the front of his T-shirt, recognized the tribal name he had been seeing everywhere since he had arrived, and brushed his fingers across it. Now he would see the other Indian players, he thought. They would be shooting with the rest. He remembered Coach Dodge often saying, "Wherever they's a bunch of Alabamas and Coushattas and a goal, they'll be putting the ball up."

The gym itself was filled with young men with skinny necks, some of whom Sam recognized from the day before. Most of them were gathered at either end of the court in front of the main goals working on their various moves and shots. Sam picked up a loose ball and moved to a practice goal on the side where only one other person was shooting and put up a twenty-footer. It hit the back of the rim and bounced away with a vibrating sound. A bad sign. It had felt right when it left his hand. He had missed the first warm-up shot he had taken in the University of Texas gym in Austin at his first state tournament, and he had known then the Old Ones weren't to be with him so far from home. The back of his neck felt cold, and his armpits itched. He retrieved the ball, swerved to the left and tried a bank shot. It fell cleanly, and he felt a little better.

He worked another twenty minutes or so, looking out of the corners of his eyes from time to time at the other man shooting at his goal and watching for a glimpse of an Illini Indian. None showed, but the old rhythms of the shots began coming and the ball stopped feeling heavy and strange in his hands. The tall man worked with his back to the goal, pivoting back and forth on hook shots and little turn-around jumpers. Once he asked Sam if he could slam and when Sam said nothing, he demonstrated his own ability by going up high and putting the ball through the goal with a great grunt and a shower of flying sweat.

In the center of the main court, the man with the dead smile from yesterday blew a whistle and everybody began walking toward him, basketballs trickling away from their hands toward the out-of-bounds lines. Sam turned at the head of the circle and shot a left-handed jump before he joined the crowd. The sound of its snapping the net was loud enough in the silence to cause heads to turn toward him. The man with the whistle had put his smile away again. He looked at Sam but said nothing, and the others began their study of the area in front of their feet again.

"Agility drills," the man said and began dividing the players up into groups of three or four. Sam found himself standing next to two others, both about his size and both with shaved heads and darting eyes. The air was sharp with sweat. Another man with the word *Assistant* lettered on his shirt led them off to the far wall of the building, bouncing a basketball in front of him as he talked over his shoulder.

"You know the scramble drill?" he asked.

"Yes sir," the other two said together. Sam rubbed his left thumb against the tips of his fingers and watched the ends of his shoestrings flip as he walked. They reached the wall and stopped, and Assistant pointed to one of the others.

"You first," he said.

The shaved head turned his back to the wall and crouched, hands outstretched and eyes glazed over like skim ice in January. Assistant stood behind him and suddenly threw the basketball he had been tossing from hand to hand hard against the wall behind the crouching man, who whirled and dove for the ball, managing to touch it with his left hand as it bounced past him and onto the floor. Twice more he was able to reach the ball, and once he stopped it and dribbled it twice. Assistant began to throw harder and further away from the shaved one, and three balls in a row got by him. Sweat began spotting the floor as he stood in his crouch waiting for the ball to slam against the wall. Sam could see from where he was standing at the side that the tendons behind the shaved one's knees were jumping up and down as he waited.

After another minute or so of this ritual, Assistant walked around in front of the man and crouched until he was looking into his eyes. He lifted his hands up in front of the shaved one's face and suddenly jerked the left one to the side. The player whirled to his right and faced the wall, his feet chattering up and down in place. Assistant tried the same thing again to the left and then twice to the right. By the time the process was stopped, the shaved one was huffing and blowing like Thomas Two Tongues at the end of a two-hour sermon.

As Assistant took the second shaved one through the same routine, Sam looked about him at the gym where the same thing was happening with the rest of the groups and considered what he would do when Assistant pointed to him. Once before, a coach had wanted him to do something which didn't involve his trying to put the ball through the basket while other people tried to stop him, and he had refused. The coach had been a young man working on a physical education degree at Stephen F. Austin University. He had been assigned to work with Coach Dodge at Big Muddy to get his "practice teaching" done for certification as an officially approved teacher in Texas schools. He was promoting something he called "wind sprints," and he had directed Sam, along with the other Coushattas, to join in with the white players

running back and forth between the wall and the middle of the
court. A couple of the Indian players from the Alabama tribe half-
heartedly took part, finishing always behind the panting sons of
white farmers and sawmill workers. Sam and the other Coushattas
had stood to one side talking quietly in the language of the Nation
and waiting to play basketball after the foolishness was over.
Coach Dodge had later confided in the young coach-to-be that
these Indians didn't have enough gumption to do anything tough
like "wind sprints." "They don't want to put out a-tall," he said.
"That's why none of them ever gets to be coaches theyselves, or
politicians or dentists."

"You do have some white kids here with what it takes,
though," the young man from S.F.A. had said, watching Shirald
Hendrix and Don Ray Popp dash back and forth between the
boundary lines, teeth gritted and hair flying.

"Well, yeah," Coach Dodge had allowed, thinking of the sum
total of four points the two had scored between them against
Milby High the week before.

Before Sam, the second of the group finished his last dancing
whirl to the right and dropped into a squat to rest. Assistant turned
and looked at Sam and gestured with his right hand in the direction
of the wall. "O.K.," he said. "Last man up." Sam looked from the
man's face down to the letters on his shirt and then back up again.
The deep breathing of the last shaved head was the only sound for
a half-minute or so.

Assistant Coach Tom Chudy studied the dark face of the
Coushatta standing before him and began to realize he had a little
problem building up. Here was a minority kid of some kind who
would have to have special handling or the usefulness of the drill
would be lost completely. Coach Chudy had done a semester
course in his M.A. program in physical education on just this kind
of player, the sort that had begun cropping up more and more
these days since things had started becoming strange in the country, in the universities, and in basketball. He had learned that most
of the time these little breakdowns in discipline occurred because
of the minority player's fear of not being able to match the
proficiency of the white players, not because of any real desire to
rebel. At least that's what the seminar in Coaching the Special
Player had taught. Blacks, for example, lots of times just didn't
understand what the directions meant and covered their fear of

failure by acting mean and sulky. This fellow with the straight black hair and dark skin probably just didn't understand or want to be showed up by his inability to match the performance of the two others in the group.

"Well, son, aren't you going to try to get with it?" Coach Chudy figured a fatherly semichallenging tone would be best to start with. Then he could move on to a harsher command-situation, if he had to. "It's not hard to do this little scramble drill. Nobody's going to think the less of you if you don't pick up the little tricks of it right off the bat. You saw Perkins and Sullivan do it. You just give it a try, and we'll help you when you screw up, and we'll set you right."

Chudy felt proud of his tone and wished Professor Nagel could be there to appreciate his handling of the minority kid. He looked at the other two players to see what effect he was having on them. He had learned that lots of times the ones who really benefited from good coaching procedures were the bystanders themselves. Perkins and Sullivan were looking steadily at the minority player's knees, their eyes set and their faces slack.

Sam looked at the wall and then at the point on the floor where the others had crouched to begin their drill. He imagined himself in the same position, waiting to hear the splat of the ball behind him before he turned to swat at it as it bounced past him. He could see McKinley Short Eyes watching him do such a thing, the old man slowly rubbing a turkey feather back and forth on the sleeve of his coat while he waited for Sam to finish the act. Short Eyes, he knew, would not speak as he turned away to climb the steps back into his house.

"Assistant," Sam said, "I cannot."

"Sure you can. Give her a try. We'll work with you on it. This drill's important for developing hand-eye and anticipation."

Sam made a sweeping gesture with his right hand and let it drop to his side. It was decided. Chudy could see that the two shaved heads were beginning to realize that a breakdown in discipline was taking place. He ordered them to take some laps around the gym and turned back to Sam as they trotted off, putting a lot of rolling action into their shoulders as they moved away. Neither one spoke to the other until they were well out of range of the coach.

"Now, do you want to try it while nobody but me's watching?" Coach Chudy craned his neck to look around Sam in the direction of the head coach at the far end of the gym. He didn't seem to have noticed that anything was wrong yet. Chudy probably had five minutes to use before he had to report discipline breakdown and take the ass-reaming that would result. Back to the minority kid.

"Now look here, son. You've got to get over there and try that scramble drill. I'll tell you one thing for certain. You won't play a minute of Illini basketball if you don't. We have a program here that works, and you've got to fit into it or you're out of here." Chudy looked hard at the dark-skinned kid to see what effect some tough talk would have. He seemed the same as before, staring straight ahead with nothing showing in his eyes. Chudy fingered the whistle hanging around his neck and tried to think of something else. Won't talk back to me. Hell, almost any kid will give you back some lip. You can handle them fine once you get them to explaining themselves.

In the middle of wondering what to do next, Chudy heard his name called over the sound of the bouncing balls and the squeaking of rubber soles. He looked up the court and saw Thompson looking his way. He felt his sphincter tighten and his throat go dry. "I'll talk to you later," he growled at Sam and trotted off.

Sam picked up the loose basketball by his feet and began dribbling it in tight circles, alternately changing hands and directions. His mind was empty. Now McKinley Short Eyes would speak to him before he went into the door of his house.

The drills ended, and student managers began gathering up the basketballs. In the middle of the court the coaches stood conferring about the opening lineups of the scrimmage to come. Knots of the well-drilled scramblers stood around at the edge of the boundary line, waiting for whatever would happen next. Sam bounced the ball he had been dribbling to a short blond manager with his hand out and walked toward the edge of one of the groups where he saw F. D. Jones/Akbar Ameer standing. In a few minutes two of the assistant coaches picked out ten players from the sidelines and started a scrimmage at one end of the court. Akbar caught Sam's eye and looked knowing.

The two teams were nervous and jittery and took bad shots and missed good ones. Coaches darted in and out of the shifting mass, pushing an arm here and kicking at a leg there, all the while shouting orders in loud voices. "Don't you see he's eating you alive, number twenty? Don't you see he's eating you alive?" Assistant Chudy kept asking one player over and over. Cries of "move your ass" and "jam him in there" came from various others of the men with silver-colored whistles bouncing off their chests. Every couple of minutes the coach with the dead smile would sound a blast, and the action would stop until the players were repositioned and the ball handed to one of the guards. "Now," Thompson would say, and the shuffling would recommence. Sam began to be bored by watching the guards work the ball to one of the tall forwards or the center, and he began observing the feet of the guards rather than the passes they were trying to set up. All of their movements were predictable, he saw, like most of the big Houston teams the Big Muddy Bobcats played in nonconference games. There were a lot of head and eye fakes, but the feet plodded straight ahead. Nobody passed off-balance, nobody tried to drive very far into the key.

The coaches began making substitutions, and after three or four of the original ten had sat down, Sam realized that everyone was looking at him. "Blue nine, blue nine," one of the smallest of the assistants barked at him. "What's your number, blue nine?" Sam looked at his chest and then walked toward the center of the court. "Listen up, now," the little coach continued, glancing at Dead Smile for approval, "you got to always know what number you are and where you are." Someone flipped Sam the ball, and the coach told him to see if he could move it inside. The man guarding Sam, a stocky blond with thick thighs and close-set eyes, stuck his hand up toward Sam's face, and Sam began to work.

Dribbling with his right hand, he moved toward the right boundary and waited until his man began to come over to pinch him against the line. As he did, Sam slowed until the blond guard was overcommitted, and then he spun to his right, reversed the dribble coming back left and found himself with no one between him and the goal except the center. He drove directly at the tall man, lifted the upper part of his body as though he were going to go up for a jumper, and then as the center left the floor to block, scooted around his left side and passed off to his forward standing alone three feet from the goal. The ball hit him in the chest and bounced out of bounds as the center fell across Sam's back and slipped halfway to the floor.

Whistles blew, and the assistants began screaming at the guard assigned to Sam, at Sam's left forward, and at the opposing center. "Keep your eyes open, blue eighteen. That ball came to *you*, and you never even saw it, did you?"

"Hemmings, don't you let him sucker you like that. You ended up on your fat ass out of bounds after you thought you had him pinched!"

"Red center, why in shit's name did you go up so damn quick? Did you ever consider he might pass off?"

Sam walked back to the half-court line and waited for the ball. As he passed some of the coaches he saw Dead Smile leaning down to talk directly into Chudy's face. Chudy wore an earnest expression as he listened and nodded.

The small coach handed Sam the ball again, and Hemmings moved a step back and widened his stance as he waited for Sam to start it up. His cheeks looked like someone had pasted two spots of red just below his eyes. Sam hesitated, dropped his right shoulder and dribbled left a few steps, waving the other blue guard back. Hemmings' eyes flicked toward the right side where Sam had gestured, and Sam accelerated to the right, gaining a step on the guard as he lunged to recover. By that time Sam was able to whip a pass just over Hemmings' left hand to his center. Hemmings' legs were crossing as Sam ran by to take the short return on his drive toward the basket. As the ball settled though the net from Sam's lay-up, the big-legged guard cracked into Sam's back driving him across the out-of-bounds line almost to the wall. As Sam picked himself up and walked back to the midline, the coaches yelled at Hemmings and praised the center for his "good assist." Hemmings looked hard at the floor, and blue center acted as if he hadn't heard a thing the whistle-blowers were saying.

For the rest of the scrimmage Sam continued to start the plays, facing first one then another of the guards Dead Smile motioned in. He shot little for the first few minutes, but after he broke a good sweat, he began to drive more, either unassisted or after one return pass. He found it relatively easy to thread his way past the guards and around the center, and it wasn't until the forwards began to bunch the middle that he began to pass off a good bit, finding his forwards for short jumpers and occasionally working the ball across to the other guard coming behind him or across the corner for drives down the backline. The more the session went on, the more the assistants yelled, whistled, and ran in and out of the pack to shove the various body parts into new positions. The scrimmage ended with Chudy standing toe-to-toe with a tall center talking fast in a low voice into the general vicinity of the man's collarbone.

"Showers," Chudy finally said, and the shaven heads broke into a trot toward the door. "Just a minute, blue nine," Chudy said in Sam's direction. "Coach Thompson wants to talk to you first." He looked over at Dead Smile and back to Sam, trying to judge how sharp a tone to use. "You got something to explain," he added and waited for directions. Dead Smile nodded and Chudy turned away, walking with his head reared back in the direction of the last man disappearing through the door. Chudy liked always to come into the shower room only after all the players were already there. The sudden hush was sweet every time.

Sam waited to hear what Thompson wanted. A drop of sweat trickled into his left eye as he looked at Dead Smile refix his face and start to speak. The air in the gym felt clammy, like the mist that rose off the salt lick in the Nation on summer mornings.

"Well, number nine," he said. "Sam Leaping Deer, isn't it? From near Houston?" Dead Smile gathered his face.

"Yes," Sam said. "I live in Texas. In the Alabama-Coushatta Nation."

"You fellows play some good basketball there at Big Muddy," Dead Smile said in a friendly voice. "What is that area? Oil, or cattle country?" Sam double-translated the question, saw no sense in it, and finally answered.

"Hogs, I guess."

"Uh-huh. Well." Thompson fingered the silver whistle on the chain around his neck before he spoke again. He was going to move slowly. He had concluded long ago that rural kids, particularly minority ones far from home, didn't respond well to fast talk or sudden movements. The less spooked they got, the more you got out of them.

"A couple of things we need to talk about. First one is did you ever use a pattern offense in your high school days?"

Sam had heard the term before. Coach Dodge would use it every time he came back from one of the coaching schools he attended in the summer in Lufkin or Nacogdoches or Huntsville. The coaches from Houston and Beaumont seemed to think it was important to talk about a lot, so Dodge would offer up his version of it during the first few practices of each fall at Big Muddy. By the time the Bobcats had played an actual game or two, he would forget about pattern offense and go back to depending on the Indians' hitting the basket more times than the other team.

"Some," Sam answered Dead Smile.

"Fine, fine. Now if you did, you had to learn something about discipline. About giving yourself up to a larger thing. You know, striving for a team effort as opposed to gunning away individually." He regarded Sam to see what effect he was having.

"Now the same thing applies to all our drills here. Agility drills, sprints, tips and taps, all of it. A little while ago Coach Chudy told me you refused on the scramble drill."

Sam gave Dead Smile a white-man nod and thought about the door of McKinley Short Eyes' house. He could see the rotted-out screen swinging slowly shut.

"We can't have that here at Illinois. I liked what I saw of you directing the attack in the scrimmage a few minutes ago." Praise at the right time was essential, Thompson knew. "And I think with some work and discipline and commitment you can play some basketball for us here. In fact I'm thinking about working you with the starters next week to see what happens. But you've got to be willing to participate in all our drills at practice. Otherwise, you'll never play a minute in the Assembly Hall."

Sam remembered the large saucer-shaped structure he had seen in the picture given to him by Coach Dodge. Another image, the one of the Indian chief balanced on two basketballs, also came into his mind.

"Well, Leaping Deer," Dead Smile said, "I've given you something to think about, and I don't want you to give me an answer now. Those are the terms, though. I want you to understand that. You let me know soon."

Thompson looked around for his smile and found it again. "Any questions?"

"Yes," Sam said, carefully shaping his words in the language of the white man. "The other Indians. The Illini players. Where do they practice?"

"What do you mean, Leaping Deer? The Fighting Illini basketball team is right here around us. And you can be a real member of the group if you get your thinking straightened out."

Thompson figured he'd said enough to motivate the young Indian by now, so he turned to walk away. Sam called after him.

"Where do they live? The Indian players?"

"Listen, Deer. You'll see them all later. Go on in now," Thompson said over his shoulder.

Sam started slowly toward the door where the others had gone, picking at the letters on the front of his shirt. He would have to ask one of the shaven heads later about the Indians.

Sam Leaping Deer began his classes at the University of Illinois by following M. M. Myers, his Athletic Department guide, from one large building to another, stopping in each for an hour in a room with many other people. Most of the people were dressed alike with little to say to each other. In one room he sat with about fifty others for an hour, watching his choice of three television sets, each tuned to an image of the same man talking about pieces of rock which he alternately showed to the camera and scratched at with a small tool that looked like an ice-pick.

After each hour Sam would walk out into the hall and be met by Myers, who always asked, "How did it go?" At first Sam tried to answer, but after Myers only repeated "right, right" several times, he quit trying to comment on what had taken place in the classroom.

The last class of Sam's first-day schedule met in a smaller room than the other ones and had fewer people in it. Myers got him there just as the bell was ringing, and Sam had to sit in the last open seat, one in the circle of chairs near the front of the room. The seats were arranged so that all the people there were formed into a ring facing inward. Sam looked around him for the seat where the teacher would be sitting, but he could see no one who looked the part. On his left sat a young woman with long blonde hair knotted into braids. She was fiddling with some books and papers when Sam looked at her, but she noticed him anyway. Sam nodded when she said hello and then looked back across the room to the other side of the circle. No one spoke for two or three minutes, although there was a good deal of twisting and flouncing in the seats and rearranging of pencils and notebooks. It became quieter. Everyone watched a fat freckled girl light a cigarette, blow out the match, and drop it into her purse.

"Whoosh," somebody said, and people laughed.

"I like that," a woman sitting three seats over to Sam's right said. "It sets an easy tone, a feeling that's right for beginnings." Heads swung to look in her direction.

"I am Sally Smith. I am your teacher. A flat name and a flat title. A name I once deplored and a title I once feared the implications, the connotations, the vibrations of. Now a name and a title that I've come to accept, embrace, live with. Words of designation that I have domesticated. Words setting limits within which I live, work, and exist. Limits which have lost the power of constriction because they are limits that have imploded."

"Oh, wow," the girl with braids next to Sam whispered breathily, shifting in her chair.

Sally Smith was dressed in jeans and a colored flowing blouse covered with small patterns. Sam noticed that large silver rings swung back and forth from her ears as she talked. Now and then she would put both hands up to her head, seize two handfuls of hair just above her ears, and toss it back away from her face. Her voice became louder as she went on, lifting and swelling as she neared the end of sentences.

"Meet my gaze," she told the class, swaying a bit in her chair. "Meet my gaze. That is our goal in our study, in our engagement with literature this term, and in our engagement with each other. We will learn to meet the gaze of those here, and the gaze of those authors whose work we will experience. Really to meet the gaze of anyone gives us an overwhelming flash of pure existence."

Sam could hear the girl to his left writing rapidly in a notebook as Sally Smith talked. She hunched forward over her lap, her braids swinging as her hand moved across the page in little jerks. Mrs. Manning, the senior English teacher at Big Muddy, had warned Sam many times that he would have to take notes now that he was going off to college. "Write down as much as you can of everything you hear," she had said, "and then get it all by heart." Sam took a pencil out of his shirt pocket and thought of what he might write on the notebook in front of him. He leaned forward and wrote the word *gaze* at the top left of the first sheet of paper. He stared at what he had put down and felt a little light-headed. He took a deep breath and lifted his eyes to the faces of the people on the other side of the circle.

The man directly across from Sam was looking right at him. He lifted his eyebrows, turned the corners of his mouth down, and cut his eyes toward Sally Smith. From the look on the man's face, Sam had a feeling that he knew what Sam was thinking. He tried to place where he had seen the face in the last few days and couldn't.

"I will never talk again as much to you in one class as I have done today," Sally Smith was saying. "Our times together will be spontaneous, open to whatever directions seem most fruitful to us. Our interchange will be creative, flowing, as unstructured and as organic as we can allow. I will hush now, and for the rest of our first session, depend on you to supply whatever subject, mood, or movement seems inevitable and right." She threw her hair back once more, lowered her arms, and leaned forward in her seat, her eyes sweeping around the circle like a mother hawk's.

Sally Smith knew that the first class meeting was all-important, even though she had been teaching freshman English only a year and a half. You had to break through the inhibiting structures the students brought with them, the kinds of structures that Sally herself had conquered when she finally broke free from Curtis and the mindless life of married slavery she had had with him. These students, like she herself had been, were at a critical point in their lives. A false start, and they would be plunged into the sort of patterns she had earned her way out of. Now they sat exposed and vulnerable, their unconscious lives closer to the surface than they had been since prepubescence. She must encourage this cluster of trembling awarenesses to launch out into the unknown, the possible, with no stays, no screens between themselves and the true state of creative flux which defined existence.

That dark one there, for example, with the badly-cut hair, looked to be a perfect emblem of the state of mind she sensed in the group. He looked older than most of the others, but, of course, with primitives it was hard to tell. The counting of years did not in a real sense apply to the lives of the dark peoples of the earth. Sally could tell by looking that the dark one in question was more alien in this environment than any of the people around him. He even held his pencil strangely, upright in his hand as though it were a sign of something. She must get to know him, draw him out of the lonely psychic space he occupied and lead him into a creative interchange with the other young men and women around him. And with herself.

The fat girl who had smoked the cigarette raised her hand and asked about paper assignments. Another wanted to know about the reading lists. The rest of the hour was spent in talking about "nuts and bolts," as Sally Smith called it. Sam rose to leave as the bell rang, but before he could gather the books and papers together that had been given to him by M. M. Myers, the woman in the colored blouse caught his eye and asked him to wait for a minute. He stood by his desk as various other members of the class clustered around the teacher, among them the girl with the blonde braids. She left last, smiling broadly and hugging an armful of books to her chest. Sam watched the braids swing back and forth across her back as she walked out.

"Now," said Sally Smith and turned toward Sam. She gestured toward a seat, but Sam remained standing. He focussed on the silver ring in her right ear as she began to talk.

"Which one are you on my list?" she said, pointing to a green sheet of paper covered with letters that looked like they had been made by a strange typewriter. She turned the page toward Sam, and he looked at it. About four or five lines down he saw S. H. L. Deer printed in letters all the same size.

"There," he pointed. "Leaping Deer."

"What do your friends call you?"

"Sam. Sometimes Leaping Deer," he said warily.

"Is that a Chicano name? Perhaps a translation from the original?" Sam studied her face for a minute.

"It is what it is," he finally said.

"Oh, I like that. The way you put it. The acceptance. The refusal to question the sign." She threw back the two handfuls of hair, and Sam caught a whiff of perfume. It smelled not sweet, but heavy, something like watermelons late in the season.

"I hope you like poetry," she continued. "Probably you come from a culture with a well-developed oral literature. Later, as the class goes on and grows in awareness, perhaps you can share some of the legends of your people with us. You know, your version of the creation myths and like that." Sally Smith regarded Sam closely. He looked back at her eyes, large and blue with sharp pointed lashes. "Listen, Sam," she said, putting a hand on one of his, "I don't want to push you at all just now. But later, I believe you can be of great service to all of us in the class. You'll know what I mean then, when the time comes. For the present, just *be*."

Sam nodded and began to ease toward the door.

"Before you go, tell me where you live. I mean on campus

here. I'd like to be available to you for counsel. And, of course, to all the rest of the class too." Sam told her and took another step toward the door.

"We'll be meeting sometimes at my place for classes. I'll give you directions later. Please feel free to talk to me. I like to think I'm sympathetic." She smiled, and her earrings jingled as she leaned forward to watch Sam leave the room. Outside in the hall he found himself clutching his pencil so hard that one of his fingers tingled.

He stopped to get his bearings, and as he looked down the hall to see which direction to take, he saw somebody leaning against the wall by a bulletin board covered with notices. It was the tall man with the familiar face. He straightened up and lifted his hand in Sam's direction.

"Leaping Deer," he said. "How's your overwhelming flash?"

"What?"

"You know. What she said in there." The man walked toward Sam and pointed down the hall. "I believe it's that way. If you're going to Huff Gym now, that is." The two began walking down the hall together toward the open door through which Sam could see a large green yard filled with people throwing plastic saucers back and forth to each other. As they went down the steps of the building to the sidewalk, they had to walk around a big red-bearded man talking intently to a smaller gray-bearded man in a suit about someone's "deep images." Sam tried, but didn't catch the name.

"Who is she?" Sam asked the man walking beside him.

"Sally Smith? Oh, she's a teaching assistant who's found Freud. We've got it made in there, though, man, if we can stand that much flux and gaze-meeting."

"What will she teach us?"

"You name it. A few poems. Some symbolic stuff. A little touchie-feelie psych, maybe, if we're lucky. Maybe how to get in that blonde's pants, if we're *real* lucky." He turned his mouth into the upside down smile Sam had noticed earlier in the classroom.

"I don't know which I like more," the man said. "A class like Sally Smith's or the TV lectures. You can sleep in one and you can vibrate in the other. Whatever does it for you."

"You go to Huff Gym too?" asked Sam.

"Sure, yeah. Don't you remember the first scrimmage? You

must have given me three assists. Hell, I'm blue twenty-four," the man said and then threw his arms up in the air like a referee signaling. "Shit," he said in a different voice and let his arms drop back to his sides.

Sam remembered why the face was familiar, thinking back to a particular play in which the man walking with him had taken Sam's pass, started, stopped to shed his man, and then gone up for a clean jump shot. "Good move," Assistant Chudy had yelled.

"Chudy," Sam said for no particular reason.

"Yeah, you could get papers on him. He's a certifiable ass-hole. He must be permanently sore from all the reaming he gets from Thompson."

Sam looked at the man in deep surprise. He had never heard a white player at Big Muddy say anything like what he'd just heard spoken about Coach Chudy. The players of the Alabama tribe were bad to mock Coach Dodge in the language of the Nation, but the Coushattas usually expressed their low feelings about white men in small hand gestures. The white players at Big Muddy were generally second-rate enough at basketball to feel pride in Dodge. They called him the "old man" in low, serious voices when he was pissed at them, and usually after a winning game two or three of them would try to hoist him to their shoulders as they'd seen done in moments of triumph in movies and on television.

"Where did you play before," Sam asked. "Some other state?"

"It felt like it sometime. I mean, you know when we were playing those big Chicago teams. But no, I played in Illinois. Up-state." He slowed to let someone pass the two of them at an intersection in the sidewalk.

"Did you play all your high school ball right there deep in the heart of Texas, Leaping Deer? Or did you ever get out of state?"

"Once," Sam said. "We played a team in Louisiana. Fenton. They won their state that year. We ran them hard."

"Yeah? Why'd you play them? Couldn't find enough people to beat in Texas?"

"No," said Sam, remembering how excited Coach Dodge had been to be able to say that Big Muddy had beat the state champions of both Texas and Louisiana in one year. "Our coach had a plan."

"They've always got a plan. The coaches," said the tall man. "And the plan generally involves running somebody else around in circles. But hell, it comes with the territory."

"You must not think about them too much, the coaches," Sam said. "Just win enough to keep them quiet."

The tall man laughed and made a sweeping gesture with both arms, wide enough to alarm two women passing them from the opposite direction.

"You shit me not," he said. "That keeps everybody quiet. Winning enough."

The two walked on in silence until they reached the edge of the large green space. As they stopped to let some cars pass before they crossed the street, the man turned to Sam.

"I've got to split off here for a few minutes," he said. "I'll see you later. Tonight's Friday, you know."

Sam nodded and started to cross the street.

"You want to have a beer then later on? I got a car, and I think I know of a party."

"All right," Sam said, even though he didn't want the beer.

"After practice, then." Sam stepped out into the street. From half-way up the block, the man called something to him.

"What?"

"Name's Art Wallace. Art Wallace, that's me."

Sam waved and went on, remembering to look both ways before he crossed the street.

Sam sat in the passenger seat of a low dark-green car being driven very fast by Art Wallace. The automobile reminded Sam of one he had seen in bits and pieces alongside Highway 190 a couple of years back. That one had been driven by a Houston hairdresser who had swerved to miss a cow in the road and ended up taking out one and a half young pine trees. The hairdresser had refused to be consoled by the fact that he was still alive and had complained about the condition of his car right up to the time the ambulance from Franklin had arrived to take him off. The super-charger of his machine now lay under the back side of Cooper Leaping Deer's house waiting to be joined to something that would move.

"You sure you don't want a beer," Art said, flipping an empty can over his shoulder into the back seat.

"No beer," Sam said. The headlights picked up the silhouette of a dog trotting across the highway ahead. Sam sat leaning forward to miss part of the rush of air pouring through the window into his face. Art's new beer made a pop-sizzle noise as he opened it.

"Leaping Deer," Art said, "you know why you didn't play in the scrimmage today at practice?" Sam said nothing.

"Well, I'll tell you why. But you already know why, anyway. It's because you won't do the little shit drills they give us."

Again in practice, Sam had refused to scramble, to listen in a crouch for the ball being thrown by Assistant Chudy against the wall behind him. McKinley Short Eyes remained fixed in his mind, turned at the door of his house about to enter, deciding whether to speak. This time Chudy had said little to Sam, but he had been extra tough on the other two assigned to him for drill, running them until they were both blowing like steam engines. Sam had watched the scrimmage from the sidelines, sitting alongside two other players who were never told by Dead Smile to take some-one's place in one of the lineups. One of the two was Martin, the tall sandy-haired man from the first day. "Look like you're real eager to get in there," he had whispered to Sam. "They really like it when you show desire."

The green car went into a long curve, and Art shifted into a lower gear. "What do you think you're going to gain by not doing the drills?" he asked.

"The drill is not basketball. There is no goal."

Art took a drink from the can of beer. "Right. But see, they're not really thinking about basketball at all when they have us doing the drills. That's not the point of the drills. Not the point at all." He drove for a couple of minutes without speaking.

"Agility," he said. "They call it agility training. How to kiss ass with style." Art looked over at the outline of Sam's face in the light from the dashboard. Sam sat staring straight ahead as though he were the one driving through the Illinois night.

"But you know what, Leaping Deer? I do them. I do all of them. The scramble, tips and taps, wind sprints, anything they can dream up I do. And you know why I do all that shit? Run around like a poodle on a leash? Because," Art paused and looked back at the Indian's face, "because that's all part of the course. All that's part of what I have to put up with before they'll let me do what I want to. It's just the cost. The price I've got to pay to buy what I want."

Art finished the can of beer and let it drop into the back seat. It made a clanking sound against the others already there.

"Now you, Leaping Deer, you're luckier than most people. You have to pay a lot less than most of us do."

"How is that so?" Sam asked.

"Look at it. You know how you did the first day in scrimmage. You're good enough that they're going to ask you to eat just a little bit of shit before they let you do what you want. Think about what's-his-name. That tall kid that hasn't played any yet."

"Martin?"

"Yeah. Now he'll be here the full four years and probably never play a full half, total, the whole time. But they won't run him off. You know why?" Art waited for a minute and then went on. "Because he'll eat any amount of shit they want to dish out. And they always want to have one champion shit-eater around to be a good example for everybody else. Hell, Sam, Illini basketball's like everything else. It's mixed up with shit. It's not pure, man. What you have to do is take what's left after you squeeze the shit out of it."

Sam rolled his window up and hunched forward in the seat. The night air coming off the Illinois cornfields had become colder.

"But, Leaping Deer," Art began speaking again, "that little bit of shit they do want you to eat, you got to eat. It's important to Thompson and Chudy. Especially Chudy. Hell, boy, it's important to all us Illini." Art slid into an imitation of some kind of accent, one that Sam associated with the voices of radio disc jockeys.

"It's just a question of priorities. What would you rather do? Not pay the admission price and go back home, or go ahead and let them think they won and get to do what you want to?"

Both men became silent for a few minutes, the only sounds those of the engine and the wind. Sam watched a farmhouse with a bright light standing in the yard whip by and disappear. The light quickly became a dull glow in the mist behind, then vanished as the car went around a curve.

"Let me ask you something, Leaping Deer. Why do you play basketball? I mean *really* why do you. You know, I don't mean because you can or because you're good at it, but what about it is really the one thing that keeps you doing it?"

Sam considered the question. He imagined himself with a basketball in his hands somewhere in range of a goal. He saw the goal, a round hoop high above the floor, hanging alone away from all other things. He appreciated its roundness, the curve of the metal continuing to flow into itself forever. Its plane was fixed parallel to the earth, matching the balance the Nation's elders claimed Abba Mikko had given the world to start it. From the goal a white net hung, its bottom open and smaller than its mouth. The hoop waited in its roundness, solid and unmoving, while all around it things moved and slid and fell away.

In Sam's hands the basketball, a sphere, a circle perfected each way it could be beheld, looked at the goal. It had no eyes but roundness. Circle needed circle. The ball stirred alive in his hands, found its true weight and balance, and focussed its roundness into its float toward roundness. Sam watched the arc of the curve the ball made in the air coincide with the plane the goal occupied in its balanced relation to the earth. The curve of roundness entered the circle suspended above all the sliding movements. The white net flicked to show what had happened, to testify to the act just completed above it. For an instant the roundness of the perfected circle of the ball had found itself exactly intersected by the plane of the circle of the goal. Sam stopped the movement of the ball through the hoop and looked at that moment. In his mind, it hung forever.

Art was speaking to him, and Sam let the ball drop through the net again before turning his attention to the man driving the car.

"I didn't hear you."

"I just said why do you really play it? I wondered if you even thought about it much. I realized a couple of years ago what I actually get out of it besides the publicity and scholarships and nooky. You know what it is?"

"No."

"Think about it this way. Imagine yourself with the ball, up against somebody guarding you and you beat him somehow. You know, you get by him, fake him the wrong way, catch him leaning, get him up off the floor when he shouldn't be. Shoot over him. Something. Well, you know that look that comes in his eyes when he sees he's beat? I mean even before the ball goes through the fucking basket? Well, that's what I play for. To see that bastard realize I beat him."

Art laughed and downshifted into a sharp curve coming up in the two-lane highway.

"Didn't that sign say Philo?"

"I don't know," Sam said.

"Yeah, I think we're almost there. I believe it said Philo. Hey, but you haven't answered me yet. Is it the same reason? Does it get you off the same way it does me? That look in the eyes?"

Sam pictured the goal with the ball half through it again and hesitated. Finally, he answered Art. "Yeah, that's it. The look."

"I thought so. I could tell that first day watching you come at Hemmings. God, you whipped his ass."

Sam grunted and looked at the street lights of a small town the car was entering. On each side of the road large white wooden houses stood between flower beds and shade trees. Art slowed the car after a third block and leaned across the seat to look at a street sign. "Yeah, right up here," he said and turned. He drove a few hundred feet and pulled in behind a Volkswagen van parked with several other cars in front of another white house like the other ones on the main street. He switched off the engine and opened the last beer of the six-pack he had bought in an all-night store near the university.

"Thing is, Leaping Deer, is that the coaches can stop you from beating that fucker if you don't go along with their drills and stuff. We've got no alternative now, man. High school's over. Can't play there any more. Who wants to play in pick-up games in schoolyards? That's all that's left besides this." Art drank from his beer, and Sam thought about a question to ask him. Art had a lot to say. Maybe he would know about the Indian players that Sam had yet to see any sign of.

"One thing. Where are the Illini, the Indian players?"

"I heard you've been asking the coaches that, Leaping Deer. What do you mean by it? You're not talking about the goddam mascot, are you?" Art took a hard look at Sam's face in the street-light.

"What did the fuckers tell you?" he asked. "That there were Indians playing basketball here?"

"The pictures," Sam said and stopped.

"Look, Leaping Deer, as far as I know, you're the only Indian ever recruited by the U of I. There's not a single Indian playing basketball here and never was. If they said different, they just lied to you."

Sam looked out of the window at a large shiny purple ball sitting on a white plastic pedestal in the yard next to the car. The reflection of the green car in the ball was distorted by the curve of the glass so that his hand lying on the window edge looked huge and powerful while his face was tiny and bunched together. He flexed his hand, and monstrous fingers pulsed on the side of the purple ball. He leaned his head away from the window, and the reflection of it on the glass vanished.

"To tell you the truth," Art said, "the only Indians I've heard of around here's that Red Power bunch. You know about them? They started up last year and got in all the Chicago papers. I read about them when I was still living at home."

"What nation . . ." Sam began and then, remembering that the white man didn't seem to be able to understand the term, changed it. "What tribe is that one?"

"No, it's not just one tribe. I don't know much about it, but what they do is appeal to all the Indians on campus. Seven or eight, maybe, in all, I guess. Maybe more. I remember the head man's name, though. Walks Dead." Art shook his head. "Jesus! Walks Dead—can't you hear his mother calling him to dinner?"

Art finished the beer and opened the car door. "Let's go to the party," he said. Sam followed him up a sidewalk made of bricks so cracked and crumbling that he had to watch where he stepped. Art knocked on the front door of the house and opened it. "I hope the guy I know is here," he said.

The room they entered was lit by two lights, one blue and the other red. Sam's head was pounding so hard that the two lamps slowly danced up and down as he looked around him. He felt like either grabbing the lights to hold them still or throwing them against the wall to make them stop shining. The darkness itself would be better than this.

He moved toward the far side of the room to get out of the way of somebody pushing in behind him. Between him and the record player in the corner two people were dancing slowly to the sound of a woman's voice accusing somebody of talking about talking and loving about loving. The hand of one of the dancers rested on the back of the other one's neck, working its way up and down the spine as though it were trying to find a way to get inside.

Sam got past the couple and stood leaning against the back of a chair, thinking about what Art had told him. He took a glass of something offered to him by a short bald man dressed in a tight suit and drank from it without tasting. The short man stood talking up into Sam's face over the sound of the music and seemed satisfied with the occasional nod Sam gave him as he drank. As more people crowded into the room and different songs came out of the speaker, Sam steadily emptied the glasses the short man kept putting into his hand. Now and then he saw Art among the dancers, a head higher than the people around him, but Sam didn't try to get his attention.

The short man left to put some more in the glasses, and Sam felt somebody looking at him from close up. He turned to his left and saw a woman standing at his elbow, pulling at the beads around her neck and staring at the side of his nose.

"It's my birthday," she said. She was wearing cat's-eye-shaped glasses he couldn't see through. Some of her piled-up hair had broken loose on one side of her head and hung down across her face. She blew out of the corner of her mouth to dislodge the strand stuck to it, but it held on.

"How many?" Sam asked.

"How many what, honey?"

"Years. How many years old?"

"That's something you don't ask," she said and pulled the hair away from her mouth. "That's for me to know and you to find out."

The short man came back with two glasses and poked one at Sam. "I see you met Myra," he said and punched a finger into Sam's ribs.

"No formal introductions, please," the woman said. "Just go with it. Let things slide as they will. I mean, when you get to know somebody, it's better without labels, right?" She tilted her head back at Sam and showed her teeth, blue in the light.

"You live in this house?" Sam asked and looked around the room.

"Who, us? Me and Myra? Naw, but our aunt does. She's upstairs somewhere, huh, Myra?" The man leaned toward Sam to laugh and spilled some of his drnk.

"She's my aunt, and yes, she's upstairs somewhere. As you well know." Myra gave the short man a hard look and took Sam's arm, pulling him around to face her. The strand of hair had crawled back toward the corner of her mouth.

"Dance with me," she said. Sam tilted back his head and threw the rest of the drink down his throat. Somewhere in the back of his head he could hear the sound of water dripping off a roof onto a sheet of tin. The splash was slow and regular, and it seemed to him it would last a long time.

"Yes," he said to the water and put the empty glass on the speaker behind him. He put his arms up to the woman, as the whites did in their dancing, and moved toward her. She wrapped herself into him and began slowly swaying to the music.

"Watch her, boy," the short man said. "She won't let loose until it thunders."

Several songs passed. In between the drips of water Sam listened to a voice singing about time, another worried about somebody named Tommy, another one lost and glad of it. Myra steadily moved closer in, standing tiptoe until her face was jammed between Sam's jaw and shoulder. Her left hand wandered up and down the back of his neck, while her right held the cat's-eye glasses tight against the small of his back. At first he had tried to move his feet in a pattern as he had seen done before by people dancing at Big Muddy and at a couple of the cafes in Franklin, but since Myra had seemed not interested, he had settled for swaying back and forth to the rhythm of the drops of water on the tin. At one point as Myra moved her body against his, he had felt his groin come alive and had tried to pull back, but she had moved even tighter against him.

A new song began on the record player, and Myra spoke into Sam's ear. "I feel really strong psychic vibrations from you. You know what I mean? What I'm talking about is the other side. The dark powers." She moved in a slow squirm and blew her breath against the side of his face.

"God, I feel all fogged in," she said.

Sam listened to the drops on the sheet of tin and thought about what was in the glasses. "Some more drink," he declared.

"All right," Myra said and broke her hold. She pulled Sam by the hand after her toward the back of the room. He followed, bumping into people as he went, none of whom seemed to notice. Art Wallace stood by the door they were headed for in conversation with a small blonde woman balanced on six-inch high heels. As Sam passed, he could hear Art telling the woman that something was sudden all right, but real.

After Myra had poured some clear liquid into another glass for Sam, she led him out of the kitchen into a room that opened off it. It was a large room with many fixtures and its own history.

When Ben Bevis, the only child of Aunt Nelia, the eighty-four-year-old woman living upstairs, had finally been talked into marriage by Lucille Statts, she had moved into the big house in

Philo with Ben and his mother. She had soon realized that the old lady was going to live longer than she had expected, even though Ben himself was already fifty-two years old. Lucille was one soon to get bored, so she had talked Ben into approaching Aunt Nelia about making some modifications to that old bedroom that nobody ever used. "It is a sheer disgrace not to be active and make some use of wasted space," she had told Ben, lying beside him in the bedroom next to Aunt Nelia's and sipping at a rootbeer float. "I want to set up my practice right here," she had told Ben and let him kiss her somewhere near her mouth.

So after several scenes with Mama in which she called him a great big sorry thing not fit to polish his own father's shoes, Ben had talked the old lady into allowing Lucille to bring in her equipment and punch holes in that nice hardwood floor in order to mount it. The pity of it all was that Lucille didn't operate the business for more than three or four months before she met a hybrid corn salesman at the Rosebowl Inn in Urbana and ran off with him to Iowa. She had left everything right in the house where it was, even the two parakeets, which soon died, and especially all the alterations to the back bedroom.

For a long time after she left, Ben Bevis would come to Lucille's old place of business and sit in first one, then the other of the big hair dryers mounted there and run the hot air on his head while he thought of the way she used to look lying on the sofa in her pink slip trying to cool off in the summer heat. The warm air from the dryers felt good blowing over his face and chest, and he had kept coming to the room for little crying sessions until Aunt Nelia had caught him there once and put a stop to it.

So what Sam saw as he entered the room behind Myra was a line of six recliner adjustable hair dryers down one wall, two large shampoo sinks jammed up against another one, and several small flat tables scattered among sofas and wicker chairs. While she was still living downstairs and before she had moved to the big room upstairs for good, Aunt Nelia had tried to disguise Lucille's use of the room by hanging big lampshades painted with rural scenes over the tops of the dryers. Some of these had dried out with the heat and had flaked away, so now what was mainly left were the wire frames.

The far dryer seemed to be in use. A man and a woman had hit the recliner button and were lying side by side in the seat facing each other. As Sam watched, the woman took a drag on a cigarette and passed it to the man, who looked to Sam a little like Superintendent Purkey back at Big Muddy. The man puffed the cigarette and flipped a switch on the side of the chair. A hum started in the head of the dryer, and the woman lying in the seat leaned her head back to catch the warm air flowing toward her. "Oh, shit," she said in a dreamy voice. "Oh, shit."

Sam took a sip from his glass and listened for the water dripping on the sheet of tin. It was there, regular and strong. Myra was saying something to him and pulling at his arm.

"What?"

"Don't you want to sit down for a minute? This sofa's comfy," Myra said, pointing to what looked like a sleeping whiteface steer. Sam let her lead him over to it and flopped down. His glass was almost empty again. Myra shook the bottle in front of his nose. "Look," she said, "more where that came from."

Sam noticed that the strand of hair had moved toward Myra's mouth again, wider this time and more determined to crawl down her throat. In the dim light, it looked as though she was about to eat part of her own head or as if she were slithering down inside herself. He reached over and brushed the clump away from her face, but it swung back almost to where it was at the beginning. Myra looked pleased.

"Why don't we just take it all down," she said and started pulling pins, barrettes, fasteners from the top of her head and throwing them toward one of the tables near the sofa. One or two hit and stayed. When she finished, the clump on top of her head had shifted to one side and hung, now and then releasing a snakelike strand to join the other ones gone before. At the opposite end of the room the dryer purred hot air through the cigarette smoke. Sam looked into his empty glass and reached for the bottle. His hand touched Myra's shoulder instead, and she jerked toward him. He leaned forward, took the bottle from her hand and tilted it to his mouth. The liquid gurgled like spring water over smooth stones as he drank.

He twisted the bottom of the bottle against the rug to level it and leaned back against the arm of the sofa, pulling Myra with him. Her first kiss missed his mouth, but the next found it, and Sam felt teeth searching for something, his lip, no, his tongue, no, something deeper. He laid his hand against the front of the woman's dress, found an opening, and pushed beneath. His body turned to one side, and he felt the length of her against him. He closed his eyes and slipped away from himself, the water on the sheet of tin in his mind falling dark and alone and sure.

The next time he reached for the bottle Sam found it on its side in the middle of a wet spot on the rug. He drank what was left and saw that Myra was gone. The only sign she had left was a couple of hairpins and a green plastic barrette. The couple under the hair dryer seemed to be asleep under the steady blast of hot air from the top of the machine. When Sam got up from the sofa and stood weaving for a minute to get his bearings, the woman of the hair-dryer pair rolled over and looked at him. "Bye," she said, and Sam walked toward the door into the kitchen. As he opened it and left the room, she called after him. "Come again."

The party was dead in the kitchen. All the ice was melted, and the bottles and cans were empty. Sam stepped over a cardboard box blocking the way and walked toward the sound of voices in the front room. Art Wallace sat on a sofa beside the blonde woman with the high heels, facing a gray-haired man who squatted on a low hassock. All of them turned their heads toward Sam as he stood in the door.

"Leaping Deer," Art said. "Sit down and join us."

"What kind of name is that?" asked the blonde woman. "Must be a nickname, huh?"

"No, it's not a nickname. It's a patronymic," Art told her. "Do you know what that means?" The blonde giggled and smoothed her skirt over her knees.

Sam's eyes felt tired. It seemed to him that it might rest them if he leaned his head against the door facing. The other man swivelled around on his hassock so he could look at Sam. He had shaved recently, but missed a spot of gray stubble just above the knot in his tie. In the war between the blue and red lamps, his shirt looked the color of the lemon extract favored by Sam's father.

"Hi," he said. "Anybody else still in the drying room?"

Sam lifted his fingers.

"Are they about ready for a comb-out? You look like you already had yours." The man looked rapidly back and forth from Art to Sam, showing his teeth and sucking in and blowing out long whistling breaths.

"This is Ben Bevis, Leaping Deer," said Art. "And that's him laughing."

"Yes sir, my name's Ben Bevis, and my Mama lives upstairs. Has for several years now. Tell him what I like best, son."

"You tell him, Ben," Art said and cut his eyes toward the blonde. She punched him on the shoulder and strained her upper body against the sofa and let the springs in it bounce her forward again.

"All right, I will. I like two things best of all. Number one. Movies. I like almost any movie if I can get the bus schedule right to see it. I don't mind coming in at any time during it, neither. Whether it's just started or about to end. I don't care one way or the other. Number two. I like to shoot little boys in the seat of the pants with my BB gun."

"Why's that now, Ben?" Art asked.

"Oh, you know. I already told you and the young lady why I like to do that."

"Yeah, but Leaping Deer didn't hear it. When you were telling us about that, he was back in the what-you-call-it room getting the kinks out."

"Well, all right." Ben Bevis spun around on the hassock with his feet lifted. "The reason why is when I sting them with the BB gun they jump and twitch and slap at their little old boo-boos.

"Lots of times I catch them stealing apples out of Mama's orchard," he explained to Sam. "That's when I like to do it. Either when they're up in a tree or when they're running off to climb over the fence."

Sam lifted his hands to the sides of his head, poked at his temples and wondered if he was going to be sick enough to vomit. Looking at the door to the outside, he judged its distance and began walking toward it, making sure to lift his feet high enough to step over anything that might be in the way.

"You going to the car?" Art asked. "I'll be there in a minute." As he left the house Sam could hear Ben Bevis admitting to Art and the blonde woman that sometimes he missed the little boys' behinds when they dodged too fast or were too little to draw a fine bead on.

Sam traveled with the sun, hurrying to keep pace so that his journey would be over before the darkness came. In the first part of the morning he came to a tall tree, a sycamore with a wild turkey perched on its highest limb. He used one of the three arrows he carried in a bark sling over his shoulder to shoot at the dark bird. It fell with a loud noise, breaking small branches as it tumbled to the earth and landing with a heavy sound on the far side of the trunk. Yet when he ran to the opposite side of the scaly tree and reached down to pick up the turkey, he found only a dead mosquito with his arrow lying across its back.

The sun was high over his left shoulder, and when he turned to judge how much time was left to him, Sam caught sight of a black bear reared up to claw at a pine. He took a step backward, and the bear dropped to all fours and shrivelled until it became a black hairy caterpillar which buried itself in the leaves on the forest floor.

Sam reached for the two arrows in the bark sling and found them changed into pieces of polished bone. He moved toward the edge of a clearing just ahead of him and found when he reached it that the country opened before him into a large flat plain with a high humpbacked mountain in its center. Yet when he neared the mound after a long time of running against the speed of the sun, he discovered the mountain to be only a small land turtle crawling slowly over the ground. He touched it with the tip of the bow in his right hand and was not surprised when the turtle collapsed into grains of black sand.

Suddenly the plain became a deep forest, dark and quiet like the woods between the Nation and the white man's settlement at Big Muddy. Around him, crawling among the rotting leaves of the earth and hanging on the low limbs of the tree, rattlesnakes of many sizes lived by the thousands. To protect his legs Sam used the knife from his belt to strip the bark from a slippery elm and made leggings which he tied to his thighs with cane lashings. He sighted the sun through an opening in the treetops and moved ahead, ignoring the snakes which pulled at the bark of his leggings as he ran.

He came to a place where the sky seemed to join the earth and found that he had left the dark woods behind him. Now he stood on the edge of water so wide that he could see no end to it. The rays of the sun flashed so brightly off the water that he had to shade his eyes to look. He could see no way to cross to the other side, and he threw his bow into the water in despair. When the

bow touched the surface, a great wallowing splash followed, and a
huge Horned Snake appeared swimming toward the shore.

In a buckskin bag over his left shoulder Sam found three ears
of corn and threw one into the edge of the water. The Horned
Snake, its body as large as a tree, with glowing horns on its head
and scales that flashed like sparks of fire, lay before him to eat the
corn. He straddled it like a horse, and it turned back into the
water, swimming toward the place where the sun was sinking
toward the world. The air moved against Sam's face so quickly that
he reached with one hand to hold on to the horn on the side of the
Snake's head. It became easier to ride, although once Sam had to
throw another of the ears of corn ahead of the Snake when it began
to slow. He fed the last ear to the Horned Snake when he saw the
opposite shore of the water come into view, and he thanked the
beast in the language of the Nation after he had jumped off its back
onto the solid earth.

Ahead of him the sun shone at an angle through the tops of
the trees, and Sam quickened his pace. The slippery-elm bark leggings, which had been shredded by the fangs of the rattlesnakes,
made a dry rustling as he ran. The sound was loud enough to
drown out for awhile a louder noise that came at regular intervals
as Sam chased the sun. Finally, as he moved quickly through
stands of cane and low underbrush, Sam became so conscious of
the loud clashing that he had to stop and stuff the puffballs from a
thistle into his ears before he could go on.

He broke free of the cane thicket and stopped to look at what
was causing the deafening clanging noise. Ahead of him, beneath
the sun, which had sunk away almost completely, Sam saw the sky
rising at its edge, falling back to strike the earth, and then rising
again to repeat the movement. Each time the sky rose upward, an
open space between it and the earth appeared. Sam saw that the
battle between earth and sky had always been and would always
be, and that the only way out was through the open space which
came for an instant, vanished, appeared again and would do so
forever. He moved toward the open space and tried to judge the
movement of the sky as the sun dropped lower.

It seemed to him that if he could slip through the small space
which came and went like the marks rain made on the surface of
Long King Creek he would be able to reach the place he needed to
be. He shook the buckskin bag and the bark arrow sheath from his

shoulders, let go of all he was holding, and readied himself to dash through the opening the next time the sky lifted from the earth. Edging near the place the earth and sky intersected, he endured the loud noise and then leaped. But he missed his timing and collided with the blue edge of the sky, banging his head against the hard surface and falling back. He jumped again, then again, each time miscalculating the gap and ending up short of the open space. His head was beginning to ache, and he felt himself slipping further back from the place which would let him move into the other world. The crashing sound grew louder, and the sky darkened as the sun slipped from his view, the last glimmer of its top edge fading toward black. He gathered himself, made one last leap so strongly that sound and darkness became one thing. He whined in his throat and flung his arms out in front of him.

"Goddamn, you trying to knock you brains out against that wall?"

Akbar was leaning on the edge of his desk, looking from across the room with great interest as Sam rolled away from the wall beside his bed. His head was pounding in waves, and as he looked from the wall toward Akbar the light from the window struck into his eyes like two hickory wedges. Akbar's form was too painfully outlined against the far wall to be able to bear looking at. Sam squeezed his eyes shut and put a hand to his forehead. For some reason he felt as though things would be better if he held on to something with the other one, so he fumbled awkwardly until he found the leg of a chair near his bed. He seized it tightly and took long breaths carefully through his nose. The bedcovers were twisted around his upper body and neck as though they meant to strangle him, but he lay still and did nothing to loosen anything.

"Man, what did you O D on?" Akbar asked. "Must have been gin, cause you come in this morning about three smelling like dead flowers. Me and that white dude had to talk you out of your shoes. I heard of lots of kinds of drunk. Knee-walking, name-calling, telephoning, arm-wrestling. But I ain't never heard of shoe-saving before. What you think we's going to do with them, man? Sell them to somebody?" Akbar talked a good bit more, but Sam tried not to hear him, preferring instead to remember the open space he had seen in his dream and to try to ignore the sound of the sky meeting the earth in that series of endless flat reports.

"Well, I can't hang around here all day watching you suffer."

Akbar strolled to the door, digging at his hair with the wide-toothed comb he always carried in a back pocket. He opened the door, made a choreographed exiting gesture, then turned back to speak.

"Hey," he said. "Somebody came by last night to see you, Leaping Deer. Fucker was wearing a modified headdress, man. Looked like he was your homeboy. Beads all over his shirt. Moccasins. Little bitty axe stuck in his belt. Said he was the walking dead, something like that."

"Walks Dead." Sam spoke for the first time in several hours and was sorry of it. The words of the white man's language seemed to take off a layer of the back part of his throat as he said them.

"Yeah, that's right. Walks Dead. You already know the dude?"

Sam started to shake his head but thought better of it.

"Said he'd be back. Maybe tonight." Akbar put the comb back into his pocket and stepped out into the hall. "You gonna make practice today?"

Sam lifted two fingers from his forehead and held tighter to the chair leg with the other hand.

"Well, I'm splitting. Don't worry. I ain't gonna slam it." Akbar gave a high-pitched laugh and eased the door shut. Sam settled back into the pillow under his head and tried to think about the dream, but the crashing sound of earth and sky kept getting in the way.

How Water Was Lost

By the time he reached Huff Gym at four o'clock, Sam was feeling much better except for an uncertain sense that he had left something out of the dream he had had. Something needed to be put in before it could be complete. He tried to think of what the story lacked, but nothing came into his mind. The dream had signs for him, but he couldn't read them. It wasn't until he heard his name called twice that he put the puzzle out of his mind and looked to see who was speaking to him.

"Leaping Deer," Art Wallace said again. "Glad to see you still around."

Sam got up from the bench and walked to the door where Art was standing. They went together out to the court where Coach Chudy was dividing people into squads for the drills. Chudy looked over toward Sam and Art coming toward him and felt one of his little belly pains begin to crank up just above his belt buckle. Thompson had laid it on the line to him twice about the Indian already, and Chudy didn't know what he was going to do about getting the little red-skinned bastard to cooperate. Along with the rest of the staff Thompson had decided it could be worth coddling Leaping Deer and going along with him to a certain limit. "But, Chudy," Thompson had said, his eyes like bruised meat as he spoke, "you have got to figure some way to get Leaping Deer to take part in the drills. If you don't, he's got to go, and that means you'll have lost us one of the best freshman guards, potential-wise, we ever had a chance at. He's yours, win or lose."

"Well," Chudy said as Sam and Art stopped in front of him, "time to divide up for drills." The Indian seemed to be staring at a point just to the left of Chudy's head. Chudy restrained himself from turning to see what might be behind him. The other kid was acting normal. His head was dropped so that he seemed to be counting the number of boards in the floor. "Blue twenty-four, you go on over there," Chudy said and pointed. He listened to the sound of the player trotting off and wondered what next to say. The Indian stood quietly, giving no sign that he was thinking of anything but whatever it was he was staring at. Chudy noticed that even his eyes looked red.

"Leaping Deer," Chudy began, "the drills. The drills. Well, they're important. See, what they develop. . . ." He trailed off and stopped and slipped his left hand under the front of his pants. He pushed against his belly to see if he could definitely locate a sore spot.

"Yes," Sam said. "I know. I'll do drills."

"You will?" Chudy jerked his hand out of his pants, pulling his shirttail along with it. "I mean, good. That's the spirit. I knew you had good basketball sense. You're showing just the right kind of attitude."

Ten minutes later Chudy stood by Coach Thompson watching Sam crouch with his back to a wall against which a basketball was being thrown by another assistant. "I reasoned with him for a while," Chudy was saying. "Then I had to go to psychology and make him do some rethinking of his attitudes. I've learned that with this kind of kid a stern approach works real well."

"Yeah, right, Chudy," Thompson said. "Just relax. He's out there now." They both watched as the basketball splatted against the wall and bounced by Sam as he turned too slowly to stop it.

"He's not worth a damn at the drills, is he?" said Thompson.

"Yeah, well, we'll have to work on that and see if we can't improve his reaction time."

"No sweat, Chudy. He'll never be any good at drills. Anybody out there's better at that than he is. But the thing is, he's doing them. Now he can play some roundball for me."

Someone blew a whistle and Sam turned away from the wall.

Chudy watched him walk off to the side away from his group and stand by himself. He looks better already, Chudy thought. He's looking down at the floor like everybody else, and he's all slouched over like he's tired. Chudy took a deep breath and fingered his belly. It felt alive and well.

"Stick your shirt in your pants, Chudy," Thompson said.

Voices were coming out of the door of his room when Sam got back to the dormitory. He stopped in the hall to listen before he had to show himself to the people inside. After scrambling after loose basketballs with no one to beat and no circle of goal hanging above his head, he felt like not having to see anybody just yet, much less having to put on a talking-to-whites face. As he stood in the hall, people in small groups walking past laughing, talking, and making loud sounds, he thought of McKinley Short Eyes turning at the door of his home to look back at him before going inside. He imagined the way the old man would fix his gaze on the ground in front of him rather than seeking his face, and Sam knew he had to put something else in his mind soon. He closed the door to the house of Short Eyes and walked into what was now his room.

"Leaping Deer," said Akbar, "meet Walks Dead."

A tall man leaning against the wall straightened up and stuck out his hand white-man fashion. He wore his hair in two long braids tied with pieces of leather and was dressed something like the Indians Sam had seen in picture books and movies. His shirt was made of buckskin decorated with beads, and he had what looked like a brand-new turkey feather fastened to the back of his head with another piece of animal hide. Except for the jeans he wore, he was dressed completely in leather, down to a pair of huge brown moccasins. When he turned away from the wall to shake hands, light flashed on the cutting edge of a small hatchet in his belt which looked as if it had just come from a hardware store.

"Brother," he said and crossed his arms high against his chest. He stood in that posture until Sam nodded and then he let his arms drop. He rested one hand on the blade of his hatchet and looked around the room.

"So, Leaping Deer, they have you living in this place." Walks Dead cut his eyes to Akbar, to a desk, back to Akbar, and then to Sam.

"Listen," Akbar said. "I got to split, and you homeboys want to talk some shit." He walked to the door, looked back at Walks Dead and spoke. "How," he said.

"How, hell. Who?" Walks Dead answered.

Akbar left laughing. "Hoo wee," he said. "That's what you call *red* humor."

"They're a simple people," Walks Dead said after the door closed. "Niggers."

"We've got to get you out of here, right?" He gestured toward Akbar's side of the room. "Listen, how much housing allowance do they give you? No matter. What you can do is demand an amount equivalent to the going rate for rentals in Cₕₐmpaign-Urbana. What else? Yeah, how much else do you get?"

Sam shrugged. "Sixty dollars. For laundry."

Walks Dead laughed. "Yeah, laundry, my royal red ass. We got them on that, see, because of NCAA regulations. They'd be afraid not to continue it when you move to the lodge, if we threaten them just right."

He began walking about the room, fingering his hatchet and pointing with his left hand as he talked. "And don't forget. Don't forget your meals here. We can convert that into a cash allowance again equivalent to the going rate here in town. What we're talking about, Leaping Deer, is around, let me see, a hundred, sixty more, another hundred and twenty-five. We're talking about two hundred and eighty-five dollars a month. That's what you got coming to you, and that's what we'll get from the bastards."

Sam sat down on the edge of his bed and watched Walks Dead stride up and down. The man's eyes, Sam noticed, were a lighter color than he'd ever seen on the reservation in Texas, and his face looked thinner than the usual Alabama or Coushatta male's. The nation of Walks Dead obviously bred a different kind of human.

"I tell you what, Leaping Deer. I hope they *do* give you trouble when you move to the lodge. I hope they do. It'll give us a chance to test our strength again before the big test comes. It's always better to get a little practice before the main event. I bet that's true even in basketball, right?"

Sam thought for a minute before he answered, wondering why an Indian wanted to discuss basketball tactics. Back at Big Muddy the only ones who even talked about a game either before or after it was played were the whites, particularly the white benchwarmers, who seemed to remember every detail. They spent

so much time talking about what was already done or not yet here
that it seemed to get in their way when Coach Dodge actually put
them into a game. Most of them either stood around with the
basketball waiting for something to happen, or threw long dangerous cross-court passes or shot when there was little chance to hit.
They were so worried about what had been or was to be that what
was made them act like a blue jay stung by wasps. They stood in
one place, trembling as their eyes glazed over until somebody on
the other team took the ball away from them.

"Yes, it seems so," Sam finally said to Walks Dead, speaking
in the tongue of the Nation.

"You'll have to run that by me again, Leaping Deer. I don't
speak whatever dialect that is. Fact of the matter is," Walks Dead
said, "I only know a few words of anything besides English. I
know it gets to be a pain using the white man's language all the
time, but that's all we've got. It's all about died out with the old
folks."

"What nation is yours?"

"Oh, you know, a little Sioux, a little Cheyenne, maybe some
Blackfoot in the woodpile somewhere." Walks Dead sat down on
Akbar's bed, got up quickly and leaned against the wall again.

"But the tribal differences are not important, right? The real
thing to remember is that we're all brothers in the struggle."

"And the others in the lodge . . ." Sam trailed off.

"Yeah, right, the lodge."

"Are they of your nation?"

"Oh, well, some of it. They're a few who belong to one tribe
or the other, most mixed somehow. We got two braves that claim
full-blood Kiowa. Another one Sac. But you don't understand, I
think. See, we're all brothers in the RAMS."

"Rams?"

"Yeah, stands for Red American Movement Students. It's our
confederation to claim our rights as Indian students. We've got our
lodge, a big old house we rent together on West Illinois Street.
You know, for solidarity, meetings, ceremonies, parties, like that.
And I'll tell you something." Walks Dead stood up straight and
looked intently at Sam. "We could use you in the RAMS. All our
Red Brothers along with us, particularly somebody like you,
somebody that's got an in with the jocks. Man, think about it. To
have somebody actually on one of the teams at this place that calls

itself by a tribal name. Leaping Deer, you don't realize how useful that would be. You could really give us visibility. And, of course," Walks Dead continued, speaking a lot faster, "we'd give you something you can't get anywhere else too. I mean being with your brothers and doing something for all your people." He stopped and studied Sam for a minute, now and then fiddling with the fringe on the sleeve of his shirt.

"Listen," he went on. "I'm not going to pressure you for a quick decision. But why not come by tomorrow night for our next powwow about the U of I Centennial Celebration plans. You can meet people and talk. You know, get a little mellow. What do you say?"

"What's the U of I celebration?" Sam asked.

"Oh, in a couple of months it'll be a hundred years since they founded this great beast. A hundred years ago they made the ripoff of this chunk of Indian land official. So the university has all these plans for celebrating the hundredth anniversary of the robbery, see, and we're going to make sure the red point of view is represented. We're working on ideas for it. You coming tomorrow?"

"All right," Sam said slowly, and immediately Walks Dead stood up, straightened his headdress, adjusted the hatchet in his belt, and shook his sleeves until the fringe all hung straight. He turned to Sam, crossed his arms over his chest as he'd done earlier, and bobbed his head.

"Tomorrow, brother," he said, and strode out.

Sam read for a few minutes in a blue book named *First Steps Toward a Theory of Psychology* that he'd been assigned in one of his classes and then gave it up. He rummaged in the green trunk for a minute and lay back across his bed, a dark chunk of the root from the land of the Alabama-Coushatta Nation under his tongue. By the time Akbar came back, Sam had managed to fall asleep, although the splat of a basketball bouncing off a wall at his back sounded for a long time in his ears, drowning out the slam of McKinley Short Eyes' door.

The next day after practice Sam began walking toward West Illinois Street, following a hand-drawn map he'd found shoved under the door of his room. The directions he followed led him across part of the campus, between some buildings, and into a large open space with a patch of corn enclosed by a low fence in the center of it. As he stopped to look at it, a breeze caught the heads of the stalks and moved the tassels in a wave that flowed from one end of the patch to the other. The slow up-and-down rustle was like the surface of the water in the marsh ponds of the Big Thicket. "Sha towea," Sam said and watched until the gust of wind died away. Low behind him, the sun made long shadows of the corn-stalks through the fence. The falling breeze was cold against his back, and Sam began to walk slowly away toward the line of trees, some already turning color this early in the fall.

A few blocks over, he found the lodge of the Red American Movement Students. The house was a large frame one with turrets, protruding windows, four chimneys, brick sidewalks, and what had been a wide porch wrapped around the front and two sides. Now part of the porch hung like snaggle teeth in an old woman's mouth, holes rotted here and there, big sections missing al-together. Someone had laid a two-by-six board from the front door to the sidewalk to bridge the gap left when the front steps had vanished one night.

Homer Bentley, a hog farmer in Champaign County during the War of the Great Rebellion, had made a fortune selling pork to the Union Army. Enough to allow him to buy a substitute soldier for himself and to build a town house in Urbana away from the smell of hog shit and the drovers who moved the producers of the shit south toward Nashville, Chattanooga, and Atlanta. Unfortu-nately, just after the big house on West Illinois had been finished, Homer himself was finished by the effects of a bite from a rabid sow that he was helping through a gate with a steel rod. Homer went to the cemetery in a few weeks and the sow went to Georgia, where the Union soldiers who ate her and the other hogs she had bitten on her journey southward sickened and fell prey to vomiting and the Georgia quick-step. The sow alone slowed Sherman's march to the sea more than General John Hood's Texans. Sam's great-grandfather, along with other young Alabamas and Coushat-tas, had declined the honor of accompanying John Hood's Con-federate recruiters from Texas to the white man's war in the east.

The reigning chief at the time had put it to the warriors of the Nation this way. "If we go, they might make us take another reservation when their fight is over. Also, there's no percentage in intertribal wars."

So the house which Union hogs had built passed down

through a widow, a maiden daughter, a maiden niece, and now belonged to a distant cousin, several times removed from Homer Bentley and opposed, in fact, to the consumption of pork on quasi-religious grounds. Virginia Gouch was, as she often put it, "heavy into the occult," and she rented the big old house on West Illinois to the Indian students at a loss to herself. "I actually could get several more than eight people into the place," she told members of her coven, "but I want those Indians to have it because I see them as a psychic link to the American unconscious." Virginia, or Rayna, as she was known to her friends in witchcraft, hadn't yet been able to get the RAMS to divulge any of their dark knowledge to her or to join her in her little ceremonial sessions, but she had hope. She planned it so that her visits to collect the rent for the property always occurred after sunset, thinking that time of the day better suited for catching the red men in a psychically receptive mood, but nothing major had happened yet.

Once when she had arrived just at midnight in the spring, she had found one of the boys, who called himself Little Bird, sitting on the floor wrapped in a blanket, staring at a candle flame. He hadn't responded to her at all, though, and she had finally been forced to conclude that he was rude, if not stoned. She hadn't meant to interrupt his trance when she began chanting, and she had been hurt when he put his hand over her mouth and pushed her away. Rayna prided herself on patience—"one waits on the spirits, not the other way around," she liked to declare—so she hadn't changed her plans or lost her faith in the psychic possibilities she sensed in the RAMS because of this little incident.

So when she saw the young man standing in the front yard of her rental property looking at the house, obviously an Indian but not one she had ever seen before, she felt that the sense of premonition she had had driving into Urbana a few minutes earlier was a true promise, not an illusion. He was dressed differently from the rest of the RAMS bunch. He wore no buckskins, no feathers, no ornaments of any kind that she could see. His hair was rather long, but not braided, and his clothes seemed not exactly like the typical white student's but ordinary just the same. She turned off the engine of her car and watched him for a minute. He seemed to want to go in, but he didn't seem sure he knew where he was going. He reached down, picked up something small from the sidewalk, looked at it and then threw it toward the hole where the steps used to be. Whatever it was made a rattling noise as it skipped off the long board and disappeared into the hole beneath. The Indian took a step toward the house, and Rayna opened the car door and called to him.

"Hello, are you looking for the RAMS?"

Sam turned and saw a white woman, not young and not old, coming toward him in a long black dress covered with various colored designs. One seemed to be a picture of a yellow bird with a cup in its mouth; another was an image of a large snake coiled halfway around the dress so that it seemed to be slowly entangling the woman with its body. Its head reminded Sam of something he couldn't quite place. The mouth was closed, but a long tongue of red thread lapped out of the face. Triangles and circles of different colors surrounded the two main designs. The whole garment ballooned and deflated in the breeze, flapping about the woman as she picked her way across the yard toward him.

"Because if you are, this is the place. I own it."

She stopped in front of Sam and looked him up and down. Then she clasped her hands in front of her face and nodded rapidly three times over them, saying something in a language he didn't understand.

"Do you live here?" asked Sam.

"Oh, no. The RAMS live here, but I own the place. It goes way back in the family. It was built for the mistress of the governor of the state." The woman paused and looked dreamily at the turret on the right side of the house. A window in it was out, but someone had patched it with a piece of cardboard and adhesive tape. "She died right here. Of a broken heart. Neglected, but always deeply, passionately loved."

She reached out toward Sam's arm, and he backed up a step.

"Oh, I'm sorry. I just wanted to feel the material of your shirt. The aura of the red man sometimes can be actually felt in the cloth of his garments. It's a kind of crinkly, dusky warmth. But enough of that." She smiled and threw her head back, making the snake's head on her dress jerk higher on her chest.

"You don't look like the others of the RAMS. You're new."

"I'm not new," Sam said and began to turn toward the house. Someone was standing just inside the door looking out at him and the woman. The door swung open, and Walks Dead stepped out onto the six-inch wide board. He had a different colored feather in his hair, Sam noticed.

"Leaping Deer," Walks Dead said in a deep voice. "You have come." In a second voice he added, "Hi, Miss Gouch."

"Leaping Deer," the woman said. "It's perfect. I knew it would be." She pulled a bracelet off her left wrist, kissed it, and returned it to her arm.

"Walks Dead, please call me Rayna. It's only fair. I don't call you Larry."

"Yeah, right, Rayna," Walks Dead cut her off. "Here's the rent, Rayna." He held out several bills toward her and, looking at Sam, jerked his head toward the house. "I'll do this," he said, "and see you inside, Leaping Deer."

"But I'd like to talk to him, Walks Dead," Rayna said, holding both hands to her chest and refusing to take the money. Sam edged by her and started up the board.

"We're really involved with some stuff now. Couldn't it be later? You know, next time?"

"Well, all right," Rayna said in a pouting voice. "But I must ask Leaping Deer one thing. Is that all right?"

"Well, sure. I guess so. What?"

"Not you. Him. Leaping Deer, what did you pick up from the ground and throw into the darkness just before I spoke to you?"

Sam stopped and thought. "A little rock," he said.

"It would have to be. Yes. Something elemental. Basic. Reduced." She smiled at Sam again, and the snake moved its head. "Thank you."

Sam walked the rest of the way up the board and opened the door. As he stepped inside, he could hear Walks Dead promising Rayna something about a gathering of all the people from the lodge. "And him, and him," she was saying as Sam let the door close behind him.

He found himself standing in a long hall lined with dark wood and plaster walls. Surrounding the holes punched in the plaster were crayon drawings of various animals: a large bird with a snake in its mouth done in red and blue, a dog or a wolf with a banner flying from its neck, what looked like a buffalo sitting on a man's head, several other birds and four-footed creatures with balloons above their heads with writing in them. One balloon proclaimed that the bear totem is number one. Another declared that we got it and they want it. The largest balloon of all contained only the words *red power* painted in a lacquer material. Near the end of the hall on the right was the most well-done and largest drawing, an Indian paddling a canoe across a body of water toward a setting sun. In a hand that looked like it wasn't that of the original artist, someone had written RAMS on the side of the Indian's canoe right across the original design of emblems there. Sam touched one of the drawings with his forefinger, and some of the oily paste came off. He rubbed most of it off on a vacant part of the wall and the rest on his pants leg.

The smell of cigarette smoke came from one of the doors on the left, and Sam took a step toward it. Behind him Walks Dead banged the front door open and called to him.

"Leaping Deer, welcome, brother," he intoned in the deep voice he had used before. He paused, then added in a higher tone, "Jesus, do you believe that woman? Rayna?" He stopped just inside the door and looked into a mirror fastened on the wall.

"But it's worth it, I guess. Putting up with her crazy shit. It's cheap rent here, and she lets us do what we want to the place. Did you see our totem gallery?" He waved his hand at the walls. "It pays to keep her happy, so I guess we'll have to go out to her place soon like we've been promising for so long. Hey, Leaping Deer, she likes your looks. If you ever want an easy lay, there's old Rayna."

Walks Dead led Sam into the room at the end of the hall, where he said all of the RAMS were gathered for the meeting about the Centennial. Six or seven people were in the room, sitting on the floor or leaning against the walls. All of them were dressed more or less like Walks Dead, except for one chunky person in bib overalls and tennis shoes who was balanced in a three-legged chair. He rose when Sam and Walks Dead came into the room, and the chair fell over catching him just behind the knees. He stumbled forward and grabbed the shoulder of someone sitting in front of him to steady his balance. "Watch it, Dennis," the person on the floor said, pushing his glasses back up his nose.

"I was just trying to keep from falling," said Dennis and righted his chair for another try at it.

"RAMS, our brother, Leaping Deer, has come to powwow

with us." Walks Dead stood with his arms crossed high over his chest again. Most of the others in the room rose to their feet and assumed the same stance, Dennis this time carefully letting his chair settle to the floor without falling before he turned to face the leaders and Sam.

"Leaping Deer, as most of you have heard, is at the U of I on an athletic scholarship. Basketball, isn't it, Leaping Deer?"

Sam nodded and studied the toe of Dennis's right tennis shoe. He could hear a church bell ringing somewhere faintly, and he thought he detected the cawing of a crow somewhere farther off. Walks Dead's voice broke in again.

"We hope that Leaping Deer will consider joining us in the lodge and becoming a member of the RAMS. All red men are brothers."

The RAMS answered fairly in unison, "All red men are brothers," but a few came in late, among them Dennis and the man he had stumbled against.

"Later you all can have a chance to talk to Leaping Deer, get to know something of his totem, and we'll all smoke the pipe of peace with him."

"Dynamite," someone in the rear of the group said in a loud whisper. Walks Dead held up his right hand and shot a look in the direction of the whisperer. The room got quiet, and Walks Dead finished his talk by saying that the powwow about the Centennial must now begin.

After some scrambling and getting settled, the RAMS arranged themselves into a circle on the floor. By now it was completly dark outside, and the only light was from three or four candles scattered around the room. Sam watched from a vantage point between a boarded-up fireplace and the door. Across the circle in the pool of light from one of the candles floated the face of Walks Dead, as he began a chant which seemed to be the official beginning of the powwow of the RAMS. After a minute or two, the chant stopped and someone with his back to Sam spoke first. After a couple of sentences he stopped and somebody else began.

Looking around the room, Sam thought of how Rabbit fooled the turkeys, who could fly up into the trees and could also run faster on the ground than any other animal. Rabbit knew that turkeys are curious about things they don't understand, so he took a large deerskin bag to the top of a hill near where the turkeys were. He got into the bag and began rolling down the hill, laughing loudly to show how much he was enjoying his newfound game. The turkeys began to follow Rabbit up and down the hill and asked him why he did what he was doing. "Because I am having so much fun," answered Rabbit.

"You are lying," said the turkeys.

"Try my game if you don't believe me," replied Rabbit. "One of you get in the bag and roll down the hill."

One turkey did and liked the game. "Yes, it's fun. I like to play this way." So all the turkeys got into the bag and rolled down all the way to the bottom of the hill, where Rabbit was waiting to tie the top of the bag together and carry off the foolish birds.

It was one of the stories McKinley Short Eyes told children of the Nation as long as they would listen to him in the evenings as he sat on the front porch of his house and smoked. One summer a white man and woman had come each evening to Short Eyes' house and had used a tape recorder to collect everything the old man told the children. All the stories of Rabbit, of Turtle, the Orphan, Crow, the Man-Eater, all of them, they had gotten onto the tapes of their machine. At the end of the summer, the white people made ready to leave, and on the last night of their recording his words, Short Eyes came to believe that he had done a terrible thing. Now all the stories that made themselves the same and different as well each time they were told belonged to the white man's machine. The tales were fixed in one way of telling on the tapes for all time. "Now they are dead things," the old man said to Sam and Beats Billy. "They are in small boxes on tape that turns in a circle forever always the same. I have tied the hands of the Old Ones."

So that night when Sam and Beats Billy climbed through the window of the room in the Agent's house where the white collectors kept their tapes, they were careful to leave the same ten-dollar bill given to Short Eyes by the white man in the recorder case itself. "I will keep the Stetson," McKinley Short Eyes had said, "because of the trouble they've caused me. It's worth that much." Later after they had taken the tapes off into the woods to burn them under Short Eyes' supervision, Beats Billy asked Sam if he really believed the tales had been captured and made dead by the tape recorder. "You know," Sam had said, repeating the words his sixth-grade teacher used to urge her students on, "it's better to be safe than sorry."

As the little spools of tape flashed up in the lightwood-pine fire, McKinley Short Eyes had sat on a nearby pin-oak stump, the white Stetson pulled low over his face, and pointed out the tales as they escaped one by one with the flaring sparks into the darkness. "Why Opossum's Tail is Bare," he listed. "How the Sun Came to the Sky. Why Turtle has Bad Eyes. The Journey to the Bead-Spitter." By the time the last spool was burned, the old man was satisfied that all the words were free again, able now to live and change as they came to each new teller for his use.

"I liked talking to the machine," he told Sam and Beats Billy. "It was good to see it listen to a Coushatta. But I let it fool me. Now you two young warriors have made a fool of the machine. You are like the orphan." And as the fire burned lower and died, the old man had told them again the story of Orphan, to which they listened well, but not in the unfailing way of machines.

"Leaping Deer," someone called, and Sam looked up from the candle flame to see all the faces in the powwow circle turned toward him. It was Walks Dead who had spoken.

"What do you think of what we've been talking about for the Centennial? Do you like one better than the other? We'd like to hear if you've got anything you think would be good."

Walks Dead looked around the circle, and several heads nodded together. Off to one side Dennis was easing up out of his squat to rest his legs. He caught Sam's eye and looked earnest, his head bobbing up and down.

Sam shrugged. "Your plans are good. I don't have any plan about the Centennial myself." He looked back at the candle flame.

"Which one sounds best?" asked Walks Dead. "The one about fucking up the parade? Or the bonfire effigy?"

"I don't know," Sam said. "It's yours. The parade, the first thing you said, I guess."

"I think you're right," Walks Dead said, pleased. "That way you get more public exposure right at the time the crowd's watching."

"Yeah, but wouldn't it be more symbolic to do the effigy bit?" The thin person whose glasses kept sliding down his nose was speaking. "I mean we ought to think about working our own thing. What comes to the average white man's mind when he hears Indian? Fire, man, fire and the scalping knife." The six or seven others sitting on the floor laughed, and one of them said, "Let's steal something. That's what we ought to do. Liberate its ass."

"Wait, wait," Walks Dead said. "We're going over the same ground again. We'll do something with the parade and the effigy thing too, if it comes to that. But if we steal something it's got to be the right thing, something that means something. We obviously got more talking to do anyway." He stood up, and the circle began breaking into ones and twos.

"Braves, give Leaping Deer welcome, while I go get the pipe and the stuff."

Walks Dead left the room. The remaining RAMS and Sam traded looks. A short puffy-faced man whose buckskin shirt was tight enough to show his nipples and the indentation of his navel came up to Sam and began talking about his father and brothers who built skyscrapers. That was their line of work, he said, because Indians weren't worried about falling the way white men are. No, another one said, it's because Indians haven't got so far to fall as white men do. Others joined in and began asking Sam questions. What's your old man do? Is there a big handcraft industry with your people? How'd you happen to pick the U of I? Do they have Native American study grants in Texas? What confederation does your tribe belong to? Do your people actually speak a dialect among themselves? What's the Coushatta word for pussy?

Sam handled these requests for information as best he could, trying to focus on each person talking to him and not having the best of luck doing so. He had the most trouble with the thin man in glasses who had wanted to do something properly symbolic for the Centennial. He announced his names to Sam, Malcolm Sullivan and Counts Buffalo, and began to inquire about details of Alabama-Coushatta tribal ritual. "What shape does your coming-of-age rite take?" he wanted to know. "And," he asked, "is there a period of sequestration for women during the time of menstrual flow?" Sam looked at him carefully, shook his head, and began to slide his hand up and down the mantelpiece he was backed up against.

About then Walks Dead came back into the room carrying a long clay pipe with a bowl the size of a teacup. He began loading it with a mixture from a plastic bag, and the people questioning Sam left him to gather around Walks Dead and marvel. "This is some more of that heavy shit, right?" one asked.

"You got it," Walks Dead said. "Now sit down in the RAMs circle, and let's pass the pipe of peace."

It was only after everybody was seated in the circle and Walks Dead was about to light up the pipe with a candle that he noticed Sam still standing by the mantel.

"Leaping Deer," he said. "Sit down and puff on this baby." The light caught in his eyes and made them look even lighter than before. A couple of the others looked up and made beckoning signs. Sam felt a tickle deep in his head as though he were about to sneeze. He straightened up and turned toward the door he had come in.

"No," he said. "I must go read."

Walks Dead scrambled to his feet as Sam left the room and started after him.

"Larry," someone called, "bring back that goddam grass."

"Here," Walks Dead said, handing the pipe to Malcolm Sullivan / Counts Buffalo, "You take it. I'll go get him."

Sam was opening the front door and stepping onto the long board over the dark hole by the time Walks Dead reached the hall and called his name again.

"What's wrong, man? Where are you going?" In his hurry Walks Dead had banged his head feather into the door facing, and it slanted off to one side. The streetlight threw an asymmetrical shadow of him because of it as he followed Sam down the ramp outdoors.

"Hey." He grabbed Sam by the shoulder, and Sam turned to face him on the sidewalk. A passing car blew leaves from the street into the back of Sam's legs, and he leaned forward away from the noise.

"Did somebody say something that pissed you off while I was out of the room?"

"No," Sam said. "I just have to leave. I'm going back to my room to read what they told me."

"Man, I don't know what's going on in your head, Leaping Deer, but that kind of attitude is going to give you trouble." Walks Dead paused and adjusted some fringe. "I mean, you know, saying you're going to do something because they told you to. What's the matter? Is this just temporary, or don't you want to be with your red brothers?"

Sam studied the pattern of shadows the street light made on the leaves, the narrow ramp to the house, the open door into the hall. The wind blowing against him was stronger than it had been earlier when he had looked at the fenced corn patch. It had picked up and chilled, and the whole night felt colder.

"I want to be in my own place. In the room with my trunk."

"Look, Leaping Deer, do you mean that? Is it just a private room? We can give you that here in the lodge with no trouble. Lots of room here."

"No."

"It's no then, huh? You'd rather live where they put you. In the same room with a nigger instead of with people of your own blood. Is that it?" Walks Dead had straightened his feather, and now he stood with his right hand on the blade of his hatchet. He cocked his head to one side as he waited for Sam to answer.

"No," Sam said again. "The black doesn't bother me. He only talks."

"Let me tell you one thing then. You don't know who your friends are. Without the RAMS, you're alone here, kid. You haven't got anybody on your side. I mean nobody. And you're going to find out that you need us a hell of a lot more than you think."

Sam looked down the street in the direction he had come and then back at Walks Dead.

"I'm going now," he said.

"Well, hey now, Leaping Deer," Walks Dead said and crossed his arms over his chest. "No hard feelings, huh? Listen, don't mention any of our Centennial plans, hear. If you do, man," he stopped and let his arms drop, "we'll know who did."

"No," said Sam, "I won't."

"One other thing, Leaping Deer. You know what? When you talk English, man, you sound just like a redneck." Walks Dead checked the feather at the back of his head and turned for the house.

"Goodbye, Larry," Sam said and broke into a trot which carried him in ten minutes up the street, across the long open space, by the corn patch waving slowly in the night wind, and back to his room.

Why Opossum's Tail Is Bare

"The next time we meet, next Wednesday, will not be at the regular hour or here in this room," Sally Smith told Sam's literature class at the end of the hour. "Instead we'll gather at my apartment on Stoughton Street. You can copy this map if you need," she said, pointing to what she'd drawn on the blackboard earlier. "Officially, we'll talk some more about the alternative worlds of fiction, and unofficially we'll get to know each other in a less structured way." She gestured at the desks and walls and made a fake frowny mouth. The class answered with student murmuring sounds, and a couple of the female members giggled at Sally Smith's imitation of disapproval.

Art Wallace cut his eyes back and forth and whispered to Sam to wait for him outside. When Art joined him, Sam was reading a notice on a bulletin board asking for volunteers for a behavior modification experiment in the psychology department. "Minimum wage," it read, "with no embarrassment."

"Leaping Deer," Art said, "what did I tell you? We're all going to get to know each other." He turned to speak to the girl with blonde braids who was just coming out of the classroom, books and records filling both her arms.

"Hi, what have you got there? Language records?"

"Yes," she said, swinging her head to toss back a strand of hair that had fallen across her cheek. "French. I'm doing French."

"I could have guessed. I'd like you to meet Samuel Houston Leaping Deer, freshman guard who'll be starting for the U of I basketball team against North Carolina in the season's opener." Art spoke in a voice something like that of the TV announcer the Leaping Deer family had heard on Cooper's half-dead set a couple of years ago.

"Oh," the blonde said, "will he really? Just a freshman? Starting?"

"Yes, he will, rumor has it. And your name is?"

"Sharon Hansen. Pleased to meet you, Samuel."

Sam nodded and wondered whether to put out his hand white-man fashion. "My name is only Sam, not Samuel," he said.

"All right. But I like to be called the whole thing. Sharon. Some people call me Sherry right off the bat, but that shows they don't really know me. I hate a nickname. I mean at least for me."

"Yes, right," said Art. "And I'm Art Wallace, but I prefer to be called Arthur." Sharon nodded and Sam studied the corner of her right eye.

"Well, Sam and I were just about to have lunch and a beer across the street, and he suggested I ask you to join us."

"Oh, I have a lab at two-thirty, but I guess if I hurried." She smiled and cocked her head first to one side, then the other.

On the way to the bar Sharon walked between Sam and Art and talked a lot about Sally Smith and how she'd just opened things up for her with literature. "I mean, it all just means so much now, and it never used to."

"Oh, there are worlds, there are worlds," said Art.

Inside the bar most of the lunch crowd had gone, and they found a booth near the middle of the room. Behind the counter a large blown-up photograph of a football player wearing a slightly outmoded helmet hung above the row of bottles and cans along the wall. The name Tom Moturka was written with magic marker across the picture of the sky behind the player, and immediately below the name were the words *Rose Bowl '47*. And immediately below the picture itself and the bottles and cans stood the present-day Tom Moturka himself. Something had happened to Tom since the days he had spent handfighting off blockers and driving his helmet into the chests of ball carriers for the Fighting Illini, however, for he was a shrunken and pasty copy of the ham-faced linebacker behind him. Like John Wayne, his favorite actor,

Tommy Mo had grappled with the Big C and lost a lung to it in the battle. "Now," he often said, "I'm just glad to be alive and able to serve beer to these U of I kids."

After a minute or so, Sam noticed the man that Tom returned to talk to in between filling orders. It was because of the size of the man's head and shoulders that Sam hadn't realized at first what he was. Then he caught a glimpse of the man's feet and the length of his arms when he raised one hand to illustrate a point in his conversation with Tommy Mo. The man was what the white people called a midget and what the people of the Alabama-Coushatta Nation called poppoyom, one of the little people who lived in hollow trees or in caves. Sam watched the small man from the corner and smiled to himself, remembering what he'd heard of the time Walter Dips Weevils and some other Coushattas had gone to a drinking place in Beaumont and seen a little man like this one perched high on a stool drinking beer from a full-sized bottle.

Walter and the other two Coushattas had come down from the reservation in the cab of a pulpwood truck one of them had got to running one Saturday morning. It had no muffler, no hood over the engine, and no starter, but by parking on downhill grades, they had been able to get it started again whenever they stopped to buy more vanilla extract or to pour water from the roadside ditches into the overheated radiator. They had wandered into a section of Beaumont near the railroad loading warehouses and been attracted by the sign above a door picturing a large bottle of Lone Star Beer. Once inside the place they began drinking up the last of their money, and Walter spotted the little man sipping slowly and calmly at a quart bottle of Falstaff.

"Look," Walter Dips Weevils said to the others in the language of the Nation, "poppoyom. I will test him to see if he hates the people still."

Walter had mashed his right foot a week or so earlier when the end of a good-sized log had rolled over it on the pulpwood job, so he was sporting a walking stick that the white boss had let him borrow to get around on. He stood up from the table where he was drinking, walked over to the bar, and tapped the little man on the shoulder with his stick.

"Ho," he said. "Poppoyom." The little man looked over at him once and took another sip from his bottle. "Poppoyom," Walter repeated and looked back at his table to see if the other two

Coushattas were appreciating his bravery. By the time he had halfway turned back to the midget and raised his stick to poke him again, the little man had cocked his bottle above his head and spun his chair around. The bottle caught Walter Dips Weevils at a point on his head just over the bulge above his left eye, and as he began to topple backward he had just enough time to label the little man one last time before he hit the floor and left the world for a time. "Poppoyom," he declared.

On the way back to the reservation, stopping for radiator water in the dark, the other two Coushattas commiserated with Walter and agreed that the poppoyom, even in the form of little white men, were still enemies to the people of the Nation and dangerous to encounter. "The poppoyom said you fucked with him," one of the Coushattas said. "And this you cannot do."

"Bastard was small but quick," the other Coushatta added.

"The bratwurst is good here," Art was saying to Sharon Hansen. "With beer."

"None for me, thank you. I've got that lab." Sharon sat across from Sam and kept her hands folded on the table. She seemed to be interested in the saltshaker just in front of her, so Sam looked at it awhile himself.

"We'll have a couple of beers, right, Sam?"

"O.K.," said Sam to Art and looked away from the saltshaker to the mirror behind the bar. The eyes of the little man on the stool were fixed on Sam's reflection. He realized Sam had seen him and raised his beer bottle in a salute. Sam waved back.

"Friend of yours?" Art asked.

"Poppoyom, a tree-dweller," said Sam. "The talk of the old people," he added as he noticed how Sharon was staring at him.

"That's fascinating," she said. "Just like what we read in class last week. A legend. Oh, wow. Wouldn't Sally be interested in that!"

"Yeah," Art said. "Man interpreting nature. Here, Sam, have a beer."

The taste was bitter, as Sam knew it would be, but he took it down without showing a sign. After he had matched Art with a couple more bottles, he might as well have been drinking well-water for all the trouble it gave him in getting it down. He turned with the next bottle, saluted the poppoyom in the mirror, who returned the honor, and took a long drink.

"Thank you," Sharon said and began collecting her books and language records. "I'll see you guys in class." Sam noticed that when she said the word *guys* it almost rhymed with *boys*. She walked toward the door, and he decided to follow and tell her how she talked.

"Sharon Hansen," he said, opening the door of the bar which had just closed behind her.

She stopped at the edge of the street and looked back, her books again gathered up tight against her chest.

"When you talk . . ." he began. "When you say English words . . . Well. . . ." He decided to change the subject. "The little man can drink a lot." He jerked his head back toward the bar.

"You mean the midget? Yeah, I guess he can. It's twenty after two. Off to lab." She looked up the street to see if anything was coming. "I enjoyed meeting you. It'll be fun to see somebody from my lit class play on the basketball team."

She waved, and Sam watched her cross the street, the blonde braid of hair swinging against her back, and then went slowly back into the bar.

"Jesus, Leaping Deer. Did you get her lined up? I didn't even know you were interested until you were halfway out the door." Art pointed at the table. "Another round. We got to be at practice in an hour and a half. You got some money?"

Sam pulled a piece of paper folded up small from the pocket of his pants and unrolled it. It was one of the checks for laundry money Coach Underwood had given him.

"Haven't you cashed that thing? I get mine to the bank like it was on fire every month. What have you been using for money?"

Sam shrugged. "I don't buy things."

"I wish I could get by like that. I bet Tommy Mo will cash it. Let's ask him." He waved to the bar. "Tommy Mo. Here's a man with a check on the U of I Athletic Department. Will you trade him for it?"

"Is it a laundry check?" Tommy Mo looked up from his pose beneath his picture.

"Yeah."

"I'll cash it, but if I'd known you were an athlete, I wouldn't have served you beer in the daytime."

"It's not mine. It's his."

Tommy Mo looked Sam up and down and turned to the

midget. "He sure ain't no football jock, nor basketball neither. He's too little."

"Hell," said the midget. "You got to have heighth *and* muscle to play them games these days." He spun around and studied Sam as he sat in the booth. "Stand up, son."

Sam stood up for the poppoyom's inspection and tilted a bottle of beer to his lips.

"Maybe," said the midget. "But I'd like him three inches taller and a little heavier to play any ball for me." He spun back around and addressed his beer.

"This is wonderful," Art said. "Give him the check, Leaping Deer."

That day after practice had ended and the last freshman hopeful had dragged himself out of the locker room, Coach Chudy sat with the other assistants listening to Thompson deliver his comments on the day's work and his plans for things to come. Chudy sat on a blue plastic chair and picked out the hairs just behind his right ear one by one, a habit his wife said would finally result in his being as bald on the side of his head as he was on top.

"Nobody showed much today," Thompson said. "Nobody."

Chudy felt compelled to raise his hand. "Coach Thompson," he said, "not to differ with you on the essentials, but that Indian kid, Sam Deer, looked a lot better on the drills today than he ever has." Thompson turned to regard him.

"Yes, he looked like he wanted to put out today." Thompson paused. "On the drills. On the drills. Yeah, you're right, Chudy. He really went after the ball when somebody was bouncing it off the wall behind him or having him dribble it in figure eights."

Chudy sat back, pleased, and glanced down at the two hairs he held between the first finger and thumb of his right hand. He opened his hand, and they drifted to the floor.

"But, Chudy, did you notice how he was a shade off on his passing in the scrimmage and how he kept fouling on his drives? He wasn't too much better than any other guard out there today."

"Yes, sir, but his heart's in the right place with the drills, don't you agree?" Chudy began to feel light-headed from speaking out so much in post-practice. He felt encouraged to go on. "And if a kid's got heart, especially a minority kid, well, that's the main thing to look for." Chudy looked around him to see how the other

assistant coaches were taking his statements, but they all seemed to
have their heads dropped forward to look at something on the
floor. A bad sign. They sensed something that he hadn't gotten
wind of yet.

Thompson held up one hand, and Chudy hushed. "All I
know is that the better the best guard I've got gets in the drills, the
worse he seems to get in the scrimmages. At least today. And
beginning Monday he's going to go at point guard, and two weeks
from Monday he's going to be in against North Carolina."
Thompson put on his smile and swept his gaze around the room.
"We don't want him to slack off now, do we?" The coaches shook
their heads together and said no. The word reverberated in the
steel locker room like a moan.

Outside the building as they walked toward the dormitories,
Sam told Art one of McKinley Short Eyes' tales about the poppoyom and their dealings with the people of the Nation. The one
he chose to relate was about the time the little people and a hunter
of the Alabama tribe traveled together through the deep woods to
another village. They killed small and large animals together, rab-
bits and bears, and the little men ate all of the large animals and the
member of the Nation ate all of the small ones. They helped each
other cross small streams and large ones, the little people solving
the problems of the big rivers and the Alabama that of the small
creeks. They worked together this way, each doing what the other
couldn't, until finally the hunter was able to save the small men
from an attack by small things, a hive of yellow jackets.

For some reason that he couldn't state and didn't want to
think much about, Sam didn't tell Art another of the stories about
the poppoyom, and it was one of the tales most favored by Short
Eyes. This account of the Nation and the little people the old man
always saved until last when he was recounting the cycle of poppoyom stories. It warned of the effects that the contact by an
ordinary member of the Nation with the little men might have.
Many times such a human being would afterwards be made the
victim of a kind of craziness, a state of mind that left him bewil-
dered, not knowing who he was and unable to remember the
location of the center of the Nation. Always, as a child, after
hearing this story from McKinley Short Eyes, Sam would leave the
circle of listeners and walk quietly away into the woods. Then
when he was out of hearing range of the others, he would run as

quickly and as straight as he could to the place of the yearly corn dances and stand at the very center of the Alabama-Coushatta Nation, certain where he was again, listening to the blood pounding in his ears until it slowed and died away.

Now walking with Art Wallace away from basketball practice, Sam closed the poppoyom out of his mind and fell silent, the afternoon's beer dead in him and the occasional words of the man beside him nothing in his ears. The only sound that came through to him was the flat clanging of a chain being blown against a campus flagpole by the north wind.

Sally Smith's apartment was the top floor of an old house that had once belonged to a chiropractor. Sally had been able to salvage the sign he had kept in the front yard advertising his services and hours, and it now hung on one wall of the main upstairs room. "T. C. D. Gutters," it declared in black and red. "Consultations and Adjustments, 9–5 by Appointment." Beneath it was a large section of tree stump which Sally had had students lug upstairs for her. The stump now served as the base for an old cash register she had found in a foreclosed country store. It had worked for a while, but some visitor had banged the keys too hard, so that all that showed now in the glass window was the 2¢ and the No Sale signs.

Scattered around the floor were small rugs, large cushions (homemade), and candle holders fashioned from straw-covered wine bottles and the insulators off of telephone poles. From the ceiling in the corner hung a straw chair fastened to a chain, and against one wall was a single bed covered with cushions to serve as a sofa. The rest of the room, apart from the paintings done by friends and the hangings made of pieces of string tied into various kinds of granny knots, was made up of phonograph speakers and books sitting on arrangements of bricks and boards.

Sally kept all of her books on the shelves in a completely random pattern. "You're likely to find Sartre next to a book on gardening," she liked to say to her students. "I refuse to organize, and I refuse to be Dewey-decimalized. I know my books, and I know where they live." Sally figured she knew what students needed to hear. It simply wasn't true that they were waiting to be pressed into shape and to assume new definitions. What they really suffered from was already having been thrust into straitjackets of conformity. They were culture-bound, tied to preconceptions, their entire selves pressed into molds. Her job was to disorganize, to unstructure, to cut off, as she liked to put it, "their life-support systems." The poor children, as physically and emotionally mature as many of them were, were struggling in their sweet inarticulate way to deprogram themselves when they protested against the impersonality of the university and the society of which it was the arm. Her duty as teacher was to give them "positive feedback" and "unconditional positive regard." Something as simple as refusing to categorize books or not wearing shoes in nice weather did more to break down old patterns-for-patterns'-sake than one might realize.

So the first thing Sam heard from his literature teacher as he and Art entered the door of her apartment was a command to take off his shoes. He looked down past the notebook in his hand to his feet and then at the feet of his teacher. She was wearing bright red paint on her toenails and a golden chain with bells around one of her ankles. Her toes looked very pink.

Art immediately dropped to the floor, threw his books to one side and began unlacing his shoes. Sam wondered why he wasn't wearing socks.

"Come on, Sam," said Sally. "Relax. I bet back in Arizona you people go unshod as a matter of course."

"I don't come from Arizona. Texas."

"Oh, is it Texas? All right. In the barrios of West Texas then."

"It is East Texas," Sam said softly so as not to embarrass Sally Smith. "The Alabama-Coushatta Reservation."

Sally grabbed two handfuls of hair and tossed it away from her face. "I can't get anything right, can I?" She cocked her head to one side and pursed her lips into a smile. "Now tell me the truth. Do all of your people wear shoes all of the time in East Texas, then?"

"Most of the time," Sam said, thinking about the diamondback rattlers, the bull nettles, and the palmetto frond points of the Big Thicket.

Sally Smith moved off to greet somebody at the door, and Sam walked across the room and sat at one end of the sofa. At the other end was the fat girl who smoked so many cigarettes in class. Art sat down between them and leaned toward Sam.

"Hey, did you see those little bells? I'd love to hear them start chiming. Can't you imagine them moving up and down your back as you stroked? Ah, the bells, the bells, the tintinnabulation of the bells."

Sam looked at the fat girl to see if she'd heard Art, but she was staring hard at her opened book. He remembered that once some of the white boys at Big Muddy had claimed that during the senior trip to New Orleans, Mrs. Kilroy, the math teacher, had stayed in her room at the big hotel and let anybody that wanted to get in bed with her. "I ain't shitting you," Glenn Adams, a tall senior with a badly scarred face, had said, "ever damn one of us put it to her." Most of the whites at Big Muddy believed what the seniors said about their math teacher, but not many of the Indians, including Sam, thought the story was true. Why would a teacher want her students to do the thing, even if she was ugly and married to a skinny sick man as Mrs. Kilroy was? Sam shook his head and opened his literature book and began reading the poem Sally Smith had assigned the students, the one about the man looking at a bowl.

"Here comes your girl, Leaping Deer," said Art, nudging Sam in the side with his elbow.

Sharon Hansen came across the room toward the sofa. She declined to take Art's seat when he offered it to her with a sweeping gesture and said that she would just sit on one of the cushions on the floor. Her hair was unbraided and looked much longer, Sam noticed, than it did the times he had seen her before. He looked at her once and then fixed his eyes again on the page he'd been reading.

"You're still wearing your shoes," Art said.

"Don't you think it's cold?" asked Sharon. "Sam seems to think so." She looked at his shoes.

"That's strange, isn't it? Sam usually doesn't have cold feet." Sam looked harder at the poem in front of him and began using his forefinger to trace beneath the lines as he read.

"Is everybody here?" called out Sally Smith, looking around from where she was sitting near the cash register on the stump. She was pleased to see that so many had come and that among them were the most interesting people. Too often some of the people she most wanted to encounter outside the confines of the classroom didn't show up at the meetings in her apartment. Tonight, though, the most psychically promising ones all seemed to be there. How, she wondered, would the American Indian from—where? Texas?—respond to poetry so removed from his experience? She looked at him over in the corner on the end of the sofa intent on his book, sitting so tightly composed that he looked ready to spring up. Would his hair feel as stiff to the touch as it looked?

Sally Smith shifted her weight with a little tinkle of the bells on her ankle and began to read aloud. By the time she had finished the poem Sam had been staring at, most of the people in the room had found the right page and were following along. Sharon Hansen sat in front of Sam and a little to his right, so that he could look down on the part in her hair. It seemed very white. He looked back at the last line of the poem and listened to the silence of the room in the pause after Sally Smith stopped reading.

"Responses?" asked Sally Smith in the way that she did after everything the class read. One by one the same people began to say the same things they had said before about other poems and stories, and Sam felt his mind sliding away from the words on the page.

He began to picture a large brown bowl on a small hill in a clearing in a thicket. All around the clearing were hackberry bushes, poplars, saw vines, and youpon, grown together in a wall so close and tight that not even a piney-woods boar hog would be able to cut through the green mat. It was noon, the sun standing directly above so that all parts of the clearing were brightly lit, and the shadows of each thing were hidden beneath it. The brown bowl was empty and had always been and would always be. Around the side of the bowl were markings like the ones a few old women of the Nation still worked into the buckskin garments worn at the corn dances. The bowl was still, the sun unmoving, no one stood in the clearing to see what was there. The only living thing was the thicket, the mass of green vine, thorn, and branch that slowly grew inward and would finally erase the clearing and cover the brown bowl. But under the youpon and hackberry, the saw vine and creeper was the bowl still, Sam thought, and the markings of the Alabama-Coushatta people were still on the circle of the bowl, cut in by someone's hand deep enough to stay forever.

"But how do we punctuate the last two lines?" Sally Smith was asking. "Does it make any difference where we put the quotation marks?"

"Sure," Art said. "It determines the object. It tells who he's speaking to."

"Yes," said Sally Smith. "We don't know who's talking to

what or what's talking to whom, do we? So we have to take it whichever way we like it best. Whatever satisfies us is what we take. And I mean both aesthetically and emotionally. We can call it whatever we want to. And we can make it be what we want it to be."

"Doesn't it have to be one way or the other?" Sharon asked Sally in a small voice, ballpoint pen ready above her notebook.

"No, Sharon. It's just like life. It's both and neither, and you take your pick if you want. But you don't even have to choose at all, if you don't want. You can have it both ways at once. But you can never have it no way. Again, it's like the existence of any one of you. It isn't all or none; it never is that."

Sally leaned back, pleased at the way the discussion had led and proud of her statement about the last few lines of the poem. Ambiguity. That's what they all needed to learn to live with. If she could give them that, the realization that nothing was definite, there was no black or white, no right or wrong, she had done what she should do as teacher. All around her she could hear the satisfying scratch of pens and pencils as her words were recorded.

Looking about the room, Sally Smith could see only two heads not bent over notebooks. They belonged to Art Wallace, slouching on the sofa with his large white feet sticking out into the middle of the floor, and Sam Leaping Deer, still bolt upright in his place on the end. It wouldn't do to question him about the poem in front of the others, she thought. It would be counterproductive to try to draw him out if he lacked the linguistic equipment necessary to comprehend written poetry. I'll ditto some chants, she told herself, and use them in class. Maybe I can get him to open up and do some oral things for us.

After most of the class had talked for another thirty or forty minutes about whether or not it was right to talk about things they'd read or movies they'd seen, Sally Smith brought out some red wine, paper cups, cheese, and several currently popular record albums. She had learned not to try to introduce students to too much cultural excellence at once. It only turned them off, and besides, Sally herself liked the same kind of music the kids did. It was emotional, basic, "good to dance to," and Sally had a need to let her body move the way rhythm wanted it to go. She liked the way dancing made her feel so fully inside herself, so little divided into actor and perceiver. I wonder, she thought, as she passed the wine around, how the Indian would move.

All around the room people were beginning to drink the wine out of Sally's paper cups, to stand in little clumps and circles, to smoke cigarettes, talk in loud voices, and laugh in unison. The literary discussion was rapidly changing its shape and direction. Somebody flipped off the overhead switch, and the light level dropped to that of an Angelina County honkytonk. Over near the record player two people who had a few minutes earlier been arguing about what a word meant faced each other and began moving themselves around in time to the voice of a man on the record begging to be allowed to tell somebody—anybody—about oo poo pah doo. They looked to Sam like two people who had stepped on a soft blacktop road in August and were trying to scrape off their feet in the gravel shoulder of the highway. Now and then the female member of the pair would lift a foot and give it a little kick to the side. Sam kept half-expecting her to dislodge a small rock or two and send it ricocheting across the room into somebody else or one of the little glass bottles on the bookshelves.

He looked around for Sharon and discovered she had left her place on the floor near the sofa. She stood near a window talking to Sally Smith, a book open in her hand and a forefinger marking her place on the page. As he watched, Sally leaned toward her and said something he couldn't hear, her long gold earrings swinging as she spoke. He lip-read Sharon's response, "Oh, really? Wow," and looked down at the cup in his hand. He knocked back the wine, holding his breath, and looked around for the bottle. It was being lifted from a low table by Art Wallace, bending over to tend to his cup.

"Here we go, Leaping Deer," he said, topping off the drink in his hand, "bust-head red." Somebody dancing behind him jostled his arm and the wine slopped out and ran down his hand, dark blood in the half-light of the room. Art licked his fingers and took Sam's cup.

The song on the record player changed, and further outbreaks of dancing began to take place. To Sam's left, the fat girl with the cigarette habit gave a little hitch and shuffle, moved even in her solitude by the wail of the music. She reminded Sam of Mary Ethel Matlock at Big Muddy's senior prom, the only dance he had actually gone inside the building to see during his whole four years there. Sam had stood for five or ten minutes near the door with two or three other Coushattas and watched the white graduates of Big Muddy spin and tussle on the basketball floor. Mrs. Peebles' prom committee had decorated the gym with purple and white streamers and big letters cut from silver cardboard that spelled out *Au Revoir, Bobcats.* Mrs. Peebles had worked for a French motif throughout the whole of graduation week, from having the cafeteria serve some mushrooms in the salad at the senior dinner all the way to slipping some French songs into the stack of records played at the prom.

In fact, the loudspeakers were pouring out "The Poor People of Paris" when Frank Shoes pulled at Sam's arm to get his attention where they stood in the doorway to the gym. Frank Shoes had been chewing a pecan-sized piece of root all the way from the reservation, and his eyes, as he spoke, were straining out of their sockets as though they wanted to leave his body and go off to live on their own somewhere.

"Sam Leaping Deer," he said in the tongue of the Nation, "there is Matlock. If you want to wrestle, she will let you dance with her."

The other two Coushattas sniggered at the vision the words of Frank Shoes called up. Sam glanced over at Mary Ethel in spite of himself. She was wearing a white dress made of crinkly material over many layers of petticoats, so many that they kicked the edge of the dress up like a stiff breeze. Although she was a large girl, her breasts were small, and on the left side of her chest, the big bunch of carnations dyed purple, which she had had to buy herself, rose up high enough to interfere with the operation of her neck, if she wanted to lower her head to look at something, like maybe her purple high heels dyed to match the purse on her right arm.

Mary Ethel caught Sam's glance as she stood swaying to the beat of the music. She gave him what she thought was a forgiving smile and let her hands drop to her side, remembering to keep her fingers extended parallel to the floor. She hummed to the music and increased the tilt of her sway, the petticoats yielding a mild thrashing sound.

"She is ready. Now you must wrestle her or be called a coward," Frank Shoes had said, while the other Coushattas stumbled out of the gym, hands over their mouths to keep from laughing too loudly in front of whites.

"Eat the warm droppings from an armadillo," Sam had told Frank Shoes, treading right on the heels of the first two out.

Sam took another slug of the wine and looked around him.

The roof of his mouth itched, and the music was beginning to make his head throb. He leaned back to stretch his neck and felt the buckskin pouch beneath his shirt slide up his chest. Lifting a hand to it, he squeezed it between finger and thumb, gauging the amount of mikko root it held. He wondered if Walks Dead and the RAMS were smoking their pipe of peace tonight. Maybe they had all gone to the house of the woman in the snake dress, as Walks Dead said they must do soon. They seemed to owe her something, and she appeared to be a woman who would collect what was hers. White women always seemed to want something and to know that they wanted it, he was coming to believe.

Other than his own mother, the wife of Cooper Leaping Deer, Sam had been around few women of the Alabama-Coushatta Nation. The ones he saw, the mothers of his friends and the wives of the men of the Nation, were always busy feeding small children, chopping wood to burn in the cookstoves, singing in high quavery voices in one of the two white man's churches on Sundays, boiling clothes in iron washpots in the front yards of shotgun houses, hoeing weeds among the squash, beans, and corn of their small gardens, and tending to their husbands when they had had too much whiskey or extract to make it up the steps into the houses. All these activities left them with little time to relate to the young males of the Nation, even if there had been the desire. With the young girls it was somewhat different, but most of them were kept so busy helping the women and were watched so closely around the young men that it was not easy to know them much either. None of the women of the Nation, old or young, as far as Sam could tell, seemed to want anything. If they did, they did not show it, and if they wanted something they didn't already have, no man could guess what it was.

The white women in Illinois, however, as Sam observed them, left no doubts about their desires, even less doubt than Mary Ethel Matlock back in Big Muddy. Myra, the woman in the country in the room of many hair dryers, was the first to come to his mind in connection with the subject. She had been his first woman, but when he thought about it, Sam was left with the feeling that it was the other way around. In some strange way he had not had her at all, and she was not a person he could call a first for him in any way. No, he had not been her first man, certainly, either, but something about the episode in the dark room with the strange drink in his head and the sound of the warm air from the hair dryers in his ears made him think about McKinley Short Eyes' stories about the yotonah, the cannibal tribe who lived near great water and devoured careless members of the Nation who strayed into their territory.

Uneasy, he put the story out of his mind to consider later. Across the room from where he leaned against the wall with a new cup of wine in his hand stood Sharon Hansen, still talking to Sally Smith. What made these women act as they did and gave them their concerns was much harder to understand than the case of Myra. The two were interested still in the book Sharon held in her hand. At least they put their heads close together to look at it, nodding together and listening to each other speak. Sally Smith did most of the talking, but now and then Sharon would lift her right hand, say something, and the teacher would nod and laugh as if pleased.

Sam watched a tall man with a big nose and many sores on his face refill Sally Smith's wine cup and be refused by Sharon. "No?" he asked. "Aw, come on." Sharon turned away from him and began talking again to the teacher, tossing her hair back so that it fell over her shoulder.

"Flash after overwhelming flash, hey, Sam?" Art stood watching him regard the two women. He stepped sideways out of the path of a dancer and turned his wine cup upside down.

"This literature is having a terrible effect on me. I think I've had too many quatrains. Maybe just a couplet more." He went off searching for the wine jug, and Sam headed for the bathroom, the rawhide thong on the buckskin bag of mikko root tickling the short hairs on his neck.

When he returned from studying the pictures of naked women and the printed slogans on Sally Smith's bathroom wall, Sam felt better for the chunk of root under his tongue but puzzled by one of the statements he'd just read. "Things are in the saddle and ride mankind," it said in a delicate handwriting in green ink on a white card pinned to the wall. He tried to imagine a thing in a saddle fastened to the back of a large white man, but didn't like what his mind came up with. All he could see as he stood in the hall leading to the bathroom with his eyes fixed on a smooth black door knob was a creature whose body kept changing shape like the fog off a marsh pond. The hands at the end of its wavering arms were long and skinny as bones, and the fingers were covered with gold rings that were tarnishing to green even as he pictured them. The fog creature, with a head so thin and misty that Sam could see through it to a far-off line of gray horizon, held tightly to leather reins fastened to a bit in the white man's mouth.

He saw the white man struggle for a minute against the thing riding the saddle strapped to his back, then drop his hands hopelessly to his sides and begin to move off toward the far edge of the flat country, slowly at first, and then faster and faster. As the white man and the creature riding him shrank into the distance, the wind of their progress whipped at the body of the creature, tearing little puffs of mist away. But the more the creature's head and body thinned in the breeze of the journey, the tighter it fastened its grip on the reins controlling the white man's head. The last look at the vision Sam permitted himself gave him a view of the pair dipping into the darkness of a low swale and moving soundlessly out of sight of the place where their journey began.

"Leaping Deer," Art said, "I'm about to get shit-faced on this wine. You ready to go?" Art spoke slowly, shaping each word with care. He was holding a shoe in each hand.

"Are you O.K., Art?"

Art looked to Sam as if he were about to topple like a lightning-struck pine any second now. His hair stood out on one side of his head as though he had tangled with an electric fan, and his huge bare feet seemed to have lost some essential contact with Sally Smith's floor.

"Oh, yeah," said Art. "I'm smooth and slick. Just gonna float on home."

"Watch out for the berdache," Sam answered. "It's dark enough tonight for them to be roaming."

"The what? Is that something that'll get you?" Art moved a shoe back and forth like a club. "Don't you worry, Sam. I'll just use these size fourteens on them."

"Don't offer to trade anything," Sam said. "You do and you'll be naked in the morning."

"Got you, Leaping Deer. Look, don't drink all that stuff. Leave some for breakfast." Art left the hall and followed several other people out the front door, bending over on the way through to say something to a short dark girl wearing what looked like a man's army uniform. She shook her head and let the door slam.

When Sam made his way over to the table where the jug of wine was sitting, he saw that only Sharon and the man with the sores on his face were left talking to Sally. Plenty Sores was saying in an excited voice that he loved the theater and just everything about it.

"I mean it has to all come from you, right? When you're acting, you show what you're really like behind all the false fronts you have to put on in society. The real *you* can come out. I mean you can reveal your emotional depths."

Sharon started to say something, but Plenty Sores kept talking.

"Don't you agree, Sally? By the way, I just love being able to call my teacher by the first name. It's just like we're equals. Of course, I know we aren't. You know just everything about literature and art and music." He swept his arms wide apart and then brought them together again with a little hand-slap that ended up with his pointing with all ten fingers toward his chest from a range of about two inches. "Me?" he asked. "I don't know anything yet, but I will, I will. Don't you agree, Sally? I just love to say your name."

"You mean about?"

"About acting. You know. What you reveal of your emotional depths when you do a role."

"Yes, that's certainly one well-supported theory about the dynamics of acting," said Sally, holding out her cup toward Sam as he stood with the bottle in his hand. He poured her some wine and looked back toward the actor, who was lighting a cigarette from a green package. When he dropped the pack on the table Sam saw on the side a picture of a man and a woman holding hands and running up a hill through some woods. Both were smiling very happily and had sweaters tied around their bodies.

Sharon stood up and said she had to go before it got any later but thank you very much she enjoyed it. Plenty Sores agreed and gathered his things about him.

"Which way are you walking?" he asked.

"Pennsylvania."

"Oh, I'm going the other way. I've got miles."

Sam set his half-empty cup down and began looking around for the book he'd brought with him. By the time he'd found it where someone had kicked it back under the sofa, Plenty Sores had gone and Sally and Sharon were standing at the door watching him. He felt like he ought to speak.

"My book," he said and lifted it in the direction of the two women. He looked at Sharon.

"Do you go to Pennsylvania Street?"

"Yes," she said. "I'm in McBride."

"I wonder," Sally said and put her hand on Sam's arm, "if I could go over some of your writing with you, Sam? I know it's a little late, but it'll take just a few minutes and save you a trip to that awful office of mine." She squeezed Sharon's arm, and Sam sat back down on the sofa and reached for his wine cup. He could hear Sharon's footsteps going down the first few stairs. "Goodbye," Sally was saying, "see you in class. Keep reading Keats." Sharon said something Sam couldn't make out, and Sally laughed.

She walked back into the room smoothing her hair back from her face, ready, she had almost convinced herself, to go over Sam Leaping Deer's first two essays with him.

On one of them, she remembered, she had asked the class to write an argumentative essay supporting some assertion with reference to evidence and logical cause and effect, and what the young Indian had written was a mood piece about what seemed to her a dreary landscape, and it was filled with sentence fragments. The other had been an assignment to write a comparison-contrast paper, and on that one Leaping Deer had presented only one side and never got around to the contrasting view at all. He had far to go, rhetorically.

"Now," Sally said, "where are those papers?" She began to rummage around in the drawers of a bright blue desk, shuffling papers and making bumping noises in the half-lit room.

Sam watched his right hand pick up the jug of wine, tilt it over his cup, set the jug back down, and lift the cup to his mouth. He drank what his hand offered him and waited for it to fetch him some more from the bottle. His blood made a low pounding in his ears, as regular as the steady flow of the water of Long King Creek over one of the little waterfalls on the reservation land. A beam of light from the kitchen lay across the table in front of him, touching the glass of the bottle as it tilted to transfer more wine for his hand to bring him. He was pleased to see how well his hand was working, careful when it lifted the bottle, slow and steady as it poured, and sure of the location of his mouth as it brought the cup near his face.

"Here they are," said Sally, sitting down beside him on the sofa. "Both of them. We'll need some more light, though, to see, I think." She lifted one of the papers so that the beam of kitchen light lay across it. The writing on that paper was made by the same good right hand, Sam thought with pride, and waited for his loyal servant to bring him some more drink. Instead, he noticed, it stopped pouring the wine, set down the bottle, and began touching the hair that Sally had just pushed back from her face. His whole body began to cooperate with the hand and turned toward the woman. The left hand, the holder of what the good right hand operated on, placed itself on the shoulder of the woman and turned her toward Sam. The right hand carefully cupped the back of Sally's head and brought her face up to his. Grateful, Sam drank what the hand offered him as though it were wine from the bottle. The tongue of his mouth went forth to taste and met a foe which it wrestled with briefly and defeated.

Someone said "Oh, God" in a shaking voice unfamiliar to him, and Sam's hands and tongue, his lips and arms became so busy in their smooth movements that he found it difficult to see just what all these good parts of himself were doing. All at one time, both hands were helping the woman remove her blouse and pants, were moving to caress the breasts whose nipples seemed to have a fascination for them, were holding the woman's back up away from the sofa, were venturing down her belly in a long slide that ended in a thicket of wet marsh land which parted to let the fingers of the good right hand slip through, were along with the hands of the woman pulling at his own clothes until they lay twisted and discarded on the floor, were tugging at the woman's parted legs until they fit tightly around his body, bringing her against his belly, were reaching behind the woman's hips to squeeze at the warm hills they had uncovered, were moving back to the woman's face to pull it away from where it was jammed into the wall, a pillow half over it, its teeth clenched as air whistled through them with a sound like water boiling in a large pot, were turning the face up so that tongue could retrace where it had been, were finally searching around the upper body of the woman to lock together and hold as if to save themselves from slipping with body into a suckhole in a dark thicket of the Nation.

All these movements of hands, tongue, legs, body, Sam tried to watch, falling further and further behind in keeping track of them as the sound of hissing water, the jingle of bells, and a woman's crying somewhere mixed faster and faster, hurrying his attention from place to place until finally he heard himself cry out in despair and failure as all the separate parts, sounds, and movements became one thing and he fell, turning and turning in ever tighter circles through the half-darkness back at last into himself again.

"Oh, Jesus, Jesus, fuck, fuck," Sally Smith was saying beneath him, her face wet and twisted once more against the wall beside the sofa. Sam pushed away, trying to pull himself off her, but she held tightly to him, one arm around his neck and the other across his shoulders, while her legs seemed to be entangled so complexly with his that he couldn't move from the waist down in more than little shivers. "One minute," she said. "Just one more minute. Please, oh, God, please." Slowly she began to stretch her upper body back over the end of the sofa as though she meant to force her head from her neck, she took a long shaky breath that rattled in her throat, and, as at a signal, suddenly went so limp that her right arm slid from Sam's neck to the floor as though it had been chopped off.

Sam's back, tingling in long stripes, felt like he had been run up and down a barbed-wire fence. His breath whistled in his throat as though he had just led three fast breaks in a row down a basketball court, and the muscles of his thighs and arms trembled as if in fever-chill. As he stood up and began putting on his clothes, he discovered that the jug of wine lay on the floor knocked over so that most of what was left in it had poured into one of his shoes. He turned it upside down and watched a little spurt of wine splash onto the rug. He dressed quickly and remembered to pick up his literature book. On the sofa a bare foot stuck out from the cover Sally Smith had pulled over herself. She looked to be asleep, her head turned away from the kitchen light and a mass of hair across her face. The door to the outside stairs squealed when Sam opened it, but he eased it shut, once on the other side, and it didn't make another sound.

D. T. Donovan looked up again from the cornstalk he was detasseling at the young fellow hanging over the fence around the Morrill Experimental Cornfield. Usually, whenever he entered the area inside the fence to work with whatever special hybrid was in cultivation at the time, D. T. Donovan became so lost in the world of corn genetics that he wouldn't have looked up from his work if somebody had dropped a bomb on the library buried less than a hundred yards away. The fact the library *was* sunk into the ground and not looming above the Morrill plot had been the result of D. T. Donovan's campaign against the shadows a building would throw over the corn late in the afternoon. How in the world could you maintain natural conditions in the cornfield with an artificial environment of late afternoon shadows, he had asked everybody at the university and finally the Governor of Illinois himself. Well, they had dug the building into the ground finally, and the hybrid strains could grow with a fair chance of showing what they would really do in an ordinary field.

The young fellow leaning over the fence—dark skin and hair, must be some kind of a foreign student—continued to watch D. T. Donovan as he moved from stalk to stalk of the King Diamond 240-X, carefully detaching the tassels and checking them against the electronic pollen counter slung around his neck by a leather strap. Most young people never gave the Morrill plot a second look as they passed, but this foreign student had been studying D. T. Donovan's progress from plant to plant for fully thirty minutes.

"You interested in corn, young man?" asked D. T. Donovan, placing a tassel in a cloth bag tied to his waist.

The foreign student nodded his head and kept his eyes fixed on the tassels moving in slow ripples in the light breeze.

"This hybrid here we're kind of proud of. It's unique, the only one of its kind in the world right now. We've been breeding it to this point for four years, and we're going to let it ripen and dry here in the field. It'll be another two months before we harvest the ears. Then next spring we plant right from that seed. We can stop having to cross-pollinate then, you see, and go directly from the new kernel itself." D. T. Donovan caressed one of the tassels, sniffed at it and sneezed.

"Why do you use the machine?"

"Pollen counter. Electronic counter developed right here at

the U of I. That's how we got to this point with King Diamond. Machines did it all. Without machines, we'd still be floundering around."

"You make the corn grow with that machine?"

"Well, not exactly," D. T. Donovan answered and patted his power source. "But this hybrid wouldn't be here without this machine." He flipped a switch and the machine began clicking, its silver case glinting in the late afternoon sun. D. T. Donovan pushed back his baseball cap to get a closer look at his dials.

Sam moved back from the fence and looked down at the indentations the strand of wire had made in the palms of his hands. From across the campus came the sound of bells, and he turned to begin walking toward the gym for the afternoon practice. When he looked back over his shoulder at the corn patch, he could see D. T. Donovan again moving from stalk to stalk questioning each plant he came to with the little silver wire attached to his machine.

Ten minutes later, in the locker room, Sam came upon Art Wallace, who was half-lying across a bench as his ankles were being taped by a student trainer. Art looked down in the mouth.

"Hello, Sam," said Art, and winced as the man doing the tape job got too high on his ankle and jerked some hair loose from his calf. "You're sure kicking some ass these days in practice. I want you to know your old friends on the bench miss you and remember when and all that crap."

"Well, not so much," said Sam, picking up his gear and walking toward a room filled with weight-lifting equipment. He liked to change in there because usually no one else but him was in the room at that time of day.

"Hey, Sam, are they that much better than us, the returning guys?" Leaning over to tie his shoes, Art looked up and jerked his head in the direction of the gym.

"Some are better, but not too much," Sam said, trying to put his answer in a way that would make Art feel better. Even the way Art was lacing his shoes looked sad, Sam thought.

"Yeah, I think it's just a matter of confidence and getting a chance to show what you can do." Art stood up, ready to go join the other players.

"Oh, yeah, Leaping Deer. One other thing. I know you're running with a higher class of people these days, but why haven't you been in lit class?"

Art grinned and Sam shrugged and looked at the wire basket he was holding. He focussed on one eyelet of the left basketball shoe, four up from the bottom, then counted four up from the bottom on the corresponding side of the other shoe and looked at that one.

"Sally Smith told me to tell you when I saw you something about some papers. Said they were all right, you did a good job, and she wants you to talk to her about them again. And then guess what else she said? She said she hopes you don't isolate yourself. How about that, man? She's gonna do a little psychological number on you about why you cut class."

Sam hadn't known what to do all week about Sally Smith's literature class after having watched his body do all the things it had done to her in the apartment that night. Even after hearing the message Art brought from her, he still dreaded the thought of seeing her again in the bright daylight in the classroom with Sharon and the others around. But what she had said to Art made it sound as though she was not angry and would say nothing to him about all the things he had seen himself doing. Maybe being with a man in that way meant nothing more to a white woman than the handshakes white men were continually offering meant to them. He might think about going back to the class in a few days if nothing more happened to convince him of how strange this thing was.

"I have many things to do," Sam said to Art. "Tell Sally Smith I will come back when I can do it."

"O.K. I've got to go hit it," said Art, starting for the door to the gym. "See you around. Hey, Sam." He looked back and lifted an eyebrow. "Sharon wants to know if you're sick or anything. I told her 'anything'."

If Sharon Hansen knew the thing he had done with Sally Smith, she would not want anything more to do with him again, Sam thought. Sharon wanted to listen to her teacher, write down what she said about the things they read in the class, and make the careful lines under certain words and groups of words that Sam had seen her trace in her literature book as he sat beside her. She would be afraid of him and think of him as not a serious person if she discovered that he had watched himself do all those things to Sally Smith, his teacher, and had done nothing to stop his actions. He wondered what name she would have for such a person as he had shown himself to be. Sam could hear exactly the name that La

Wanda Two Tongues would say was his if she could learn of his drunken fornication back where she lived in the Nation. "Toksati," she would call him, the Nation's word for tie snake, the creature that lurked in deep small waterholes and used fermented cane to lure small helpless animals back into its den to be eaten alive.

Right then and there, as he trotted out to join the starting lineup in practice, Sam promised himself that he would that night consult his deerfoot talisman and cast the sabia beads to change the direction his life seemed to have started taking. He hoped that he wanted to change it enough to make the charm work. He thought of Sharon Hansen, her thick blonde hair, and wondered how she would look naked like Sally Smith had been. Would she make crying sounds as she loved, he wondered, and by thinking that, he knew himself to be more of a toksati than he had at first thought.

"Blue nine," called the coach with the dead smile, "after warm-up, I want you to start working on setting up the forwards on turnarounds." Sam nodded and joined the straggling crowd taking laps around the gym before shooting practice. Sometime during his third circuit of the court, he felt himself breaking into a light sweat, and he stopped thinking about women, white or red, for the next two hours.

A Journey to the Sky

The sixteen thousand seats in the Assembly Hall were only about a third filled at 7:30 when the team trotted out of the dressing room to take warm-up shots before the opening game of the season. At the other end of the court, the players from North Carolina, dressed in light blue, were banging away with jump shots and pretending not to notice that the home team was now on the floor, even though their entrance had caused several hundred in the audience to applaud. "Go, Illini," some local insurance salesman or associate professor of history or soybean farmer bellowed. "Trip the Tarheels." In front of the home stands eight men and women dressed in matching costumes went into a letter-perfect dance routine, waving orange pompoms and kicking up their legs high enough for people in the front rows to be able to see the women's blue satin underpants.

Standing at the bench Sam took off the brand-new warm-up jacket he'd just been given by a clubfooted man in the dressing room who everybody called Ears. Sam carefully folded the jacket so that the sleeves of it hid the profile of the Indian's head embroidered on the back with orange thread. The nose on the figure reminded him of the picture he'd seen on one of the walls of Big Muddy High School of Thomas Jefferson in the act of signing the Declaration of Independence. The Indian on the jacket had been given no eyes by the machine that stitched him, but his headdress made up for the lack. It was full, rich, and elaborate. Each feather drooped in perfect symmetry, and each feather ended in a lacy puff that looked like a dandelion's head.

Sam laid the decently-covered blind Indian on the bench and picked up a basketball from a wire rack. He heard somebody call his name and looked up to see Art, not suited up, sitting a couple of rows up behind the place the team would be occupying during the game. He had a pair of crutches beside him and he pointed toward his taped ankle.

"Leaping Deer," he said again, "whip some ass tonight." Sam extended his right arm toward Art, the palm of his hand down, looked toward the nearest goal and saw that the curve of its circle flowed as it should, apart from everything around it, untouched by the practice shots falling through it and bouncing off and away from it. It hung in the light, bright in its roundness and larger than what a measurement of it would show it to be. The cries of the cheerleaders, the voices and movements of the people in their seats, the squeaks and thuds of rubber against the wooden floor and the glass backboard were melting into a thin hum, diminishing in the presence of the circle in the air even as Sam regarded it. He moved toward it in its quiet, gathering himself for his first offering to it of the roundness in his hands tonight.

I hope he doesn't fly all to pieces in the first two minutes, Coach Buck Thompson thought as he stood in the team huddle just before tip-off. He looked from the stack of hands in the circle before him, the brown ones of the Indian lying limply atop the clenched and entangled fingers of his four veterans, and tried to get a close look at the ethnic's eyes. They looked murky and glazed over to him, unfocussed and sunk deep in his head. He's probably going into shock. Won't be able to do a damn thing. You really can't trust these off-breed kids, no matter how good they look in practice. I'll probably have to jerk him before he passes out.

"Now, listen," Thompson addressed his troops, "slow and careful. Don't try to run with them or they'll blow us out of here. Leaping Deer, set them up every time you come down the court. Don't hurry." The Indian didn't give a sign that he'd heard, and Thompson felt something small kick in his belly as though it was just waking up and would soon start trying to claw its way out. I'll pull him, I'll pull him in ten seconds, he thought and waved his players off onto the court. He made himself sit down and grab a towel to chew on.

Sam joined the cluster of men around the center circle and began to position himself in relation to the two players about to go up for the referee's toss. When the man in the blue uniform next to him stuck out his hand, Sam laid his fingers limply in the palm noticing that it felt damp, and fixed his eyes on the ball balanced on the referee's fingertips. The two players on either side of the short man in the striped shirt grunted and strained, going into deep quivering squats, waiting for the ball to be released, their right hands held head high. The ball left, turning slowly on an axis and floated up until it hung for an instant above the court, the players and referees on the court, the cement and steel foundations, the ground beneath it all. Then the centers released into their jumps, the two right hands stretched for the ball, and the man in blue reached it first, sending the tap deep into the opposite court where one of the North Carolina guards caught the ball and began to dribble it slowly across the center line.

Sam moved to pick him up, noticing that as the man bounced the ball between his hand and the floor, the height of the dribble was a few inches more than usual because of the man's size. Moving slowly toward him, Sam timed himself so that as he faked a quick lunge at the ball, the blue uniform changed hands across the front of his body leaving the ball unprotected enough for Sam to get the tips of two fingers on it. Deflected, the ball bounced off the man's right knee, and Sam batted it away in the direction opposite to the way the other player was leaning. The ball was his, no one was near him and Sam dribbled at a moderate pace toward his goal, leaving the floor at the right moment to allow the roundness carried by his hand to intersect with the smooth flow of the circle above him. Looking back over his head he watched the white net flick up to acknowledge what had just passed through it.

The next time down the court, the guard who had coughed the ball up passed off before he reached the center line and went by Sam empty-handed. He had a determined look on his face and didn't do much dribbling in between the times he and the other guard passed the ball around the perimeter of the circle, working to their forwards and trying to get the ball inside to the center. It wasn't until one of the North Carolina players tried a jumper and missed that Sam got his hands on the ball again. The Illinois center retrieved the high bounce off the rim of the basket and flipped the ball off to the other guard, who got it to Sam just in front of the time line. The North Carolina players were hustling down into defensive positions, and as Sam dribbled near the sideline, he heard Dead Smile yelling to slow it down and set it up. Sam looked around for his guard, realized that the defense was sagging back on him beyond the free-throw key, and decided to take it in closer.

As he neared the top of the key, the thin freckled guard in blue moved up to meet him, looking nervous and quick. Sam slowed, gave the man in front of him a head-fake to the left, and drove hard off his left leg to the right. The path to the basket was clear for about a eighteen-foot jumper, so Sam went up, loosed his shot and knew from the feeling of weightlessness as the ball left the tips of his fingers that the shot was in. He had half-turned his body in the air to land headed back away from his goal toward the other end of the court by the time the ball fell through the circle of steel and into the hands of one of the North Carolina forwards.

"Goddamn it, I told him to set it up," said Coach Buck Thompson to one of his assistants as he sat squirming on the bench.

"I know," the assistant answered. "What about the game plan?"

Thompson groped around for his chewing towel where it had fallen to the floor. He hadn't gotten a good purchase on it yet before the North Carolina center hit a hook shot and the action moved again toward the Illinois goal. This time the Indian worked it inside to the center who passed off to the right forward who got it back to the Indian coming around behind through the back door. He was stopped by a defending forward, seemed to be about to kick the ball back outside, but on the way up to pass off to his left, shifted the ball to his right hand and got off a bankshot over the shoulder of the North Carolina man, who had been fooled into dropping his hands. The ball squeaked against the glass, changed direction and bounced through the goal, dribbling off the back of the North Carolina forward's head on its way down.

Thompson looked at the clock. A minute and twenty-five seconds gone, and North Carolina was coming down the court at a slow trot, the guards working the ball back and forth with short passes while the front line set up. "Slow it down, Jimbo," the taller of the two in the backcourt urged the one with dime-sized freckles and the quick moves of a neurotic. "Take your time."

By the time six more minutes had passed and North Carolina had finally called a time-out, Sam had scored twelve more points on six of seven shots, among them two goals leading fast breaks, three on long one-hand set shots taken when the defense had collapsed into a zone, and the other on a give-and-go drive up the center of the lane when the defense came back out into man-to-man coverage. The shot he missed was one on which he had put too much spin working backwards over his head on a drive down the back line under his goal. Two other players on Buck Thompson's Illini had contributed eight points between them, so the score stood at twenty-six to ten just seven and a half minutes into the first half.

"Leaping Deer," said Coach Thompson, "you're not leading the slow-down game a team's got to play to beat North Carolina. Haven't I told you they're a fast-breaking team and they just love to run with you? We've got to make them play our game or they'll burn us out of here."

Sam nodded and wiped his face with the orange towel a student manager had draped around his neck. He looked back at the huddle of players across the floor and then at the goal he'd been working to. The circle looked even bigger to him now than it had at the beginning of the game, ten feet above the shining floor but close enough to touch, waiting for the ball he must give it, a basket that was never filled, that was always hungry to be fed the roundness that fit it.

Dead Smile was still talking to him, gesturing with a towel held in his right hand and holding a notebook tight against his chest with the left.

"Coach," said one of the tall players who had been scrambling for rebounds and who had missed the two shots he had tried, "shouldn't number nine try to work the ball inside more to the front-line people? My man was giving me lots of room. I really think I could sting them inside if I get more help." He gazed earnestly down at Coach Thompson with an injured look on his face.

"What have I just been saying, Kolchek? Move around more

in there, and maybe you'll get more inside passes. Leaping Deer, remember what I said now." Thompson raised his voice so he could be heard over the sound of the band thirty feet away ripping its way through a song Sam had never heard before. When it had begun, people in the audience had started yelling and whistling even louder than they had when the time-out had been called. Now the music stopped, and the cheerleaders, who had been shaking their fists at the crowd and turning flips backwards and landing on their feet, began to chant something together. The crowd got quiet, the cheerleaders finished saying whatever it was they had been saying and then joined the crowd in screaming together again.

Sam looked down at the rolled-up towel in his hand and watched sweat drip from his nose and fall onto a large letter I. He moved his head around in little jerks to make the sweat fall into the rough pattern of a circle. He needed one more drop to make the circle complete when the buzzer went off to end the time-out, but when he shook his head nothing else fell. He touched a finger to the depression above his collarbone, transferred a drop of sweat and flicked it at the I on the towel, and then trotted, satisfied, back out onto the court to find his man.

For the next several minutes the North Carolina team threw a full-court press at Illinois, what the coach of the Tarheels, Charles "Bubba" Longmire, liked to call his "reducing program." "Hit most teams with it," he often said, "and the bastards'll blow a gasket." The first couple of times down the floor the press worked for the Tarheels, once when a long pass thrown by a badgered forward went out of bounds and the next time when the other guard in the forecourt with Sam let himself get pinched and tied up in the corner. After that, Sam began dribbling the ball down the court alone, refusing to pass off until the two North Carolina guards would converge, figuring they could squeeze him. Twice in the last second left before having to cross the time line, Sam passed off through the whirling arms of the two guards and hit one of his men open enough to drive in close for a short jumper. The third time down the court he drove through the two men guarding him and hit a shot from the top of the key, and the fourth and fifth times he drew fouls and made the free shots.

"Shit," said Bubba Longmire. "That fucker's gone foul Jimbo or Billy one out." He motioned to one of his assistants, who bellowed a couple of numbers at a guard on the way by, and the reducing program petered out and changed to a sag with one rover following number nine everywhere he went.

For the rest of the half, number nine looked to Bubba Longmire like he was pleased to entertain the rover, a senior guard from Asheville who, if he didn't score much, did stick like a tick on defense. Usually. This time he had his troubles, taking fakes, heading the wrong direction, stepping off the wrong foot, leaning forward when he ought to be backing, getting caught for fouls, jumping up into the air to block shots that didn't come until after he'd landed, being too quick, being too slow, standing around, running around, letting his attention wander, watching too close.

In one of the several time-outs Bubba Longmire called, Thurman tried to explain it, scrubbing at his face and neck with a towel while he cursed. "Sumbitch is holding me. Ever time I crowd him close and about get him, he'll reach down where the referee can't see it and push against my knee with his off hand. You know that time I fell down backwards? Well, he give a little pull to the bottom of my pants and tipped me off-balance. Hardly ever touched me, but it threw off my timing."

"I's you I wouldn't talk about timing, Thurman. He is whipping your ass. I don't know how much he's made by hisself, but I know what the scoreboard says." A few of the people in the huddle lifted their heads to study the twenty-point difference stated in a huge display of light above.

"Don't you look up yonder. You ain't gone learn nothing to help you there." Bubba Longmire raised his voice higher to be heard over the crowd, which the cheerleaders by this time were trying to catch up to in pitch and frenzy.

"Now listen, Thurman. Can't you, you know, slow him down any? I mean your back ain't broke."

"Hell, Coach, I already got three fouls on me. One of them wasn't even a real one, neither. He made it look like I was holding his arm, and it was him holding me. Referee hadn't even seen him a single time."

"Jimbo," said Longmire, looking at the freckle-faced nervous guard who had been watching Sam work on Thurman and who was grateful that he was guarding who he was, "you gone have to start cheating over and helping out with this little sumbitch."

"What about my man, Coach? He'll be open."

"Your man ain't shot shit and won't, and you know it. There ain't nobody out there scored nothing but that little Mexican-looking bastard. Thurman can't handle him by himself. He's done showed me that." Coach Bubba Longmire paused and looked across the court at the Illinois bench where everybody was standing up and jiggling around like they had fever. He looked for number nine and at first couldn't see him with the taller players clustered in a knot around Thompson. Then he dropped his eyes to their legs and picked out the pair of dark ones among all the pale ones surrounding them. Looks like some kind of a goddamn weed, he thought. "What is he," he said out loud, "a Filipino or something?"

In the locker room at half time, Sam sat in a row of blue plastic chairs and studied the scratches on the backs of his hands where the North Carolina players had gouged him reaching in for the ball. Dead Smile stood at a blackboard in front of the row of chairs, pointing with a piece of chalk at X's, circles, and dotted and solid lines. Beside him was Coach Chudy, his gut sucked up tight, nodding solemnly every minute or so as Thompson lectured the team on the half a game still to come. The players lined up in the plastic chairs were listening carefully to their leaders, especially the ones in the dry uniforms who hadn't played in the first half at all and wouldn't in the second unless something major happened. They were also the ones, Sam imagined, thinking back to half times at Big Muddy, who would yell the loudest and scramble hardest to get back to the court when the time came for the game to start again.

Once when Big Muddy was down by eight at the half in a district game with Leggett, Don Ray Popp, the son of the woods foreman for Carter Lumber Company, had gotten so fired up hearing Coach Dodge plead with the Indians on the team that he had run his foot against the doorjamb fighting to get out of the locker room and had broken two toes. Don Ray was bitterly disappointed at being lost for the season until Dodge started letting him sit on the bench anyway even though he wasn't dressed out to play. Don Ray liked to tell his daddy that even crippled he added something to the spirit of the Bobcats by just being there as a kind of inspirational presence.

Dead Smile finished drawing and erasing and redrawing the

lines and circles and asked if there were any questions. Someone asked him to repeat a point he'd made and after he did that, the tall player who had talked before in the first time-out raised his hand.

"Coach Thompson, I've been wondering if we shouldn't try to concentrate a little more on working the ball inside in the second half. It's getting real fluid in there. I mean, we're looking kind of sloppy."

Sam licked at the blood on the longest scratch on the back of his left hand and then dabbed at it with one of the orange towels scattered all over the room. He heard the click of Dead Smile's chalk as he laid it down in the blackboard tray.

"Kolchek," Dead Smile finally said, "I believe we might be going in for a period of adjustment. I'm afraid we just might be." No one else said much before the buzzer blew to call them back outside.

As Sam refolded the jacket to hide the Indian's head again, he looked up in the seats behind the bench for Art. He was there with a paper cup in his hand, just turning to say something to Sharon Hansen. She grabbed Art's hand and pointed in the direction of Sam. They both waved, and Art yelled something that Sam couldn't hear for the noise of the crowd. Sam noticed that for the first time since he'd met Sharon she wasn't carrying an armload of books. He covered the Indian's head well and turned toward the circle of players, rubbing the backs of his hands against his jersey to feel the sting.

In the first few minutes after the second half tip-off, Sam was called twice by the referee for charging, but he drew five more fouls himself, two on Thurman and three on the freckle-faced guard called Jimbo. After Thurman fouled Sam the second time and fouled out of the game, he threw up his hand to acknowledge the violation and spoke to Sam as he turned to leave the court.

"You can shoot all right," he said, "I'll give you that. But you held on to my britches twice when you got by me."

"Three times," Sam said and turned for the free-throw line.

Soon after Thurman left, Jimbo and the new North Carolina guard began going to pieces, trying wilder passes and taking less time with their play. The defense spread out, the game speeded up, and Sam found himself leading fast break after fast break, throwing long passes to open men, stealing loose balls and bad throws, and slipping into the North Carolina passing lanes again and again for pick-offs. With a minute or so to go, he had just slapped a ball loose at the North Carolina end of the court and thown it ahead of the other guard streaking for the Illinois goal for a lay-up. The buzzer sounded a long blast after the score, and Sam looked around to see who had fouled.

"Ladies and gentlemen," a voice came through the loud-speaker. It stopped and then continued in a few seconds with the speaker talking to someone beside him in the media booth. "Is that it? There? All right. Ladies and gentlemen," the voice began, formal and solemn again. "With his last goal, Sam Leaping Deer, a freshman playing in his first game for the Illini, has just broken the single-game scoring record for most points by a player in the Assembly Hall. That record was held by Don Freeman, fifty-one points, and Sam Leaping Deer has just scored his fifty-second point."

The band broke into "Hail to the Orange," the cheerleaders began building up and tearing down body pyramids like berserk carpenters, and most of the spectators rose to their feet to clap, stomp, cheer, and ask each other who in hell was Sam Houston Leaping Deer and what *was* he anyway. Down on the court Coach Buck Thompson called a time-out in the midst of all the noise and addressed himself to the five people standing in a circle around him.

"You're getting your applause right now," he told Sam and moved his hand in a circle, "so I'm not going to take you out for that. We also got North Carolina beat by twenty-five points, so there's nothing else to worry about. You've got about a minute and a half to see if you can't get a few more points. The rest of you get the ball to him." Dead Smile waved them back out onto the court, thinking of the headlines tomorrow what with the Indian scoring so much and Illinois beating a team picked a ten-point favorite over it. The news would certainly hit the Chicago papers, and since it was so early in the season probably it would go nation-wide. And, Jesus, it was sweet to put it to Bubba Longmire. There he was now, sitting on the North Carolina bench with a towel around his head, staring at the floor like it was interesting. There'll be reporters around this week to talk about this game. Hell, Buck Thompson told himself, I'll just tell them that our game plan was to beat them at their own game, run with them and just blow them out. "Shit," Thompson said out loud, causing Chudy to cut an eye at him, "maybe even *Sports Illustrated.*"

The next morning as Sam stood in front of his mirror dressing and wondering whether he ought to shave the sprinkling of black hairs which slowly began to show up on his face every couple of weeks, Akbar Ameer came back into the room waving something in his hand.

"Hey, brother, you got them where you want them now. Listen to what Charley's saying in his daily rag, man. Here's what the *Daily Illini's* got in it this morning." Akbar sat down on the edge of his bed and began to read aloud from the paper. His voice as he did so sounded almost like a white man's, Sam noticed.

" 'Indian Leads Illini to Victory over N.C. in Season's Opener. Sets Assembly Hall Scoring Record of 56 Points.' That's the headlines," Akbar said. "Listen to this shit in the story.

" 'Sam Houston Leaping Deer, a freshman starter for the Illini and an Alabama Indian from Texas, showed Illinois the way to victory over North Carolina last night in the Assembly Hall. He went on the warpath against the Tarheels to the tune of fifty-six points, a single-game record for the Assembly Hall. Asked about the sensational performance of the freshman Redskin, Coach Buck Thompson stated that he and his staff had been planning just such a departure from the usual careful slow-down basketball of the Illini. "We knew we were going to run with North Carolina," he said. "Our entire attack was predicated on the fast break, the quickness of our guards, and what we knew we were ready for— all-out run-and-gun basketball. Young Leaping Deer was just the spark we needed to ignite our new strategy." ' "

Akbar stopped reading to laugh. "Listen to that mother lie. Sounds like you made a believer out of him, Leaping Deer." He looked back at the newspaper and then up at Sam. "Rest of it's just about the game. What you think about this shit, man?" he asked, folding the paper crosswise and throwing it on Sam's bed.

Sam shrugged. "I'm not Alabama. I'm of the Coushatta tribe. It said that wrong. My father and mother are Coushatta. The father of my father was Baxter Leaping Deer, also Coushatta. It goes back that way."

"I believe you, I believe you. You don't have to tell me. But you know something? From now on, they gonna call you another tribe, man. They gonna call you Illini. Hell, they even gonna call you *Chief* Illini." Akbar cackled again. "Hey, you ought to seen that crazy fucker last night at half time."

Sam shook his head and looked at a picture of himself in the newspaper. It showed him high in the air, his left arm extended, the ball just leaving his hand as he passed off to somebody not pictured. The caption at the bottom read, "Caution: Warrior at Work."

"One of the brothers told me," Akbar was saying. "Half time when we was in the locker room. You ought to see the cat, man. Place got dark, and a big spotlight hit that big circle in the middle of the court. You know, the big old blue I in the middle of the orange. Band start playing, sound like tom toms, drums. Cowboys and Indians music. Then out comes this big dude dressed in leather clothes, look like Roy Rogers in drag. Had a big headdress on full of feathers, and he's leaning way back while he's drawing his knees up to his chin. They figure he's going to fall over backwards and bust his ass any minute. He got out to where the spotlight was shining, he just cut loose and *danced*. Feet flying every direction. Them white folks in the stands was just going crazy hollering and screaming at that dude carrying on. You know the funniest thing was when he got up close to where the brothers was sitting a little later on. Somebody hollered at him, and you could see him when he looked up in the stands. He's a ghost, man. Just as white as a sheet, had blue eyes and blond hair. Them black loveknots was just a wig sitting on top of his yellow hair."

"Chief Illini?" Sam asked. "Did he have two basketballs?"

"Yeah, right. They told me about that. That's one thing he was good at. He balanced on them balls and rolled all over that big blue I. Talk about something look crazy, man. That must have been it."

Sam looked over at his green trunk and thought about the picture of Chief Illini that Coach Dodge had given Cooper Leaping Deer last spring. He couldn't remember whether Cooper had kept it or passed it on to one of Sam's younger brothers to admire. He promised himself to find out what had happened to the photograph the next time he found himself on Alabama-Coushatta land. Slowly, as he sat on his bed, the image of his father tracing the outline of Chief Illini's headdress on the picture with his forefinger began to rise up in Sam's mind like stone.

"Akbar," he said, "there's not a real Illini Indian around here anywhere, is there?"

"The only real red man in this place is you, baby, looks like," said Akbar. "But, shit, you knew that already, didn't you?"

"Yeah, I guess so," Sam answered and slowly lay back across his bed.

"Well," said Akbar, "I'll let you read your reviews. Looks like you done become the red hope of the Fighting Illini. If we don't see you no more on the bench, at least we can read about you in the newspapers." He left the room in an exaggerated shuffle, looking back over his shoulder and rolling his eyes. Sam sat on the edge of the bed for a long time after Akbar was gone, looking back and forth from the picture of himself in the paper to a blank white spot on the far wall, rising to leave finally just before the bell rang for his literature class.

"You were just super," Sharon Hansen was saying as she and Sam walked away from the English Building. "Art *said* you would be good, but he was surprised as much as I was by how many points you made. I never saw anything like it." On the sidewalk ahead three men dressed in identical sweaters with strange markings stopped chasing a hollow plastic ball they had been hitting to let Sam and Sharon pass. One of them, a pudgy man with close-set eyes and heavy front teeth, took a close look at Sam's face as he stepped past.

"Hey," he called out, looking around at the one holding the over-sized plastic bat and then back at Sam as he moved off. "Great game, guy. Great game."

"Everybody's talking about it," Sharon said across her stack of books. "You must just be really proud." From behind them came the flat sound of the plastic bat meeting the ball again. "I don't mean egotistical," Sharon went on. "You know, just a feeling of accomplishment."

Sam reached down, picked up a dry branch from the sidewalk, and began stripping the bark off it as he walked along beside her. When he reached a knot he couldn't dislodge with his thumbnail, he threw the stick toward a small puddle of water in a gravel driveway. He watched it kick up a shower of drops that glittered in the sun.

"You and Art go places together?" he asked.

"Like the game last night? Oh no, not really. Art just asked me in class one day if I'd like to go see you play in the first game. I'd never been to a college basketball game before. It's really different, isn't it?"

"I don't know," said Sam. "They were taller. I think the music was louder."

"I guess you see things about it I wouldn't. I really enjoyed it, though. It was nice seeing it with Art too. He told me things to notice." They stopped at a curb to let some cars pass. "I mean," Sharon said, "he told me how to watch it, you know? Don't you think he's fun to talk to?"

"Yes," said Sam, thinking of Art and Sharon sitting together watching him play basketball. He wondered what Art had told her to look for.

"I wonder why he wasn't in class today," said Sharon. "I missed hearing him joke around with Sally. I guess she's probably the only person there who hadn't heard about last night."

Sam wouldn't have been able to comment at all on the behavior of Sally Smith during this first day back in literature class. After one quick glance at her, which had caught her eye on him, Sam had spent the rest of the hour studiously regarding the book on his desk and the footwear of the people around him. She had sounded no different to him, from the things she said about the poems they looked at to the way she said them. As the class ended he had scrambled up from his chair to be one of the first ones out of the room, glad the hour was over and thankful she hadn't asked him any direct questions which would have caused him to speak. Maybe it was true that to white women what they called making love meant so little as to be forgotten as soon as it ended. He could go back to the class now, even see her and speak to her directly, and nothing would be meant by it. In some ways it was easier to live around these women than those of the Nation. If this thing he had seen take place between himself and Sally Smith had happened with him and La Wanda Two Tongues on the reservation, they would both have been made different people by it, never able to live again with their spirits unmingled in some way, as they did before. They would have seen each other, and the selves that had lived before the seeing would never live in the same way again.

"Sally's so involved with literature and her ideas that she doesn't even notice most of the things going on around her. I wish

I could be more like her." Sharon slowed to step around a pile of leaves somebody had raked into the middle of the sidewalk. "She's just so dedicated, and she just refuses to let herself be distracted by petty things. Don't you notice that, Sam? I think that anybody that hears her talk for a while just has to realize how dedicated she is. And she really cares about her students. She has helped me so much with my papers, and her insights!" Sharon made a wide gesture with her right hand that she hoped would indicate a complete inability to put into words a feeling of great awe. Sam helped her pick up the two books she dropped, and they continued their walk under the leaf-shedding trees, threading their way through the clots of people moving with and against them.

The more Sharon talked about her admiration for Sally Smith the more she pursed her lips in thought between statements, Sam noticed, and each time she did so, he became more interested in the smooth balance her chin, lips, and nose made together in the late afternoon sun as it cut through the red and gold maples. As they walked, it was getting harder and harder for him to decide what he liked better, the way her face looked in these moments or the way her hair, the heavy yellow of corn tassels, shifted in the light breeze from the north.

"And she really is helpful, just in a practical way," Sharon said further of Sally Smith. "I told her I want to move out of the dorm because of the noise, and she's found me a room on the first floor of the house her apartment's in. Isn't that great?"

Sam allowed that it was and stopped to turn off toward Huff Gym. "I go this way," he said.

"Oh, all right." Sharon shifted her books and tossed her hair back from her face. "Congratulations again."

"What?"

"The game. It was great. You were great."

"When will you move to the room?"

"Saturday, I guess. I'm going to try then."

"I will help you."

"Oh, really? I do have some heavy stuff. A trunk and this girl's giving me an old chair. It needs that. The new room. But I hate to spoil your Saturday afternoon."

"I'll do it."

"Well, thanks. Really, thanks a lot. See you."

Sam nodded and left for practice, deciding to take the long

way that ran by the corn patch. He would have enough time before
the sun fell too low, he thought, watching the shadows creeping
out from the trunks of the trees.

He reached the locker room after most of the others had
already dressed and begun wandering out one by one to the practice court. As he picked up his basket of gear he looked around for
Art Wallace but didn't see him. Off to his left Martin Kroeber was
sitting on a bench carefully tying and retying the laces of his shoes
so that they both had the same length of string left dangling. He
was hunched down so low that his spread knees stuck up to the
level of his ears. After Sam had spoken his name twice, Martin
heard and poked his head up and craned his neck to see who had
called him.

"Hi, Sam," he said. "Long time no see." He jerked his head
back and reflected for a second. "Hey, man, no offense, huh? Just
a, you know, figure of speech."

"Has Art gone out already?" Sam asked and gestured toward
the door with the pair of white socks in his hand.

"You mean Art Wallace?" said Martin, dropping his voice and
looking quickly over each shoulder.

"Yes, Art Wallace."

"Yeah, I guess you wouldn't know. He's hitting the bleachers
again today, man." Martin got the shoes tied to his satisfaction,
kicked each foot up one at a time, and let the heels bounce against
the concrete floor.

"Hitting the bleachers? What is that?"

"Ah, you know, up and down them. I don't know why they
got him out there exactly. Some guys say he was dogging it in
practice, but I never noticed if he was. Maybe it's his attitude or
something. All I know," said Martin, leaning toward Sam and
pitching his voice even lower, "is that he's been out there at the
stadium for two days in a row now. Looks to me like some of the
coaches are down on him. Maybe Chudy. Maybe Thompson himself."

Martin looked over his shoulder again and jumped up,
stretching his arms above his head toward the ceiling. "Hey, Sam,
how high do you think this roof is here? It's over ten feet, I know.
How close am I getting to it from where you're standing over
there? You got an angle on it." He jumped toward it again, but

Sam didn't bother to judge how high Martin could get. He picked up the pair of socks he had just put back in the basket when Martin had begun to talk. Like the jersey and shorts of his practice uniform, like the basketball shoes beneath them in the wire basket, the socks looked perfectly clean and new.

The U of I football stadium, capacity 71,500, was a good mile from the gym, across four or five baseball diamonds and open fields, so that as Sam trotted toward it after practice, he couldn't in the gathering darkness pick out the features of the people moving up and down its bleachers. They looked to him like four or five dots, a little blacker than anything around them as they climbed slowly to the top of the last row of seats, turned, and came down much more quickly toward the bottom. When he got near enough to see better, he noticed a man sitting on one of the steps a little to the side dressed in the white T-shirt and blue windbreaker worn by the group of young men who swarmed in large number about the gyms, locker rooms, and playing fields of the Athletic Department. Graduate students in phys ed, Art had told him, studying to be coaches when they grow up.

As Sam reached the steel-mesh fence around the stadium, the man in the blue coat with the orange I on the back blew a blast on the silver whistle hanging around his neck. The four people running down the bleachers had reached a point about halfway to the bottom, but at the sound of the whistle they all came to a stop, turned around and began running slowly up the rows of seats again. One of them, a burly skin-headed man in gray shirt and pants that had turned black with sweat, fell further and further behind the other three as they climbed.

"It's getting late," called the man with the whistle. "But unless you stay up with the other ones, Palmer, I'm gonna run all of you all night." He raised his voice so the others could hear. "And if you three dog it to let him catch up, I'll sure know it."

Palmer put on a burst of speed which lasted only three or four rows, and by the time he had reached the top of the stands, the other three had turned and passed him on his way up. One of them said something to him as he went by, but the words were lost somewhere in the tons of concrete.

"No talking," said the man with the whistle. "You know better than to say anything to each other." He looked down at his watch and began to hum, tapping with his fingers on his knee to keep time. This time he let the runners reach the bottom of the stands, Palmer lagging seven or eight rows behind, before he again blew his whistle. When the whistle sounded, Palmer turned back for the journey up even though he hadn't yet reached the bottom of the rows of seats.

"No, Palmer, not you. You haven't made it down there yet. You've got to earn that turnaround, boy. You're just getting further behind all the time."

Palmer hesitated, stopped, turned back, and trotted to the bottom. From where he stood outside the fence, Sam could hear Palmer's deep ragged breaths coming as he reached the bottom of the stands. They reminded Sam of the wet whistling sounds he had heard once when Cooper Leaping Deer had slit the throat of a hog for slaughter and had sliced through the windpipe with the same stroke of the knife. The hog had had its head crushed by a blow Cooper delivered with a sledgehammer as it fed on some loose corn Sam's mother had thrown in front of it. As it lay on its side, its legs quivering and its breath coming through the hole in its throat with the slobbering sound of air escaping a torn rubber inner tube, Sam had stood with his young brothers watching. Finally, he had picked up the bloody sledgehammer himself and pounded the top of the hog's head until the wet whistling had stopped. It took so long that when it finally became quiet, Sam's arms were weak and shaking from swinging the hammer. "White girl," Cooper had called him and laughed as he split the hog's hind legs just above the hooves so he could slip a rope through to hoist the carcass to a tree limb.

At the bottom of the last row, Palmer swung his body around to face the tier of seats climbing one by one toward the top of the stadium, alternating blue and orange as they mounted before him. Almost halfway up now the three others drove themselves from one level to the next, their heads down and their arms swinging back and forth as they moved higher. Palmer lifted his shaved head in a long quavery look like a blind man trying to see a flash of light, planted one leg and then stepped with the other toward the first level. He made that one, the next two, stumbled on the row after, caught himself, and finally with his next step jammed the toe of his right foot against the edge of the next row. He fell forward off-balance, and tried to catch himself with his sweaty hands but slipped off the edge of the metal seat and jammed the top edge of his shoulder into the concrete step with the sound of a side of beef falling off the back of a flatbed truck. He lay still for a few seconds and then rolled over on his back, one hand over his eyes and the other reaching for his shoulder. From where Sam stood holding to the steel mesh of the fence, the pale soles of Palmer's shoes looked as big and as fixed in place as tombstones in the white man's cemetery.

"Coach," said Palmer in a voice that sounded small and full of bubbles, "Coach, I can't. I just can't anymore."

"Palmer," said the man in the blue and orange coat, leaving his seat and running up the rows to lean down into the fallen man's face, "get up, you son of a bitch. You yellow quitter. You piece of shit. You've got some more running to do in this stadium tonight, pus-face."

"I can't, Coach. I can't," Palmer said and started to cry, his sobs loud and wet among the empty seats. About then the ones still running passed near where Palmer had fallen as they made their way down. All were in lockstep side by side, and none of them looked at Palmer as he rolled his head back and forth and scrubbed at his eyes with the heels of his hands.

"You guys keep going," said the graduate-student coach in a yearning voice without looking up from Palmer's face.

"What does this shit mean, Palmer? Are you refusing to obey my order to run these seats?" He had taken the whistle from around his neck and was now swinging it by the chain in little tight circles that made the whistle bounce off his left hand each time it went around.

"Answer me, turd-sucker."

Palmer, by this time completely given up to sobbing, his legs splayed out and his bald head sunk down into the darkness between two rows of seats, could only groan in response.

"Palmer, you know what this means, don't you? If you don't obey me in one minute, I'm going to have to tell the Athletic Department that you have quit, you gutless piece of shit. Do you hear that? Quit. I said quit."

"Yes," said Palmer finally, sucking in long breaths and gritting his teeth so he could talk. "Yes, Coach. I quit. I quit."

"Did I hear you right? Did you say you quit? Did you?"

"Yes," Palmer said in a long shaky groan. "I quit. I quit." He rolled himself over and spoke with his face jammed into the cement of the stadium. "I quit. I quit. Oh, Daddy, Daddy, I'm sorry, I'm sorry, but I quit. I quit."

"Oh, well, then, Palmer. That's a different case, isn't it?" the man with the whistle said, straightening up from where he'd been crouched over Palmer's head. "You just go on in now and come back tomorrow and sign the release. Be at Coach Barlow's office at four, and we'll take care of it." He stepped back and replaced the whistle around his neck, studying Palmer as he lay on his belly with his hands over the back of his head.

"Palmer, this is the last thing I'll ever say to you." He spoke in a slow, careful voice. "One thing I want you to remember. You quit because you can't take it. You'll never play Big Ten football because you, you yellow shit, don't have the guts to take it. See you tomorrow at four." He turned away and blew his whistle, a sharp bright sound in the empty concrete bowl.

"You guys," he said to the other three, who had stopped halfway up the stands at the signal, "see you here at four-thirty tomorrow. Be ready to run." He walked off toward the far side of the football field, zipping up the blue coat as he went.

Sam watched Art and the two others come slowly down the stands. One of them, Sam couldn't tell which in the darkness, made a move toward where Palmer was still lying, but somebody pulled at his arm and he continued to the bottom with the others.

"Hey, Leaping Deer," Art said, splitting off from the other two, who began to walk slowly in the same direction the graduate assistant had taken, "I thought that was you." He came over to the fence and leaned against a concrete post and started to shiver as the breeze hit him. He looked wet from his hair down to his shoes.

"Here," Sam said and stripped off his jacket. He threw it over the fence, but it caught on the wire at the top, and Art had to jump twice before he was able to pull it loose on his side.

"I hope I didn't snag it. I left over there in a hurry and didn't bring one."

"Why?" asked Sam, looking from Art to the stadium bleachers. He couldn't hear any more sounds from Palmer, but he could make out his bulk in the same position between the two rows of seats.

"You mean why about the coat, or why about us hitting the bleachers?"

"The bleachers."

"Well, Sam," said Art and hawked up from deep in his throat and spit. "I don't know the technical reason, I guess, but the real reason we've been running over here for the last three days is that they're trying to run us off."

"Run you off? Make you leave here?"

"Not leave the U of I, no, they don't care about that. What they want us to do, see, is what that football guy just did." Art looked up at the stands toward Palmer and leaned his forehead back against the post. He zipped up Sam's jacket and crossed his arms. The sleeves were way too short for him, Sam noticed.

"You mean say you quit?"

"Yeah, they want our scholarships. Poor old Illinois hasn't got enough to go around." Art began speaking in his radio-announcer voice. "It's all a matter of economic necessity in this everchanging world of ours."

"What do you mean?"

"Oh, they're only allowed a certain number of athletic grants-in-aid, and they've decided that the four of us are depriving somebody they might like better. If they can make us do what Palmer just did, there's three more people they can bring in."

"Can't they just tell you to leave?" Sam asked after a minute or so. He felt very conscious of an imperfection in one of the fence wires beneath his hand, and he began to pick at it with a fingernail. Was it just a blob of extra paint, or was it a bubble in the metal of the wire itself?

"Oh, no," said Art. "They play by the NCAA rules. You can't just take away an athlete's scholarship. He's got to ask them to take it away. He's got to say he quits, and he's got to say it in writing before they can give it to somebody else."

Up in the stands, Palmer had sat up and swung his legs over the edge of the row of seats. Sam could see him sitting with his elbows on his knees and his face in his hands. His bald head was whiter than anything around him. From where Sam stood outside the fence, it looked like a pale basketball on top of a big pile of something dark and wet.

"How long will they do this bleacher running?"

"I don't know," Art said through the fence. "Until we quit or until they change their minds." A truck drove slowly up Stadium Road, its motor roaring in a low gear. Sam read the words on its side in the light from the streetlamps: Mayflower Moves the Country.

"It's that fucking Thompson. I think he believes he's got too many forwards. Small quick guards. That's all he talks about now, I hear. He figures he'll run me and Kendall and who's the other guy off. Then he can go for some more quickness."

"Why do you not want to quit?" asked Sam. The hump on the steel wire was more than just paint. His fingernail had yet to budge it or even to make a dent. "Because of the scholarship?"

"Oh, I guess part of it's just to spite the bastards. But it's not all that." Art turned his head to the side and spit again. "I could go on to school without the money, so it isn't just the full ride that I don't want to give up. You remember when we went to that party in Philo and we talked about what we really like about the game? I mean about playing it. The one thing?"

"I remember it, yes."

"Well, that's why I haven't let them run me off yet, I guess. I still want to have the chance to see the look in that fucker's eyes when he knows I've beat him. You must have seen that look fifty times the other night. You know what I'm talking about."

"I guess so," Sam said, and thought back but couldn't picture the look on a single face in his game against the team dressed in blue.

"Well, I hope I can last a while longer," Art was saying. "I don't think I'm that slow." He wiped his forehead on the sleeve of Sam's jacket and straightened up. "Fuck it," he said. "I'm tired. I'm going in. I'll be seeing you."

Sam made one last hard flick with his nail against the bump of metal, but still nothing gave. He stepped back from the fence and looked up at the rows of bleachers. The pale basketball of Palmer's head still balanced on the dark mass beneath it, and no sound but the wind came from the concrete hollow of the stadium.

"Hey, Sam," Art called through the fence between them. "Thanks for the jacket."

Sam waved and walked toward the sound of a motorcycle going up the lighted street. He stuck his hands in his pockets and listened to the motor fade until it sounded like the whine of a mosquito in Lost Man Marsh. He felt cold.

When Sam arrived at the dormitory on Saturday morning to

help Sharon move, he recognized Art's low green car sitting at the curb near a side entrance to the building. As he got nearer, he could see Art's feet sticking out beyond the end of the car from where he was lying on the ground trying to do something with a rope.

"Can you catch this other end?" he said from under the car. "We've got to figure some way to tie that trunk and that other stuff on here."

Sam dropped to one knee beside the car and began fishing for the rope end. Neither he nor Art mentioned anything about the bleacher episode as they loaded the car with the cardboard boxes, lamps, books, and clothes on wire hangers which Sharon and some other woman kept bringing out to the curb in relays. Sam was sure that Art had been going out to the empty stadium for the sessions with the man in the blue coat all week, though, because he had seen no sign of him in the dressing room before or after practice on any of the days. Martin Kroeber had seemed not to know any more about what was going on than he had on Monday and had told Sam the second time he asked him about what was happening with Art and the other two first-year players that he figured what he didn't know wouldn't hurt him and he was going to keep it that way.

"Is that it?" asked Art, tying down the last end of the rope and stepping back to look at the load piled up on the back of the car.

"That's all I own in the world," Sharon said. Although a chilly wind was blowing, she kept patting her forehead as if she was hot. She caught Sam looking at her and smiled. "It's awful, isn't it?"

Sam nodded and looked up at the maple tree near the car where only a few leaves still hung on the top branches. As he watched, two or three more broke loose and were swept down the street by the breeze. Everywhere he looked after they had all three gotten in the front seat of the car and driven slowly off toward Sharon's new room, Sam could see only a few more leaves still between him and the black limbs against the sky, and these grew steadily fewer as they moved along. Even when I am not watching them, Sam thought, these leaves are taken off by the wind. When I am inside and when it is dark, one by one they are carried away, and the sky gets bigger each minute. Soon there will be no leaves to hide it at all.

He forced himself to look over at Sharon where she sat jammed between him and Art, the right side of her body from her knee to her shoulder pressed tightly against Sam. But even this pressure of her weight, shifting slightly here and there as the car bumped over the brick streets, couldn't take his mind off the difference between the sky here, opening up each day wider, and the sky of the Nation, always fixed by the green needles of the pines and cedars. These trees of the Thicket, unlike the oaks and sweetgums, the sycamores and beeches, contained the sky all year and didn't let it show the true depth and emptiness hidden behind the green mask of needles. Here in Illinois in this land of cornfields reaching like the sea past all trees, where the ears of the corn were fed only to hogs and where the few trees that grew gave up all their foliage to the wind, the sky behind reached each day further, naked from horizon to horizon, nothing in it but a low sound of moaning.

"There it is," Sharon said, pointing to a brown house with several doors across its face, all of them bearing a different metal number. "Remember? Sally's up those stairs."

They began to unload the car, taking turns with the boxes and Sam and Art working together on the trunk and the upholstered chair covered with a pattern of pink roses as Sharon held the door open. Each time he passed the foot of the stairs leading up the outside of the house to the apartment of Sally Smith above, Sam kept his head turned toward the side door leading into Sharon's room on the first floor. As he struggled with the last box from the car, a bulky one filled with what felt like pillows and blankets, he heard the squeak of a screen door spring come from above his head. He lost his purchase on the door with the toe of his shoe and it slammed shut, forcing him to turn again sideways and fumble blindly for the handle with two fingers of his left hand. His hand slipped, the box slid in his arms, and he had to let the whole thing settle to the step in front of him.

"Do you need some help?" asked Sally Smith from where she stood at the top of the stairs holding a book cracked open in her left hand.

"It's hard to open," Sam said, leaning forward to try again.

"Yes, you've got your hands full, don't you? Let me just slip by you and see what I can do." She lay the book on the rail and came down the steps. As she reached around Sam to pull at the handle, he caught again the scent of something like watermelons late in the season. He dropped his head forward to clear his nostrils and when he lifted the box again up to chest level he was able to plug them with the smell of wool and cotton.

"Hello, hello," said Art, coming up from behind with a lamp in each hand.

"Here is a large part of my literature class," Sally Smith said, smiling and holding the door open for Sam and his box of bedding.

"We just can't stay away from our teacher, can we, Sam?" Art answered and followed the two of them into the room where Sharon was setting a small table first in one place and then another.

"Hi, Sally," she said. "Just put that box anywhere, Sam. I've got to empty it anyway."

Sam looked back at Art and Sally behind him in the doorway, the light coming from behind into the dark room so that the outline of Art's bulk beside Sally made it look as though his head was missing.

"I think you'll like it here," Sally said. "It's quiet and warm in the winter." She pointed to the ceiling. "I suppose you'll hear me moving around some, though. I'll try to tiptoe."

"Thanks so much for telling me about this place. It's really great to be out of that dorm. I'm just going to love being here."

Everyone stood quiet for a minute and watched Art tip a small glass ball filled with oil and fake snow back and forth in his hand. "Part of the furnishings," he said. "A portable blizzard for those long winter nights." A tiny plastic farmhouse appeared and disappeared as bits of Styrofoam swirled about it.

"You know," said Art, "if you put all this into scale you'd have snowflakes as big as basketballs bouncing off the roof. And that wouldn't be fun, would it?" He put the ball down on the arm of a sofa and patted it.

"Why don't I go upstairs and bring down some wine for a homecoming toast?" asked Sally, looking from one to the other and ending up with her eyes on Sam. "Do we need some glasses?"

"Oh, I've got some," said Sharon and began fumbling in one of the smaller boxes. "Where are they now?"

Sam pushed at one of the boxes on the floor with his foot and spoke in the direction of the heating grate it was sitting on. "I have to go now." When Sharon looked up at him from where she had been searching for glasses, he added, "On a trip."

"Do you have to? I wish you could stay."

"Where do you have to go?" asked Sally Smith, studying the way the hair lay on the back of Sam's head. "If I'm not prying."

"Let me tell her, Sam," said Art. "I don't believe she's heard about the exploits of Sam Leaping Deer, member of English class one oh one.

"Sam is moving in fast company," he said. "Flying to Madison, Wisconsin, this afternoon with the basketball team to play tonight. They thought about sending him by himself, but they need somebody to throw the ball in to him." Art reached over and pushed Sam's shoulder, knocking him off-balance enough to make him have to catch himself.

"What?" said Sally. "Are you on the basketball team?"

"Is he!" Sharon began, but got quiet when she saw how Sally was shaking her head back and forth and regarding Sam with a solemn look on her face.

"I suppose I knew, but never really allowed myself to articulate it. I should have known you were being exploited. The university doesn't bring anyone here from another state without designs on him." She moved a step closer to Sam and laid her right hand on his shoulder, looking earnestly at what she could see of his face. "I sincerely hope you aren't too diminished by the whole sorry scheme they're perpetrating."

"If you think Leaping Deer is diminished or exploited, you ought to have seen North Carolina the other night," said Art. "There's guys on that team who had their whole lives changed by what Sam did to them. I bet by now half of them's become better Christians because of it." Laughing, he picked up the glass ball of snow and began tossing it back and forth from hand to hand.

"Oh, Art," said Sally, looking sorrowfully down at him, "the more accomplished Sam is as a player, the more they'll try to take from him. They're insatiable. The system always is. It uses up the best it can find with no concern for waste, material or human." She looked back at Sam who had started easing his way toward the door and the light outside.

As he reached the street, walking fast and checking his shirt pocket for the sheet of instructions about road games he had been given by Coach Chudy, he heard the door open and slam behind him. He looked back and saw Sharon coming down the sidewalk toward him. Sometime during the course of the move from the dormitory, the scarf she had been wearing over her hair had come loose at one side and slipped back, allowing some strands of hair to fall down over her forehead and across her face. Brushing them back with one hand, she called to him.

"Sam, I wanted to thank you again for helping me move. I wish you could stay longer."

Sam stopped and watched her walk up to him. She looked ready to speak again, but when she stopped at the edge of the sidewalk, she dropped her eyes instead and looked toward some pebbles which the last rain had washed against a grating.

"I know you're in a hurry," she said. "Good luck tonight."

Behind her the side door to the house opened and Sally Smith came out just ahead of Art. Art said something that Sam couldn't hear, and Sally laughed and looked toward the street. In her hand she was carrying a glass which she turned upside down and shook over a pale green bush growing near the sidewalk. Sharon looked back toward the other two and turned to Sam.

"Please come by and see me," she said. "You know where I live now."

"I will come again," Sam said and watched his hand move toward Sharon's as she stood facing him. Just in time he stopped it and put it in his pocket for safekeeping.

"Goodbye," he said and left, hearing behind him the voices of Sally and Art as they came toward Sharon. All the way to the meeting place for the basketball team he matched his steps to the sound running through his head of a Coushatta chant about Rabbit, one of the first songs that children of the Nation were taught by the old people.

The main thing Sam remembered about the trip to Madison to play basketball against a team that shot worse than many high schools he had seen was the airplane ride there. After the plane had climbed to a few hundred feet, it banked to the left and Sam had looked across the person sitting next to him, a second-string center who didn't talk much, and saw the fields, parking lots, and highways beginning to fall into a pattern. Everything looked worked on. The huge patches of corn, browning now in the fall, were arranged in squares and long rectangles. The trees, most of their leaves gone so that they looked like the skeletons of small animals, were arranged in orderly rows and clumps near the buildings and along the fencerows separating the fields. Straining to see past the large nose of the man next to him by the window who was dozing off as the plane climbed, Sam caught a glimpse of the far horizon or at least the place where it ought to be. What he saw was a dark line edged in red fading into a bank of clouds so heavy that they covered all the sky but for a clear space where the plane was flying. As he watched, the red line faded quickly into the black and the light in the plane seemed to glow brighter as the sky outside vanished into mist.

Sam shifted in his seat and looked around him, but no one else seemed to be noticing what was taking place as they all continued together the process of leaving the earth and entering the empty sky. Across the aisle, three or four people were arguing over the playing cards they held in their hands, one of them laughing and shaking his right hand as though he were trying to fling off something that had bit him. Two of the men on the plane were standing in the aisle a few feet up from Sam's seat, blocking the path of a black-haired woman in a light blue suit who was trying to push a cart loaded with bottles and cans past them. One of the men, the guard who played opposite Sam in the backcourt, kept asking her if she lived around here. Each time he did, the other man would laugh in a high cackle and the woman would shake her head and give the cart a little bump against the legs in her way. Outside, the mist grew heavier, and as Sam turned back to see what was left of the light, the window clouded over so thickly that nothing was visible but a layer of fog as deep as any he'd ever seen on the earliest morning he'd spent hunting the farthest swamp of the Big Thicket.

He had fallen back into his seat and closed his eyes, refusing the black-haired woman's offer of drinks and food, and even when Dead Smile had come up to him later and asked if he was feeling sick, he had done nothing more than shake his head in response. It was only after he had felt the wheels of the airplane rolling along the solid ground again that he had allowed himself to look out at the lights of buildings and lampposts sliding by the window.

Outside the plane as they boarded a bus, Sam had looked up at the black sky with no moon and no stars, and had checked the leather pouch about his neck. He did not think of the game waiting to be played, and he tried not to consider the plane ride he would have to take back up into the air later that night. At least it would

be dark all the way back to Illinois, and he would not have to
watch the light being sucked up into the mist and blackness and
emptied into the sky's open mouth.

"Sit down, Chudy," said Buck Thompson and moved his legs
to make room in the aisle seat. Chudy looked pleased and sat
down, careful not to spill his cup of Sprite and ice on the head
coach's knees.

"Well, Coach," he said. "A nice little workout. They sure
weren't North Carolina, but they gave us a chance to polish some
of our patterns. We looked pretty slick inside there, several times."
He looked over at Thompson for agreement, his drink halfway to
his open mouth.

"I guess so." Thompson looked up the aisle to where he knew
Leaping Deer was sitting. By leaning his head toward Chudy he
could see part of the side of Sam's head, the hair so black that it
looked almost navy blue in the yellow overhead light.

"He didn't shoot nearly as much tonight," Chudy said.

"Didn't have to. We were getting inside all night on passes.
His, mainly."

"Yeah, right. Right, Coach."

"Does he ever say anything to you? Not that I care if he even
talks at all. At this rate, anyway."

"No," Chudy said. "Well, I mean now and then he'll say
something. But you know how quiet he is." Chudy thought for a
minute and added something he'd heard once in a coaching clinic at
Lexington, Kentucky. "These kind of kids are not at ease with
language, you know." He cut a glance at Thompson's face and hid
his mouth with his Sprite glass.

Up ahead of the two men, the Indian's head stayed still, the
same swatch of hair fanning out from the seat back in the same
amount and at the same angle as it had been since Thompson had
been watching it. Most of the other players scattered in the seats up
and down the aisle were asleep, though from a couple of spots
Thompson could hear conversation.

"I've got a feeling, Chudy," he said, leaning back in his seat
and letting his eyes half-close as the cool air from the plastic nozzle
above his head washed over his face. Chudy stayed quiet, waiting
to hear what the head coach was about to say. Maybe it would be
something he hadn't said yet to the other assistants. Later on

Chudy could drop it in conversation, and then if Thompson repeated it, people would think that he and the old man thought along the same lines, had the same kind of basketball mind.

"Now it doesn't pay to get excited too soon about anything. Especially basketball." Thompson stopped and looked over at Chudy. "And especially kids like this one."

"Right, Coach," Chudy allowed and sipped at his Sprite.

"But on the other hand, he showed us tonight he can be more than just a gunner. How many assists did he have? Ten, eleven?"

"Twelve," Chudy spat out, glad he'd happened to talk to the scorer. He rewarded himself with a chunk of ice from the plastic cup.

"So, all right. He can do that too. But the thing I'm really thinking about is the kind of visibility he can give us. Look at the color he's got. He's just perfect to come along just now with this centennial year and all that stuff. See, the P.R. office has been pumping out copy for over a year about it, and we've got this game scheduled for Centennial Day with Ohio State. You see what that means."

"Uh-huh," said Chudy. "Yeah, of course. I see all right." He busied himself with the last chunk of ice, trying to dislodge it from the bottom of the cup. Just as he tongued the ice loose and considered whether to say something else, Thompson began talking again.

"The word's already starting to get out about him. The connections are just perfect. Look, he's some kind of Indian, he's a freshman, it's the Illinois Centennial, we're the Fighting Illini. It's all matched up. We've already had all this publicity to get it set up. What all this means, Chudy," said Thompson, shifting in his seat and craning his neck to look up the aisle, "is that there'll be all kinds of media people there. And if he puts on the kind of show he's been doing so far, it'll be all over the country."

Thompson caught the stewardess's eye and held up two fingers. She straightened up from where she'd been sitting on the arm of somebody's seat and went toward the back of the plane. From his aisle seat, Chudy riveted his eyes on the flexing muscles at the backs of her knees as she moved away.

"That'd be good for us then, wouldn't it?" he asked, looking away from the stewardess after she'd stopped at the drink cart.

"It'd be good for us all right. If the Indian does his stuff that night, it'll mean the most notice for Illinois basketball since I don't know when. What I'm talking about, Chudy, is television interviews, UPI and AP headlines, and cover stories. Cover stories, Chudy. When's the last time you've been associated with a basketball program that made the cover of a national magazine?"

Thompson took the two miniature bottles of Wild Turkey from the tray the stewardess was shoving at him and cracking them one at a time, poured the bourbon slowly over the ice in the plastic glass.

"Thanks, honey," he said. "You give good service."

"Always glad to serve the Fighting Illini," she said, pouting her lips into a little bow and stepping back from the side of Chudy's leg where he had let it drift into contact with her thigh as she leaned across him with Thompson's liquor.

"It never happened," Chudy said, watching the hips move away from him up the aisle.

"What?"

"I mean what you said. Being associated with a program that made the cover of a magazine. Unless you count *Coaching Clinic.*"

"No, Chudy," Thompson said, feeling his first drink of the Wild Turkey take hold in his throat and chest. "I don't mean *Coaching Clinic.* I'm talking about national visibility. I'm talking about *Sport.* Hell, I'm talking about the cover of *Sports Illustrated.* And I say, fuck the cover jinx. I'd like to have the damn jinx to worry about, for a change, by God."

Up the aisle the stewardess had resumed her perch on the arm of the seat and was again allowing the side of her thigh, high up near the hip, to jiggle with the plane's vibrations against the forearm of the man sitting there, Tom Duncan, agriculture major from Mattoon and president of the Illinois chapter of the Fellowship of Christian Athletes. Tom felt a little guilty about not moving his arm, but it was dark in the dim aisle lights, and besides, they were talking about Duroc shoats and whether or not Jesus Christ was coming again soon. So until the stewardess got up to tell the Indian freshman to fasten his seatbelt for the descent into Champaign-Urbana, Tom sat in the same position, having a good discussion with the young lady while his arm went dead and the coaches talked in their seat down the aisle behind him.

Dirty Boy and Rabbit

"Is there much, you know, camaraderie among the guys on the team? I mean especially between you two." The reporter from the Chicago newspaper pushed his glasses up the bridge of his nose and looked back and forth from Sam to Akbar. The nose seemed to be the biggest thing he owned, jutting out from his face and hanging over his top lip like an outsized beak. From the side, Sam thought, he looks like Red Bird. He tried to remember what Red Bird said to the Coushatta youth who was trying to get back across the ocean in the story McKinley Short Eyes used to tell the children of the Nation. He came up with it in a second or two. *"Coushatta warrior,"* Red Bird said from his perch on a huckleberry bush, *"something big is coming after you."*

"Say what?" asked Akbar, and Sam looked away from the reporter's beak toward the notepad and pencil in his hand.

"Camaraderie. I mean, you know, do the guys horse around a lot with each other? Is it a tight bunch? Do you have nicknames you call each other? Stuff like that."

"I dig," said Akbar. "You mean like in the locker room or on the court when we jest with each other." He cut his eyes toward Sam and leaned back to ponder the question just put to him.

"Oh yeah, man. It's a real feeling of closeness among all us dudes. Right, Leaping Deer?"

Sam made a short humming sound in his throat and tried to remember what happened next to the Coushatta in the story. Somewhere along the way he found three magic chunk stones, but was it before or after Red Bird's warning?

"Could you give me an example of some of this closeness, Ameer? Like what do you and Leaping Deer talk about here together, you know, being roommates and all?" The reporter poised his pencil to write and looked down at his pad with a serious face.

"Shit, man, you can call me Jones," said Akbar. "Well, you see, the typical thing we two like to discuss of an evening is our individual moves. Understand, it's a highly intellectual game." Akbar stood up and began to walk around the room as he talked, gesturing with his right hand and using his left to stroke his chin in thought. Each time he passed the chair where Sam was sitting, he either let his chin drop or raised his eyebrows as though he were scared or surprised. After the first couple of times, Sam had to look off to keep his face straight.

"What we do," Akbar was saying, "is plan our movements to the basket, away from the basket, with the ball, without the ball, our passes, our dribbling, and our general court strategy. We choreograph our game. One thing we never forget, though." Akbar interrupted his stroll and looked down at the pad where the reporter was scribbling. "One thing we never forget. You gonna want to get this down right. And that's latitude for ad libs."

"You mean like when an opportunity opens up you hadn't planned for?" The reporter looked up, his eyes shining. His glasses had slipped again, but in the heat of his note-taking he didn't bother to fix them.

"Right. You got it. We sorta retain our license to free-lance. We ain't gonna lock ourselves into a system. Uh-uh."

"Great," the reporter said, feeling relaxed and warmed up. He turned toward Sam and cocked his head back so that his nostrils seemed to be taking aim at Sam's chest.

"What do you say to all this, Leaping Deer? You must have something to add to the topic." The reporter smiled encouragingly.

Sam studied the Red Bird beak for a minute and shook his head. "No," he said. "Akbar says more than I can."

"Well, all right, then. Something else I want to ask you about. Several things actually." Pausing, the reporter looked at Sam and then swung back toward Akbar. "I want to level with you fellows," he said, thinking to himself that from the look of things, he'd won the trust and confidence of these two guys by now, strange pair though they might be.

"O.K. What I'm interested in and what any reader would like to know is this. Here you are together, roommates. A black dude and, well, what'll I say, an Indian brave. You're thrown together by fate or by chance at the U of I to play basketball. You're both freshmen, you're both at a predominantly white school. One of you has made the starting lineup in his first year and is setting scoring records. Now, the question for both of you is what's your response? There's gotta be problems, right?"

"Uh-*uh*," said Akbar in a loud voice, wagging his head back and forth, "no sir. There ain't no problems at all. Not none at all for me anyway. No sir. I'm just proud to be here. Improving my skills, looking forward to being able to start some day, and getting myself a good education. That's the main thing for me."

"That's great to hear," the reporter said and wrote rapidly on his notepad. "What about you, Leaping Deer? Any problems of adjustment, or do you agree with your roommate?" He swivelled his nose back around in Sam's direction and waited for an answer.

It was after Red Bird had warned him that the Coushatta had found the magic chunk stones, Sam remembered. Then he had armed himself with the stones and climbed into the branches of a long-needle pine to hide from the spotted panthers and their master, the Man-Eater. But what about the Coushatta's three sisters? They belonged somewhere in the story, but just where Sam couldn't come up with. The reporter lifted his eyebrows above the Red Bird beak and flashed Sam a grin that showed a lot of small teeth.

"Yes," Sam answered the question, "what Akbar believes is true."

"Dynamite," said the reporter. "Just goes to show, huh? What a fine comment. I mean really fine." He flipped a page in his notebook and made underlining motions.

"Now, a question or two just for you, Leaping Deer." He looked back over his shoulder at Akbar who grinned and nodded his head up and down. "Your time will come, son. With your kind of ability and attitude, you're bound to play a lot of roundball for the Illini in seasons to come." He turned back to Sam, glad he'd thought to say something encouraging to the black kid.

"Here's the situation, Leaping Deer. Tomorrow, you're the

starting guard against the Ohio State Buckeyes on Illinois Centennial Day. The university is celebrating its hundredth birthday, and you're an Indian playing for the Illini against the defending Big Ten Champs. You're representing your university, and you're representing your people with all their fighting spirit and spunk. This early in the season you've got the second highest scoring average per game in the nation, and you're only a freshman. The pressure, face it, is intense. Maybe paralyzing. In a couple of sentences, what's your response to all this?" Leaning forward in his chair, the reporter looked ready to charge something, no matter how big or mean it was.

Sam dropped his eyes to the toe of his right shoe and studied a long grass stain along one side of the rubber sole. Across the room Akbar leaned against his desk and looked from Sam to the reporter and back, his lips pursed tightly together as though he was trying to restrain a sound that badly wanted out. When he saw Sam glance at him, he rolled his eyes back in his head until all that showed were the whites.

"Let's put it this way," the reporter said, scratching behind his ear with the business end of his pencil. "How do you feel right now?"

"The same," Sam said. Were the three sisters in the story lost or were they being held prisoner, he wondered. There was another animal in it somewhere, too, some other kind of bird maybe.

"Calm, confident, ready," the reporter said in a steady tone, pausing after each word for a full two seconds. "Unflustered, cool," he added and stood up, flipping his notebook shut and slipping it into a coat pocket.

"I know the story I'm going to write," he said, "and I believe I know the game you're going to play, Leaping Deer. It's been a pleasure meeting you. And you too, Ameer."

"Jones, man. Feel free." Akbar offered the reporter his hand like a white man, Sam noticed, not like he did with the blacks who occasionally came by the room to play cards, talk, and smoke grass. The reporter was hip, though, and came back at Akbar with a soul handshake after the first one was finished.

"Good luck," said the reporter. "I'll be there. I wouldn't miss the chance to see you in action." He turned and with one last push of his glasses up the bridge of his nose, he slipped through the door and left.

After he was gone, Akbar sat on the edge of his bed for almost five minutes, laughing and saying the word *shit* over and over in various inflections, durations, and strengths. Sam thought about Red Bird beaks and continued trying to reconstruct the half-remembered story about the Coushatta, the three lost or captured sisters, and the vague animal that seemed to be the key to something important. Finally, Akbar stood, reached for a jacket and looked over at Sam.

"Let's go see that torchlight parade. Gonna start in a little while. Say it's going to be a big deal, man. Once in a hundred years."

Sam picked up a book entitled *Structure and Meaning*, rippled its pages twice and tossed it onto his desk next to three or four other volumes. It landed at a slant on a pile of papers, and he had to move fast to keep it from sliding to the floor.

"All right," he said and followed Akbar into the hall, trailing his fingers along the top of the green tin trunk as he passed it and remembering to switch out the light before he closed the door.

By the time they got within eight or nine blocks of Green Street, the route of the U of I Centennial Parade, they began passing cars parked in haphazard patterns everywhere: along the sides of the street, nosed up into the yards of houses along the way, in the way of other parked cars, three or four abandoned in the main line of traffic itself. As they passed one driveway blocked by a large blue Dodge with a white vinyl top, a man in yellow pants, probably the owner of the house, was bending over next to the front of the car with a screwdriver letting the air out of the near tire. Over the hiss of the escaping air, they could hear him urging two children to go into the house for crayons to mark on the white vinyl top. "Don't you want to draw some pictures?" he was saying.

The nearer they came to the street where the bands and floats and torchbearers would be marching, the thicker the crowd of people became. At one point Sam climbed up on a mound of dirt in front of the construction site of a new hamburger place and looked forward toward Green Street. The bobbing heads, moving up and down randomly in the dim light from the streetlights and the solid line of car headlights, looked like the surface of Lake Tejas being broken up into rises and depressions by a heavy rain. The mass of heads was so thick and constant you could skip rocks off it, he thought.

"Look at them mothers," Akbar said. "Listen at them."

They stood together on the mound of dirt for a minute, lifted above the men, women, and children locked in the slow flow toward Green Street, and paid attention to the sound around them. It was low and high, sharp and dull, a compound of voices, cries, and laughter. It put Sam in mind of the way Long King Creek roared and gurgled under the state highway bridge when the spring rains brought its level up high enough to rip at the tree roots along the bank and tear the pale early leaves off the lower limbs. But the sound of the torchlight parade was more various than that. Now and then it had sirens in it, screeching brakes, car horns, an occasional low thud as one vehicle tore into another one's bumper or fender or radiator. Nearer the parade route itself, the sounds included the bullhorns of the police trying to control the crowd and keep the street clear, the high voices of women and girls shrieking either from pain or great joy, it was impossible to tell which, and from far up the street the first faint rattles of drums and pealing of bells as the Torchlight Centennial Parade got under way.

As the crowd, eight or ten deep on the sidewalk where Sam and Akbar stood, heard the first sounds of the first unit in the parade start up, it gave voice to a deep roar which lasted for a full minute. It was the same sound a home crowd made when the best player on the other team happened to foul out late in a game, Sam thought. It had blood in it.

"What these fuckers so worked up about?" asked Akbar. "They sound like they drunk or crazy." He pointed from where he and Sam were standing on some concrete steps set into the front of a yard to a family group just below them. "Look at that dude. He's wearing a full Peoria. White shoes, white belt, white tie." As they watched, the woman standing next to the man leaned toward him, poked her face up to the side of his head as though to whisper something, and then sank her teeth in his ear until the blood came. The man bellowed and started swinging around in a little tight circle, but the woman held on gamely to her grip until he managed to slug her on the side of the head and neck three or four times with his right fist.

"Dad hit mom," their eight- or ten-year-old son said in a flat voice to his sister, but nobody else around them seemed to notice anything. When Sam looked back at the couple in a minute or two, they were holding hands peaceably and looking expectantly up the street for the parade. Every now and then the man dabbed at his

ear with a neatly folded handkerchief and looked down at it to see
what he'd gathered.

As the first contingent of the parade got nearer, its torches
winking and bouncing in long uneven lines like lightning bugs, the
crowd began to shift and shudder, unraveling at the edges into
groups of two or three which ran out into the middle of the street,
challenging the police lines for three or four seconds before they
either came back to where they'd begun or crossed over to the
opposite curb. At one point, one of the street crossers, a bearded
long-haired man wearing a colorful strangely cut shirt like the ones
Akbar favored, even though the man wasn't black, slipped on a
patch of oil and fell flat on the street. The crowd sucked in its
breath with a deep sighing sound, and when a policeman near the
fallen man reached down and grabbed him by the hair at the back
of his neck, let the breath go in a great shout of approval.

At the foot of the steps below Sam and Akbar, the man with
the bitten ear and the full Peoria turned to answer his wife, who
was too short to see what had happened. "They got one," Sam
heard him say. "They got one down in the street." Putting his
hands to his mouth, the man turned back toward the street where
the policeman had the bearded man up now and was moving him
toward the curb at a fast clip. "Hit him," yelled the father of the
family. "Hit that dirty scum."

The wife jumped up and down beside her husband trying to
see, and the son pulled at his father's arm demanding to be lifted up
to see the policeman hit him. As the man leaned over to pick up the
boy, the woman grabbed her husband, kissed him full in the
mouth, and began jumping up, trying to get a clear view over the
heads in front of her. By the time the father got the boy up into the
air, though, the policeman had shoved the bearded man back into
the crowd and the first torchbearers of the parade were within a
hundred feet of the steps where Sam and Akbar were standing.

Sam looked away from the family scene and sucked at the
bitter piece of root he held beneath his tongue. Before him, what
had looked like lines of lightning bugs from several blocks away
was now a string of half-grown boys in military uniforms carrying
wooden poles with burning cans on the ends of them. The black
smoke trailing off the flames smelled to Sam like the oily material
the Texas Highway Department used to repair holes in the road
that cut across the reservation. He tried not to breathe too deeply
and looked farther up the street to see what was coming behind the

first wave. The crowd around him had become quiet now that the parade had actually reached it, and it became even calmer as various officials in limousines crept by in low gear, waving their hands out the windows and pretending to recognize people in the throng.

"That dude's the president, man," said Akbar, pointing toward a long orange vehicle sporting large I's on the hood and doors and carrying four elderly men and women. Sam looked, but couldn't distinguish any faces, so he turned back to see what was coming next, something the crowd liked, judging from the cheers, whistles, and screams that kept pace with its advance.

The float came into sight over the heads of the crowd, first a large green John Deere tractor, then the flatbed platform it was pulling. Along the sides of the float were large signs proclaiming the same thing as did the cloth banners strung from posts at the front and back of the platform. "Walt Disney's Abe Lincoln," it said in big letters, and beneath that another line of print: "From New York's World's Fair." A different hand had added another line in a different colored paint: "Illinois, Land of Lincoln."

On the platform itself someone had built a small version of a log cabin with a window and a door and a chimney out of which curled the white fumes from a large bucket of dry ice. Around the platform in two neat stacks and a couple of looser piles were split rails weathered gray from the elements and a stump with some wedges and a splitting maul. Abe himself sat in the same chair he'd occupied at the World's Fair, but his clothing was not the same as it had been there. Phil Rodgers, the man who had contracted with the Disney Studios for the right to borrow Abe for the U of I Centennial Parade, had been able to persuade the Projects Committee to dress Abe in the kind of clothes he would have worn as a young man learning his trade as politician and railsplitter in the State of Illinois. So what Sam, Akbar, and the rest of the crowd saw as the float slowly crept near was Abe sitting in his chair attired in blue denim pants and a lighter blue workshirt. In his right hand, firmly fastened with wire so tightly that it was beginning to cut through the latex flesh, was a child-sized shiny double-bit axe.

At about the time the float drew even with where Sam was standing, a small boy who had been crouched down behind Abe's chair reached over and rabbit-punched Abe on the back of his neck, setting off the switch hidden beneath the hairline. Abe dropped his head forward, raised it again, and began to shift in his seat, squirming first to the left, then to the right. He began to rise slowly with a series of little jerks, pushing off from the chair arm with his left hand and chopping at the other side of the chair with his axe. Sam watched a small chip of chair wood sail off the platform and be seized by a middle-aged lady whose legs were wrapped in several yards of Ace bandage. She held the chip up high above her head, and the crowd gave her a short, but hearty, cheer.

About halfway up out of the chair, Abe hesitated and began to rock back and forth as though he had something on his mind, but after the boy with him had given him a push from behind, he straightened up with one last click, rather louder than the others, and stood facing the back of the John Deere tractor. He turned his head from side to side a couple of times, raised his left hand to his face and stroked his beard, dropped the hand to his side and opened his mouth. His lips curled and flexed, he slashed the air with the axe once, and he began to speak in a low rasping voice full of static and electrical noises. "Shhh," hissed the crowd, and it got quiet enough to hear Abe fairly distinctly.

"Our forefathers," he was saying, "brought forth upon this continent a new nation, conceived in liberty and dedicated to the proposition that all men are created equal." At the word *equal*, Abe made what sounded like a mechanical hiccough and began to stretch his mouth open wider and wider. He lifted his axe high in the air and acted like he wanted to bring it down briskly but was being restrained by an invisible force. In a series of tremors that began at the level of his body where the large belt buckle held the jeans tightly cinched around his belly, Abe began to shake as if he were having fever chills. The chills got harder, and the axe in his right hand trembled as though Abe were holding back a blow only at great emotional cost. By the time his upper body had begun to collapse in on itself, then straighten and collapse again more and more rapidly, the boy on the platform had walked around to the front of the sixteenth president and faced him as if he were used to this sort of behavior. Staying carefully away from the axe in Abe's hand, the boy reached up toward his face, touched a button disguised as a mole, and Abe relaxed enough for the boy to ease him back into his chair, bending his legs at the knee one at a time and pushing him on the tops of his shoulders until he was well seated. Abe seemed calm, but being cut off in the middle of his speech had left him with his mouth open and just the tip of his blood-red tongue sticking out.

"The poor man," said a woman standing near Sam, "what he had to go through with the Civil War and all."

"Yes," said the woman next to her. "His wife was supposed to be crazy, you know."

The boy on the platform crouched down behind the chair again, and the float moved away, pulling Abe on toward his next speaking appearance.

"The Great Emancipator," Akbar said. "Look like he done developed a little hitch in his get-along."

"Yeah," said Sam. "Sad and happy. Enemy and friend."

"Say what?"

"Nothing," Sam answered, thinking of Mrs. Hubbard every week or so pointing out the two faces of Lincoln in the picture on the wall of the American history class back at Big Muddy. He wondered if seeing Disney's version of the president would have meant a lot to her.

After Abe's float had moved on, several high school bands playing different selections marched along the parade route, all headed up by heavy-thighed girls twirling batons and all sounding just the least bit flat. Now and then Akbar would lean over to Sam and point out the various pluses and minuses of the majorettes strutting by, speaking loudly to be heard over the bands' horns and drums and the noises of the crowd. Sam was looking closely at the backs of one set of legs to see what Akbar meant by doughmarks, when suddenly Akbar stopped talking right in the middle of his explanation of the phenomenon.

Sam looked away from the silver-clad bottom he had been studying and saw a large open space behind the last line of marchers in the Tolono High School Band. What had caught Akbar's attention occupied the center of the space. It was an old black woman, tall and large-boned but skinny in the way only a formerly heavy-bodied person can be. She was wearing Converse All-Star basketball shoes and a red, white, and blue costume made up of patches of many different materials arranged in no particular design. On her head was a large cardboard hat shaped like the headgear Sam had seen Pilgrims wearing in history book pictures and trimmed around the crown with tiny U.S. flags and what looked like Coca Cola bottle caps.

As the two watched, the woman moved in a half-shuffle, half-step from one side of the street to the other, dancing in time to the tune being played by the Tolono band, the theme from a TV show interspersed periodically with *America, the Beautiful.* She came close to the curb, working her body up and down in a tight little pattern, and several voices in the crowd called out, "Mama Freedom." The old woman opened her mouth and cackled, flapping her elbows vigorously, and picked up her step a beat or two. "Boogie down," she shouted, throwing back her head and letting her mouth drop wide open. Sam could see that her gums were blue in the light.

"Jesus," said Akbar, watching the old woman work away from them to the other side of the street, the cardboard sign with *Mama Freedom* crayoned on it now visible on her back. "You see that, man? Aunt Thomasina. That's what you call that shit. Old hanky-headed bitch." Akbar jiggled up and down on the concrete step, looking nervous and sticking out his lower lip as he shifted around.

"Look there," Sam said to him, pointing to the next line of women, dressed in sequins and carrying silver clubs. By the time that group had marched by, Akbar seemed calmed down and satisfied to watch some more of the Centennial Parade, although now and then he would look back up the street in the direction Mama Freedom had gone as if by concentrating he might still see her.

In a few more minutes Sam began to feel restless and started looking here and there to spot a way out of the massive clot of people crowded around him on the steps. Just about the time he thought he saw an opening, the sound of some kind of chant from the parade route itself made him turn back and again regard Green Street. Two groups, one immediately behind the other in the line of march, seemed to be trying to outshout each other.

The first was made up of four lines of dark-skinned men, some bearded and wearing long robes and cloths tied to their heads, some clean-shaven and dressed in the uniform of jeans and shirt any student might wear. What they all had in common was what they carried in their right hands, gesturing with it as they slowly moved along behind the parade unit in front of them, a flatbed truck lined with Gold Star Mothers in long pastel dresses, staring grimly straight ahead from their steel folding chairs. It took

Sam a few seconds to recognize the objects the dark men were shaking at the backs of the Gold Star Mothers, and when he did, he still felt puzzled.

The four or five feet of rubber tubing each held were pieces cut from a garden hose, and the oversized wooden gas-pump nozzles at one end of each piece had been made from flat sheets of wood by someone with a saw. So at about the same time some unit far up the parade route broke down, causing the group of dark-skinned men to stop their advance and begin marching in place, Sam got a good chance to look closely at them.

As the men stepped in rhythm, they chanted in unison and shook their gas-pump hoses together. "Oil, oil, U . . . A . . . R," they said over and over, giving the sections of hose a classy little lift at the end of each sequence. "Oil, oil, U . . . A . . . R . . ." Most of the voices, chanting in what was obviously a foreign tongue to them, were baritones and basses, but there were some pitched high enough to give the cheers a raw cutting edge. One of the sharpest of these, sounding to Sam like a young fox with its foot caught in a trap, came from the man nearest the curb, a man small and drawn-up and dressed in a striped robe. Each time he chanted a syllable, his body hunched and jerked as though he were coughing up phlegm. The dark bearded face looked familiar beneath the white cloth framing it, and at one point, as the man swung himself to the right in his marching strut, Sam was able to get a good look at him head-on.

His eyes seemed to settle on Sam's face, glittering, and in the middle of his shout, the man opened his mouth in a wide grin. Raising his hose toward Sam, he shook it in a little salute and yelled something in his high voice which cut through the deeper shouts of the other marching men. At the sound of his voice, they hesitated for a couple of beats and then shifted into another cheer from their arsenal, the high voice of the small man setting the pace. "Third World Brothers, Third World Brothers, Third World Brothers," they began to shout, having a hard time with the *th* sound, Sam noticed. At the end of each sequence of words, they all shook their hoses and wooden devices in the air above their heads, all but the small hunched-up man near the curb. Instead, he swept his hose toward Sam in a beckoning gesture, his eyes fixed and shining.

Up ahead in the parade route, whatever had been clogging the

progress on Green Street moved, and the truckload of Gold Star
Mothers jerked into motion, shaking a couple of the Mothers who
happened to be sitting in wobbly chairs and causing the others to
raise their hands either to their hairdos or their eye-glasses. The
float crept ahead, and the dark men with hoses began to move off
in pursuit, still chanting the Third World Brothers cheer. As long
as the little man with the high sharp voice was able to pick Sam out
of the crowd, he continued to look back and make gestures with
his hose, pointing now with his left hand to his own chest and then
to the line of men next to him.

"What are they?" a woman in the crowd asked her husband
standing with his hands on his hips as he watched the group move
off.

"It's some of them foreigners," he said. "Goddamn A-Rabs.
They got all our oil." He hawked up a big wad and spit.

"Leaping Deer," Akbar said. "That little scrunched-up fucker
kept looking at you and making signs. He know you, man?"

"That's Fawzi Kahwli," said Sam, leaning back into the crowd
so that he was blocked from view by a woman next to him in a long
cloth coat trimmed with what looked like possum fur. "Naw, he
doesn't know me."

"He sure act like he did," Akbar said, rocking back and forth
on the step beside Sam and cutting his eyes at him.

"He knows less about me than Rabbit knows about Buzzard," said Sam, borrowing a proverb from one of McKinley Short
Eyes' stories, this one about the time Buzzard fooled Rabbit into
letting him practice medicine on a wound that Rabbit had made in
his own hide. Buzzard had killed Rabbit and eaten him, of course,
and Rabbit's last scream, which Short Eyes liked to demonstrate
with a high quavery bubbling sound from deep in his throat,
couldn't have been too different from what Sam was now hearing
from the group passing in front, the one whose yells had been
drowned out earlier by the Third World Brothers.

This unit of the parade, which Dr. Philip Rodgers, Parade
Marshal, had included in the official Centennial Parade Program
under "Opinion, Advocates of," was all female, and despite the
coolness of the Illinois November wind, all the women were wearing T-shirts. The emblems on the fronts of the black shirts were
large white circles with what Sam judged to be arrows jutting
down from them in the direction of the street. Most of the women

had matching designs on their foreheads drawn in either dark brown or red, depending on whether the artists had used blood or paint.

The organizer of this parade unit, Letty Ford from Chicago, Madison, Berkeley, and points east, had urged all the marchers to use blood in making their designs. "If it isn't your time," she had said, "some sister will share her statement of blood with you." Only a handful of the sisters had taken her suggestion, though, some refusing on philosophical grounds which they explained at length and some for reasons of squeamishness which they didn't state at all.

As the women passed, led by two people with a cloth banner proclaiming in large letters "U of I Chapter W.O.M.B.," the crowd on either side of the street accompanied their progress with a mixture of catcalls, hisses, and shouts. A large, well-dressed man to Sam's left, whose face was so clean-shaven it looked skinned, leaned forward and bellowed at the line of women walking closest to the curb near him. "What these dykes need," he said and paused to draw another breath, "is a good hard reaming."

Whirling from where she walked in line, a thin sharp-featured woman whose breasts through her black T-shirt were all nipple stopped to face the man who had yelled. "Who's going to ream us, buster?" she asked in a voice that didn't match her size. "You?"

"Lady," said the man in the business suit, "I wouldn't fuck any one of you with his dick." He pointed to a bald man next to him who grinned and looked down modestly at the pavement.

"By the looks of him," the woman answered, "the asshole hasn't got one." She skipped back into line and regained her place, and the bald man gazed up with a hurt look at the man who had pointed at him.

"Why you pointing at me?" he said and tugged at the man's coat sleeve. The man who had yelled shrugged, jerked his arm away, and moved off a couple of steps.

The two women holding the banner at the head of the group began to shout in unison, and the women behind answered them in one voice. "Women Only," the leaders said. "Men Begone," came the reply. Below where Sam stood on the concrete step, the woman who had bitten her husband's ear slipped her right hand under his white belt and gave it a hard pull. He reached down with both hands and began bending her fingers back one by one to pry himself loose, not saying a word or looking back.

"Here comes your homeboy," said Abkar, tapping Sam on the shoulder and pointing past the float in front toward the next unit coming down Green Street. Sam looked away from the woman below him, who had now grabbed her husband's white belt with her other hand, and turned to see what Akbar was talking about. He was beginning to feel that too much was going on to stand all at once. It was like watching the small children of the Nation clubbing catfish in the shallows of Long King Creek late in the summer when the water fell low enough in places to show the backs of the fish as they burrowed deep into the mud. Here one child was methodically pounding a fish head into jelly, there one had cut himself on a sharp spine on a fish's back and had sat down in the mud to squall, in another place a six-year-old had prized a fish over on its back and was haggling its belly open with a butcher knife as it flopped beneath him. It was something that made you dizzy, but something you had to watch.

What Akbar had seen was another flatbed truck moving slowly toward them in the parade line. On its door were painted the words "Amber Dawn Farm, Homestead, Illinois," and on its bed stood several people in a circle around a big wooden stake to which was tied Rayna Gouch. On her head she was wearing a long black wig knotted into two plaits, and she was dressed in a buckskin outfit covered with colored beads in an intricate pattern. A white cardboard sign around her neck on a string declared her to be Mother Red America, and the cloth banners at the front, sides, and back of the truckbed proclaimed in script letters "Red Man's Country, White Man's Rape." Walks Dead stood immediately in front of Mother Red America, and like the other seven or eight RAMS, his face was painted a dead white with a black stripe across the mouth. In place of the little axe in his belt, Walks Dead now carried an uncased pocket calculator, and he wore high black rubber boots on which were painted a series of letters: ITT, CIA, IBM, ATT, FBI.

About every twenty feet or so of the truck's progress, Walks Dead would whirl from his position in front of Rayna Gouch and turn toward where she stood tied to a four-by-four stake with bits of red, white, and blue bunting and make cutting motions on her throat with a huge white slide rule. Each time he did, Rayna would let loose with a scream that had in it something of the sound of a circle saw cutting through knotty pine. Then she would stretch her mouth open, stick out what looked like half a foot of tongue, and let her head roll to one side. During this performance, the rest of the RAMS kept up a steady chant to the rhythm of a couple of drums being pounded by the man Sam remembered as Dennis and another person he couldn't recognize behind the white paint.

As the truckload of RAMS moved along, somebody in the crowd began clapping his hands in time to the drumbeat, and others began joining in until the drums themselves were almost drowned out. "It's their native chant," a woman standing on the other side of Akbar hollered. Just about then, somebody lit a string of firecrackers and threw them out into the middle of the street, disrupting the hand-clapping and causing one of the drummers to lose the beat. The other one, Dennis, slowed, tapped a couple of more times, and stopped. Then he looked up for directions from Walks Dead, who had just finished cutting Mother Red America's throat again and was standing in the middle of the truck-bed slowly extending his arms to full length in front of his chest.

"He's either gonna fly or do a deep kneebend," Akbar said to Sam.

Now that the drummers had stopped, the crowd had quit clapping and was beginning to push in toward the street a little, causing Sam and Akbar to teeter on the edge of the concrete step where they were standing. Sam leaned back against the chest of whoever it was pushing from behind, but he felt no more effect than if he had been a wood chip in an April flood. He spread his arms and balanced himself as best he could, noticing from the corner of his eye that Akbar had given in and moved down a step in between two ladies with blue hair and large purses swinging from their shoulders. One of them gave a little snort and shuffle when she felt Akbar push into her from behind, and when she looked back and saw who had moved in on her, she swung her purse around toward the front and squeezed it to her chest with both hands.

The RAMS float had come to a halt, and Walks Dead had reached full extension on his pose. All around the truckbed, the rest of the RAMS fell into prechoreographed stances, some squatting with their arms folded across their chests, one or two looking stoic as they knelt on one knee, and at each side of the truck a single man stood as a lookout, hand to his eyes as though shading against the prairie sun as his gaze fastened on something moving on the far horizon. Still fastened to her stake, Rayna stood in the middle of the float, chin lifted to make her neck look smoother and mouth set in a firm line. Every now and then her lips would move as she chanted something low and dark, and at one point she got enough volume into it to cause a couple of the RAMS to look around at her.

"Hey, chief," somebody in the crowd yelled at the float, "you play basketball?"

"Naw," another answered. "Him hunt buffalo. Drink firewater. Humpum squaw."

The Amber Dawn Farms truck jerked ahead a couple of feet, causing Mother Red America's stake to shiver and upsetting the posture of several of the RAMS. The lookout on the near side of the float stumbled, caught himself, and then saw Sam just as he was forced from his place on the step to the next one down. To keep his balance, Sam had to flail his arms out, catching the man just below him a glancing blow on the side of the head with his right hand. The man jerked his head around to see who had hit him, caught a glimpse of Sam's face, and then looked back to the front as though he wished he hadn't seen what was coming up behind him. By the time Sam had found his footing on the new step among all the other feet, the lookout had said something to Walks Dead and was pointing into the crowd in Sam's direction.

"Them fuckers see you, man," said Akbar, leaning across to Sam and speaking through the swatch of blue hair separating them.

Back on the float, Walks Dead and the other RAMS were all coming to the side of the platform, and as the truck began to move off up the street, they leaned forward together and began to chant something at Sam. Even Mother Red America began to struggle against the red, white, and blue cloth binding her to the stake as she tried to break free and join her children at the edge of the moving truckbed.

"Leaping Deer," they said in unison, "Join us, join us. Leaping Deer, Leaping Deer, join us, join us."

The heads of the crowd began to wobble, turning first one way, then the other, as they looked for the focus of the RAMS' chant. As Sam stared at Mother Red America's right hand, which by now she had worked loose and was using to tear at the bonds around her chest, one by one the faces of the crowd began to fix in place as they found him. To his left, the blue-hairs began to push themselves away and down to the next step, and the other people immediately near Sam and Akbar started sagging back to leave an open space around them.

The half-grown boy in front pulled at his father's white tie and spoke up into his face, his eyes turned toward Sam. "Is that our basketball Indian, Dad?" he asked, squirming in a little circle as though his bladder were full.

"Yeah," said Akbar to Sam in a low voice, "and this here's one of their basketball niggers." He took a step backwards up to the next level of cement and began to turn away from the street. "Let's leave here, man."

The RAMS on the truck raised their voices as they moved farther away, joined now by Rayna, who had finally freed herself from the stake and was waving Walks Dead's fake slide rule rhythmically up and down as everyone on the float chanted. Several people in the crowd had picked up the chant too, so that as Sam and Akbar moved in their little cleared circle up the embankment of the yard and toward the street leading away from the parade route, the sound was becoming loud enough to be heard several blocks away. More and more people joined in, even those too far away to have seen what caused the cheer to begin in the first place, filling the cold Illinois night with the repeated words: "Leaping Deer, Leaping Deer, join us, join us. Leaping Deer, Leaping Deer, join us, join us."

As they reached the crest of the little hill and began to move through the mass of people into the middle of the street, Sam broke into a trot, dodging the outstretched hands of first a man in an orange sweatshirt and then two people whose faces he didn't even see. He kept his eyes on the legs of the men and women ahead of him, moving from side to side as he slipped past them, making hard cuts as he squeezed through clots of bodies that reached out to slap at him as he ran by. A couple of times he had to deliver hip and shoulder bumps to people who suddenly rose up in front of him, moving as though to get in his way and bring him to a halt. At one point a woman whose face seemed to be all teeth jabbed at him with long fingernails and left a tear in the skin of his right cheek. He reversed direction, spun off his left foot, squeezed between two parked cars and cut across a yard between two houses, leaving the streets and sidewalks to the crowd.

From behind him, the cheer the RAMS had started was still being kept up by the white people, but it grew fainter as he moved through the dark back yards between the houses, putting distance between himself and the route of the Centennial Parade. After running at a good clip through six or eight yards, scrambling over three sets of fence in the process and upsetting the sleep of several dogs, one of them a chow that just missed taking a chunk out of his leg, Sam came to a street separating him from another long block of houses. He looked around him and then decided to go on as he had started, keeping to the darkness in the rear of the houses and trusting to luck in the case of dogs and high fences.

After a while, he came to one yard which extended for a long way back from the dark house sitting on the front edge of it. He slowed to a walk and then stopped by a child's swing set that looked big enough to have come from the playground of an elementary school. Leaning against one of the steel supports, he listened to hear what the crowd was saying now. He could hear nothing but car engines in low gear, horns being honked, and the sound of voices from people walking down the sidewalks and the side streets. Now and then a car would backfire or a firecracker would go off and a woman or two would scream, but the crowd had stopped chanting his name in unison, and there was no real pattern to the noises he was hearing from where he stood in the darkness.

The wind cut him, and Sam shivered and looked up. Across the face of the three-quarter moon, the clouds drove in ragged pieces, moving too fast for him to be able to make out their shapes. From time to time the light dimmed as a cloud thicker than usual came between the moon and the earth. Once when this happened and the back yard became even darker for a moment, the supports of the swing set and the leafless tree limbs fading into the sky behind them, Sam lifted his right hand in front of his face and strained to see its outline. Nothing seemed to be in his line of vision, and it wasn't until after he had closed first one eye, then the other and stared a little to the side of where he knew his hand to be that he was able to pick out the dim difference between himself and the black air around him. Even then he felt uncertain he had really been able to see himself. Maybe he had wanted to see the hand so much that he had imagined its shape, blacker than the blackness beyond it.

He dropped his hand to the level of his belly and pulled at the leather belt cinched around him, fingering a small imperfection that he knew to be in the leather, a depression that had been left when something sharp made a gouge there. Near his head the chain holding one of the swing seats began making a regular clinking sound in the wind, continuing for a time even after the gust had died down. He listened to his breath come and go for a while, concentrating on the difference in the sounds the air made depending on the direction it took in his body. It seemed to be louder as it left him, he noticed, and he considered the reason why.

Somewhere from beyond the roofs of the houses behind him came the sound of several loud cries that seemed somehow connected, but Sam tried to put them out of his mind. He felt he had to think about the direction which events in his life had been taking before he would be able to go back to his room and listen to Akbar go over the things they had seen tonight in the parade. Trying to begin systematically, he squatted in front of one of the swings where children's feet had worn a patch of ground into bare dirt. He picked up a small stick and began drawing straight lines on the ground, leaning forward and trying to see by the beams of light from the moon, interrupted every few seconds by the clouds driven across its face by the wind.

The more Sam tried to think about one thing and the way it related to another—the way he saw Sharon Hansen, for example, and what he had done with Sally Smith, or playing basketball on a white man's team that called itself an Indian name and yet had never had an Indian other than himself playing for it, or the fact that all around him lay huge fields given over to corn grown with the aid of small clicking machines and intended to be eaten not by men but by hogs—the less sure he felt about any connection between one part of what he saw and another or between one bit of his life and the rest of it or between himself and the things he saw himself doing.

Hunkered down by a man-sized children's toy and drawing lines he could only half-see in the dark earth, he worked to focus on some single thing he could be sure of, one object or event that brought some other thing with it and made their joining together real enough to live with. But whenever he felt he was on the way to making some move in his mind toward sifting through the people he had met, the things he had seen them do or heard them say, and coming up with something central enough to begin considering, his thoughts started to scatter in all directions like a flushed covey of quail.

He would seize on one thing, the fact of the little axe in Walks Dead's belt, or the white line of the part in Sharon Hansen's hair that came into view when she leaned forward over one of her books, or the way Art Wallace looked running up and down the empty stadium seats, and then there in the dark back yard of some white man he had never seen, Sam would feel his attention begin to shift and blur, whatever he had been thinking dissolving into a mist as light and lasting as seed thistle. Each thing he regarded, quiet enough there in the dark to count his own breaths, finally seemed to lead him to one or another of the stories he had been told by McKinley Short Eyes. And of these, the one that came to Sam's mind most frequently, and finally the only one he thought of, was the story of Dirty Boy, the Coushatta youth whose name meant Orphan and who had been fooled by Rabbit and made homeless in his own village.

After the third time thoughts of something in his own recent life led him to Dirty Boy, Sam straightened up from his squat in the dirt, found a tree to lean against, scooped himself some root from the leather bag around his throat, and began to review the events of Dirty Boy's tale.

The youth had entered the Coushatta village, playing the flute given him by the old woman and wearing the headdress she had made him of feathers from Bluejay and Red Bird. But Rabbit had stolen these things when Dirty Boy had dived into the river to fetch turtles from the bottom. When he reached the village no one was friendly to him, refusing to look at him because of the mud covering his buckskins. Only one young woman spoke to him, seeing him standing outside her hut and finally asking him to come inside. He had lived with her, ignored by the people of the village until he had begun leading them to the places in the river where the fish were easy to catch and bringing back meat from the many deer he was able to kill. Then the people of the Nation began to welcome him, and Rabbit returned to try to imitate Dirty Boy's good deeds.

Sam shifted his weight against the tree trunk which had begun to cut into his back and tried to remember how the rest of the story went. Somewhere in it Dirty Boy combed his wife's hair into two parts and split her head with a club so cleverly that she became two wives instead of one. When Rabbit tried the same trick, he killed his wife and had to flee the dogs of the village which chased him to a hollow tree where he was forced to live. Where did Dirty Boy's magic house come into the story? It was somewhere near the end when Dirty Boy gathered some bits of wood, arranged them into a square, and kicked them over, causing a beautiful hut to arise from the scattered pieces. Rabbit tried the same thing, and the pile of wood collapsed around him, falling into large chunks which fell on him, crushing him beneath them until he screamed once in a high-pitched voice and died. Even now, McKinley Short Eyes would say to the listening circle of Alabama and Coushatta children as he reached the end of the story of Dirty Boy, when Rabbit is caught by Hawk or killed by a trap, he screams once in just the same way he did then.

Yes, Sam thought to himself in the language of the Nation, that is the story of Dirty Boy, but what does it want to say to me? Leaning his head back against the tree until the rough edges of the bark dug into his scalp, he looked up into the bare branches lit now by the moon, its face clear of clouds for a few seconds. He listened with his breath held to whatever the story might speak to him, but he could hear nothing but the clink of metal from the swings and the sounds of engines as the traffic in the streets began to loosen and speed up.

Nothing else spoke, no matter how well he listened, and after a while he left the darkness of the yard and his place by the leafless tree and headed back to where he would spend the night. Buttoning his jacket tightly to his throat, he faced into the chill wind and began trotting down the middle of the street, hoping that by the time he reached the room, Akbar would already be asleep.

VIII

Poppoyom and Big Man-Eater

Dressing in new orange and blue uniforms for the Illinois Centennial Game in the Assembly Hall, with its polished drinking fountains, its wide benches and its eight wall-sized blackboards covered with diagrams, the Fighting Illini basketball team felt good. A little nervous and shaky in its legs and bellies, but good. The last of the Chicago reporters that Coach Thompson had allowed in for a few minutes before the game, breaking one of his rules in the process, had gone, and only two strangers were still in the room. Word had it that the one with sleepy eyes and the small cigar in his mouth, standing off to one side being talked at by Coach Chudy, was a writer from *Sports Illustrated*. The other one, a small young man with a camera around his neck and a habit of drumming his fingertips on whatever was handy, was a photographer from the same magazine, a man who had taken famous pictures of athletes in stressful situations all over the world.

Every once in a while, as Chudy talked and supported his remarks by jabbing at the chalk marks on the nearest blackboard, the writer would take the cigar out of his mouth, spit little pieces of tobacco off the tip of his tongue, and look around the room as if he thought he might see somebody he knew and was trying to avoid.

Pete Koloski, the starting strong forward, who was standing

fairly close to the *Sports Illustrated* man anyway, began working his way nearer to him, trying to hear what was being said and hoping that maybe his own name was being mentioned in the conversation. He dropped his right shoe, leaned over to pick it up and took two steps forward and eased into a seat on the bench just behind the two men.

Chudy was talking game plan and the writer was nodding and looking at his cigar. His left shoe had come untied, Koloski noticed, as he bent over to fumble at his own laces and strained to hear.

"They're big, they're fast, they're tough," Chudy was saying. "Coach Thompson and I know the problems we're up against tonight. O.S.U. can always be counted on to do whatever it takes to win." He picked up a loose piece of chalk and underlined one of the circles on the blackboard twice.

"Right," said the *Sports Illustrated* man, "right." He looked around the room again for whoever it was he didn't want to see and studied the wet end of his cigar.

"Say, Coach," he said. "Chudy, isn't it? Other than the Indian kid, Leaping Deer, you got anybody else here on the team that's, you know, strange, or flaky? Maybe a little off to one side?"

"Well, sir," said Chudy, "these are a fine bunch of young men. Most of them's got B averages in their studies. Lot of them majoring in hard stuff, too. You know, industrial engineering, secondary education, things like that." Jiggling the piece of chalk in his hand and looking just the least bit puzzled, Chudy paused for a few seconds and then went on. "Some of them's campus leaders, too. They're in fraternities, blood drives, one of them's a real good golfer and sings in a choir."

"Yeah, I get you," said the writer and looked at his photographer, who was alternately fiddling with his camera lens and trying to balance a film can on the tip of his index finger. The photographer spoke for the first time.

"Sounds like a wonderful group of young men," he said.

Just about then Koloski decided he ought to make his move. Straightening up from his shoe-tying, he surged up off the bench and whirled to face the roomful of Illini. "O.K., guys," he shouted. "See red. Bust the Buckeyes."

Behind him the photographer's film can fell to the floor with a clattering noise that was immediately drowned out by the yells of

most of the team, starters and substitutes too, the substitutes loudest of all, in fact.

"That's what I mean by the spirit of this team," said Chudy,
leaning over to speak into the ear of the *Sports Illustrated* man.

"Uh huh," said the writer.

Walking deliberately around the room from one to the other
of his fellow players, Koloski felt full of desire and inspiration. To
each man he came to he offered his outstretched palms, which they
loudly slapped, and in return all offered their own. Returning the
slaps, Koloski imagined himself getting more and more in control.
Cool, set, ready. Not only was he about to start against the Buckeyes in the U of I Centennial Game, he was being observed in a
team-leader role by a writer from *Sports Illustrated,* and he had
heard just a few minutes ago that some of the pressure behind him
was being relieved. The two freshman strong forwards had finally
been run off, and it would be a whole year before he had to worry
that some hotshot would push in and take away his starting job.
And by then he'd be a senior anyway. The sting of the slaps on his
hands was sweet. He was fired up.

"See red, Leaping Deer," he said to the Indian guard and
stuck out his palms toward him. "Bust the Buckeyes."

Sam looked up from where he sat on the end of the last bench
in the room, the one nearest the door into the long tiled room lined
with orange toilets and blue shower stalls. As he looked at the
numbers on the chest of the man in front of him, he could hear
someone just beyond the doorway gagging and heaving over one
of the commodes.

"Leaping Deer," number seventeen repeated, "see red." The
hands in the front of him looked splotched and mottled with blood
just below the skin, Sam noticed, and one of them was trembling a
little. After a time, seeing that the hands were going to wait, Sam
finally took one of them in his right hand and gave it a white man's
shake.

"No, man," said the voice coming from above the blue numbers on the new orange jersey, "show me some spirit. Give me
some skin."

Sam dropped the hand, folded his arms across his chest and
leaned back, raising his eyes to the man's face. A couple of the
other Illini close enough to see what was happening, began to
snigger, and Koloski's ears turned a bright red.

"Hey, man," he said, looking quickly back toward the *Sports Illustrated* pair and then back to Sam. "Don't be like your buddy, Leaping Deer. Show some spunk. You got to get with it, boy."

"Who?" asked Sam slowly. "My buddy?" Behind him, the man in the roomful of toilets finally got a good purchase and brought up a heave that made a wet solid sound as it hit.

"Yeah, you know. What's his name. Wallace. He quit today. Him and that other forward, the guy from Moline. Wallace and him both quit today."

"Run off," Sam said as though he were the one telling the news and not the man in front of him.

"That's right," said Koloski, dropping his hands and moving back a step. "Run off today. No spirit. Yellow quitter couldn't take it."

The back of Koloski's calves were just beginning to touch the bench behind him when Sam's forearm caught him in the throat right above the collarbone. The momentum of Sam's spring from where he'd been sitting carried both of them over the bench, and they ended up between two other people, Koloski underneath trying to yell past whatever it was that had suddenly risen up in his throat and Sam working quietly for a hold that would allow him to cut off completely the sounds from the mouth gaping in front of him.

By the time Koloski had pushed himself up underneath the next line of benches and managed finally to get another breath, the photographer from *Sports Illustrated* had jumped up to the bench nearest him, run from one row to the next and was snapping pictures from directly above the two as they rolled around on the floor, the regular machinelike clicking of his shutter almost drowned out by the yelling of the players and the cursing of Chudy and Thompson.

"Get up from there, you crazy guys," Chudy kept saying over and over as he tugged at the back of Sam's uniform with one hand and tried to keep himself from being pulled down with the other.

"Koloski," yelled Coach Thompson, bending over and poking at Sam's hands, "let go of his fingers. If you sprain one of his goddamn fingers, you're through. I mean that, you stupid bastard."

In another minute both men were up on their feet on opposite sides of the room, surrounded by players and coaches, Koloski trying to explain to anybody who would listen what had happened and Sam allowing the head trainer to inspect his hands. "Now close the right one," the gray-haired man was saying, "make a fist. Flex your fingers back and forth."

"Well, what is it, damn it?" asked Thompson. "Are they all right?" He looked ready to turn and go after Koloski depending on the answer he got.

"Nothing wrong except for that split fingernail," said the trainer, dabbing with a cotton ball at the blood oozing from beneath Sam's right thumbnail. "It'll be sore all right."

"Shit, fuck it to hell," said Thompson. "Tape it up, and we'll see what he can do." He pushed his hair back out of his eyes just as the five-minute buzzer went off, and then he looked around the big room. The writer from *Sports Illustrated* was listening to Koloski while the photographer fiddled with his camera and Chudy walked around acting as though he was trying to remember where he was.

"Get them out on the court, Chudy," Thompson yelled and turned back toward Sam.

As the players began to shuffle into place near the door, Koloski at the front of the line looking back over his shoulder every few seconds in Sam's general direction and the *Sports Illustrated* men talking in low voices near the wall of lockers, Coach Thompson put on his Dead Smile face and regarded Sam head-on.

"Gee, Leaping Deer," he said, dropping his voice into the low sincere range, "what happened? Did Koloski say something to offend you? You shouldn't think anything about that. He's just a big dumb kid who gets excited. Listen, I'll give him a real earful when this game's over."

At least the Indian was looking at him, Thompson thought, but the worst thing about this kid was his eyes. You could never see anything in them. Right now the look in Leaping Deer's was about as expressive as a couple of pecan shells. They were so brown they were black, and as Thompson looked, the eyes seemed to get blacker.

"We got about a minute, son," Thompson said, looking over Sam's head at the large blue clock on the wall behind him. "Is there anything you want to say before you go out there?" The big orange second hand had swept past the twelve.

"Art," Sam said. "Art Wallace. Is he run off?"

"Oh," said Coach Thompson and licked first his bottom, then his top lip. "I don't know what kind of rumors you've been hearing, Leaping Deer, but let me tell you the truth. We don't run people off. Wallace just decided in his case that he wasn't cut out for Big Ten basketball, and he decided to leave our program. You see, son, not many people your age are like you, no matter where they played their high school ball or how good they were when they did. It's a different game at this level, and Wallace just doesn't have it. He'd be the first to tell you that. We had a nice talk, Wallace and I did, about his career options, and he told me that for the good of Illini basketball, and for his own good too, he wanted to leave us. With no hard feelings on either side, too. Those were his very words, no hard feelings. That's what he said." The orange hand had completed its circuit and was moving steadily through a new one, not hurrying and not slowing down as it counted off the seconds in the locker room.

"Well, son," the coach said, getting his smile fairly well set back into place, "are you ready to go out there and play some basketball for the Fighting Illini?" He put a firm, friendly hand on the Indian's shoulder.

"I'll let you know, Buck," Sam said, stepping back and starting for the door into the Assembly Hall. As he went through it, he lifted his right hand to his mouth and bit at the piece of tape the trainer had wrapped around it. The little answering pain felt right as he thought it would, and he gave the thumb another bite as he walked out onto the court.

The starting lineups of the two teams were milling around the center circle, one player short, and as Sam came into view, the captain of the Illini said something to a referee standing with a ball in his hands and pointed in Sam's direction. At about the same time, the crowd caught sight of Sam and gave a great shout which the Illinois cheerleaders began efficiently organizing into a disciplined chant. After about half a minute everyone in the Assembly Hall, which seemed to have every seat filled for the Centennial Game, was saying Sam's name over and over again, while the band punctuated each repetition with horn blasts and booming drums.

Sam stopped at the Illinois bench and removed the warm-up jacket which the trainer had thrown over his shoulders in the dressing room. Folding it carefully to hide the embroidered profile of the Indian with the perfect headdress, he looked up into the row where Art and Sharon had been sitting during the first game he had played in the Assembly Hall, but he could see no one he knew. In the seats where he was sure they had been were now a middle-aged man and woman dressed in matching orange jumpsuits trimmed in blue. Across their chests were the letters U of I and below that in script were the words "One Hundred Years of Giving." The woman, whose hair beneath her small blue beanie looked like it had been varnished and whose face was a shade lighter orange than her jumpsuit, saw that Sam was looking at her and began elbowing her husband in the side. "Look," she said, not turning away from Sam, and then leaning forward over the heads of the people in the row in front of her, she began mouthing something at him, speaking slowly and with enough lip action for Sam to understand her over the continuing cheers of the Assembly Hall crowd. "Go get 'em, Little Beaver," she was saying, her elbow digging hard into her husband's side, "Go get 'em, Little Beaver."

Sam finished folding the jacket, adjusted one sleeve that had fallen loose, and laid the orange-headed Indian on the floor near the bench. The force of the kick he gave it was hard enough to send it off the edge of the floor beneath the team bench, and as he turned to cross the out-of-bounds line onto the court, he could see people in the first row of seats scrambling and clawing to claim the jacket.

Going out to join the men clustered around the center circle, the sound of his own name coming at him in waves, Sam felt again like he had in the dark back yard after the parade, puzzling over McKinley Short Eyes' story of Dirty Boy. Surely back in the youpon and pine thickets of the Nation, one thing in his life was tied to another: the way a man ran said something about the kind of man he was, what food he ate meant more to him than just stuff to stretch his belly full, the way even he played the white man's basketball belonged only to him and was apart from why the whites wanted him to play it. But here, he thought as he watched the centers go up for the tip-off and maneuvered himself against the man beside him, all that he had been doing was a collection of one thing and then another thing and then another. There was no middle around which these things circled. And what he had thought he could always make his own, no matter how the whites fooled themselves into believing he did as they wanted, he saw himself giving up and trading away. He saw himself receiving in barter not the sense he had always had before—that though things shifted and slid around him, changing and crumbling all the while as he remained apart, knowing where the center was and knowing always how to reach that place where all movement stopped—but getting instead in return what had happened to Art Wallace and having his name come over and over again from the mouths of people who he had thought could never know him. He had to find again that place in the circle where nothing was, where the shadowy things around him could not reach in and touch.

For the first ten minutes or so of the game, Sam played automatically, taking shots when he was open and passing off to the other guard or the center, occasionally finding one of the other Illinois players streaking for the basket. He gave no real attention to where he was, concentrating instead on the scene of Art Wallace running up and down the bleacher seats of the stadium in the darkness and on the random faces of the people at the parade which came by bunches into his mind. He found himself trying to attach each face or group of faces to the particular place and time he had seen them, but finally gave up the attempt when each one seemed to dissolve into another as he tried to fix it somewhere solid.

It wasn't until someone called a time-out and he found himself standing alone in the middle of the court holding the basketball with no one else around him that he finally gave up for good trying to control what was going through his head. It was not a thing for him to do, he told himself, as he headed for the group of people gathered around Coach Thompson in front of the Illinois bench. He would struggle alone no more to place one thing with another as he thought it ought to fit. Instead, he would allow the Old Ones to decide what he must do, and he would let their casting of the clear sabia beads touched with red direct his actions.

When he reached the circle of people standing with Thompson, all of them but one or two twisted around to look at him and the coach with the Dead Smile drooping off to one side as he stared hardest of all, Sam felt nothing troublesome move in his mind. Even the steady yelling of the crowd being whipped on by the cheerleaders and the war-dancing of Chief Illini himself seemed to Sam to be dropping away as he stood facing the coach, waiting to hear whatever it was the Old Ones would have him do.

"Leaping Deer," Thompson was saying, shouting to make himself heard above the noise of the people and the band, "where the hell are you? Do you know you've been playing like you're in a goddamn trance or something?" He swept his gaze around the men standing near him, fighting to control the bottom half of his face, and then looked back at Sam with burning eyes.

"Look at that," he said, pointing to the bank of lights on the four-sided electronic scoreboard suspended over the center of the basketball court. "Do you even know what the fucking score is?"

"Yes, Dead Smile," said Sam and pulled the basketball under his right arm away from the official who had walked up to him and begun tugging at it. "Here."

Taking two steps back from the circle of blue and orange men to give himself room for full body extension, he leaned back, putting everything he could on the ball, and threw it squarely into the center of Coach Buck Thompson's face.

The coach dropped like something had cut both heel tendons, falling backwards into the man behind him and grabbing with both hands at his mouth and nose as he went down. Just before he turned to leave, Sam noted with no surprise that in among the blood and snot Dead Smile was coughing into his hands and examining was a pink plastic appliance studded with several sharp white teeth.

Everybody was too busy with Thompson to try to stop Sam, either offering towels or bending over to study what the coach was catching in his hands, so Sam trotted down the edge of the floor undisturbed toward where the cheerleaders were strung out in an orderly line. Only a part of the Centennial Game crowd had seen what happened to the coach, so most of them watched Sam approach Chief Illini puzzled but not alarmed.

When he saw the Indian coming closer to him, weaving his way around the cheerleaders between them and obviously going somewhere he had already picked out, Chief Illini began to edge out of his place in the formation. As the Indian passed the last cheerleader, a cute little blonde from Kankakee, and swerved to avoid stepping on her dropped pompoms, Chief Illini was able to get a good look at the red man's eyes. Something he saw in them caused him to begin to turn and run, but by that time it was too late.

All in all, people in the crowd later agreed, the Indian was fairly gentle with Chief Illini. He didn't actually hit him or twist his arm or run over him. He just helped the Chief sit down on the basketball court about twenty feet from the hoop, about where a good jump-shot shooter would hit from on about half his attempts. With his left hand he removed Chief Illini's six-foot headdress, the upkeep of which cost the State of Illinois over four hundred dollars a year, and then, getting a good chunk of the black wig-hair in his right hand, he gave a hard jerk.

"Jesus," several people in the crowd said almost at the same time, watching the wig come off in the Indian's hand, "he's scalping the Chief."

Chief Illini immediately threw both arms up and covered his blond nakedness as best he could until one of the cheerleaders brought him her warm-up jacket to wrap around his head. By the time that happened, the Indian was gone, exiting through the nearest door, carrying the headdress and long plaited wig slung over his left shoulder while he used his free hand to push off the two or three people who approached him gingerly as he left, trying to stop him maybe or at least slow him down a little. As the heavy glass and metal door swung shut behind the Indian wearing the blue nine on his back, the buzzer signaling the end of the time-out went off, but no one in the Assembly Hall made a move to start the Centennial Game again.

Outside in the parking lot Sam shifted his burden to a more comfortable position and looked up at the sky. The night, which had begun overcast, was clearing, and he could see among the stars above him the constellation Old Man Sylestine claimed as a monument to the original Leaping Deer's great vault from the bank of Long King Creek. Even the two little dim stars which supposedly represented the pigs from the white man's settlement carried by Sam's ancestor with him into the heavens were visible, and fixing the position of these with reference to the horizon, Sam began working his way through the hundreds of cars parked on the vast cement plain, careful not to let Chief Illini's headdress or hair brush against any of the vehicles.

Traffic on the streets was light, and although at first in the cold November air he had felt chilled wearing only his basketball uniform, it was not long before the running warmed him. By the time he reached the street where Sharon Hansen lived, he had broken into a light sweat, slowing his pace only now and then to adjust the load he was carrying. As he rounded the corner of the block where her apartment was located, he passed an old man and woman dressed like twins in black who turned to stare at him going by. The woman called something out to him which he made no effort to understand, and the old man pulled at her arm to get her started up the street again. "Come on, Mama, he doesn't look right," Sam heard him say. Glancing back over his shoulder as he came to a halt in front of Sharon's house, Sam watched the couple scuttle through the circle of light from a streetlamp like two beetles swimming across the stagnant water of a Big Thicket stump-hole.

The top floors of the house were dark, but Sam could see a dim lemon-colored light coming from one of the windows on the bottom level. Thinking back to his earlier visit, he decided the window was the one to Sharon's room and began to walk toward the house, his basketball shoes making no sound on the concrete path. He swung Chief Illini's headdress around in front of him at arm's length and shook it to let the feathers fall straight, wondering what Sharon would think of what he had brought with him.

He reached the door at the side of the house leading into Sharon's room and lifted his hand to knock, but paused, thinking he had heard something. The door itself stood open a crack, and as he waited, listening, the sound again came to him from inside the room, a sound made by someone groaning as though suffering from pain or great loss. It reminded him of the way Palmer, the football player who had collapsed on the stadium seats that night running the stands along with Art, had moaned as he lay between the rows of bleachers, the heels of his hands digging into his eyes and his large belly quaking as he cried. Giving the door a little push and moving to the side so that he could see through the crack as the beam of light from inside grew wider, Sam peered inside, half-expecting to see someone alone in the room grieving aloud.

The light came from a small lamp on a table just to the left of the single bed on the far side of the room. The shadow cast by a bookshelf made it difficult at first for Sam to see exactly the shapes before him, but their general outlines were clear enough. The moaning was coming from Sharon Hansen, who lay back across the single bed at an angle so that one foot, still wearing a tennis shoe, rested on the floor. One of her hands lay across her eyes as though to shade them from the lamp, and the fingers of the other moved one by one in a slow rhythm as they wound their way deeper into the hair of Sally Smith, who kneeled on the floor with Sharon's other leg thrown over her shoulder and crooked at the knee about the back of Sally's neck. Sally had slipped her hands under Sharon's naked buttocks, yellow in the light, and was alternately lifting and relaxing her shoulders, moving Sharon from side to side in slow rolls at each contraction. Each of the moans Sam had been hearing came just at the moment when Sally's head finished its long slow movement up from where she began each of her grazing tongue motions.

For half a second the scene brought to Sam's mind the story of Cannibal and the young girl of the Nation whose flesh he longed to eat, but here the young girl was trying no escape and would want no help from magic chunk stones or the series of three ripe huckleberries, three blackberries, and three pieces of cane which alone could save her.

Stepping back soundlessly from the door, Sam slipped the long plaits of hair made into the wig for Chief Illini off his shoulder and carefully hung the thing on the outside doorknob. He adjusted the wig so that each plaited strand lay separate and straight, hanging parallel to each other on either side of the doorknob. When he was satisfied with the way it looked in the dim light, the peak of the wig rounded like a skull and the face, which should have been between the plaits, nothing but empty air, he stepped back softly and eased his way down the steps of the low porch. After he had moved a few feet from the door, he knew he was too far away to hear the regular moans Sharon was making with each long slow movement of Sally's tongue, but even after he had gotten three blocks down the street he still seemed to hear a whisper of her cries floating in the air around him.

The Old Ones took Sam at a fairly good pace on through the cold Illinois night, the six-foot length of the perfect headdress bouncing against his left shoulder as he ran. In a few minutes he found himself passing the open space of campus near the fenced patch of corn which the white man valued so highly and named in strange ways, and Sam slowed to see if there was something there he ought now to do.

The stalks were brown and withered, rustling together dryly as the night wind swept across them, each plant loaded with ears drying for harvest, and Sam stopped to watch them for a minute.

He stood in the shadow of a tree and quieted his breath, open and waiting to hear, but nothing spoke to him about the Old Ones' plans for that particular moment. Yet something about the white man's field of corn was important, he felt, and in time he would be allowed to know what that thing was. Then he would be brought back here to carry out the rest of what it was he had to do in this spot.

He looked up again into the sky at the patterns of stars and began to move off, picking up speed as he trotted across the open space of ground toward the next destination waiting for him. He was not surprised when, after threading his way among several buildings and crossing a couple of empty streets, he saw dead ahead of him a large electric sign spelling out in red and white letters the words *Tommy Mo's*. He saw it to be the bar where he and Art had sat together in the booth drinking beer and talking to Sharon Hansen for the first time.

Art's small green car was parked in front of the building, its cloth top down and mud splattered all the way from one end of the machine to the other. When Sam stopped to look inside it, he noticed that the near front wheel was run up on the curb at such a hard angle that the hubcap had popped off and was leaning against the street edge. He reached down, picked it up, and hammered it against the side of the tire to knock off the worst part of the mud. When it looked as though all that was going to come loose had, he threw both the hubcap and Chief Illini's headdress into the back seat among some empty beer cans and a couple of pairs of basketball shoes. He covered the headdress with a wrinkled tan jacket he found in the driver's seat and walked into Tommy Mo's, squeezing by some people who were having a hard time finding their way out. "Trick or treat," one of them was saying to nobody in particular, "trick or treat."

The room was about two-thirds full, and it wasn't until Sam had worked his way through the crowd to the middle of the aisle between the bar and the line of booths that he was able to pick out Art. He was sitting at the end of the counter drinking beer and engaged in a conversation with the man beside him. When Sam got nearer, he recognized that the man talking to Art, a brown hat pushed to the back of his head and his stubby fingers jabbing the air as he spoke, was the midget he had seen there the first time he was in the place. The poppoyom was drunk, and Art looked drunker. He was talking with a lot of lip action, opening his mouth wide for each word he said as though he was afraid it was going to get stuck in his throat on the way out and choke him to death.

"Norman Mailer's a fucking lightweight," the poppoyom was saying, moving his right hand back and forth as though to brush away fruit flies, "a fucking lightweight, I tell you."

"That's," Art said, pausing after each word to get his bearings, "easy for you to say."

"Art," said Sam. "Art Wallace. I found you." He moved up until he was standing right next to the little man on the stool and then lifted his hand in Art's direction.

Art put down his bottle of beer and swung around to get a better look, knocking over an ashtray full of peanut shells in the process.

"Jesus," he said. "It's Sam. Hey, Leaping Deer, I came in here to watch you on TV, but somebody's stole Tommy Mo's set." He spun halfway back around on his revolving stool and pointed, blinking, in the direction of a shelf on the wall above the bar mirror. "See? That's where it was. That's where Tommy Mo kept it."

Sam studied the empty space between two rows of whiskey bottles and nodded. "Yeah, it's gone now," he said. "Maybe a cannibal got it."

"A cannibal?" said the midget, leaning even further back to look up at Sam. "You say a cannibal?"

"Ho, poppoyom," Sam answered the little man and touched him on the brown hat with the tips of his fingers. The midget looked pleased and reached for his beer.

"Game's not over already, is it?" asked Art. "Hell, you still wearing your uniform. Why? What's the matter?"

"Oh, nothing," Sam said. "I just got run off."

"No shit? I did too," shouted Art, spreading his arms and rearing back so far he almost fell off his seat. "Have a beer, Sam, goddamn it. Come on in here."

While Art yelled for one of the bartenders, the poppoyom looked Sam up and down and shook his head sympathetically. "Well, son," he said, "you remember what I said first time I saw you. You needed a few more inches, didn't you?"

"Poppoyom," said Sam, "you were right. You know how it is."

"Shit, son. You learn to live with it." The little man sighed gustily and bubbled his bottle of beer.

"Here's your beer, Sam," said Art, shoving a full bottle toward him.

"O.K., Art. We'll drink one more and then we have something to do," Sam said, reaching for the bottle and speaking loudly to be heard over a country song that had just started on the jukebox. He took a long swallow and shivered, the cold air in the bar starting to chill the sweat in his uniform. He could feel the Old Ones beginning to move in him.

"What we got to do besides get drunk?" Art asked, beginning to pause again for an extra beat between his words.

"First I need a hog," Sam said.

"A hog?"

"Yes, I want a hog. We need to find us a hog first. You already have your car here."

The poppoyom finished his beer and peered up at Sam with an interested look on his face. When he opened his mouth to speak, his head looked as big as a two-gallon jug. "What kind of a hog do you need, son? Poland China? Duroc?"

"A good-sized one," Sam said. "Pretty big. Hungry, though. It's got to be a hungry hog. I don't care what his white-man name is."

The poppoyom hunched himself forward on his bar stool and began drawing with one of his stubby fingers in the water on the bar top. "I believe what you talking about then is a gilt right before slaughter. What a hog man does, see, is he won't feed a gilt the last couple of days before he kills him. That way you ain't got all that shit to contend with. He's clean then, and his guts are slick and white. Hell, I've seen them as white as a lace tablecloth."

"All right," Sam said. "A gilt then. Where can we get him?"

"We really gonna get a hog?" Art asked, putting down his empty bottle among all the peanut shells on the bar.

"We got the car, we got the poppoyom, now we need the gilt hog," said Sam and looked down at the little man for an answer.

"Hell, boys, let's go," he said and leapt off his bar stool, catching himself expertly on the way down so that he hit the floor in a half-run, half-waddle. By the time Sam and Art began to follow him, the poppoyom was several feet ahead, elbowing his way among the forest of knees and thighs between him and the door, hardly slowing down even when his way out seemed completely blocked. As Sam and Art followed the little man out the door, somebody near the front of the room recognized Sam and called out his name, but after getting a better look, decided not to come out the door of Tommy Mo's after him.

Art and Sam got into the front seat of the green car, and the poppoyom clambered up over the rear bumper and the trunk like a fox squirrel and flopped into the back beside Chief Illini's headdress. Art fired the machine up, jerked it out into the street with a loud whump and a squall of rear tires, and made for a main street. After he had pulled his hat low over his eyes with both hands, the poppoyom leaned over the back of the front seat and gave directions.

"You know the U of I farms," he said, "out on Philo Road. Turn off on that little road by the sheep pens and go to the third building. The Swine Enclosure." Art nodded and began winding the engine through its gears, taking each one to the limit as he whipped the car past the long rows of university buildings.

Sam leaned back in the wash of cold air blowing over him and looked up at the star patterns, clear now of the last few clouds. Behind him, in the back seat, the poppoyom had found the headdress beneath the tan jacket and was working to smooth out the feathers as the wind whipped at them, singing at the top of his lungs some song Sam had never heard before. Was it from the white man's jukebox, Sam wondered, or was it a magic chant of the little people of the woods? One thing was sure: he knew what McKinley Short Eyes would call it. He could see the old man now, dressed in overalls with his hair grown out too long from a white man's haircut, sitting on the ground in front of his house as he told Sam of the tricks and wiles of the poppoyom, the small friends of the Alabamas and Coushattas.

When they reached the turn-off, Art stopped the car and looked into the back seat. His hair was blown up around his head against the grain, and his eyes were watering from the wind and the beer. "Now what?" he said.

The midget had donned Chief Illini's headdress and was trying to adjust it to fit his outsized head. "Turn off your lights," he said struggling with a buckskin drawstring, "and drive slow and quiet up to the side of that third building over."

"Ho, poppoyom," Sam said. "I'll help you fasten it, but first take some of this." He drew the leather pouch attached to the rawhide string from under his basketball jersey and prized it open. Enough of the dark root for three healthy-sized chews remained inside, and he divided it between himself and the other two men. "Just hold it under your tongue. Don't swallow it."

"What is this stuff?" Art asked as he packed it into his mouth. "Some kind of mushroom?"

"No," said Sam. "It's mikko root. The poppoyom first showed the Nation how to use it."

"Sounds good to me," Art said. "Now where's that goddamn hog?"

Driving in low gear with the lights off, Art pulled the car close to the side of the long metal building the midget had pointed out, and cut the engine.

"You sure this is it?" he asked. "I don't even smell any hog shit."

"There ain't much around any more, that's a fact." The poppoyom sucked at the mikko root and adjusted his warbonnet. "What they do is process it and feed it back to the hogs that shit it in the first place."

"They make them eat their own shit?"

"It's nutritious, them hog-scientists claim. Don't want to waste nothing no more." He gestured at a door toward the back of the building. "We can get in right through there, I believe, if I remember right."

"How do you know this place so well?" asked Art and yawned so widely he almost dropped his mikko root.

"Aw, when I was a kid, I used to come out here with Buster Wainwright and Jimmy Conder to mess around with the sows at night." The poppoyom spat and looked pensive. "When you're a little person, you got to make do with what you can get."

"Hogs, huh?" Art said. "Tell me, how is hog?"

"Well," said the poppoyom, leaning back in the car seat and studying for a minute. "About like goat."

Sam crawled out of the car and headed for the metal building, followed in a short time by Art and the little man, who kept looking over his shoulder to avoid catching his headdress on something as he trotted along behind the other two. As Sam neared the wall of the building, he could hear grunts and snuffling sounds coming from inside, and he slowed to let the poppoyom catch up, but he still reached the door first. It was fastened shut with a heavy padlock threaded through a steel bar, and when he saw that, Sam began looking around on the ground for something large and solid.

"Never fear, son," the poppoyom said and went for his pants pocket, coming up in a few seconds with a ring full of keys. The third one worked, opening the padlock with an oily click, and Art and Sam stepped inside the building as the little man held the door open.

High up on the wall at the far end of the building was a single bulb throwing hardly enough light for Sam to make out the two rows of pens with a sawdust aisle running between them. What he couldn't see he could hear, though, and as he walked between the pens, he had the feeling that lines of old people were sleeping on each side of him, snorting and snuffling through their open mouths as they dreamed bad dreams about other places and other times. As he passed one enclosure, the animal moans coming from it reminded him of what he had heard earlier that evening as Sally Smith worked on Sharon, and he gave his head a hard shake to clear it of the thought.

Several feet behind him the poppoyom had stopped in front of a pen and was lighting a match. "Here's your hog," he said, "you want one hungry."

Sam joined Art and looked over the top of a wooden gate that the poppoyom was looking through. In the flame of the little man's second match, he could see a hog that was up on its feet restlessly rooting about the floor of its pen, moving from side to side and back and forth as it searched the cement as though it had lost something. Now and then it would rear up and stand with its front hooves on the edge of the side boards, sniffing the air with its head thrown back, its small eyes darting about in the dim light. Then it would flop back to the floor and resume its snuffling from one side of the pen to the other. Its wide flat back was an off-white color splotched with black, and as it reared up at the front of the pen and looked through the boards at the poppoyom, Sam could see a heavy metal ring punched through the tip of the grayish snout.

"That's good," the little man said. "That's gonna make it a lot easier."

"What you mean, Byron?" Art asked in a far-away voice that told Sam the mikko root was taking hold.

"That nose ring. We can handle that fucker, I don't care how big he thinks he is."

The little man slipped off the belt holding his pants up, and the next time the speckled hog rammed its nose between the boards at the front of the pen, he slipped one end of his belt through the steel ring with a short deft motion so quick the hog had no time to back off and Sam and Art barely saw what had happened.

"I got him now," he said, pulling at the belt until the hog's snout protruded several inches between the boards. "He's ready to join our club. Jimmy Conder was here now we'd be fighting over who's first."

"Let's open that gate and get him out of here," Sam said and began fumbling at the latch in the darkness. "You have a match, Art?"

"Yeah," Art said, going carefully through his pockets until he found a matchbook from Tommy Mo's. "What we gonna do with him?"

"This is Big Man-Eater," said Sam, translating the name into English for the benefit of the rest of the raiding party. "We're going to put him in the car."

At first the hog was reluctant to go along, but after the poppoyom had given the nose ring a couple of hard twists to get the animal's attention, it followed quietly as the three men left the Swine Enclosure, Sam and Art leading the way to open the door for Byron and Big Man-Eater. Sam stopped to refasten the padlock through the steel hasp, and as he did so, he could hear the snuffling moans and bubbles of the breathing inside going on in a regular rhythm. Terrible things must live in the dreams of the white man's hog to cause that kind of grieving, he thought.

By the time he caught up with the others, Art had opened the door of his green car and the poppoyom had clambered into the front seat and was pulling at the belt through the nose ring of Big Man-Eater. The hog got his front feet up onto the edge of the seat easily enough but was having a hard time getting a purchase with his back hooves. They kept slipping on the metal at the bottom of the door, and it wasn't until Sam and Art had each grabbed hold of a back leg and heaved that the beast was able to make it all the way into the front seat.

"That's the easy part," said Art. "Now how are we going to get him into the back of the car. He must weigh four hundred pounds."

"Just over three hundred," said the poppoyom and gave the belt a twitch. "He ain't but half-grown yet. I'm gonna get on the trunk, and you two encourage him." Letting the belt slide to its limit in his right hand, the little man scrambled over the top of the seat, reached the trunk of the car and stood up. He leaned back, put his full weight on the end of the belt, and Big Man-Eater came alive in Sam's and Art's hands, surging over the top of the front seat as if it had been born to do it, its hind feet flailing and a high-pitched squeal like metal tearing coming from somewhere deep in its guts.

"Sounds like a fucking linebacker," said Art, dodging the hooves a couple of inches from his face and beginning to laugh. "He sounds like Dick Butkus whipping Michigan."

As the hog came over the seat in a tumbling rush, the poppoyom gave an expert twist to the nose ring, and the animal turned in the air and landed lengthwise in the tiny back seat crushing dead beer cans and filling up the empty space as though it were a package specially made just for it.

"Now where are you gonna sit, Byron?" asked Art in a voice blurred by mikko root. "On the trunk?"

"Naw, I'm gonna sit on Big Man-Eater's back. I'm gonna ride this hog." Adjusting his warbonnet, which had lost a few feathers and become a little tangled in the process of loading the hog, the poppoyom spun himself off the trunk of the car and landed with a whoop on the hog's back.

"Ready to roll," he said, and gave the belt-end in his hand a twitch. "You got a man ahold of you now, Big Man-Eater," he addressed the hog. He turned in the saddle and patted Sam on the shoulder.

"Son, this Indian chewing tobacco you gave me don't make me want to spit a drop, but it sure smooths things out."

"Ho, poppoyom," said Sam.

Art started the engine and began to back the car in a tight arc, stopping just short of the side of the Swine Enclosure building before shifting gears. "What are we gonna do with Big Man-Eater, Sam?"

"We're gonna feed him," Sam answered. "We're going to give him all the corn he can eat. Go to the corn patch."

"Corn's all gone. It's all been harvested by now except for the seed corn."

"That's right. Go to the U of I corn patch. That's what Big Man-Eater wants to eat."

"You mean the Morrill Plot on the Quad? Right there on the campus?" Art looked wide-awake again.

"Yeah," said Sam, "where the white-haired man uses the electric machine to count it. That's the right corn for this hog. That's what he was born to eat."

"Shit, let's go," said Art and headed toward Philo Road, his small green car full of hog hitting bottom at each bump it came to.

On the way to where the corn patch stood in the large open piece of ground, Sam leaned back in the front seat and let one of the Nation's harvest chants run through his head. It was a song with no words to it, just three syllables repeated over and over in varying lifts and falls of the singer's voice, and something about its simpleness seemed exactly right to him as he rode under the bare stars of the Illinois sky. From behind him came the sound of the poppoyom singing something to Big Man-Eater about helping him make it through the night, and from time to time Art would twist around to yell over his shoulder to the little man that he better not let the goddamn hog bite him on the ear. Sam rode and listened to the chant.

In a few minutes Art pulled the car up behind a parked Volkswagen van and cut the engine. The street was deserted except for a few parked cars and up ahead a couple of blocks a man walking a small well-trimmed poodle on a leash. As Sam and the others sat quietly watching, the man and dog walked out of the circle of light cast by a streetlamp and vanished into the darkness. The gilt hog snuffled deep in its throat and the poppoyom spoke in a loud whisper. "He'd like to eat up that damn little white dog. He smells him."

"Big Man-Eater needs corn, not dogmeat," said Sam and stepped out of the car into the street.

"It's over behind that line of elms," Art said, pointing into the darkness beyond them. "Just about a hundred yards."

"Wait just a minute," said the poppoyom, taking Chief Illini's warbonnet off his head and beginning to tie its leather strings around the hog's neck. "We got to dress him up right first." Somewhere during the journey between the Swine Enclosure and Emancipation Street, the headdress had lost about two feet of feathers and trim, but it was still the most impressive and elaborate one Sam or any other Coushatta had ever seen. So that when the poppoyom gave the nose ring a good hard two-thirds' revolution causing the hog to rise up out of the back seat like an alligator breaking water to snap at a mallard duck, the visual effect of Big Man-Eater's headgear and the little man riding its spotted back was enough to make Sam and Art look at each other in deep appreciation.

"I thought he'd be hard to get out of that back seat," said Art, stepping well out of the way.

"Hell," said the poppoyom, speaking in the middle of a series of bucks by the gilt, "I can *ride* this fucking Man-Eater. You boys lead on, and we'll follow."

After another couple of hard bucks and a maneuver that Sam had heard cowboys at the Polk County Rodeo call "sunfishing," the hog seemed to get used to having a rider and settled into a quick trot, heading across the sidewalk toward the line of trees as if it knew where it was going.

"Guide him, Byron," Art called to the poppoyom, who was leaning forward on the back of Big Man-Eater and drumming his heels against its sides.

"He won't have to guide him," said Sam. "Big Man-Eater smells sha towea."

Everybody arrived at the fence surrounding the Morrill Experimental Cornfield at about the same time, the poppoyom and his mount just a shade ahead of Art and Sam. The hog immediately dropped his nose to ground level, almost pulling his rider off his back as he snorted and snuffled at the bottom strand of wire, trying to find a way to root under the barrier between him and the stand of King Diamond 240-X seed corn. The little man leaned back on the belt through the nose ring, and the hog began shaking its head from side to side and prancing in tight little circles as he fought to get at the fence. At one point in his struggles he got a front hoof hung in the trailing headdress and ripped several more feathers loose, but the rawhide strings tied around its neck continued to hold the warbonnet on.

"Here," said the poppoyom, throwing his ring of keys toward

Sam and nearly losing his seat as he did, "get that gate open. He's getting to be hell to hang on to."

Sam picked up the ring from the grass by one of the keys attached to it and then counted seven keys over from the first one he had touched. It slipped into the padlock holding the gate closed as if it had been greased, and as the hasp sprang open in his hand, he took a quick look at the constellations above him to acknowledge the help of the Old Ones.

"Ho, poppoyom," he said and swung open the gate to the white man's corn patch. "Let Big Man-Eater feed."

The hog circled away from the steel fence and made a dash at the open gap, Chief Illini's warbonnet streaming back from its head in a long curve of feathers lit by the streetlamps. The poppoyom, pulling the belt free from the nose ring, gave Big Man-Eater its head, and just as it reached the gate, he threw one leg over its back and dismounted with a flourish, hitting the ground on his feet in a dead run.

"Goddamn," he said with a whoop. "I ain't had so much fun since I left Decatur."

The hog hit the first row of King Diamond 240-X in a rush, knocking over six or eight of the dried stalks before it came to a halt and began feeding in short telling jerks of its head. It began working its way from ear to ear of the seed corn, blowing at the leaves temporarily blocking its way and chewing through the kernels and cobs with a steady grinding noise. Chief Illini's headdress bobbing up and down as Big Man-Eater fed looked to Sam like an unfamiliar harvest dance of some tribe he had never before seen. He stepped back from the gate and closed it, carefully fitting the padlock through the steel hasp and clicking it shut. He gave the cold metal two hard jerks to make sure everything was fastened down tight.

"I tell you one thing," said the poppoyom, peering through the fence and speaking in a thoughtful voice, "what he don't eat up, he'll shit all over." He rethreaded his belt through his pants loops and looked up at Art, standing beside Sam with his arms crossed and his elbows on top of the fence.

"Boys," he asked, "have you ever seen a happier Duroc gilt?"

"No," said Art, "nor one more deserving of happiness."

The three men stood by silently for several minutes, watching Big Man-Eater chew its way across, through, and up and down the rows of seed corn. The occasional people that passed on the dark sidewalk near them, mostly graduate students coming to or from libraries or laboratories, gave the three a wide berth, thinking it best not to investigate why a midget, a man well over six feet tall, and another shorter one dressed only in a basketball uniform in the forty-degree weather were staring intently into Morrill Plot toward the source of those regular, dry, crackling sounds.

"Art," Sam finally said, well satisfied so far with the November night, "take me to get my green trunk and then to one more place." He stepped back from the fence, motioned to the poppoyom, and headed away from the corn patch back toward Emancipation Street. It wasn't until all three men were back in Art's small car with the engine fired up that the last sounds of Big Man-Eater grew too faint for Sam to hear. And even then, as he rode through the night toward his room, he could picture exactly the look of the broad black and white back of the hog moving steadily ahead as it ate ear after machine-counted ear of sha towea grown by the white man in that special place.

When they reached the dormitory on Pennsylvania Avenue, Art pulled the car into the shadow of a large bush as far as possible from the corner streetlight. The poppoyom said he was tired from hog-riding and would wait in the car, so Sam led Art through a side door of the building and up some back stairs to the corridor his room was on. The lights were off and the door was locked, but in the room Akbar was awake and listening. He opened the door before Sam had time to knock and stopped him from switching on the light.

"Don't let nobody know you here, man. Come on in and be quiet." Akbar looked nervous in the dim light of the room, pacing back and forth and running his big wide-toothed comb through his hair was he talked.

"They done been here, Leaping Deer, looking for you, man. Three of them fuckers in this room. Got so filled up in here I couldn't get my breath."

"Who was it?" Sam asked as he put things from his side of the room into the green trunk. He stopped to study the back of a book titled *Meaning and Structure in Art* and then carefully set it back on the shelf above his desk.

"*The* man, that's who it was. The Uni-Cops was here, Leaping Deer. Three of them asking to see you and rubbing on their billy clubs like it was their dicks."

"The cops?" Art said. "What the cops want with Sam?"

"Where you been, man?" asked Akbar. "You mean to tell me you don't know about the Centennial Game? Leaping Deer he done give it a name Illinois ain't never gonna forget." Akbar looked hard across the room at Sam leaning over the trunk and decided to stop talking.

"Well," he said, "I guess I let him tell you about it. You all probably ain't got time now anyway."

"Akbar," said Sam, holding out a large chunk of mikko root that he'd just broken off the supply in the trunk, "try some of this. The poppoyom says it smooths him out."

"Don't mind if I do," said Akbar. "What do you do with it? Eat it, or stick it in your nose?"

Sam put on some long pants and a blue shirt and jacket and finished putting things in the green trunk. Wadding the basketball uniform up into a little ball in his left hand, he straightened up and looked around the room one last time.

"I told them you done come and gone," Akbar said around the chunk of mikko root in his mouth. "They ain't gonna catch you leaving if you hurry it up."

Sam nodded and began pulling his trunk from the foot of the bed so he could lift it to his shoulder.

"Well, you on your way, I guess," Akbar said as Art helped Sam get the trunk up and they started for the door. "I tell you something, though, Leaping Deer, I ain't never seen nobody drive the lane the way you did. Never nobody. I mean that, man."

"Akbar Ameer," said Sam, pausing in the door and then making the flat sweeping gesture with his right hand parallel to the earth. "Don't swallow the mikko root." As they left, Akbar watched them all the way down the hall, the forgotten comb stuck into his hair so hard that it looked like it was welded to his head.

When Art and Sam got the green trunk to the car, the poppoyom was asleep, and he began to grumble when they woke him and made him move over to make room. "If it ain't a fucking Duroc gilt, it's a tin box I got to sit with," he complained, but he quieted down when Sam gave him the Illinois basketball uniform. In all of McKinley Short Eyes' stories about the little people of the woods, the poppoyom always liked new clothes and preferred them as gifts in return for favors they did the people of the Nation. Some things are the same always, even here, Sam thought as he watched the little man put the orange jersey with the blue number nine on over his brown jacket.

"That looks just fine," said Art, "if you let it out a little." He started the engine and turned to Sam.

"Where to now, Leaping Deer?" he asked. "You got any more animals you want rode?"

"The last place we must go," Sam answered him, "is the little store in Champaign close to the bus station. Look for the sign of the greyhound." In the back seat the poppoyom was humming a country song to himself as he solemnly leaned forward to regard the blue nine on his chest.

"O.K.," said Art. "But you're not going to break into somebody's store, are you?"

"No, I just want to trade something at a store. Find the greyhound first, and you'll see what I do."

It was late enough when they reached downtown Champaign for most of the store lights to be off. Here and there a bar was still lit and open, Maysies and The Place and Strange Pleasures, and just as they drove past The Capitol Steps, three men tumbled out the front door as though they'd been dropped by a large hand and began randomly fighting among themselves, each man trading weak, pushing blows with the other two.

"Damn, I wish I was out of this car," said the poppoyom. "I'd show them fuckers some fighting." He tapped Sam on the shoulder. "You got any more of that Indian chewing tobacco, son?"

Sam broke off another piece of mikko root for the midget and, as he turned to hand it to him, caught sight of a blue neon greyhound in full stride in the empty air about two blocks up and one over.

"There's the dog sign, Art," he said. "Where I have to go is on this side of it."

The store that Sam remembered still had the sign up saying it was closed until further notice, and when he walked up to the window, he could see among all the embroidered pillows, steerhorn ashtrays, and Bowie knives that it also still had what he had come for. Near the back of the display, half-hidden by the rubberized fringe of a blue cowboy vest, was the kaosati, the yellowed human skull, its eye sockets plugged with hardened white clay painted with blue and yellow designs. Whoever had made the markings had done a good job of it, Sam thought, noticing how well-matched each eyehole was, the paint beginning exactly at the same point on each side of the chalky moldings set into the eyes and ending exactly at the correct spot above each cheekbone. McKinley Short Eyes had demonstrated the proper way of marking the skulls of conquered enemies to his audience of young Alabamas and Coushattas by showing them both good and bad examples of the art. One of the ancient skulls in his collection had been poorly done, the yellow lines uneven on the dried white clay and the blue circles flattened instead of rounded. "The man who did this job," he had said, pointing at the flaws with a silver ball-point pen some white man had lost on the shoulder of Texas Highway 190, "is having many problems in eternity. The man he killed is not happy with the painting of his kaosati and will never give the man who killed him any peace. If you don't paint the blue and yellow designs the right way, your enemy will be ashamed and will never forgive you."

Each time at this point, the old man would put aside the example of faulty magic and then pick up the best skull from his collection and begin lecturing on the fine points of its brush work. "Bold strokes," he would say, "but not sloppy." Turning the kaosati from side to side before the eyes of each student, he would talk about the art that had gone into it until he was sure that each one of the young members of the Nation would know how to proceed if the occasion for such precise, close work ever again arose.

"What are you looking at, son?" asked the poppoyom beside Sam, standing on his tiptoes to peer into the window of Marty's Treasure and Junque. "You gonna buy your mama one of them nice pillows? That there's the only reason I always regretted the armed services don't accept little people. Them pretty pillows. That sorry little brother of mine must have sent back ten or twelve of them things to Mama from all over. Places like Hong Kong and Japan and Little Rock. Everywhere." He stepped back from the window and started rocking back and forth on the heels of his little boots, looking like he was about to cry.

"Don't get down on yourself, Byron," said Art. "Take a good hard suck on your mikko root. I notice that'll pick you up."

"Poppoyom," Sam said, looking down at the bald spot on the

top of the midget's head, "we'll get you a pillow for your mother.
Give me your keys again."

This time Sam counted three over to the left from the first key
he touched and then nine over to the right. When he inserted the
key into the padlock on the door, it was harder to turn than the
ones on the Swine Enclosure and the Morrill Plot had been because
a leak in Marty's drainpipe directly above the lock had been allowing water to pour over the lock each time it rained. But by jiggling
the key a couple of times, Sam was able to get the rusty tumblers to
fall into place, and he had the door open in a few seconds.

Once inside the store, Sam walked around to the back of the
display window and reached over the piece of plywood nailed
across it and picked up the kaosati. It felt light and dry in his hand,
and when he tested a couple of the teeth in the upper jaw, he found
that they were still firmly set in place. He reached into the pocket
of his jacket and took out the clear sabia bead touched with red.
Rubbing it between his finger and thumb, he looked at it for a
minute before he leaned over and placed it in the spot where the
kaosati had been. "Fathers," he said in the tongue of the Nation, "I
leave the sabia in exchange for this warrior. I take him home."

"Where's Mama's pillow?" asked the poppoyom, chinning
himself on the plywood backdrop and struggling to see over into
the display case.

"Here's a good one," Art said and reached past a set of drinking glasses inscribed with Masonic emblems to get at a purple and
gold creation. He handed the midget a flat rayon-covered pillow
trimmed with yellow fringe and bearing across its face two jet-
fighter planes and the words "Strategic Air Command." At the
bottom worked in with silver thread was the legend "Chenault Air
Force Base, Tolono, Illinois," and in black curly letters the pillow
stated it was the Terror of the Skies.

"Aw, yeah, she'll love it," the poppoyom said in a choked-up
voice. He held the pillow gently at arm's length for a minute while
he studied its details, and then he began fumbling with his belt
buckle.

"I'm gonna trade them my hog halter for it," he said. "I wish I
had the ring out of that Duroc's nose to leave them too. I'd purely
love to do it."

"The thought's as good as the deed, as my dear old daddy
used to say," declared Art. "Let's get out of here."

Back outside, Sam opened the green trunk, and after wrapping the kaosati in a couple of T-shirts he placed it carefully under some clothes. He almost forgot to refasten the padlock to Marty's Treasure and Junque, but remembered just as Art began to pull away from the curb and had him wait while he went back. The sabia bead that he'd left for the skull took up little space beside the blue cowboy vest, but as Sam gave it a last look, it caught a shaft of light from the streetlamp behind him. He stared at the glass bead dotted with red, feeling that if he could look long enough he would be able to see through it to whatever lay behind the paint. It was like the water of Long King Creek, easiest to read when the spring rains muddied it and hardest to know when the summer made it run clear. Squinting, he leaned near the window so that his breath began to fog it.

In a minute Art Wallace called his name from the car. Sam slowly clicked shut the lock, turning his back on the sabia glowing behind him, and climbed into the front seat of the car. "Take us to the big highway," he said and began buttoning his jacket against the cold.

On the way out of town to the interstate, nobody said much. Art paid close attention to his driving, and Sam let himself sink low enough to rest the back of his head against the car seat, while the midget riding in the back now and then made crooning sounds as he stroked the embroidered pillow and thought about things long ago and far away.

"All right," said Art as he reached the access road to the highway and pulled off to the side. "We're here. Now what, Sam?"

"Now," Sam said, "now, I'm leaving this country."

"Where you going? Back to Texas?"

"Yes," said Sam. "Home. Back to the Nation."

"That's what I figured," Art said after sitting quiet long enough for five or six cars to pass headed south on the four-lane highway. He killed the engine and turned to face Sam.

"Leaping Deer, you didn't get run off," he finally said. "I'll find out tomorrow in the daylight what they say about it, but what do you say? Why are you leaving Illinois?"

In the back seat the poppoyom had curled up beside the trunk with the Strategic Air Command pillow under his head and begun to snore. The basketball jersey had worked its way down his body so that all that showed beneath it were the children's shoes on the little man's feet. Taking a last look at the blue nine on the orange shirt, black in the moonlight, Sam turned back to answer Art.

"There's no middle for me here, Art Wallace. Nothing holds still inside the circle. Everything is strung out in a line." He spoke slowly, trying to choose the words that would make the translation right. "And it's sha towea, the corn. Something about the corn is not good here." He turned his right hand around twice to include all the open fields around him. "Too much corn. Too much bad corn. Not the place for a Coushatta."

"I don't understand what you mean," said Art after a long pause. "But I do see you're going to go." On the highway three trucks loaded with stacks of steel pipe thundered past, running nose to tail like dogs after a rabbit. Both men watched them until the red taillights dwindled into nothing far down the interstate.

"What about Sharon?" asked Art. "Last time I looked you seemed to be getting pretty tight with her."

"Sharon Hansen," Sam stated as though he were labeling a tree or bush in the Big Thicket that someone had asked him the name of. "I believe she wanted a cannibal to get her and it did." He studied for a minute and added, "It almost got me too, but I didn't want that, and I got away from it."

"I don't know what any of that means, and I don't think I want to," said Art after a while and looked back at the highway again. "You going to hitch back home then?" He spoke softly as though not to wake the little man sleeping in the back.

"Yes, I'll get a ride," Sam said. "And you, Art Wallace. What will you do now?"

"Aw, at first I was so pissed when I finally let them run me off that I promised myself I was never going to touch another goddamn basketball. Who needs it?" He leaned back, stretched his arms above his head and let out a groan. "But you know, I think I'm getting over it. What I'm going to do, I think, is transfer from here to some dipshit place and be a real studhorse. Maybe Northern Illinois or somewhere like that. I can see the headlines now. Art Wallace, All Bleeding-Gum Conference Forward. Hell, I'll probably set some scoring records myself." He laughed for a minute and bounced a fist on the steering wheel.

"Really, though," he said in a quiet voice, "I guess it's still like what I told you before. Remember? I still want to see the look in that fucker's eyes when he knows I've beat him. I still need to get some more of that." Art shook his right fist above his head and then, taking a deep sigh, let it drop.

"No use waiting any longer. You got to catch a ride, Sam," he said and, getting out of the car, began lifting the green trunk from its place beside the sleeping midget.

"Didn't old Byron do good tonight?" he asked Sam, looking down at the little man in the basketball shirt. "You got to hand it to him."

"Yeah," Sam said. "If you treat the poppoyom right, he's always a good friend to anybody from the Nation." Leaning over the little man, Sam stuck his index finger into the snoring mouth and hooked out the mikko root from beneath the broad tongue. "He might swallow it," he told Art and deposited the black chunk in the pocket of the midget's discarded coat. "A sick poppoyom can get pretty mad."

Art took one end of the green trunk and Sam the other, and they carried it up the access road to the shoulder of the south-bound interstate. Stopping by a roadsign that said "Champaign Exit 3," the two men stood looking down the long stretch of white cement leading out of the cornfields of central Illinois. From the embankment, they could see the lights of Champaign off to the east and now and then a car or two leaving the state highway beneath them to circle up the access and join the flow of machines on the four-lane. The wind from a passing truck blew against them hard enough to make them lean forward for balance, and Sam put one hand on the roadsign support to steady himself.

"Well," Art said after the truck had gone by, "I better go get Byron home. He's married, you know." He kicked at the gravel of the roadbed and looked back toward Champaign. "Got three kids. And you know something? They're all normal size. Every one of them's taller than he is. Even his little girl."

Sam nodded and opened his mouth to speak, but found he didn't have anything to say. The little sliver of pale moon he had noticed earlier was gone, but the night was still clear, and he could make out most of the star patterns he had first learned a long time ago. After a while, Art stuck out his hand, and Sam shook it without looking. Art turned and began to walk slowly back down the access road toward the green car and the sleeping poppoyom.

"All right, Leaping Deer," he said over his shoulder. "I'm

going to come see you someday. I want to find that place they grow that funny chewing gum. You wait and see."

"All right," Sam said and watched Art Wallace all the way down the curved road and into the car. It drove off slowly, and Sam was able to follow its taillights for what must have been well over a minute, but finally he lost them among some other lights on the highway to Champaign after another truck had passed in front of him. He turned slowly away to face the interstate, and sticking out his right thumb, looked north up the long highway toward the line of approaching headlights. Suddenly, he felt as though he'd left something. He looked through all his pockets, but it wasn't until after he had hefted both ends of his trunk to make sure the weight seemed right that he was able finally to settle down to finding himself a ride down the road toward home.

Circle Looks at Circle

In a few minutes a truck running at the rear of a clump of five others slowed and peeled off from the group to the shoulder of the highway about a hundred yards up from where Sam was standing. As Sam moved up the gravel roadbed toward it at a trot as fast as the green trunk on his shoulder would allow him, he could see by the glow of the bank of red and orange taillights that the letters ETMF were painted across the rear double doors. When Sam reached the cab, the driver had already leaned across the seat and pushed the door open.

"Put that thing back there in the sleeper," he told Sam, pointing at the trunk. "It's plenty of room back yonder. I don't never even use it."

Sam stowed the trunk and crawled up into the passenger seat, pushing a pile of work gloves, pencils, and paperback books out of his way.

"Where you headed?" asked the driver as he pulled out into the lane of traffic and began working his way up through the gears, double-clutching after each one to get as much as he could out of the engine. "Down to Cairo?"

"No," said Sam, looking away from his reflection in the window glass, "not there. I'm going to Texas."

"Well, boy, I tell you. You're in luck tonight. This here

jimmy belongs to East Texas Motor Freight, and it's being herded by none other than Cowboy Reeves all the way to Houston. We're gonna be there in twenty two hours and seventeen minutes with a load of heavy-duty blow-out gaskets."

Cowboy wore a new white Stetson and a fringed two-colored shirt with snap buttons, and as he worked the pedals on the floor, Sam could see that he was shod in flowered black boots that reached clear to the knee. As the big semi moved past the last sign pointing to Champaign-Urbana, Cowboy looked over at Sam and asked him if he had been working the harvest. He was wearing dark glasses with gold rims which picked up red and orange reflections from the dashboard lights as he talked.

"No," Sam said. "I missed the harvest."

"Just as well. There ain't no percentage in stoop labor." Cowboy Reeves pulled out to pass a slow-moving passenger car and gestured with his right hand.

"You know something?" he asked. "I was on that Candid Camera show one time. That thing on TV? Yeah, it was just this side of Memphis. You know where that old boy's got the cafe right next to that wrecking yard where one-oh-six comes across? It was right there." He put the semi into the next highest gear and stubbed out his cigarette. "See, what it was, I walked up to the counter and ordered me a cup of coffee, put my money down, and this waitress I never seen before she got it for me and every time I lifted it up to take a sip the damn thing dribbled down the side. You know, spilled kinda like. It happened three or four times and that damn shit was getting all over the table and running down on my shirt and my britches and I finally just got ahold of it with both hands and it still poured down the side like a cow pissing on a flat rock. Know what I mean?"

"Yeah," Sam said. "I get you."

"Well, I called her back on over there and she give me some more coffee and it kept on spilling until I got plumb mad and started to leave, and right then's when that little fat-faced fellow talks funny turned around next to me on the other chair there and says, smile, you're on Candid Camera. They had that damn camera in behind a bunch of them peanut butter crackers on the back shelf and was taking my picture the whole time." Cowboy stopped talking and lit another cigarette, driving down the Illinois interstate with a half-smile on his face. "That's when I was on TV," he

said in a minute or so through the cloud of tobacco smoke surrounding his head.

"Must have been funny to see," Sam finally offered.

"Yeah, that's the only machine besides a truck engine I got
any use for. A television set. You can see whoever's talking on it,
and that's all right. You know who's saying what then." He gestured toward a small microphone hanging from a hook beneath the
instrument panel. "Not like that damn thing. That fucking CB
yonder."

Sam studied it in the light from the dials and said nothing.

"Truckers is supposed to like them things, but I don't," said
Cowboy Reeves. "You know why?" He took off his dark glasses
and looked across at Sam with a sad expression on his face. "It ain't
real, that's why. I don't get no comfort from it. You see I got it
turned off. And it's gonna stay that way too. That there's the way I
keep it ninety percent of the time."

Neither one said anything for a while, and Sam let himself
settle back into the seat, closing his eyes against the lights from the
passing cars and the occasional high-intensity lamps in the front
yards of the passing farms. By the time Cowboy Reeves had driven
the East Texas Motor Freight truck past the exit roads to Mattoon,
Sam could feel himself sinking into sleep as though he were slowly
falling through thick layers of soft white smoke. The last thing he
could pick out was the voice of the truck driver either singing or
talking in a blurred high-pitched tone. And in another minute or
so, the white mist curled around that and smothered it too.

Somewhere ahead of him coming from beyond the edge of the
cane thicket was a regular booming sound, repeated over and over
again as he moved toward it. This time as he stopped to gather puff
balls from a thistle to stuff in his ears against the clanging noise, he
knew what he would see when he came to the end of the dark
woods. And he knew this time that he could not hesitate and try to
judge the speed of the lifting edge of the sky and the duration of
the open space between it and the earth. He would have to trust
himself and the Old Ones and run directly at the place where the
elements of sky and earth intersected, showing no fear or caution,
and leap as strongly as he could for the brief open space. He
stopped at the edge of the open grass clearing, dotted here and
there with yellowing youpon bushes, and removed the bark leggings he had worn for protection against the fangs of the rattle-

snakes. The shredded leggings came off in pieces which turned to dust and disappeared as he dropped them to the ground, and by the time he had removed the last torn strand, there was no sign left of what had saved him from the snake poison.

As stuffed as his ears were with the puff balls, the noise of the sky slamming against the earth was still so deafening that he could feel sharp pains deep inside his head as he gathered himself to run. He broke into the clearing and halfway across the open ground he reached full speed, moving faster than he had ever been able to go before, passing the youpon bushes so quickly that he had no time to feel the slap of their sharp edges against his bare legs. The slamming noise of the sky and earth became so loud that he felt he had to cry out, but he knew he must not, and with one last thrust he launched himself from the earth in a leap toward the place where the pain was worst, remembering not to try to judge. Instantly, the air blew cool against his body and the terrible noise stopped as though it had never been, and he found himself walking quietly in a green plain beside a small stream of clear water.

All about him deer grazed quietly on the long green grass, not lifting their heads to sniff the air for danger and feeding unafraid as he passed near them. Flights of brightly colored birds like none he had ever seen before drifted from tree to tree above him, singing clear notes as they fed on ripe fruit and berries. A family of foxes played near the trunk of a large pine in front of him, the young ones scampering about the mother and nosing at squirrels which ate undisturbed the oak mast which lay scattered about everywhere on the ground.

Looking down at his feet, Sam Leaping Deer saw that he was wearing moccasins decorated more finely than any he had ever seen in the corn dances of the Nation, and when he lifted his hands, he saw on his wrists bracelets made of a hard beautiful metal.

"Abba Mikko," he said, and at the words, the scene before him blurred and changed, leaving in place of the green plain of animals a lodge more massive and beautiful than he could have imagined, built of perfect yellow and brown timbers. He walked to its door and did not forget to touch the carved supports on each side of the opening before he entered. Approaching the sleeping platform in the middle of the room, he slipped the moccasins from his feet, although they were clean and perfectly dry, and lay down

across the cushions of moss covered with the soft hides of unknown animals. He pulled the blanket of blue and green design
over him and fell immediately into undreaming sleep in the large
room filled with light.

"Hey, don't you want something to eat?"

Sam roused himself and looked across the truck cab at Cowboy Reeves who had replaced his dark glasses and was fanning
himself with his Stetson. The hat brim had left a permanent circle
in the slicked-down black hair on his head just above where his
sideburns started. He had pushed open the door on his side of the
truck, and he looked red-eyed and hot in the flat early-morning
sunshine.

Sam nodded at the driver and looked around to find that they
were parked along with eight or ten other big rigs in front of a long
flat building about two-thirds covered with white shingles. The
rest of it was exposed tar paper which was torn and faded where
the weather had been able to work on it. Inside, he and Cowboy
Reeves were served grits and sausage and eggs by a middle-aged
waitress who seemed to be the victim of new dentures. Most of the
time she kept her lips stretched shut over her perfectly white regular teeth as she walked back and forth between the tables and the
serving slot cut into the wall of the kitchen. Now and then,
though, when she thought she had her back turned enough for
nobody to see, she would lift both hands to her face and push at
the plates as though she were trying to set them in cement. Once
when she stopped near the jukebox to make a selection, Sam saw
the waitress draw her top lip back, close her eyes and shoot the
upper plate halfway out of her mouth into her right hand with a
slight gagging sound. When she looked around to see if anybody
had been watching, Sam dropped his eyes to the grits and egg yolk
on his plate and paid close attention to his breakfast.

Sam dozed for most of the rest of the day as the ETMF truck
roared through Tennessee and on into Arkansas. Cowboy Reeves
seemed satisfied not to talk. Instead, he sang medleys of country
and religious tunes, finishing one and hardly pausing before beginning another. Now and then he popped small white pills into his
mouth and washed them down with slugs from a thermos of iced
tea. At one point Sam was awakened by the static and chatter of
the shortwave radio as they came into Little Rock. Cowboy ex-

plained that he had to get some help against the highway patrol and that he wouldn't use the thing at all except to help keep his Estimated Time of Arrival in Houston solid. "That's the only use for this damn thing. Listen at it spitting and popping. It'd shock the piss out of you if it could get at you."

"You go through Franklin?" Sam asked.

"You mean south of Lufkin on fifty-nine? Sure do. Hell, that's almost close enough to Houston for me to start gearing down. That where you going?"

"Close to there. Let me out at the big red light," Sam said and settled back to nap, hoping that Cowboy wouldn't have to use the radio again.

At about midnight the East Texas Motor Freight semi full of heavy-duty blow-out gaskets from Chicago pulled up beside the Franklin County Courthouse with a long hiss of airbrakes. Sam had been awake for the last couple of hours looking out the window at the loblolly and long-needle pines outlined against the night sky. The fact that there were no leaves on these branches to be lost was somehow deeply satisfying to him.

He reached back behind the front seat into the sleeping compartment and pulled out the green trunk and stepped down onto the curb, feeling suddenly a little dizzy as his feet touched the ground. Something in his belly did a little dip and roll as he eased the trunk to the grass just over the curb and then stepped back to close the truck door.

"Hey," said Cowboy Reeves, leaning across the seat toward Sam and pointing to something behind him. "What's it say on that big old monument yonder?"

Sam looked at the marble soldier standing atop the square piece of stone in the middle of the grass plot behind him and shrugged. "I don't know," he said, turning back to Cowboy. "I never read it."

"Well, don't make no difference. I'm gonna be in Harris County in forty-two minutes. You take her easy." He left in a great cloud of diesel fumes, gunning the engine and racing through the lower gears to beat the next red light four blocks up.

Before he picked up the trunk and crossed the street to start down Highway 96 toward the land of the Nation, Sam walked over to the monument to read the inscriptions carved around its base. Squinting in the dim light, he read on one side of the soldier's footrest that Franklin County had furnished more soldiers to the Confederacy than it had voters. On the other side of the stone foundation, far enough away from the light that he had to read over it three times before he was sure he had it right, Sam finally made out the words whose edges were beginning to blur away with the elements. "Defeat does not always establish the wrong," it stated in rain-softened stone. He stood still for a minute and watched a car full of drunk high school boys circle the square a couple of times and then roar off up the highway toward Lufkin. Then, by standing on tiptoe and reaching high above his head he was able to touch the tip of the soldier's right foot. He rubbed his fingers across the slick stone and looked at them, but nothing of the surface seemed to have come off on them. He walked back to his trunk, got it up on one shoulder and crossed against the light.

He caught a ride in a pickup truck with a farmer who was coming home late from hauling a load of piney-woods hogs to the Huntsville auction. The farmer turned off about two miles short of the reservation, and Sam took up the green trunk again for the rest of his journey, its contents rustling softly back and forth by his ear as he walked down the shoulder of the road between the banks of pines.

By the time he got to the cattle guard separating the reservation from the rest of Texas, the moon had dropped below the line of trees, and he had to step carefully to keep from slipping into one of the spaces between the iron bars. Once across the barrier, he began to walk more quickly, looking toward the dark mass of thicket to his right to find the opening he wanted to take to get away from the highway and into the woods.

About the time he thought he saw it, the headlights of a car on the highway behind him swept past and picked out the bulk of something lying in the ditch a few yards ahead of him. When he got a little closer, Sam saw that it was the Alabama youth called President Polk, flat on his back with his arms outspread as though he had just fallen out of a sweetgum tree. President Polk had an empty vanilla extract bottle in his right hand, and under his head was an American Ace coffee can that he was using as a pillow.

"President Polk," said Sam, stopping on the bank of the ditch and speaking in the tongue of the Nation, "are you resting well there?"

President Polk opened his eyes and lifted his head from the

coffee can, craning his neck to see who had spoken. "Is it one of the Old Ones?" he asked, spreading his hand over the extract bottle to try to hide it. His voice sounded weak and far-off, but the words were clear in Sam's ears.

"No, it's me. Sam Leaping Deer."

"Leaping Deer," President Polk said. "Didn't we whip the ass of Crockett?"

"Yes," said Sam. "We did. Do you want to get up from there?"

"No," President Polk answered in a thoughtful tone, moving the can under his head to a more comfortable spot and settling back on it. "This is a good place, I think. It's dry and not too soft. I'll talk to you later, Sam Leaping Deer. In the daylight."

"All right," Sam said, moving off toward the opening into the thicket. "Good dreams to you, President Polk."

"Good dreams to you, Sam Leaping Deer," President Polk said with a sigh, his voice fading away as he nestled himself back into the rocks and gravel of the road ditch.

After he had walked for fifteen or twenty minutes along the narrow trail through the pine thicket, using his free hand to feel ahead of him for tree trunks and low branches, Sam began to hear the sound of water in the stream bed of Long King Creek, and he knew he was near the place he wanted to find. He stopped and lowered the trunk to the ground, almost overturning it on a stump in the dark, and then straightened and rubbed his right shoulder before bending over again to open it. The kaosati had worked its way to the bottom of the pile of clothes, and it wasn't until after he had rummaged in the tin box for almost a minute that he found it when his fingers grazed the teeth in the upper jaw.

In a place far in the back of his head, one of the spring chants of the Nation started up and began to repeat itself, faintly in a slow peaceful way, and he stopped in the darkness near the running water to listen to it for a spell before looking for the tree he knew would be somewhere there close to him. The words of the chant and the taps on the drum accompanying it built steadily in volume until he looked about him to be sure it wasn't there in the world as well as inside him, but in a few moments it began to fade and finally vanished, leaving only the sound of Long King Creek water and far off the short scream of some small animal caught by an owl hunting in the darkness.

"Kaosati," he said aloud. "Warrior." Walking away from the trunk toward the creek bank, he lifted the skull painted with blue and yellow designs up before him and turned as he reached the place where he felt the earth crumbling under his feet and sliding toward the water. He took several steps along the bank of Long King, balanced on the line between earth and water, and with one last stride, stopped and put out his left hand until it touched the scaly bark of a large tree, the sycamore that had served as the most western point of the burial platform of McKinley Short Eyes years before.

The length of telephone wire that had once lashed the sapling of the platform to the sycamore was still there, and when Sam felt above his head on the trunk, his hand found it still wound around the lowest branch of the tree. The end of the wire slipped easily through one of the openings in the skull in his hands, and with a few twists and knots he fastened the kaosati firmly to the tree, high enough from the ground to be out of easy reach and hidden in the angle formed by the branch and trunk.

For the rest of the night he squatted beneath the kaosati on the bank of Long King Creek, his back against the sycamore trunk, and listened to the unseen water flow by him. At first light, he bathed himself in the stream, standing hip-deep in the cold water as he scrubbed his body with the dark brown sand from the creek bed. He dressed again and took a last look at the skull fastened to Short Eyes' tree as it took definition in the growing light. Here in the air of the Nation, the designs on the clay filling the eye sockets looked to Sam even more perfect than they had behind the store window in Illinois. Turning away, he took up the green trunk one last time, and before the sun was fully up in the sky he was turning off the sandy road toward the house of Cooper Leaping Deer. His clothes were completely dry, and only a little dampness from his bathing in Long King Creek still remained in his hair.

When Sam came around the last bend and walked up into the yard, he saw that Cooper's collection of injured automobiles was changed somewhat. The Ford coupe was still where it had always been, the weeds a little higher around its tires and bumpers and a new hole in one of the side windows, but where the '50 Ford pickup had been was now only a large yellow patch among the young saplings and bitter-weeds. The most important change in the landscape, an addition pulled up near enough to the house for its left front fender to graze the end of the porch, dominated the scene.

It was a yellow Plymouth with the Taxi sign still attached to its roof and with only one of its doors torn off. When Sam got a little closer, he saw that the tires were all up and that the grass and weeds under the machine were no higher than what was growing around it. It looked as though the car had actually been driven up to its present position and deliberately parked, resting in place until somebody would come out of the shotgun house, get into it and drive away.

Sam put down the green trunk on the edge of the porch with a thump and stopped to study the emblem on the side of the left front door. "Corrigan Taxi Service," it proclaimed above a picture of a longhorn steer with a puzzled but happy look on its face, "Give Us a Call and We'll Give You a Honk." Something moved in the house behind him, and he turned to see his mother standing in the doorway, her hand thrust through where the screen used to be as she unlatched the hook holding the door closed.

"Sam," she said, stepping onto the porch and coming toward him, "the cooking smoke told me yesterday you were coming."

"Mother," said Sam, speaking to her in the tongue of the Nation, "wife of my father. Yes, I am here now." They came together, and each of them touched the hands of the other and stepped back a pace.

Sam looked at his mother for a minute and thought that she looked smaller than he had remembered, so small in fact that he almost leaned forward to kiss her on the forehead like a white man, but he was able to stop in time.

"And do you cook for my small brothers and my father?" he asked. "And do you go to the fall corn dance?"

"Yes, I do those things," she said. "Will you take food now?"

"In a while." Sam looked from his mother back toward the taxi from Corrigan and saw that one of the headlights had been broken out. "Where is Cooper Leaping Deer?"

"The yellow car needs gasoline, so he walked today," she said. "He has gone to the village for rehearsal."

"Rehearsal," Sam said and nodded, and then waited politely as he knew to do for her explanation.

"Yes," his mother said. "He has what the white man calls a leading role in the Nation's pageant." She stopped and looked off

for a while toward the line of trees surrounding the Leaping Deer
yard before she began speaking again.

"The white men came from the school called SMU to show us
how to do it. The little white man who moves quickly calls it
Beyond the Sundown. Every day your father goes with other men
of the Nation to the village dance ground, and they practice to
learn how to tell about the time when the Alabamas and Coushattas came to Texas to live."

Sam sat down on the edge of the trunk and picked up a neck-
lace made of Seven-Up bottle caps and string that one of the children had left on the porch. It rattled, but felt light, like nothing, as
he tossed it from one hand to the other.

"Why do they do this pageant?" he asked, watching the neck-
lace carefully so that he wouldn't let it fall to the ground.

"They say that the white people will come in their cars and
pay money to see the Nation pretend to be the old Alabamas and
Coushattas. The clothes the men wear when they rehearse are very
pretty, and the white men have given new drums. It says about it
on the big sign on the highway. Did you read the words on it?"

"No," said Sam. "I came home through the woods. It was
dark." Tossing aside the string of Seven-Up caps, he rose from his
seat on the trunk and pointed at the taxi. "Did my father trade for
that machine?"

"The white man in Franklin will let him pay for it each
month. Brother Two Tongues says the white men who make the
pageant will give the Nation some of the money that the other
white people pay them to see us."

The screen door swung open, and the youngest brother of the
family walked out onto the porch and fastened his eyes on Sam.
Except for a pair of rubber-soled shoes, he was naked.

"Ho, little brother," said Sam, pointing at the rash of chill
bumps across the child's chest and belly, "you will be cold like
that."

"Sam Leaping Deer," said the boy as he awkwardly made a
circle with the thumb and first finger of his right hand. "Two
points."

"Where is La Wanda Two Tongues?" Sam asked his mother,
looking away toward the basketball goal in the front yard.

"In the booth. She stays there in the red booth with her sisters
to sell the things for her father."

"What are these things?"

"That's on the big sign on the highway too. It is called curios. Many beads and small dolls and moccasins with red and yellow thread on them. Some little drums made of rubber." She shrugged her shoulders and set one bare foot on top of the other one.

"I will go see her," Sam said, "and I will eat after then."

As he passed the parked taxi and walked across the yard, Sam's mother opened the screen and went back into the house, and his little brother crawled under the porch to fetch the basketball that had rolled there. Before he trotted out of range, Sam could hear the springy sound of the ball bouncing against the rim of the basket and its splat against the wood of the backboard as the naked child circled from one side of the dirt court to the other, working on his moves.

The tall white woman was leaning over the counter of the booth so far that she seemed about ready to lift up one leg and crawl into the building itself. She was wearing a piece of patterned cloth tied around her head, and when Sam walked up to within a few feet of her, he could see it was a state map of some kind. Iowa, maybe, or Nebraska. It looked to be one of the square-shaped ones, though from where he stood he couldn't tell exactly its true geography. In a minute or so, she found what she wanted among the boxes of small items piled up in front of her, and she shoved a bill across the counter and stepped back to admire her buy. It was a rubber axehead fastened to a length of varnished bamboo and decorated with chartreuse and purple feathers.

"He'll love it," Sam heard her say to one of La Wanda's sisters. "He'll just go crazy over this little tommy-hawk. Does it say on it the name of y'all's tribe?"

When the sister said that it did, the woman walked off toward the corn dance ground, counting her change without watching where she was headed. Stepping up to the booth, Sam laid one hand on the counter and looked past the sister toward La Wanda, who was bent over a cardboard carton against the back wall. A radio on the shelf above her head was tuned to a song he remembered having heard somewhere in one of the truck-stops on his way down from Illinois with Cowboy Reeves. As the singer on the radio hit a high note, La Wanda straightened up and turned toward the front of the booth, her hands filled with small black-haired dolls dressed in little swatches of cloth cut to look like buckskin. One of them slipped from between her fingers, and it wasn't until after she had reached down and picked it up that she caught sight of Sam standing on the other side of her sister.

"I see you, La Wanda Two Tongues," Sam said formally and folded his hands in front of him.

"Sam Leaping Deer," she said and, stepping to the front of the booth, tumbled the double handful of dolls into a flat tray beside two other ones. "Are you back home now?"

"Yes," Sam answered. "I have come back to the Nation." He paused while he looked at La Wanda's face and tried to decide what looked unfamiliar about it. As she began to speak, arranging the dolls before her into straight rows in the tray while she did so, he decided that since he had seen her last something about her hair had changed and also the way she talked was somehow different. It was faster, and she seemed to have developed a habit of tilting her head back as she spoke.

"A lot has happened here," she was saying, patting her forehead as though she were hot. "Do you see the men on the dance ground rehearsing with Mr. Allison? He's from SMU. That's where he's a drama director."

"He tells La Wanda to call him Allie-Baby," said the younger sister and collapsed against the side wall, sputtering through the fingers she had raised to her mouth. "And he calls her Pocahontas."

"You talk too much, goose-face," La Wanda said and made a pushing motion toward her sister with one hand. "He's a real joker, Mr. Allison," she explained to Sam and tossed her hair back from her face with two little jerks of her head.

"Things are really going on these days in the village, Sam. Even my father's different. He lets me and my sisters go out now." She looked down at the plastic tray and straightened a few more dolls as her sister snorted her way through another fit of giggling.

"I live here now," Sam said slowly, staring at the last unarranged doll in La Wanda's tray. When he saw her jostle it into place beside the rows of others, he felt suddenly short of breath as though he had just caught an elbow under the ribs while going up for a rebound. He shifted his weight a quarter of a turn and looked toward the circle of men and boys standing around somebody in the middle of the corn dance ground. They were all quiet, listening intently to words being spoken by a white man Sam couldn't see from where he was standing.

"Well," La Wanda was saying, "so you'll live on the reservation again. Didn't you like it up there?"

"No," Sam said in a careful voice, "I didn't like it."

"That's him," La Wanda said, gesturing toward the cluster of Alabamas and Coushattas. "Mr. Allison. He's telling them what to do. They've been rehearsing for a long time, but maybe you can still get in the pageant too, if you ask him. I mean if you haven't got anything to do."

Sam turned back and stared for a long time at a point on La Wanda's forehead just above where the curve of her nose blended into the skull. It seemed hard to focus his eyes in the shadow of the booth, and he was having a hard time keeping them fixed straight ahead. Finally, he spoke again, asking the question he knew he had to and waiting for the answer he knew would come.

"Do you see me, La Wanda Two Tongues?"

"Yes, Sam," she said quickly. "Sure I do." She tilted her head further back. "But look around us here." She waved her hand in a circle which took in the red booth, the clump of Alabama and Coushatta males who had begun to move in a well-organized circle around a bearded white man moving a white wand up and down in a bouncy rhythm, and the three ladies with blue hair who were bearing down on the counter lined with curios.

"Things are finally happening here, Sam. You know what I mean. Something's going on that's, like, fun for a change."

"Yeah, something besides church all the time," the younger sister added, straightening up from her lean against the wall and speaking for the first time in a deadly serious tone.

"Can I help you?" La Wanda asked in English, turning away as the three white women came crowding up to the counter. She showed her teeth in a smile and touched her hand to her hair against the little breeze which had just sprung up and begun to give her trouble.

"Yes, miss," said the smallest of the blue-haired ladies. "Is everything here authentic?"

Sam was halfway to the dance ground at the center of the village before La Wanda looked up from the rows of trays and saw that he was gone. She started to call his name, but the first lady who had spoken asked her about a piece of turquoise jewelry from

Arizona which looked just like what she was searching for, and in a few seconds La Wanda found herself bending over the piece, completely involved in indicating some of the finer points of its craftsmanship.

A couple of young Indians were sitting at the edge of the beaten-down dancing area, their backs toward Sam, watching the ring of men moving around the white man with the beard, and as Sam walked closer, he thought he recognized them. And at about the same time he did, it came to him what he wanted to do. He took a long breath and stopped for a minute to watch the circle of men from the Nation as they moved their feet together in a little hop and shuffle in time to the white man's regular counting. His father must be one of them, he thought, but he didn't try to pick him out from the bunch. Finally, he bent down toward the two people sitting in front of him and spoke.

"Beats Billy," he said. "President Polk."

They turned to look back over their shoulders, and President Polk's eyes popped out as he saw who had called his name.

"Sam Leaping Deer," he said and scrambled up from the muddy edge of the dance ground. "I saw you in a vision last night. You were carrying a big dead man on your back. He was green and stiff, and his spirit was restless. And now you are here as yourself." He turned and spoke to Beats Billy. "It was a true dream I had, just like in the old stories."

"And in this dream were you in a deep ditch, sleeping on a hard pillow?" Sam asked him.

"I don't know," said President Polk, hitching his pants up over his belly and looking thoughtful. "I don't remember settings too well. But the rest is true."

"Come with me," Sam said and began walking toward the woods away from the circle of Alabamas and Coushattas wheeling about the man in the green jumpsuit. "I want you to help me fix something."

They left the village clearing, and after leading the way directly south until the sound of the rehearsal drums had faded away, Sam began to angle off toward the east a few degrees.

"Where are we going?" asked President Polk. "To my house? There's nothing over there."

"Yes, there is," said Sam. "Your basketball and goal. I need them. Do you ever use them?"

"Well," said President Polk, grunting as he hit the ground after jumping off a fallen sweetgum trunk in their path, "I might someday need to work on my jump shot." Beats Billy made a snorting sound in the back of his throat, and Sam took a quick look back at President Polk who had dropped his eyes to the ground.

Like his namesake, President Polk weighed well over two hundred pounds, but he stood just a couple of inches over five feet and had never in his life put up a jump shot that couldn't have been blocked by an ordinary twelve-year-old Coushatta.

"All right," said Sam carefully, "but I could really use it. What would you take for it?"

"Basketball *and* goal?" asked President Polk.

"Yes," Sam said without looking back.

"Well, let me see," said President Polk between strides as he stretched to follow in Sam's trail. "Two dollars, I reckon."

After they had dismembered the backboard and the goal from the post supporting it by standing on a kitchen chair and pounding away with a wood maul, Sam and Beats Billy got the thing up between them and headed again for the thicket while President Polk came behind with the basketball, the chair, and a hammer and nails. By the time Sam had led them to the huge pin oak in the middle of the clearing near Long King Creek, all three of them were winded even though they had stopped several times to rest.

"Will you mount it here?" asked Beats Billy, looking around the small clear space from where he was leaning against a long-leaf pine.

"Yes," said Sam. "I remember this place from one time before."

"Look at these roots," Beats Billy said and kicked at the one sticking up out of the ground closest to him. "You can't dribble and move around in among all these roots."

"No, I can't," Sam agreed and began lifting the backboard into position against the pin oak.

"How are you going to work on your moves then?"

Sam let the backboard slide back to the ground and began looking around for something that would leave a mark on the tree trunk. Picking up a handful of whitish pieces of stone from the ground, he turned toward Beats Billy and began sorting through the chunks for the right one.

"I'm not going to move any more," he said and threw away most of what he had been holding in his hand. "I'm going to stay in just one spot and shoot from there. I'm going to do everything from just that one spot." He discarded all but one piece of white stone, and walking back to the pin oak tree, reached above his head and drew a chalky line.

"That's the bottom of it," he said.

After the three young men of the Nation had fastened the backboard with tenpenny nails where Sam wanted it on the trunk of the pin oak, Beats Billy and President Polk took turns shooting for a few minutes. The protruding oak roots and the uneven ground made it almost impossible to move to the left or right for jump shots or hooks, and the dim light under the cover of the pine needles was too much to contend with as well. So after a few times of retrieving the ball from where it had bounced away from the clearing into the youpon thicket and after President Polk had fallen heavily over a pin oak root, both of them decided they had had enough.

"Here," said Beats Billy, tossing the basketball to Sam who had been standing back out of the way watching the other two shoot. "It's your ball, and it's the worst court I've ever seen."

He stood watching Sam for a minute, rubbing the elbow he had banged against the pin oak trunk when he had tried a lay-up and looking puzzled. "Leaping Deer," he said, "are you going to shoot any?"

"Yes," said Sam, "later. From my spot." He moved his hand in a small circle, and settling back against the bole of the pin oak tree, he smiled at President Polk and Beats Billy.

After a few minutes, when they had left, headed back to watch some more of the rehearsal in the village, Beats Billy in front and President Polk a few steps behind laboring to keep up, Sam moved to a place directly in front of the goal and in line with it. Except for the steady murmur from Long King Creek, it was completely silent where he stood. By leaning his head back, Sam could look up into the branches of the pin oak, bare now of all its leaves and gray and black against the afternoon sky. To the right and left of the naked hardwood, though, were the loblolly and long-leaf, the tall and short pines in front of him and behind, their needles as green now as they had been in the spring and summer and as they would be all year round.

Sam Houston Leaping Deer shifted his feet on the damp ground of the thicket at the heart of the Alabama-Coushatta Nation, finding his true balance before he lifted the basketball before him. In one smooth movement he dipped his knees, straightened his arms, and put the sphere into the air. Circle looked at circle, and the roundness sought the roundness it knew. Spinning slowly in the weak light of the winter sun, the ball moved in its arc through the plane of the metal rim, and Sam stopped it to see the circle within the circle, the roundness intersected by roundness. For a moment he kept it there, suspended in the clear air near the trunk of the pin oak tree, and then listening to the steady play of the water of Long King Creek, he let the perfect roundness drop on through.